Even though this story is inspired by my love for dragons, South Korea, and Japan, it is its own fantasy world. I hope you love it!

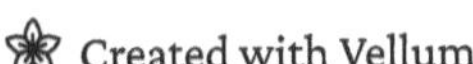 Created with Vellum

TRIGGER WARNINGS

Thank you for picking up my book. There are a few triggers that I want readers to be aware of:

Contemplation of suicide
Abuse
Bullying

If you're thinking about suicide, are worried about a friend or loved one, or would like emotional support, National Suicide Prevention Lifeline is available 24/7 across the United States. Please call 988.

Please know that you are not alone.

TORMENT
DRAGONS OF TENGHUA

MARI DIETZ

To my sister, Nicollee, a woman with fierce determination and the kindest loving heart. Thank you for believing in me even when I don't believe in myself.

CHAPTER
ONE

The pain of hunger only helped Mei focus on the storefront of Fat Choi's outdoor fish display. The sharp tang of raw fish should have put her off eating, but despite the overwhelming sourness in the air, her mouth watered.

Turn your back. Go on, Mei thought. With unblinking eyes, she studied Fat Choi. He worked briskly for a chubby man. His fat rolls vibrated under his shirt with his back-and-forth movements as he bickered with customers over the price of the latest catch. She swirled the saliva around in her mouth and swallowed, hoping it would trick her stomach into thinking she'd fed it. Her body had weakened in these last few days.

Mei thought Fat Choi was the perfect target since she didn't see his dendragon roasting the raw fish to perfection in its usual spot. She scanned the area one final time to make sure she hadn't missed it. Only bright silver fish scales gleamed in the early morning sun. The dead eyes could stare at her all they wanted. They wouldn't tell tales.

I must be insane. The old vegetables Mei had found in nearby trash piles couldn't satisfy her or her father's hunger. She pretended not to notice the way his hands trembled or how the cloth was sometimes tinged with red when he coughed. They needed meat, and the scraps she'd found last week had made them both violently ill. Mei gagged at the memory of having spent a day near the hand-dug privy. She chewed the inside of her cheek and leaned onto the balls of her feet. Shivering in the chilly morning breeze, she planted her hands on the soft dirt road.

Fast. Go fast! Every time Fat Choi turned his back, Mei froze, her body tense. It couldn't be wrong to steal to stay alive.

She tucked a greasy strand of hair behind her ear. *You can do this. Don't think about the punishment. You won't get caught.*

Fat Choi turned again, this time his arms waving in argument, probably over money. *Now.*

Mei pounced toward the stand, snaked her hand out, and snatched the fish by its slimy fin. She turned and rushed down a neighboring alley. Her heart pounded in time with her frantic gait. Hoping to get away before anyone noticed the theft, she passed the stands hidden in the shadows. The smells promised herbs that could heal anything. Those who couldn't afford treatment from homdragons were the only ones tempted to shop. The dirt turned into mud the farther she ran, and the mud squelched between her bare toes. Just ahead, Mei saw the light at the end of the alley that led to the busier section of the Market district. A small smile formed as her escape into the bustling crowd approached.

Her legs stretched out, and then they flew even farther forward, while her head and neck were jerked back. Mei choked and gasped as a long chain tightened around her neck. She landed backward in the mud.

Dropping the fish, Mei clawed at the chain around her neck. Footsteps thudded behind her in the alley's muck. Flakes of mud sprayed her face as people stopped near her head. She could only see the deep blue uniforms of the city guard. Mei went numb, and an empty feeling entered her chest. *It's over.*

"Is this it?" a deep voice said from behind Mei's head.

Wheezing came from behind the guard. "Yes." Mei recognized Fat Choi's voice. "That scab watched my stand for over an hour. I knew the gutter trash would strike eventually."

A loud squawk came from Fat Choi's direction—the dendragon agreeing with his words. Mei silently cursed herself. *Shelling baka, you are. It was there all along.*

Mei closed her eyes and tried to breathe around the tight chain of the kusarigama. Only a little air came through. A muddy boot nudged her shoulder, and she remained limp.

"Did you snap its neck?" Fat Choi asked.

"Nah, playing dead."

She jerked when a sharp pressure shot through her left hand. Mei's eyes opened, and she tried to sit up, but someone held the chain tight and yanked her neck back down. Something popped loudly in her hand; bones had broken. She bit her tongue, refusing to give them the satisfaction of screaming, but there was no controlling the tears leaking out of her eyes.

She met Fat Choi's eyes, his face looming over her as his giant body blocked out the sun by the exit of the alley. He stood on her hand, applying pressure to the broken bones.

The guard hoisted her up by the chain, and Mei sputtered for air, but thankfully, it released her hand from Fat Choi. Her left hand burned as they pulled her like a dog out into the open street. The dull fish lay discarded in the alley. *I'm sorry, Father.*

Mei bowed her head in the sun, and Fat Choi led her and the guard back to his shop. They halted in the front of his stand, and he turned around to face Mei, her head still lowered.

"That will be fifty silver." His hands rested on his fat sides.

"I don't even have the fish anymore," Mei muttered. "Way overpriced."

Fat Choi backhanded Mei across her jaw. "Thieves don't get to decide the price."

The salty taste of blood fueled her. She resisted the urge to spit. "I don't have any money." Still studying her feet, she heard whispers from the crowd gathered around them. What would her punishment be? There would be no trial for an eta like her. Some thieves lost their hand, others were beaten, and some were hanged in the center square.

If they decide to cut off my hand, hopefully they will take the broken one, Mei thought. A calm filled her. Her fate would be decided soon.

The guard took out a short leather strap and led her to a wooden pole covered in splinters. With quick movements, he latched her hands down so he could remove the chain from her neck. His sky-blue dendragon clutched his shoulder, and its sharp eyes kept watch.

Mei flinched with pain as she wiggled her left hand. Not daring to tug at her restraints, she stood hunched over, her back to the crowd.

"Fifty silver, fifty lashes?" the guard asked Fat Choi.

Fat Choi's face scrunched up, making his triple chins wiggle. "It shouldn't be alive anymore."

Mei finally saw the guard's face as he stepped next to Fat Choi. "With people disappearing, even during the non-rainy season," the guard whispered, rough voice so low she could barely hear him, "a hanging wouldn't be good for morale."

The dendragon around the guard's neck hissed at Fat Choi.

Fat Choi's lips puckered, and he waddled back to his shop, grumbling under his breath. His dendragon squawked and clutched his arm.

The guard sighed and briskly lifted Mei's rag of a shirt. The kusarigama chains clanked as he went to stand behind her. The morning sun felt oddly comforting on her bare back, and Mei focused on the tiny grooves in the wooden pole in front of her.

So this is it. Mei closed her eyes as the first strike hit her slight frame. The chains weren't sharp, but the bruising blows made her gasp. Red sparks entered her vision with each thud of the chain. She spasmed with each hit. Her knees gave out and hit the dirt, but her hands stayed firmly above her head. The cool wood scraped her face as she leaned against the pole. Time didn't pass in this moment, with her back exposed, the crowd chattering, and the chain thudding. Her father would be ashamed if he found out she'd tried to steal.

The chains broke the skin on her back and warm blood leaked out of the wounds. Blackness approached, and Mei hoped she would pass out so as not to feel the rest of the punishment. Then there was no more. It was over. Mei didn't move. Even the warm breeze hurt, so she remained perfectly still.

"Let this be a warning to all thieves," the guard said to the crowd. "This eta thinks that food is free."

Mei heard him walk over to Fat Choi and whisper, "Leave her up all day, then cut her loose. I won't be around to see what happens."

A low laugh came from Fat Choi. "Thank you, sir, for your service to our city."

He's going to kill me. Mei couldn't stand, and her arms had lost blood flow from staying firmly above her. The day was still young, but she needed to leave before dark. She took slow breaths to clear the overwhelming pain clouding her thoughts. She took her time turning toward the crowded market. Each inch required effort, but the pain reminded her that she was still alive. This wouldn't be over until she breathed her last breath. Her father needed her, and if she could move, she could escape.

Sandaled feet passed by Mei while the crowd dispersed to continue their morning market shopping. They haggled over the prices of dragon fruit in square wooden stalls while light green dendragons chittered over them. The smell of fire-roasted beef mixed with the scent of fish, and her stomach cried in hunger. Most people did not even try to skirt around her, but nudged her on their way by. As an eta, Mei was less than human, a beggar without an occupation or a dragon.

Mei tilted her head up and tried to catch a passerby's gaze. Most were feu men and women, but still they paid no mind to an eta. If another eta was near, they would steer clear of her. People loved to lump together punishments. It didn't even matter if the eta was guilty. Even though eta looked out for each other, it wouldn't be wise to save her. Eta had learned long ago to accept defeat.

One man approached Fat Choi's shop, and she caught his eye. He glanced down at her, and his narrow face darkened. He lifted his puce-brown yukata away from Mei. The flowing robes hung off his thin frame, and a clashing purple obi around his waist completed the horrid ensemble.

"Choi, if you leave this here, it will hurt your business." The man kicked a pebble at Mei. When she didn't flinch, he backed away.

Fat Choi chuckled. "If I don't, more will think I'm an easy target." His dendragon squawked. "This beauty was the first to see the snipe steal from me."

Fat Choi stroked the dendragon's yellow scales. It was no bigger than a cat. The way the sun hit its scales made the little beauty glow. Even though he had helped catch her, it didn't take away from the finery of the dendragon. The dendragon took a short flight away from Fat Choi to its perch and manipulated the flames roasting the customer's fish.

"It's a shame they even let the eta out of their district," the customer grumbled. "It just makes them think they deserve things."

Fat Choi handed the man his cooked fish wrapped in wax cloth. "Maybe Emperor Xion will see to it. More and more are stealing. With the rains coming again, Jion-sho has enough to worry about, and the Emperor can take care of snipes like this."

The customer took a large bite out of the fish, and oil dripped down his chin onto his cheap robes. "The Emperor and the Sho are at odds these days. I heard rumors that the Sho disappears for days at a time. So maybe the eta can be taken care of by the people." He looked down at Mei. "It would be easier for us to just burn them out."

Mei clenched her jaw. "You—"

Fat Choi smacked her face with a long pole. "Don't speak."

The customer started to leave, and Mei quietly slid her foot out, tripping him. After he righted himself, he kicked her in the leg and walked away.

No one would help her but herself. Her tied hands faced Fat Choi, and Mei tried to find the knot with her right hand. The leather strap had stretched since this morning, but not enough to allow her fingers to work properly. She stood to lessen the pressure, and her back throbbed with each movement.

It felt like it had taken hours to get her feet in place. The sun, now high in the sky, beat down on her wounded body. The blood mixed with the salty sting of sweat on her back, and now her thin shirt clung to the wounds. The heat made her thirsty, and the smell of cooking fish left her light-headed with hunger. Fat Choi whistled merrily in the back, oblivious to her pain.

Is Father worried? She usually came home after a day of scavenging, so he wouldn't be concerned until nightfall. *He'll never know what happened to me.* No one would tell him since no one knew who she was. Dead eta usually ended up in a random hole in the ground.

Mei clenched her jaw and leaned against the pole, gasping for air. Her eyes closed as she caught her breath, and when she slowly opened them, she discovered a face mere inches away.

Startled, Mei recoiled, but the young man didn't move. He studied her, his face showing no expression. From the looks of him, he was part of the daim class. His short light brown hair was clean, and his yukata was airy, likely silk, reminding her of flowers blowing in the breeze. The bright blue fabric mixed with golden thread complemented his tawny brown skin. Most daim never got as tan as other classes. They spent their days indoors, not in the scorching sun. His wide eyes flicked to her back, and his mouth twitched. An air of importance rested around him, like most daim. She didn't sense cruelty in his posture, but that meant nothing. Daim could kill with a word, and no one would stop them.

He faced Fat Choi, who'd come out of the back.

"What crime was committed?" he spoke with a commanding tone for someone so young. The young man folded his hands into the wide sleeves of his yukata.

Fat Choi bowed his head. "It stole a fish."

"How much?"

"Um... Daim-san..." Fat Choi searched for a name while nervously tapping his fingers on the counter, his fat jowls wobbling.

"Chin," the young man answered.

"Chin-san, it was fifty silver."

"For one fish?" Chin asked, then pressed his lips into a fine line. He never sneered at the man, but his calmness scared Mei more than if he had shown anger.

Choi fumbled for an explanation. "It also took me away from my shop to catch it."

Chin glanced between Mei and Choi, then took out a round cloth purse. "I will pay for the fish and *excessive* time lost."

Mei's eyes widened, and Fat Choi shook his hands and bowed profusely.

"Chin-san, I can't take your money."

Chin's expression hardened, turning him into an angry

daim statue in the middle of the dirt road and drawing other shoppers' attention. "Why not? Is my money not good here?"

"It must learn a lesson, honorable Chin-san, and it will not learn if you let it go."

Chin scanned Mei's body, taking in the dried blood and her hands, which had turned a deep purple. "I think the lesson has been learned." He took out five coins and placed them on the counter with a snap. "Release her."

Mei recoiled as Fat Choi roughly unknotted the leather strap. Sharp pain burned through her fingers from the blood rushing back. She flexed her right fingers, enjoying the pain that meant freedom, and cradled her left hand.

Before she could run off, Chin raised his hand. "Give her the fish."

Fat Choi's eyes narrowed. "It lost the fish in an alley."

"So how do you know she took it?"

Fat Choi's mouth gaped, but no sound came out. He grabbed the smallest fish from the stand.

Chin leaned over the counter but didn't touch the wood. "This is worth fifty silver?"

They both stood, their stances wide. Mei could tell by the spasms in Fat Choi's face that he wanted to protest, but Chin was daim. With a single phrase, he could put Fat Choi out of business. Fat Choi plodded over to the largest fish and cleaned it with deft strokes. The scales flew off the body, and one landed next to her feet. It seemed that Fat Choi pictured her as he sliced the fish.

Before he could wrap it, Chin spoke again. "I think we want it cooked. Your dendragon is famous for the flavor it adds to the fire."

Fat Choi placed the fish on a spit, and the dendragon

merrily cooked it, not sensing the dismay from its partner. Fat Choi wrapped the large fish in waxed cloth, handed it to Chin, and bowed.

"Arigato," Chin said and took the large fish. He flicked his hand to the side, motioning for Mei to follow him.

Mei didn't think it was wise to follow the strange young man, but a quick glance at Fat Choi's murderous face decided for her. She briskly followed him and cringed with each step, making sure not to walk next to him as an equal.

They turned the corner of a flower shop closing for the day, and Chin stopped and handed her the fish. "Take it."

If I take it, everyone will think I stole it. She shook her head and averted her gaze.

Chin sighed. "Take it or I will throw it away."

Mei bit her lip and put out her right hand, and Chin plopped the fish in her grasp. Her back screamed at the weight, but she hugged the fish to her chest. Her mouth watered at the thought of eating something that hadn't come from a trash pile.

"Arigato," Mei whispered.

"Do you need healing?"

Mei shook her head and backed away from him. She peeked out from the corner of her eye. "Why?"

Chin shrugged. "Just stay out of trouble." He turned on his heel and walked away. His silk yukata billowed behind him, a contrast to the cheaply built wooden shops.

I don't think he understood my question. Why would he save me? He must want something. Mei awkwardly shoved the large fish under her ragged clothes and darted away. Fat Choi might have followed her for revenge, and Chin-san likely wanted a slave to work for him. She stuck to the edges of the market, weaving between fruit and vegetable stands until they thinned out and rows of clay shacks with straw roofs came into view.

Most of the eta were still out begging, but Mei walked cautiously in the afternoon light. She scanned the corners of the empty streets. The windows of empty shacks followed her like hollow eyes. She stopped in front of the larger shack of the eta leaders.

Fumi sat inside the gloomy room, making crude slashes on a wet square made with mud. Her back remained straight, even though as an eta it should have bent long ago. Her head shot up when Mei entered. She wasn't a leader, but she collected food and divided it among those who needed it. It was never enough, but it was all the eta could do. Her gray hair stayed tied away from her face, and her clothes were as clean as an eta could get them. Fumi's eyes always remained sad, even when she sometimes smiled. She had lived a long time for an eta, and she had seen so many die from hunger.

"More vegetables?" Fumi grimaced and stopped tallying in the mud.

"Fish." Mei placed the waxed package on the short, splintered table.

Fumi touched the edge of the wax paper in reverence. "How did you get this?"

"Someone bought it for me."

Mei could practically see the drool from Fumi, but the other eta shook her head. "The leaders told me not to take from you anymore. Your father needs it."

"I don't mind—"

"Take it, Mei. We know everyone's hungry, and we help when we can, but he needs it more. This is something you found."

Mei's chest tightened as she put the fish back under her shirt. The leaders didn't have to do this, and she wished she could repay them for their kindness. "Arigato, Fumi." On her way out, she glanced back. "Did they ever find Hisao-leader?"

Fumi shook her head, and Mei could tell she held back tears. Another eta missing before the rains. The rest of the city noticed but didn't care to stop it as long as only eta vanished. The monsters had come early.

She left the shack and approached the tiny single-room home she shared with her father.

Mei came into the dark room and found her father still lying on his straw mat. The packed dirt floor was cool on Mei's feet, and she knelt next to her father.

"Father," Mei whispered.

His breath slowed, and he opened his eyes. Mei could see nothing but white. Koji had been blind for some time, but he still searched for her face. Through his holey shirt, his prominent ribs showed. She fared no better, but he got thinner by the day. What was left of his hair remained white. A hard life had aged Koji to make him look ancient when he was only in his forties.

"I got food, Father."

He smiled, deepening his wrinkled face. "I thought I smelled something."

Mei helped him sit and then peeled off a small piece of fish and placed it in his outstretched hand. His fingers bent to the side from being broken in the past. They curled inward, making it painful and difficult for him to grab anything. The jade beads he held in his fingers fell back around his thin wrist. The beads were worn from his constant touch. Koji brought the fish to his nose, and his head tilted. "This is fish?"

"Yes, Father."

He didn't eat it. "How did you get this?"

"A rich daim gave it to me."

Koji's lips tightened. "From begging?"

He doesn't need to know. Mei would never tell him about the beating or her theft. "Yes."

"You're not a beggar!" Koji tried to stand, but in his weakened state, he failed. He dropped the piece of fish and put his head in his hands. His shoulders slumped.

"But I am." Mei picked up the piece of fish and pulled her father's hands away from his face. She placed the morsel back in his hands. "Eat." Would he rather eat garbage than have her beg? "We don't need to go over this every day, Father." Mei was long over the shame of her status as an eta. What else did he expect her to do? Everyone begged, and some nights, they only ate thanks to the portions other eta had donated to the community.

They both ate bits of the fish in silence. The spicy tang from the fire should have been delicious, but to Mei, the reminder of Fat Choi made it difficult to swallow. Mei took the rest of the afternoon to dry out strips of the fish. She sat and watched over it so birds wouldn't steal it. Koji sat next to her in the doorway as they enjoyed the balmy heat together.

Mei tore thin strips of cloth from her shirt and wrapped it as tightly as she could around her left hand. The throbbing felt normal now, and Mei needed healing or she might lose the use of her hand. Sometimes, Tuan set bones for a silver, but maybe he would trade for some dried fish.

She gritted her teeth at the pain. Her father needed the

fish more than she needed her hand. Mei would make do with just her right.

"What was that?" Koji asked.

"I ripped my shirt today. It's nothing."

"Mm-hmm."

Mei bit her lip at the lie. "The dragon fruit vendor has a new apprentice."

"Oh, what color is the dendragon?"

Mei smiled at her father's brightened mood over the mention of dragons. "It's a pretty pale pink. It looked like it could make the fruit much larger."

"Ah, I bet the price will go up."

"Most likely."

Then, like that, Koji was lost in thought. That happened when dragons were mentioned. He would brighten, then his mood would shift from memories he wouldn't share with her.

Koji hummed a familiar tune, and Mei softly hummed with him. He always hummed it for her at night, and today, it felt wistful.

The sun dipped behind the mountains, and the fortress of the shodragon riders glowed a deep crimson. In the distance, Mei could see the enormous beasts flying home for the night.

"The shodragons?"

"Yes, they're flying home."

"Do you see a golden one?"

She scanned the sky and named off the colors for her father. "I don't see her tonight."

"The Sho must be away." Her father reached for her hand, and she held his tightly. He smiled sadly. "I've almost forgotten what silver looks like. Maybe I have."

"Don't you mean gold, Father?"

His other hand rested on the jade beads around his neck. "Yes, gold. Keep an eye out for me."

"I will."

The cool air refreshed her, and she wrapped the now dried fish in the wax cloth. Her father shuffled back inside, but he had a cloth bag in his hand. She wanted to ask what was in the bag, but she knew to wait. He would tell her eventually.

Mei placed the dried fish in the shack's corner and covered it with flat rocks to keep out bugs.

It grew dark as the sun set in the distance, and they had no candles for light. The cicadas sang in the trees for them, and Mei went to lie down next to her father's mat.

"You've already turned eighteen ," he said in a quiet tone.

Mei sat up. "Yes."

In the dark, she could see mournful longing on his face. "I haven't taken care of you like a father should."

"Father, don't say things like this." Mei patted his arm. "Let's go to sleep."

He placed the heavy bag next to her. "This is for you."

A heavy clank sounded as she opened the pouch. There were hundreds of silver inside. "What's this?"

"Enough to get a dragon."

TWO

Mei clutched the bag with her good hand. "Where'd you get this?" Never in her life had she seen so much money. She turned her back to the open doorway. *People will slit our throats if they see this. Not all eta are good.*

"I sold your mother's items that were in the chest."

She finally noticed the shallow hole in the dirt floor. For as long as Mei could remember, the chest had remained under the ground and locked. She'd never looked inside, and her father had never mentioned what he kept locked away. That was one topic he would never tell her, no matter how much she begged.

"This whole time, we could have had the money to heal you and get medicine?" Mei stood. "I'm going to purchase the services of a homdragon for your eyes." She took the money and started toward the door.

Her father clumsily grabbed at her arm, and Mei gasped in pain. He let go when he heard. "Sit."

Mei sat down carefully. "I am going to buy food and a healer."

"No, you are not."

She had never heard such harshness from her father. "You can't stop me."

"If you do this, there will be no one here to heal. I will take the paths to the woods."

"Father—"

"Mei, I'm still your father. You'll listen to me."

The frail, gentle father was no longer before her. This man was someone Mei didn't recognize. Somehow, Koji seemed taller in the fading light. His white eyes showed determination. She didn't doubt he would leave her. The monsters roamed the woods, and he would die a horrible death.

"Yes, I will listen."

He nodded sharply. "This is for you to buy an apprenticeship. When a dragon chooses you, you will be offered a place to train. I saved this for your future. To heal a dying man would be a waste. I had to wait until you were eighteen . You had to survive until you were eighteen ." He reached out and found Mei's knee, his bent fingers gripping her. "You will have to work harder than anyone since it's rare for an eta to rise. But they'll not turn you away once a dragon has chosen you."

"There's no guarantee that a dragon will. It's foolish to risk this money on a hope." Mei's throat tightened at the thought of wasting the money when they could hire a healer today.

Her father now had that stubborn set to his jaw. "Without a dragon, you will always live here as less than human."

"I don't care."

"I do," Koji said softly. "You didn't get to choose this life. It's better that you get a chance." His blind eyes closed. "This is all I can do for you. This is all I could do for your mother."

Mei shook her head. "This is foolish."

He squeezed her knee. "Sometimes, you need to be a baka." He took his hand back. "Why are you in pain?"

"I'm not."

Koji sighed. "Is there more to the fish story?"

Mei ignored his question. "How did you find a place to sell Mother's belongings?"

"I asked."

"I'm surprised you weren't robbed."

Koji went to lie down. "Bury it in the ground and sleep over it. There are fresh clothes in there as well. Tomorrow, you will go to the temple for your eighteen -year celebration. There are only two selections a year."

With tense movements, she followed his directions. The beads clicked as her father ran them through his fingers. It was a comforting, familiar noise that always lulled her to sleep. After a short while, her father's breathing steadied. Her mind raced at the thought of having a dragon as a partner. She'd only heard rumors of what it was like to have something connected to you. Some said they spoke in your mind. Mei shuddered. It would be odd to have someone else in her thoughts.

I should just take the money to get Father healed. She got up throughout the night to stand at the doorway, her feet aching to walk beyond. But if she used the money, Father would end his life. He had always been a man of his word.

After he'd grown sick and blind, she'd seen the crushing blow of him breaking his promise to take care of her.

"Stubborn baka," she whispered in the dark.

Even if she got a dragon, Mei would have to leave and live with whoever trained her. Tears leaked from her eyes as sleep remained far away. "You'll die, anyway." He'd planned this, never telling her. He'd planned to die and leave her. Mei sat and listened to his soft breathing, a sound she might never hear again.

The hum of the cicadas lessened as the sun rose. Mei quietly watched the rise and fall of her father's chest and committed each feature to memory. She didn't know when she would see his face again. From her spot on the floor, she touched his bent, calloused hands. The skin was always worn and cracked, just like hers.

She got up and went out to the muddy creek waters. She tried her best to wash off years of grime. Arms out, she frowned at the streaks of mud lining her body. Water was for drinking, not bathing. This shallow stream wasn't used for drinking or washing; it had just made her dirtier.

Mei leaned back on her heels and watched the golden sun peer over the canopy of cherry trees. The mud dried, making her skin feel tight, and it flaked off with any movement. Mei tried her best but resorted to tying her hair up in a knot with a string. It was difficult using just her right hand and pinning the string loosely in her left. The pain in her back and hand were now part of her, and she gritted her teeth. *My legs work. That is all I need right now.* She hoped her face was less muddy. Maybe the clothes her father had gotten her would cover up her skin.

She leaned over and tried to see her reflection in the muddy water, but it was only a dark outline. It didn't matter. If dragons chose based on cleanliness, Mei was already in trouble.

On her way back home, various neighbors came out of their mud-and-straw huts. Some nodded to her, and Mei waved. Around the corner, she ran into Yui, who was panting for air.

"Mei!"

Mei stepped back. "Yes?"

Yui grabbed Mei's right arm and pulled her between two huts. Mei cringed at the pain in her back, but Yui didn't notice. Yui had grown up with Mei and was taller than her by a handspan. Both of them wore rags, but Yui kept her hair short. It was easier to clean in the rain. A deep scar ran across her mouth, giving her a permanent smirk.

Normally, Yui tried to make them laugh and forget about being an eta, but her face was stricken with fear. "Your father had me take him to the Daim district," she whispered frantically. "I thought we would get killed!"

Mei's brow furrowed. "What would he do there?"

"I thought you would know. He had an old chest that was moldy and broken, and he came out with nothing."

He'd probably hidden the money under his clothes. "You shouldn't have taken him."

Yui crossed her arms. "He said it was for your birthday, like he could afford anything from there."

"What did they sell?"

"Oh, some armor and weapons. Things we aren't allowed to buy or have."

If Father got money, that means he likely sold a weapon. "Don't take him on any errands unless it's to heal him."

"Well, excuse me for wanting to help on your birthday." Yui stuck out her lower lip in a pout.

Mei rolled her eyes. "He shouldn't be walking around, and eta aren't allowed in the Daim district."

"You're lucky I wasn't killed."

"Yeah." Mei strode out from between the houses. "Yui?"

"What?"

"If I'm no longer around, will you look in on Father?"

Yui's eyes narrowed. "Where are you going?"

"If something happens to me."

Yui glanced at Mei's hand. "What'd you do?"

"I don't expect you to feed him. The community food should help. Just... just keep an eye on him?"

Yui sighed. "I already risked death to get you a present, so I don't see why I can't give him any leftover scraps. We never have much, Mei, so stay out of trouble."

Mei nodded and walked back home, leaving Yui standing in the road. It wasn't much, but Yui would take care of her father.

I can get away and bring him food too—and some for Yui's family. She bit her lip and went inside the dark hut. He might plan to die, but Mei wouldn't let him. Mei got out the leftover fish and gently shook her father awake.

His white eyes opened, and his hand rested on Mei's arm. "Rikku?"

"No, Father."

Koji blinked rapidly, and Mei helped him sit up. He bent his head. "Sometimes I forget I can't see."

"Did you dream of Mother again?"

He smiled softly as Mei place the dried fish in his palm. "Yes. She was always so fierce."

Mei didn't take any of the fish for herself. He would need it more in the coming days if his insane plan came true. She went to sit across from Koji. "Tell me a story about her."

Koji's eyes were distant, and his face wrinkled with a smile. "The day I met Rikku, she swore she would kill me." His thumb rubbed the jade beads around his wrist. He had told her once that they'd belonged to her mother.

Mei hugged her knees to her chest and let herself forget the pain of her body and get lost in Koji's story. As he spoke of her mother, his face softened, and a slight smile lifted the corners of his mouth.

"It was right after the rains, and the blossoms were in full bloom, each petal like bright butterflies of color. I was with some of my friends that day, and we were climbing the trees and jumping into the water below."

Mei sighed at the extravagance of using water for sport.

"Then we moved farther down to where there were rumors of bathing women."

Mei played along with the repeated story and gasped, enjoying her father's lightened mood. "Father, were you a pervert?"

Koji chuckled. "Yes, and if any boy did that to you, I would cut off his head. Thankfully, even though we were idiots, we found no naked women."

"But you found a lunch?"

Koji nodded. "You've heard this too many times."

Mei's eyes were wistful, and her head filled with a world she could only dream of in her mud hut. "Yes, but I enjoy hearing it from you."

"So all that jumping made us hungry, and we didn't see an owner around. The decorative box was filled with the most beautiful and delicate rice cakes. They were in the shape of flowers. It didn't take us long to eat them. Then I felt something cold on my neck."

"What was it?"

"I turned slowly to see an avenging goddess standing over me and the empty lunch. Her long dark hair flew to the side in the wind, but I couldn't make out her face with the sun behind her."

"Who was it?" Mei leaned in, and her right finger drew the image of the sun on the dirt floor.

"I didn't know, but she had to be the owner of the lunch. So I bowed and placed my head at her feet. I think this surprised her." Koji paused. "She said to me, 'What are you doing?' And I answered, 'Oh Inari Okami, we did not know this was your food. Bless us sinners, and we will make two times the offering in your temple.'"

Mei snorted. "Did she buy it?"

Koji laughed. "No, but she did laugh at me and take her sword away from my neck." Koji touched his neck in memory. "Then placing her sword in its sheath, she said in the most commanding tone, 'No need. Just take me to the festival and let me eat all the food I want.'"

"Did you?"

"I did." Koji finished the last of the fish that Mei had given him. "I didn't have money to eat for a week after that. She could eat."

"I wish I'd known her." In front of her dirt sun, Mei outlined a woman with flowing hair.

Koji closed his eyes. "Her heart is in you."

They sat in silence again. Mei wanted to say so much, but talking about her leaving would sound too much like goodbye forever.

"Mei."

"Yes, Father?"

"You need to go."

"Yes, Father."

Mei stood, unburied the cloth bag, and took out a plain gray yukata. It was the cleanest thing she had ever owned. It smelled like dirt, but she quickly shed her rags and slid the crisp material over her body. Mei tightened the obi as much as she could and stood in the doorway with the bag hidden in the front folds.

"Father..." How could she tell him how much he meant to her? She grabbed him around his thin waist, and he clutched her to him. He smelled of dirt after a rainfall. Mei's throat thickened, and she squeezed her eyes shut to seal in the tears.

"We are very proud of you," he whispered. Then softly in her ear, he hummed the melody of her childhood. With one last squeeze, he gently pushed her away. "Go and I will know that you have lived."

"Yes, Father," Mei whispered and turned her back to him. "I love you."

"I love you too."

Tears burned her eyes as she walked away from the muddy shack that had been her home since she was young. The winding roads that many got lost on were familiar to Mei as she twisted and turned toward the mountain. She didn't look back; otherwise, she would run back to beg to stay. Mei walked with her head held high and images in her mind of her mother almost killing her father over rice cakes.

Mei forced her legs to keep moving farther away. Her father might think this was the end, but once she got a dragon, she would be back. She would make him live. The apprentices of dendragons and homdragons could take leave for home visits. She shouldn't worry. He didn't need to make it sound so final. She clutched the heavy bag. It was a curse on her life, but a hope for her father.

She arrived at the end of the eta district, and the marketplace bustled. Mei gave a wide berth to the area of Fat Choi's fish stand, and her stomach growled in pain as she passed by colorful spice displays and street food, all being cooked by dendragons.

Mei couldn't help but pause at a brown dendragon forming a clay bowl in a pottery shop. Fire manipulators were more common, but this one controlled earth. Its earth-green eyes flicked in her direction, and Mei hustled on toward the temple.

Some shoppers gave her peculiar looks. *I'm still dirty*, Mei thought. It tempted her to put her head down like she normally did. Today, however, she wasn't eta; she was Rikku and Koji's daughter.

In the distance, the white stone walls of the temple were framed by red torii gates. Mei picked up her pace, and the number of paper lanterns increased the closer she got to the walls. Symbols she didn't recognize were written on signs, and she followed others who were with their parents. They also looked to be eighteen , so she hoped they were going in the right direction.

Those closest to her sniffed and backed away. Mei bent her head and smelled herself, but she found nothing out of the ordinary. She smelled the same as she always did. They all made their way up toward the mountain, the path lined with bright red pillars of the torii gates and adorned with more lanterns. Mei could see drawings of dragons on the pillars. She took this as a sign that she was in the correct place.

The pace slowed down as everyone split up to go to different priests. The priests took the money and bowed, then gestured for the individual to go inside what looked like the entrance to a cave.

She shuffled her feet nervously. Everyone wore brightly colored yukatas. Her gray one felt like a funeral shroud. People openly pointed at her, and some shook their heads, and others snickered. She thought she saw Chin from the market, so she ducked away so he wouldn't see her.

Mei jutted out her jaw. *I'm the daughter of Rikku and Koji.* She chanted the phrase over and over in her head. It was finally her turn, and she approached the ornate table with an austere priest in a plain brown yukata. *I should have picked someone who looked kinder.*

"Who are you?"

"Mei?"

The bald priest scowled. "You don't know who you are?"

"I'm Mei."

He took in her gray yukata and probably muddy face. "The price to gain a dragon is ten thousand silver. This isn't a handout."

How much? Mei gasped at the price. She and Father could have moved somewhere else with that kind of money. "I h-have it." She pulled the bag from the folds in her clothing.

The priest poked it with his pencil. "I need a count over here."

A haggard-looking young man approached and counted the money. Mei's face flushed. No one else had needed their money counted. Standing stiffly, she waited until he'd finished.

"Ten thousand one hundred silver."

The priest snorted. "You overpaid." He handed her back one hundred silver, and Mei looked at the extensive amount of money in her hand. "Well, go on! To the left. I don't have all day to sit here and smell you."

Mei ducked into the tunnel on the left. Those in the most expensive clothes had gone to the right. She was among the feu class, but they were dressed better than her. They all rolled up their sleeves. There was a round pool of water in which others washed their hands, so she followed their example.

Her hands muddied the water; at least part of her would be clean. She rolled up her sleeves and followed them at a distance.

The farther she went in, the darker it grew. Only flickering lanterns guided them. Then they came to a large open room of carved smooth stone, probably reformed with dendragons. Priests waited inside, but square cloth masks covered their full faces and fluttered in the breeze.

Row upon row of eggs lined a narrow stone path. They glittered in the pale lantern light. The people ahead of her lifted their arms and placed a hand near each egg without touching them. They would pause for a moment, then move on to the next set of two.

She followed suit. *This has to be it.* What happened when a dragon chose you? Her eyes flicked around to the others, but nothing happened. Then a loud crack sounded, and a cry of joy occupied the quiet space.

A young woman was bleeding from her hand, but she held a tiny silvery dragon in her arms. Her face glowed, and a priest approached and took her out a door in the side of the stone room.

What was the blood for? Mei shuddered and returned her hands to her sides. She plodded along the seemingly endless path. Her back ached, and she tried to hold up both her arms until the end.

Mei didn't know how long she had been in this room, but the priests had rushed dozens of happy new dragon owners out. Then in front of her, a masked priest appeared out of the darkness, and Mei jumped. She looked around and realized there were no more eggs in front of her.

"They have not chosen you. Follow me." The voice was muffled under the mask, but the words stabbed into Mei's heart.

CHAPTER

THREE

A chill entered the cavern, and Mei shivered. She looked behind her but saw no one. *This can't be the end.* "May I go back? I must have missed one."

The masked priest shook his head. "You did not miss any. I watched you. You are not worthy."

Not worthy. Mei clutched her stomach with her good hand. "I-I'm the daughter of—"

He held up his hand, cutting her off. "The dragons do not care. They are the ones that judge your worth."

"The money." Mei's head hung limply. They had to give it back. Then she could heal her father.

"Instead of paying your master, it goes to the temple."

"No."

The priest stepped forward. "Pardon?"

Mei balled her fist and stuck out her chin. "No."

"No?"

"If I don't get a dragon, I get my money back."

The priest sighed. "That isn't how it works."

"Give me a dragon."

The priest's words were clipped as he repeated, "That isn't how it works."

Mei twisted her head around, looking for help. When she turned back to the priest, he waved his hand toward an opening.

"Come."

Mei shuffled after him. Her body went numb at the thought that she had thrown away ten thousand silver. Father's sad smile crashed into her thoughts, and before she could take another step, Mei paused. Heat coursed through her body. *I am not leaving here without a dragon.*

The priest kept walking, thinking she followed. Mei spotted another path out of the corner of her eye and ran toward it. Her bare feet made no sound against the stone. She didn't know where the path led, but any path was better than going back outside to face defeat. *I will die in these caves before going home to watch Father die.*

A voice rose behind her as she darted down the dark tunnel, but Mei didn't hear his words. She ran through the pain and the unknown. In the dark, her breath was her only companion. Her right hand lightly touched the cold stone to guide her steps. The path ahead was still dark, and Mei followed the right turns. A crevice appeared, and her thin body fit inside. Mei found herself lucky as a group of priests darted past her, holding lanterns.

She rested against the cold stone. It felt good on her sore back. Her breathing slowed, and she continued down the smaller pathway to avoid anyone else. The darkness enveloped her as she awkwardly slid her feet sideways. Her right hand spread out in front of her, feeling for a safe path.

Then a faint light appeared ahead. Mei edged toward it. If any priests were in that area, she'd need to run back. She didn't even know how to get out of here, but she couldn't go home to her father without the money.

I'll just disappear, and he'll never know. Mei swallowed against the tightness in her throat. She could let her father believe she'd gotten a dragon. He could die happy. Mei paused, and a final rebellious voice screamed in her mind, *No, I will not leave without a dragon. Do you hear me?* From the dark came a chuckle, but when she turned, she saw only darkness. She shook her head and went forward.

The light grew brighter, and Mei peered around the edge of a doorway. It was another cavern, with young men and women going through pathways. This was different. The path between the eggs was smoother, and there were fewer eggs in this room. The eggs were about the same size, however, and they glowed slightly. Mei shook her head and rubbed her eyes. The eggs still glowed.

Why were there eggs in this location? Mei scanned the room. The priests here wore bright golden robes. Then she studied the people passing through. They all wore rich yukatas. Golden thread sparkled in the candlelight, and the soft swish of silk graced Mei's ears as they walked among the glowing eggs.

These eggs were meant for the daim. Mei bit her lip and curled her bare toes over the stone. Everyone was supposed to get an equal chance at a dragon, but they kept some back.

Homdragons, Mei thought. Her fingers rapidly tapped the side of her yukata. *I can get a homdragon, and if it heals...* The phrase "not worthy" thudded in her mind.

Mei took in a slow breath and got down on her hands and knees. She winced as she crawled, but she entered the taller walkway with the others. Scraping her knees against the stone, Mei reached the first egg. She darted her hand toward it and held her breath. Nothing. Peeking around the bend in the walkway, she headed toward the next egg. As she stretched out, a shout rang out in the large cavern.

"Get her!"

Mei painfully sprung to her feet and ran, holding out her hand, hoping against hope that a dragon would choose her. Father believed in her. At least one dragon had to find her worthy.

Strong hands grabbed her, and Mei gasped in pain as they twisted her broken hand. She kicked one in the shin, and he groaned, almost letting her go.

"Get her out of here!"

They all wore masks, and two held her arms as they dragged her out of the cavern and into a dark hall. Her heels scraped against the stone, and she tried to jerk her arms away from the two priests, but they just held her tighter.

"Give me my money back!"

One of the priests snorted. "It was stolen anyway."

The other priest nodded. "Filthy eta thinks it can be one of the bonded."

Mei's eyes burned, and she banged her head against one of their shoulders, making her head smart with fresh pain. "I am the daughter of Rikku and Koji!"

The one she'd banged her head against pinched her broken hand, and she gasped and fell limp. "Guttersnipes breeding more guttersnipes."

Mei's head lowered, but her heart still burned with a potent fire. They stopped walking. She wasn't outside the temple, but in a square room that smelled almost metallic.

The room had rougher walls than the cavern, and the

walkways looked like they were covered in brown paint. In the middle of the room, a large broad-shouldered man, who also wore a mask, waited. The two priests threw her in front of him.

Mei skidded across the floor but stopped short of the large priest's feet. She heard the footsteps of the other two walking away. She turned to see them blocking the door. Why hadn't they taken her to the entrance?

She stayed sprawled on the floor, almost enjoying the firmness of the stone beneath her cheek. Since they hadn't taken her outside, they'd probably decided to beat her or kill her. To some, killing eta was like snuffing out the life of a rodent. *Is this the end?* Mei closed her eyes. She'd thought her life would end yesterday. How odd that it would end today.

It doesn't have to be, a voice answered.

Mei jerked her head up and looked at the large man in front of her. "What?"

His arms crossed. "So it speaks."

Mei glanced around, looking for the source of the voice. "Did you say something?"

The priest's enormous hands tightened. "Yes. Remain quiet."

His voice sounded different from the one she'd heard, low and unkind. He took pleasure in the pain of others. She'd met many like him on the streets. Some gangs survived by taking from others. They took enjoyment in their sport.

Her body stiffened. She shuffled onto her feet and stared at the mask that covered his face. The symbol was different, and Mei didn't know what it meant. The blood-red color of the mask twisted her stomach. She had never seen one that color.

"So this is the one who thinks it can go beyond its station."

Mei squared her shoulders. "I paid."

The priest backhanded Mei across her face. She balked but stood taller.

"No amount of money will earn you a place in our world." He cracked his knuckles and pulled an object out of the box Mei hadn't noticed. It glinted in the light and looked like a giant fishing hook. Flecks of brown told her they had used it before.

Mei pressed her lips together and stood still, then tilted her chin up. "It's my world too," she softly said. *What am I saying?* Her mind screamed at her to lower her head—eta survived by being less, unnoticeable—but she didn't listen. Something burned inside her that was tired of lowering her head. If he was going to kill her, let him look in her eyes.

The priest lifted his hand and removed the thin cloth mask. His wide, greasy lips sneered. His narrow eyes were pushed back from his broad cheeks. "We know just what to do with things like you." He slid the hook under her chin.

Mei felt a heavy pressure in her chest, a fire that wasn't hers alone. She squared her shoulders and said firmly, "I am not a thing. I am Mei, daughter of Rikku and Koji."

The man laughed loudly. "It thinks it has some sort of breeding." He continued to press the hook against her neck and slid the smooth end so the point rested under her chin, scratching her skin.

She clenched her jaw and braced for the moment he would twist the hook up. It didn't come. Instead, a sharp burning pain sliced through her right arm. Mei peered down. Blood coated her hand and dripped onto the stone floor, staining her gray yukata. Next to her, no bigger than a cat, a dragon shook its obsidian wings. Silvery eyes tilted up at Mei, and a smooth narrow nose nudged her hand.

Hungry.

Mei jumped at the sound of the voice in her head. "What?"

The dragon nibbled on her fingers and made quiet clicking sounds. The large priest stood frozen, his mouth open in a wide circle and the hook still firmly under her jaw.

Mei took a step back, and he didn't move. She glanced from the priests at the door to the small dragon in front of her. The narrow black head seemed content to lick off Mei's blood for now, but she really should find him something to eat.

"Um, should someone feed this dragon?" Mei asked. It was absurd that she worried for this creature when she was about to die. She couldn't help but smile as it frantically nibbled at her fingers and chirped softly.

Her words startled one of the priests by the door, and he came up to her and bowed his head. "Follow me, and we will get some food."

"Okay." Mei's brow furrowed, and she followed the priest but was stopped by the dragon keeling over after trying to wobble after her.

"It's better to pick him up," the priest said.

"Oh, I didn't think I should touch him." Mei scooped the dragon into her arms, and he felt so fragile. "Does he belong to someone?"

"He's yours."

Mei's lips parted, and the mark on her bloody arm and the dragon all came together. She looked down at the creature she held, and her eyes widened. "You chose me?"

The dragon blinked his silver eyes and chirped. He then continued to nibble at her skin.

"Will he eat me?" Mei laughed softly. Her fear and doubt washed away, and warmth she didn't understand filled her body.

The priest sighed and marched out of the room while Mei trailed after him.

They wove their way in the dark stone tunnels, and Mei hoped he wasn't leading her to her death. She tightened her hold on the dragon, and it chirped at her in annoyance.

"Sorry," she whispered. Mei felt something nudge her mind, but she shook her head, and it went away.

They finally came to an open room covered in thick straw mats. Colorful paintings hung from the smooth walls. Tables occupied the center, and large gold and silver bowls were filled with raw red meat. Another table off to the side contained cooked beef and platters of fruit. Drinks and more food lined the walls. Mei had never seen so much to eat. She gaped at all the food on display.

The priest directed Mei to the table of meat and left her in the room. A few others also sported bloody arms and dragons. They all took a moment to glance up at her before continuing to feed their dragons bits of food.

Mei stood frozen, until her dragon squawked at the sight of meat. She hurriedly grabbed a bowl and put in fistfuls of the meat. Then she walked to the corner and fed her new charge.

He grabbed the strips of beef out of her fingers and smacked his jaws in satisfaction. While he ate, Mei admired how his black scales glimmered in the dim light. She stroked the scales, and they were soft.

She felt content and safe for the first time in her eighteen years. Holding this frail body, she thought maybe she could finally rest. She was tempted to look closer at his wings but left him alone. Mei had never been so close to a dragon.

The dragon ate his fill and curled up in Mei's arms, promptly falling asleep. His long black tail wrapped around her arm. His belly bulged from the feast. *Did I let him eat too much?*

She glanced around the room, and the sight of the rich food tempted her. She petted the sleeping dragon and didn't want to dislodge him over her hunger. Mei could go without food and let herself relax. Her hand and back still throbbed, but maybe whoever she apprenticed with would heal her.

In the quiet, Mei heard approaching footsteps. A group of people entered the room. They all wore loose black clothing under leather armor, which Mei had never seen before. It seemed like plates stacked on top of each other. They flapped slightly with their movements. The man in front stood with authority. His sleek hair was tied back and fell in a long tail down his spine. His jaw looked cut from stone, and his eyes, which were a fierce ebony, missed nothing. She felt like she should know him. He took her in in one glance, and Mei blushed. She'd never seen such a handsome man in her life, and in all her years, she'd never felt the need to blush before.

His voice rang out in the room. "You're the chosen from this generation." He nodded. "Come."

They all scrambled up to follow the man and his entourage. Mei glanced around. Everyone was dressed in elaborate silks. The powerful stench of perfume filled her nose as she stepped in with the others holding their drag-ons. Did they know what he meant? Mei glanced at the sleeping dragon. This didn't look like a dendragon, and homdragons didn't have wings. It probably was a dendragon. It was about the same size. She wondered when she would find out what he could manipulate. Excitement flowed through her as she stood.

Mei held her sleeping dragon and followed the crowd. She wanted to ask where they were going, but seeing the look of determination on the faces of her fellow dragon owners, she kept her mouth shut.

They all exited the temple and followed a path farther up the mountain. *Is this where we will get our apprenticeship?* Mei hoped that someone kind would take her on.

As the sun set behind the trees, they continued their trek up the mountain. Feeling light-headed from not eating all day, Mei forced her feet to walk. The others, in their volumi-nous kimonos and yukatas, looked like they hadn't fared any better. There were only ten of them altogether. Mei swore the priests had taken more out. Maybe they were just the last group from the selection.

They arrived at an iron gate. It was already dark, and the chorus of cicadas trailed behind them.

Mei looked up at the gigantic fortress before her. They'd built it into the mountain, just like the temple, with the help of dendragons. Walls climbed up the side. Torchlights lit various paths that went around each level of the fortress. A shodragon flew in and landed inside a side opening and went through. The cold air blew stronger up here, and she shivered. The fresh scent was something she could get used to. She glanced around at the others as they took a moment to rest while the man talked to the guard stationed at the gate.

Mei knew of this place. *What am I doing here?* Eyes wide, she glanced down at her sleeping dragon. *Could he be—*

The man interrupted her thoughts. "Welcome, shodragon riders."

FOUR

Chin frowned at the bright jade yukata. Mother always wanted to put him in green. He sighed and shrugged on the silky material. It folded around his shoulders and brushed against his forearms. Green wasn't normal for a yukata, but he didn't have the energy to argue today. He tightened the obi around his waist and smoothed his short brown hair. Stiffening his jaw, he took a long breath and rolled out his shoulders. Today would go smoothly. His family came from a long line of homdragon bonders, with the rare shodragon. He would be no different.

He slid open the paper door to his room and walked down the long wooden halls. The air refreshed his face, and a light breeze rustled the yukata around his legs. Chin slid open another screen door and found his mother, father, and older brother already sitting on the floor next to the table, eating.

"You shouldn't oversleep," his mother scolded as she wiped down a pair of chopsticks and placed them next to his plate. She was already dressed in an immaculate purple kimono, everything neatly in place. A hair on her head wouldn't dare move out of place once she'd tied it up. Her face had the beauty of a painting, but there was little kindness in her eyes.

His father, Masuo, smiled and continued to eat. "Aiko, he has plenty of time." It was rare to see his father smile since he'd lost his dragon. Although it never did reach his eyes. Mother must have pulled out all the stops today to get his father at breakfast. His clothes were still rumpled; he'd probably slept in them after passing out from drinking last night.

Chin ignored his mother and sat across from his brother, Kazu. In Kazu's lap, a pale green homdragon sat curled up, trying to snatch food as he ate. Her lavender eyes focused on his chopsticks. His brother wore the standard green yukata with a light green obi of one training to be a healer. Kazu nodded to Chin. His brother had bags under his eyes.

"Don't you have training today?" Chin asked. He dished rice into his bowl. It had been a long time since his brother had come home. Chin couldn't blame him.

Kazu gently shoved the homdragon's head back. "Not on selection day. They know you're eighteen and gave me the day off."

Chin nodded and ate the breakfast placed before him. The rice stuck to his throat, and he washed it down with tea. The hot liquid hadn't cooled, and Chin sputtered.

Kazu laughed. "You got tea on your yukata."

Aiko jumped up and grabbed Chin by the shoulders, shoving him back. Chin's legs flew in the air, and he fell backward.

"Get off, Mother!"

Aiko didn't listen, and her dark eyes scanned the yukata. "Where did you see the spill?"

Kazu snorted. "He didn't."

Aiko clicked her tongue and released Chin. He scowled at his brother's gleeful expression.

"Are you trying to kill me?" Chin asked.

"No need." Kazu's voice lowered. "Mother will take care of that for me."

Chin stabbed at his grilled fish and chewed while glaring at his brother. Although if there was tea on the yukata, he could change into a different color. After a few bites of his meal, Chin pushed the dishes away.

His mother eyed the leftover food. "Are you sick?"

"No."

"Then finish. You're too thin."

Chin rolled his eyes and got up from the table. "I'll wait outside."

His mother said something, but he shut the screen door and briskly walked out to the front entrance. He closed his eyes and stretched his sore back, letting the calmness of the morning soothe him. Spiderwebs glittered with morning dew around the wooden pillars of the porch. His mother kept strict watch over them. No other bugs were tolerated in her home. When he was younger his mother would gently handle the spiders and place them in his palm. "No spider will ever harm you." His young heart trusted her words.

Lost in memories of better times, he sat on the stone steps and stared out over the city. Their family home was higher on the mountain, and the city of Tenghua sprawled out like a clawed hand beneath him. It seemed so still in the morning sun.

Chin rarely got a chance to go into the city. Mother occupied his days with training and private tutors. He sighed and rested his chin on his knees. Today he might get a taste of freedom away from his family. Chin didn't remember his parents shutting his brother inside the house. Just yesterday, Mother had yelled at him for going to the market.

"Not that it was an exceptional experience," Chin muttered to himself. Finding the eta girl strapped to the fish stand... Chin grimaced at the memory of the dried blood on her back and her hand that had turned a dark shade of purple.

He should have stayed out of the fish seller's business, but from across the stalls, he'd seen her fierce eyes as she'd risen to her feet. Her body had shaken, but her thin jaw had been set. Chin couldn't let someone so determined to live die at the hands of the blubbering owner. If his mother ever found out he had helped an eta... Chin sat up and shook his head. He surely would not tell, so there was no way she would ever find out. Giving the owner his actual name probably hadn't been a wise choice, though.

The wooden door slammed open behind Chin, and he jumped to his feet to avoid a lecture on getting his clothes dirty, but it was only his brother.

Chin sat back down. "I thought you were Mother."

Kazu sat next to him. "So your eyes wouldn't have popped like that if you'd known it was me?"

"Did you want something?"

"Just out here to see the precious little one before he gets his dragon."

"You are the eldest."

"Yes, but you're the baby."

Chin glanced at his brother's homdragon. "What's it like?"

"They haven't told you all this?"

Chin shrugged and looked at the ground.

His brother elbowed him in the side. "Painful, but once their eyes gaze into yours, the pain is forgotten." He lovingly stroked his homdragon's neck. She slept while curled around his neck. Her square jaw had a bit of rice on it. His brother always gave in to her.

"What's it like to have something else in your mind?"

His brother smiled softly. "Comforting."

Before Chin could ask more questions, the door burst open, and they both jumped. Their mother stood in the center, with a light purple homdragon draped around her neck. Her hair sat in a bun at the nape of her neck, and she scowled at her two sons.

"Are you out here getting dirty?"

"No, Mother," Chin mumbled.

She sniffed, came down the stairs, and scanned Chin with her dark eyes. "Where are your sandals?"

Chin grimaced and ran back inside to slip on the wooden sandals. Their loud clacking as he ran back outside accompanied the sound of the rickshaw approaching. He stood behind his mother.

"Is Father coming?"

"No. He's preparing for the celebration."

Chin almost wished his mother would have stayed to prepare, but he knew better. She would never miss the moment her son got a dragon, and his father would never leave the house.

He helped his mother inside the rickshaw and sat next to her. She sat straight, her hands folded politely in her lap. Chin tried to look as regal but slouched back when the rickshaw jolted forward.

They rolled up the narrow street to the temple. Trees spread out between different manors. Even though they were going uphill, the pace made the trees blur a bit in Chin's view. He caught a whiff of the dying cherry blooms.

"I think it would be wise to get a homdragon that can create metals."

"I don't think I get to choose." Of all the types of homdragons metal creators were the most rare. He knew Emperor Xion had one that could make gold. No other like the Emperors exsisted.

His mother blinked. "Nonsense. Just focus."

There would be no pleasing her. He could get a shodragon and she would still be unhappy. In the cramped rickshaw, Chin tried to edge away from his mother, but for his efforts, all he got was slapped in the knee by her fan.

"Stop fidgeting."

The drive felt like it took years, and when they arrived at the temple, Chin practically leaped out of the rickshaw. His sandals clacked against the stone path, and his mother sniffed and refrained from whacking him with her fan since they were in public.

"Stay close."

Chin bit his lip and followed his mother. Even though the priests were close by, Mother had to stop and talk to every other daim present. Chin stood quietly behind her and shifted from foot to foot while his mother laughed at some insipid joke. Every so often, she would drag him forward by the shoulders and display him like a prize horse, then go back to chattering.

In the crowd, he thought a ghost in a gray death shroud passed him, but after a moment, it was gone. *That would've been more exciting.*

They finally reached the priest, and his mother handed over the silk bag that contained five thousand silver. The priest gestured for Chin to continue forward, but his mother grabbed his elbow.

"What, Mother?"

She leaned in and whispered in his ear, "Remember, one that can create metals."

"Sure." He reclaimed his elbow and went into the cave behind the priest.

At the round pool, Chin rolled up his sleeves and washed his hands and arms. The faint smell of jasmine came from the water. Familiar faces surrounded him, but Chin didn't want to talk anymore, and he traveled down the dark tunnel.

The golden lanterns gave the stone halls an unearthly gleam. Chin's heart thumped in his chest, and the loud clack of his sandals on the stone unnerved him. Up ahead, the path opened to the large cavern that contained the dragon eggs. Eggs of different sizes glowed in a rainbow of colors.

Chin placed his hands out on either side of the path and ambled between the eggs. He paused for a breath before moving on to the next set of eggs. With each failure, his chest tightened. He rubbed his hands quickly over his arms and continued down the line of glowing eggs. *Please pick me.* He wanted to get away from his mother.

The minutes passed slowly, and a few of his compatriots left the cavern with blood trailing down their arms. Chin wandered at a steady pace until there were no more eggs. A priest at the end of the path met him, and his thin cloth mask waved slightly.

"Come with me to the next room."

Chin nodded and left the cavern. Disappointment sank

into his bones. There would be no homdragon for him. He could already see his mother's pursed lips when he came out with a dendragon. A larger cavern came into view, and Chin fell in line with the others. He placed his hands out for the smaller eggs and plodded along, waiting for the sharp teeth of a dragon to bite him.

Chin started when a priest was once again in front of him. He hadn't even noticed that he'd gone through all the eggs.

The priest hesitated before speaking. "Follow me."

This time, they wove through various tunnels, and Chin had to edge sideways through some passages. The priest made no sound as they walked, and Chin had the sudden urge to yank off his loud wooden sandals. The path got steeper as they walked along and finally ended at a faintly lit room with two priests standing at the entrance. They wore black, and their masks were carved of wood and painted black. If he wasn't paying attention, Chin probably wouldn't be able to see them.

They paused before the two guards. "Do you understand what lies beyond and the commitment if you enter?" one of them asked.

Chin bit his lip. *Shodragons.* "I do. I accept."

The priest nodded at the guards, and they let them pass into the cavern beyond. There were no pathways in this room, but in the cavern's front, large eggs sat nestled in silk-lined wooden cradles. The priest stayed next to Chin, and they approached the first egg. It was half the size of a human body and bright gold. He could almost feel the hum of energy coming from the egg. They walked to the next one, and it was a deep ruby color. The next few were already cracked, but the priest paused in front of the eggshells at the center and stepped back. The black shell was broken and scattered in the room, whereas the other shards had been placed back in the box.

"Wait," the priest said and went to the entrance.

Chin could hear a flurry of words, and then one of the priest guards ran off. Confused, Chin stood obediently. After the priest returned, they continued to pass by all the eggs. As they approached the last one, Chin willed its blue shell to crack open. Nothing.

The priest said nothing, but he didn't have to. A dragon hadn't selected him. He was no better than an eta. Chin dropped his head as he followed the priest. His steps slowed. When his mother saw him without a dragon, she would cast him aside.

In their journey back to the entrance, they passed by a brightly lit room, and Chin glanced inside out of the corner of his eye. In the room, people held their dragons with a sense of wonder in their eyes. A deep bitterness formed in his stomach, and his fingernails bit into his palms. The person who he'd thought was a ghost sat in the room. It was her. It had to be. It looked like she had mud on her body, but she wore a gray yukata. Chin froze when he saw an onyx dragon in her lap.

A painful numbness set in as she stared down at the dragon. A shodragon. How had an eta gotten a shodragon? The priest noticed Chin wasn't moving, and he stepped in front of the door, blocking his view.

Chin turned his head away. *That should have been me,* Chin thought. A voice in the pit of his mind wondered if he had let her die, would that have been his dragon?

He blinked at wishing someone dead. Shame enveloped him. No, the dragon wouldn't have chosen him. Some claimed a dragon selection was based on the heart. If he wished death upon a living being, then maybe the dragons had made the right choice in not choosing him.

Chin shuffled along, and the brightness of the sun startled him. Ahead, he saw the purple kimono of his mother and the sun glinting off her homdragon's scales.

She turned as the priest approached, and her eyes widened at the sight of Chin by his side. Aiko quickly left the group she was talking to and came over to them.

"What is going on? Why is he out here?"

"Come this way, please." The priest gestured to a painted wooden building away from all the gathered people.

Aiko sniffed and followed the priest. She matched her steps with Chin's. "What's going on?" she whispered sharply.

Chin turned his head to the side so he wouldn't meet her gaze. She huffed and went with the priest into the building.

"Please sit," the priest said. "The chief priest will be with you shortly."

"What's going on?" Aiko demanded.

The priest bowed. "Please wait here." He pointed to square pillows on the floor in front of a low table.

The priest left, but she stayed standing, tapping her foot. The homdragon woke up and sputtered slightly at Aiko's jarring movements.

"Chin, what's going on?"

Chin sat down and stared at his hands but said nothing.

Aiko strode up to him, bent over, and slapped him smartly on the cheek. "Answer your mother!"

His cheek burned, but he still didn't talk. He would let the priest explain to her how he was a failure and no better than an eta who had somehow gotten a shodragon. He stayed still and studied his palms. *That's funny. There is a bit of dirt on my right palm.* Chin used his thumb to rub it off.

The screen door slid open, and the chief priest entered the room. His yukata was a modest golden brown, and behind his wrinkled face, his tan eyes were full of pity. The priest gestured for Aiko to sit, and he moved with grace for one so old as he sat at the table across from Chin.

"My apologies for the wait."

Aiko crossed her arms and remained standing. "What's going on?"

"It seems that for this selection, your son wasn't chosen." The chief priest handed the money back to Aiko. "Please understand that this means nothing about your son or his character. The next selection is in six months, and he can come again when there are newer eggs. I know this can be troubling, but this is actually normal for most daim since the number of homdragons is fewer than dendragons. Also, shodragons are rare."

Chin stopped rubbing his palm clean. He didn't want to go through this again in six months.

"No," his mother responded. "He's getting a homdragon now. We're not waiting six months. Go get an egg and bring it here."

"That's not how it works," the chief priest responded calmly. "It's not possible to force a bond."

"Then he will go in again."

The chief priest stood and bowed. "I do not believe that will change anything for this selection. However, you are welcome to have him try again, and you may stand by him."

Aiko nodded sharply. "And you will be there too."

The chief priest bowed again.

Chin stood, and his face burned at the thought of going

through the selection again. This time, his mother and the priest would follow him like he was a bad pet that hadn't performed the correct trick. It was pointless to argue, so he meekly followed the chief priest and his mother outside and back into the caves.

He mechanically washed his hands and arms again as they watched. Then he shuffled back to the first room and walked stiffly between each egg as his mother and the chief priest followed. Chin hoped that the ground would sink and consume him. It would make his mother happy not to have a failure for a son. Then Kazu could carry the family and their pride.

The end arrived, and the chief priest took Chin to the next area. Chin could feel his mother's eyes boring into his back as he walked around the dendragon eggs. Once finished, the chief priest did not take them to the shodragons but back outside.

As he came out of the gloomy caves, the bright sun still shocked him.

His mother paused. "Again."

The chief priest bowed and started to take them through once more.

"No," Chin whispered.

His mother turned. "What did you say?"

"Not again. I can't go through again."

"We will go through until a dragon chooses you."

"No." The bright sun burned his back as he faced his mother in front of the cave entrance.

She stepped forward, and Chin flinched, but she never struck. "Get back in there."

Chin bent his head and followed them. They did this over and over, and after the sixth attempt, when they went outside, the sun had dipped behind the mountain. There were no people left outside the entrance, and only a few priests remained, putting away the tables. The glow of the lanterns in the trees cast skeletal shadows on the ground. Chin shuddered from the chill in the air, and he turned to go back into the cave.

This time, his mother's voice cracked through the silence. "Enough."

The chief priest bowed again. "Come again in six months' time. Some were in their twentieth year before they were selected."

The chief priest had said that as a comfort, but his mother's jaw twitched. Seeing her stony expression as they walked back to the lone rickshaw, Chin couldn't stop his teeth from chattering. He knew what was coming.

He helped his mother, and she again sat upright and tall. Chin didn't bother to pretend and curled toward the back. The lanterns blinked, waving in the breeze as they made their way back down the mountain.

They reached their home, and it was aglow with sadly festive lanterns. His father and brother waited at the steps. As Chin exited without a dragon, their mouths gaped open.

Kazu started to speak, but Aiko cut him off with a wave of her hand. "Direct the maids to clean this up. There's no celebration tonight." Her stance was stiff as she walked up the stairs and handed her homdragon to Chin's father. "Go to your room, Chin."

Chin's father said, "Aiko, not—"

"Go to your room," she said to Chin.

Chin nodded and placed his wooden sandals at the entrance. He padded to his room and slid off the green yukata. The silky material slipped through his numb fingers.

He only took off the top of the undergarment, leaving his chest and back bare. Chin knelt in the middle of the room and waited.

Then the screen door opened. He didn't turn. It was his mother. He clenched his jaw.

The first blow of the bamboo whip surprised him enough that he let out a shocked gasp. The second stung, and Chin could already feel blood dripping down his back. But he didn't dare move. Not until it was over. He remained on his knees, and with each sting of the whip, his back jerked and his fingers dug into his thighs. He gazed upward toward his window. The luminescent moon dripped pearls of light into the darkness. His eyes burned, but he knew better than to cry. Chin collapsed on the floor. He didn't even know how many strikes had landed on his back. There had never been this many before. He lay with his cheek pressed to the cool wood and closed his eyes, wanting to be anyone else. The whoosh of the whip finally stopped.

Aiko's voice broke the silence. "Never shame your family in this way again."

Her footsteps disappeared out the door, and she shut the screen behind her. Although his bed was only a few feet away, Chin didn't move. In some way, the cold ground was more of a comfort.

The reality of the day sank in. He hadn't been chosen. There would be no freedom from his mother. Quiet tears leaked from his eyes. He wanted to scream, but he'd lost his voice.

FIVE

As Mei waited with the others, the man in charge glanced at her. She felt every bit of mud clinging to her skin. He stepped toward her and stared down at her. His long hair fell over his shoulder and almost brushed against her. She cautiously stepped away from his piercing gaze.

"Apparently, you have caused quite a stir. They're questioning my authority in letting you be here. Come." The man waved to the guards. "Get them to the top of the tower. I have other business to settle before they arrive."

The guards bowed and rushed to the others. Mei followed the man to the front entrance of the fortress. He stood still, staring off into nothing. He looked back at her and saw her confused expression. "We must fly to get there. It's faster, and I would like some sleep tonight."

I guess I'm the business. She squeezed her sleeping dragon. It wheezed and fell back asleep.

The man smiled. "Are you afraid?"

Mei blinked. "No." Thankfully, he couldn't hear her frantic heartbeat.

He laughed. "Good."

Before them, a large golden dragon landed. Even in the dark, she shone like the sun. A strong breeze stirred Mei's hair, and the shodragon folded her wings. She stood perfectly still and lifted her forearm. Her dark purple eyes whirled as she took in her new passenger. The shodragon then glanced away, like seeing an eta covered in dirt was nothing new to her.

Mei gasped. She had only seen this shodragon from a distance, but everyone knew who rode her. A man who was more kami than human, in the eyes of eta, stood before her. It was Jion-sho, head of the shodragon riders. Most claimed he had more power than the emperor, and the title of Sho had been given to him a mere few years ago in battle, after the last Sho had died. He was the youngest to ever rule the shodragons.

Jion-sho gave his dragon a loving thump on the forearm. He turned back to Mei. "Coming?"

Her frozen legs inched forward. When she reached him, he put his hands around her waist and hoisted her up to the harness. She flinched, and he jumped behind her in one smooth motion. Jion-sho leaned forward and whispered in her ear, "Are you injured, other than your hand?"

"It's nothing." Mei didn't want to show him any weakness. The looks from the other recruits had given her a hint at how well she would be accepted.

His breath tickled her ear. "It's more than nothing. We'll get you to a homdragon healer after this mess is sorted out."

Mei stared forward. She sat stiffly while he strapped the harness around his legs.

"This isn't meant for two, so I will hold you tight."

"The pain doesn't bother me." Mei lived in a world of constant slaps, beatings, and shoves. Had she ever had a day where she hadn't been in pain? After all, an eta wasn't human. It didn't matter if she hurt.

With no vocal command, Mei felt the massive power of the shodragon tense under her as she sprang upward. Mei almost gasped as they dipped before the wings balanced them. The insides of her body jerked with the forward rush as they flew up the fortress. The chilly wind hit Mei in the face, shocking her, but she smiled. She was riding a shodragon.

They passed floors of lamplit windows. All the shodragon riders lived here, as well as a full staff of healers and guards. Shadows passed in the windows, but no one looked out to see the glorious golden shodragon fly. They must have been used to it. Mei turned her head to see the city behind her, and she'd never felt so free. *Father, the golden dragon flies tonight.* The air meant freedom. *I don't know if I will get used to this.* A bitter laugh almost escaped her lips, but it was interrupted by the smooth landing at the top of the fortress.

They landed in a large courtyard that could probably hold hundreds of dragons. Jion-sho jumped down and lifted Mei, small dragon and all, to the ground. The stone floor was cold against Mei's bare feet, and it made her legs twinge. Tall pillars surrounded the courtyard, and only a short stone ledge kept people from falling down the mountain. A young person lit the torches at the top of the pillars as they walked to a pair of large doors. The lamplighters closed the glass shutters before the brisk wind could blow out the flame. Mei bit her lip. Glass was expensive, and she'd only seen it from a distance. Only a few dendragons could manipulate heat to forge glass. This was something that occurred in daim homes. Most still just slid open their paper-covered shutters to get light. Mei's home didn't even have windows.

Jion-sho nodded to the two guards at the doors. The wooden doors spanned the height of the building, which dwarfed the shodragon, yet they swung open smoothly, perfectly balanced.

The chamber was well lit and filled with gray polished stone. The back angled up toward the ceiling and blended into the mountain. Stone benches were evenly spaced apart, but at the front, a group of riders sat waiting on polished wooden chairs. They all wore hakama that were split down the middle like loose pants with kimonos over top. Each rider wore a different solid color. The obis around their middle were black. Mei didn't know if the colors meant something, but Jion-sho wore pure black.

Jion-sho took long strides, and Mei had to run to keep up with him. After they reached the front, he looked down at her. "Stay here. I need to sit up there."

Mei froze, and part of her wanted to grab him and beg him not to leave her to stand alone. He seemed strict, but Mei had a feeling that behind his sharp eyes, he was on her side. "I will be fine." She was proud that her voice didn't shake. As he walked away, Mei felt colder, and the stares from the other riders bored into her. She softly stroked the dragon in her arms. *I won't let them take you.*

The dragon opened one eye, yawned, and went back to sleep. He didn't seem too worried. Mei felt oddly reassured.

"So this is the eta that got chosen by a shodragon?

What's the big deal?" The man wearing dark green on Jion-sho's right spoke in a low gravelly voice.

"The eta shouldn't even have a chance to get a dragon," said the woman in purple at the end. Her face pinched like she'd eaten something sour.

Jion-sho held up his hand, silencing her. "Watch what you say. Everyone has an opportunity to get chosen."

Sour Expression grimaced. "What I meant to ask is where did it get the money for the dragon?"

There was a pause, and then they all looked at Mei. She looked back at them.

"Speak, eta!" Sour Face yelled.

What if they found out Mei was a thief? Would they take the dragon away? "M-my father gave me the money. He wouldn't use it for healing. He sold something."

"Something?"

"There was a chest that belonged to my mother, and I never learned what was inside."

"What was your mother's name?" asked a reedy man.

"Rikku."

All the riders froze, then Sour Face said, "Rikku. Any honorific?"

"Eta don't have honorifics." Mei's arms were getting tired from holding the dragon. Shouldn't they know that eta didn't have family names?

They whispered, and the thin man in gray sneered. "She should not have a shodragon. This was an obvious mistake. The dragon should be given to someone with more breeding."

They all broke out in argument. It started quietly, until they were yelling over each other. Some stood and gestured wildly. Amid it all, Jion-sho sat and stared at Mei, like he studied a problem he hadn't seen before. The sensei seemed divided. Most didn't care, but a few wanted her gone. They were the ones who kept mentioning the Emperor. The shouts continued.

"Can she even read?"

"You can't just take a dragon once it's bonded, you know this."

"The dragon's clearly defective."

"Maybe we should throw her out and see if the dragon will let someone else ride it."

"You know it doesn't work that way!"

"Who cares if she's eta. The dragon always chooses."

"You would say that since you aren't daim."

"Snob!"

"Ass!"

"Lizard rider!"

"Enough!" Jion-sho stood, and they all fell silent. "What a waste of time. She's no longer an eta. A shodragon has chosen her. You all know the bond that forms cannot be undone. Fools, all of you." They all looked away from Jion-sho's piercing gaze. "With the rains coming, we need shodragons. You would throw out a rider because of your petty society tiers? Once a rider is chosen, tiers disappear, as do honorifics. There's only us and the battle ahead."

"But the Emperor wants us to evaluate—"

Jion-sho cut off Sour Face. "The Emperor has no power here. The Sho controls the fortress. He knows this. He's dealing with some crying daim whose son didn't get a dragon, so she will train with the rest." His eyes met each of theirs. Some of them had drawn-out pauses, and Sour Face looked away. "I expect her to be treated as an equal in training and classes."

"How will she?" the man in green asked.

Jion-sho frowned, and the man cowered. "What do you mean?"

"Well, has she had any schooling?"

Jion-sho looked at Mei. "Can you read?"

"No."

"Write?"

"Not really."

"Add?"

"Some." Mei's face fell. Of course, all the daim and feu went to school or had private tutors. Mei stole fish. She curled her toes against the cold stone floor. *Why did he pick me? I am nothing.* The dragon continued to sleep, oblivious to the drama he'd caused.

The other riders smirked. "Rider." Mei looked up at his determined face. "You will work twice as hard as everyone else. You must learn these things on your own in your free time. Do you understand?"

"Yes."

Jion-sho nodded. "You will learn." He looked away from Mei. "Any more complaints?" He glared at the other riders. "This doesn't change the fact she's now a shodragon rider. She can learn just as well as the rest." The room was silent. Jion-sho's dark gaze went to the back of the room, and he motioned to the guards. "Bring them in."

The other recruits walked in behind Mei. When they reached her, they all glanced at her and then at the riders. Their gazes contained several raised brows and gaping mouths. A girl with a broad nose curled her lip in disgust at Mei. A handsome young man with a red shodragon studied her like she was a statue in the grand hall. His gaze made her uncomfortable, but he blinked and glanced away.

Jion-sho stood, and as he walked, the large doors on the sides of the hall opened. All the shodragons entered to stand behind their riders. After the last one had entered, they shut the doors against the chilly wind of the summer night. In the flickering lanterns, the riders with their dragons made a formidable impression.

A sheen of sweat covered Mei's face. Their eyes held no kindness when they fell on her. Most looked past her like she didn't exist. Her gaze met the rider who wore green and he tilted his head in an encouraging nod. Maybe they all didn't hate her.

"Before you are the wingleaders who command their own legion," Jion-sho said, his deep voice echoing clearly in the hall. "They are here today not only to congratulate you on being chosen, but to also witness my warning."

All the recruits knelt while holding their dragons. "You had the option not to enter the cavern of the shodragons."

Mei blinked and tried to meet the Sho's eyes. He solemnly nodded at her. She glanced down at her sleeping dragon. *What have you gotten me into?*

"So you already understand the strict rules of being a recruit. I will tell you the rules again, and you will follow them without question."

A guard came in holding an ornate golden bowl and handed it to Jion-sho. From this distance, Mei couldn't see the exact stones on the sides, but they glimmered in the torchlight.

"Once you are chosen, the dragon marks you, but we take it one step further. Your loyalty is to the wingleaders and to me, your Sho." Jion-sho stepped down, holding the golden bowl. "You all know that you may not leave for the next three years without permission from me or one of the wingleaders in this room. Those who leave will be severely punished." Jion-sho drew closer. "Desertion is punishable by taking your dragon and for the rider, death."

The other recruits solemnly nodded around her, but they didn't look surprised. They'd known what they were signing up for, and they'd made the choice. Mei felt invisible chains wrap around her wrists and ankles. They might not want her here, but she couldn't even leave.

"In the past, there have been warnings, but I have seen shodragon riders stripped of their dragons and executed, their class punished along with them."

She glanced to her side. So if one of them left, all of them would be punished? Mei clutched her dragon tighter. *I can't go see my father.* The finality of her situation sank into her stomach, and the invisible chains became heavier. When she'd left this morning, she'd held a tiny hope that as an apprentice, she would get to see him. But Jion-sho had just handed out her jail sentence for the next three years.

"Loyalty above all."

"Loyalty above all," the wingleaders repeated.

Jion-sho reached out right in front of Mei. He held the golden bowl forward, and inside, the liquid was so black she couldn't see the bottom.

"Where the dragon claimed you will now stand as a reminder. Place the wound in the bowl."

Mei held up her hand, the blood now dried. She shifted her dragon to her broken hand and placed her right one in the dark liquid. It was hot, and she almost jerked her hand away, but Jion-sho held her arm with his free hand. The bite mark flared, and her eyes watered from the pain. The burning heat felt like she'd stuck her hand in an open flame.

He looked down into her eyes, and she felt lost in the darkness of his gaze.

"Loyalty above all," he said softly.

Mei nodded and repeated, "Loyalty above all." She noticed his slight look of approval. *I didn't know what else to do.* She wished he would have gone up to someone else first.

Jion-sho freed her burning hand and moved on to the next recruit. The other pledges murmured in the background as she studied the wound. From the bite mark that the dragon had left, black veins twisted out like rotting tree branches. The injury was now sealed, and the mark would not fade.

He stepped back from the last recruit and handed the bowl to the waiting guard. Jion-sho returned to his chair and stood in front, his movements sure and solid. He took in all the recruits. Then, with the other wingleaders, he bowed, and the recruits bowed in return.

Jion-sho straightened and strode to Mei. "Let's go."

She followed him silently, and without turning, she knew the recruits all glared at her back. She wished he hadn't singled her out like this. The weariness of the day sank into her bones. Everything hurt, and she yearned to be home with her father and that he could hum to her as she fell asleep. Would he ever know that a dragon had chosen her? Did her father know what she was about to face? She pictured his steady breathing while asleep and the smooth clink of the jade beads, and her heart ached. Her throat grew tight, and part of her thought she would never see him again. Three years. From the looks on their faces, none of the wingleaders would let her go visit her father.

They went out the doors, and Jion-sho lifted her onto the shodragon. This time, it was more of a long jump down to another wide ledge than a flying ascent. Jion-sho jumped off and lifted Mei down. Even though her body burned, she itched at the thought of him continuing to lift her. Her back and hand weren't that bad; she'd lived through worse. *I'm just an eta, Jion-sho.*

The doors ahead were much smaller but also made of wood. They went through and entered a long stone corridor with a few lamps in the darkness.

"These barracks are for the new recruits. You are housed by your selection day." They walked down the hall, and Jion-sho opened a door with an unfamiliar symbol on it. He pointed to it. "This is 27, where you'll sleep and keep your clothing." No one was in the room, but single beds lined the space. The walls were bare, but dimming shades were on the lamps next to the beds. Very plain but everyone got the same size bed and space. "I wanted to show you first since some of them already know." He motioned to the bed closest to the window. "If I were you, I would pick that one. The window may have a colder breeze in the winter, but you'll have more privacy."

He opened the trunk at the end of the bed. Clothing waited inside. "Everyone gets the same clothes to sleep and train in. You're responsible for washing them yourself, and there will be inspections. I would suggest you bathe before changing into them." A smaller bed was next to Mei's. "That's where your dragon will sleep for the next few days until you get assigned your den." He lifted the bed, showing black stones. "These are heated every night while they sleep here." He pointed to a long wooden table under the window. "The dragons will get hungry often, and at night, a tray of meat is placed in the room for them."

"Where do I bathe?"

Jion-sho tilted his head and took her out of the room. They went to the very end of the hall. "This is for the women." He pointed at another symbol on the door. "Tomorrow, you will report at first dragon call down in front of the fortress. Any questions?"

Mei had hundreds, but no one else would be getting a tour from the Sho, so she shook her head. "No."

Jion-sho started to leave, then he turned around. "You will not have an easy time with the other recruits. They're privileged and have years of training already." He crossed his arms. "But you have something they don't. You've had to scrap and fight for everything in your life, and that is the person I want covering my back in battle."

Mei bowed. "I won't let you down." Somehow knowing he was on her side made her feel safe. He wouldn't let them take her dragon. Although he also knew that no one else would accept her. If she surpassed them all, maybe she would have time to take care of her father. Her father. "Sho, I..."

"What is it?" His tone was brisk.

She bowed her head. "My father, he won't know what happened to me, and I can't see him."

A warm hand settled on her shoulder. "I'm sorry you didn't know what you signed up for, but you have to see it through. Your father will believe that everything is okay. Usually, in the second year, some leave time is granted. I am sorry, recruit."

"Can I send him a message?"

"You can try."

He left the words unspoken, but no one would take a message to the eta district and search for her father. She didn't even know how to write. And who could read it if she did? "I will work hard."

Jion-sho smiled, and with that, he strode out of the barracks. The sound of his boots got quieter the farther away he went, until Mei stood in complete silence.

She didn't know when the others would arrive, so she quickly grabbed a change of clothes and went into the baths. Steam hit her face. A large pool of flowing water set deep in black stone greeted her, and her eyes widened at having so much water to bathe in. She stripped off her yukata and placed her dragon down in its folds.

"Do you only sleep?" she asked the still form. He didn't respond. She shook her head and took out the string that tied her hair back. Her black hair tangled in her fingers, and she'd never owned a comb. She thought maybe she could get it cut like the sour face who wore purple, as it would be much easier to manage. Even though women in the city wore their hair long, most of the shodragon riders kept their hair short.

The scalding water made her skin smart and her wounds burn. It was nothing like she had ever experienced. The mud floated away from her, and she ducked her head under the water and pulled her good hand through her hair. Mei gasped as she resurfaced, and she let out a short laugh. "Was jumping in the water like this, Father?" Her voice was quiet in the empty room, and she dunked again and again.

The water that rushed around her ran clear as she worked out years of grime. Colorful solid soaps were in containers, and Mei used one. Now she smelled like some sort of flower. Only a hint of red stained the water from her back wounds, which had reopened. She held up her arm.

Her skin was darker than the other riders, but now it looked like a lighter tan.

The door slid open, and she jumped up. A young woman with a kind round face and a pinkish homdragon around her neck entered. "Jion-sho said you need healing?" Her green yukata swished around her curvy figure as she approached. Her hair was tied back in a simple braid that kept it away from her face.

Mei nodded and waded toward the edge. She held up her broken hand that still had the cloth tied around it.

The lady clicked her tongue. "This is more serious and will take a few days to heal." She took off the makeshift cast Mei had made, and the homdragon padded forward. Her hand looked worse than Mei had thought. It was a mix of purples and browns and a swollen mass of skin. In a few days, Mei would have needed to find someone to cut it off. The lady held out a fresh bandage, and the dragon spat out something blueish.

Mei watched with wide eyes, and the lady smiled at her expression. "Is this your first time?"

"Yes... What does it do?"

"My homdragon creates a salve that hastens healing. This one helps bones specifically, but I mixed in something for infection. It will take a while, but it should help with the pain." She wrapped up Mei's hand, and her touch was gentle. She took in Mei's tangled hair. "Would you like me to comb out your hair?"

Mei started at the question. Her face was kind, but kindness wasn't always something to be trusted. Once the lady had a grip on her hair, Mei would be vulnerable. She moved cautiously and nodded. "I was thinking of cutting it."

"Practical. Most females do, but others find that tying it

up works too." The lady grabbed a comb out of her sleeve and motioned for Mei to turn. She gasped at her wounded back. "What is this from?"

Mei looked down, not wanting to mention the stolen fish.

"Sit in the bath so your back can soak, and I will take care of your hair first." She knelt. "My name is Emiri, by the way. And you are?"

"Mei."

Emiri combed as she worked out years of grim tangles, and Mei couldn't believe how painless Emiri made the process. She glided her hands through the water as Emiri worked. After a bit, Emiri took out small scissors.

"I don't work with hair, and these are for cutting bandages, but I can trim the edges and make them smooth."

"Okay."

After a longer pause, the snips echoed in the bath. "So, that is your shodragon?" Emiri asked.

Mei peered at the sleeping form. "Yes. He seems to just sleep."

Emiri laughed. It was light and airy like bells. "They tend to do that on selection day. Don't worry. He'll be waking you up in the middle of the night in no time."

"I wonder why he picked me." Mei closed her mouth at her errant thought. She'd just met this lady.

Emiri finished and handed Mei a towel. "I think we all wonder that." She smiled gently at Mei. Emiri got out more clean bandages. "Well, let me wrap this around you, and you should be good to take these off in two days."

Mei got out of the bath, dried off, and let Emiri wrap the clean bandages around her back. She put on the plain white clothes to sleep in and followed her out of the baths.

"Now remember to take it easy with your hand. It won't heal overnight. I know recruits have it in their heads to impress the sensei, but you need time to heal. Otherwise, we might have to re-break some bones."

"I understand."

Emiri left her, and Mei was alone once more in the hall. She went back to the door with the symbol. It was still empty. She placed her sleeping dragon on the bed next to hers and looked out the narrow window. Pricks of light from the city made Mei wonder if her father had finished the last of the fish. Her stomach growled, and she curled up on her bed, facing the stone wall. It didn't take long for her to collapse into sleep.

In the night, the door opened and footsteps shuffled inside. She'd been about to fall asleep again when a harsh voice came from one of the others.

"Don't tell me they are actually going to train it with us?" Mei didn't look, but the voice sounded male.

"Is she really an eta?" a female voice asked.

The whispers quieted, and Mei squeezed her eyes shut. She stuck out her right hand from under the blanket to touch her dragon's warm scales. Comforted by his warmth, she fell back asleep amongst the frantic whispers of her peers.

The loud roar of a dragon jerked Mei awake. It was still dark outside. The others in the room also woke and changed into a white top and long baggy navy hakama that flowed smoothly around their legs. The last piece was a thick white obi. Mei changed as well.

They all took their dragons and rushed down the hall. Mei could smell fish, rice, and miso. Her stomach flipped, and her mouth watered at the thought of fresh food. She stayed behind the others, and they came into a large hall with long wooden tables low to the floor. Mei joined one of the lines for food. Her gaze flicked around the room to follow everyone else. She had never seen so much food. They all got a serving of raw meat for their dragons. Could she just eat this? *I don't know where to start. This food is all fresh and clean.*

Mei's dragon finally woke at the smell and squawked for food. She took a morsel and stuffed it in his mouth before she went to find a seat. The dining hall filled fast, and those with white obis like hers sat in one area. The other recruits had white obis but the ones in the middle table had silver on theirs and the far table had gold.

The part of Mei that believed she was eta hesitated at sitting next to those with the white obi, but they were all equal now, according to the Sho. Mei steeled herself and slowly approached the far table. Her dragon leaned over and helped himself to the meat, finishing before Mei sat down.

The moment she placed the wooden tray down, all faces shifted in her direction. Mei tensed and slowly sat on the ground. Dishes clanked and clattered as the others continued to eat, but at Mei's table, everyone just watched her.

Willing her hand not to tremble, she reached for her chopsticks and lifted a piece of fish to her mouth. *Everything is normal. I'm eating my food.* Just as the godly spices exploded in her mouth, Mei's tray flew across the table and smashed against the wall. A confetti of rice flew across the floor, and the soup spread on the wood. Now the hall was silent.

"Vermin aren't allowed in the hall," said a girl with a broad nose and narrow eyes.

Mei's dragon hissed and perched on her shoulder, and the other dragon, a light brown one, did the same on the girl. They stood there staring each other down while the entire hall watched.

Mei wanted to look down, but the squawking dragon gave her courage. His tiny claws dug into her shoulder as he leaned forward. A wiry female dressed all in white came over.

"Clean this up now! Since you wasted that, that is all you will get until lunch." Her hands stayed on her hips while she glared at Mei.

"I didn't—"

"Well, go on. Clean it up!" The lady held out a cloth.

Mei stiffened her jaw at the girl's smirk and went to clean the food. Her stomach clenched at her wasted breakfast. She was tempted to take some of it out of the hall to eat, but with everyone watching, she didn't dare. She knew what going without food felt like, and she could handle another few hours.

The wiry woman stood over her until every grain of rice had disappeared from the wooden floor and was put onto Mei's tray. Then she yanked the tray out of Mei's hands and went to the back of the kitchen. Mei faced the rest of the table, and her dragon blinked his silver eyes. She wanted to leave, but squaring her shoulders, she sat down at the table and stared at the wall in front of her. Her fingers clenched in her lap.

One by one, all the other recruits took their food and left. They ate while they stood and leaned on the wall, leaving Mei to sit alone. Mei's dragon curled around her neck and warmed her. She smiled slightly at the rejection of her class. Isolation was nothing new to her. They would need to do better than trying to starve her and not sit by her.

The others in the dining hall gradually went back to eating and talking. Soon, everyone took their trays and left. Mei followed her class with the pure white obis. They stood out in the courtyard, huddled in groups far away from Mei.

Another loud dragon roar reverberated through the fortress, and the sour-faced woman from last night approached Mei's class. She adjusted her purple robes and gave Mei a hard glare before raising her hand. The rest of the class fell silent.

"Get into one row."

They complied but left a gap between them and Mei. The lady noticed and smirked.

"I am Sora-sensei. I have the joy of being the head sensei of your recruit class."

She didn't seem too joyful.

"I also teach the class on dragon care, but every morning, you will check in with me in our classroom. I see we have the honor of notable families with us in our recruitment class. Daisuke."

Mei noted that she left off the san. She wanted to roll her eyes. They were all equal but Sora-sensei still pointed them out.

A young man with long hair and a red dragon stepped forward and bowed. "It's my honor to give my family name to become a shodragon rider."

Sora smiled, though her face was still pinched. "Yes, we are all riders now." Her smile disappeared when it landed on Mei. "And Benio, I met with your father last night. He's very proud."

Mei groaned inwardly as the girl with the flat nose bowed. "He always knew I was destined for greatness, sensei."

"As you are. I'll be watching you closely. The rest of you will do well to follow Daisuke and Benio as examples of good decorum. Follow me."

The rest of them didn't get introductions. Mei would pay attention to the others. It was best to know those who surrounded her, and she most definitely wouldn't follow Daisuke and Benio as leaders.

Two of the other girls already flocked next to Benio, one with curls that she kept fixing. She bowed to Benio. "I'm Aimi. My parents are notable shamen. This is Niko." She gestured to the pretty girl next to her who had a dusting of freckles. "Niko's parents own the shipping yard."

Yes, they were all shodragon riders now. So much so that they needed to tell each other what their parents did. Mei stayed back. Mei didn't need to be told to stay away from those three. They already gave her covert looks and whispered.

A tall, willowy girl with a sky blue dragon frowned at the trio of girls.

Sora turned. Mei waited until everyone had cleared before following behind them. She'd rather keep her eyes on them, just like when she'd wait for a gang to pass by so she could rifle through the garbage. Her stomach burned, and she sucked it in so it could feel full.

They came to a sliding door on the first floor. Inside, there was one desk at the back without a stool. She looked around for one and then noticed Sora-sensei staring at her.

"Sit down."

"There's no stool," Mei replied softly.

The other students snickered.

"I can't understand a word you are saying. Sit. Down," Sora said slowly, like she was speaking to a child or someone addled in the mind.

Mei walked past her classmates and stood at the back, glaring forward. Her classmates' eyes burned into her, and the pain of isolation crept inside her. *I can do this. I can pass and get food to Father. I don't need them.*

"My goodness, it doesn't know how to sit in a chair." The class chuckled again at Sora's words. "You're the fortunate few who have been chosen by a shodragon. This means you're part of this training for the next three years."

Sora turned her back and wrote on the board. "After your

third year, a wingleader will decide whether to add you to their division." She smiled haughtily. "I am a wingleader, and I value a quick mind and speed. You would be lucky, however, to join any of the leaders. Since Jion-sho was appointed he hasn't chosen any new wingleaders. Her gaze narrowed. "He will only take the best, and I doubt he will take any of you."

Did the woman even know any of them yet? Mei could think of a few choice words she would have called Sora-sensei on the streets. *Like Sora could survive as an eta for a day.* Mei heard a chuckle and turned, but no one was paying attention to her.

Benio raised her hand, and Sora nodded for her to talk. "Sora-sensei, does everyone get chosen?"

"Only a few have not, but their strengths proved not to be in battle."

Benio looked at Mei and whispered something to Aimi, who stroked her coral dragon. She in turned whispered to Niko and all three of them giggled.

The Sho wouldn't have chosen Sora-sensei, Mei thought to herself. *Poor man got stuck with the old Sho's wingleaders.* The minute Mei's thoughts had left her, she heard another quiet chuckle. She turned her head, but no one was there. Maybe she was addled in the mind. It couldn't be normal to hear laughter. Mei focused since Sora was talking.

"Your daily schedule for lessons will be on the board every day along with your cleaning schedule. We follow the sound of the dragon roar to break up the classes. In the evenings, you will bathe and oil your dragons. There's little free time in the afternoons, but we expect you to use that time to study."

Sora looked around the room, meeting their eyes.

"Having a shodragon means we cannot expel you, but poor grades will be punished. And if you are hoping to join a winglegion someday, you need to show good marks."

Mei stared at the lines on the board at the front. She swallowed a large lump in her throat. Those symbols meant nothing to her. Glancing around the room, she knew no one here would teach her.

"You're not allowed to leave the grounds without permission from a wingleader. I give out passes to those who show good marks. The Sho mentioned the punishment for desertion can lead to death. Also, you may not harm another recruit or dragon. Once again, if you break any of these rules, you'll be punished."

Mei's mind wandered to her father. How would she ever know if he was okay or eating? Sora would never give her a pass. A dragon roar interrupted her thoughts.

"That's your first class for the day."

If Mei had interpreted the board right, it looked like they had about six classes in total. She kept her distance and followed her classmates to the next class. Her heart sank at the sight of the thin man from last night. His boney face followed her movements, and Mei grabbed a stool before it disappeared.

The recruits all found seats and gave Mei's desk a wide berth. Mei stroked her dragon's neck and stared out the open window. It looked so nice outside.

"I am Tomo-sensei," the man said. "This is where you will learn the basics of flight formations and the commands, as well as history." He gestured to a gangly boy next to Daisuke who's hair seemed to have a mind of its own. "Name?"

"Kenta." A deep purple dragon was wrapped around his neck.

"Pass out the books."

Kenta went around, placing one on every desk but Mei's. When it was apparent that the sensei wouldn't do anything, Mei got up to get a book.

"Who gave you permission to get up?" Tomo asked. His boney arms folded across his chest as his black eyes glared at Mei.

Mei's back stiffened. "I need a book."

"Why?"

Mei's eyes traveled to every desk that had one of the frayed books.

"Why?" Tomo asked again. "You can't read."

All the students gasped, and a flurry of whispers broke out behind Mei. Her ears turned red, and she sat back down at her desk. Her dragon cooed and nipped at her ears, but she stared forward, blurring her eyes. She heard nothing of the lesson.

The dragon roar filled Mei with relief. At the end of class, pointed whispers came in her direction.

"The eta can't even read. I can't believe she's in our class," Aimi said.

Benio huffed. "We'll be a laughingstock with her." She flipped her hair and her face twisted in a sneer.

"The sensei don't even want to teach her." Niko held her bronze dragon in her arms.

"I bet the dragon isn't even a shodragon," Benio said loudly in Mei's direction. "It's probably just an overgrown lizard."

Mei clenched her fists and met Benio's eyes. "What'd you say?" She got up from her desk stiffly, her eyes narrowing on the girl.

Benio laughed. "Oh my, Aimi, it's talking to me," she mock whispered to the girl with the coral dragon. She then stood and put her hands on her hips. "Your dragon's a pathetic excuse for a shodragon. It probably can't even fly. They should just snap its neck."

Aimi giggled behind her hands. "Do you think she just put wings on a lizard?"

Mei's heart pounded in her ears. "Don't insult my dragon, and don't threaten him."

"Why? Who's going to stop me?" Benio reached for Mei's hissing dragon.

Mei's fist jabbed into the girl's flat nose. The cartilage in Benio's nose crunched, and Mei's hand made a sickening sound. Blood sprayed as the girl fell, wailing. Mei stepped over Benio's body and looked down at her. "I am."

Benio's dragon surged at Mei, and Mei held up her fist. "No." Mei's voice reverberated, and Benio's dragon stopped in its tracks, cowering before Mei.

Mei lifted her chin and strode out of the classroom. An unfamiliar warmth filled her, and her dragon rubbed his head against her jaw.

Her nose looks better now.

"What?"

That girl, her nose. It's an improvement.

Mei could hear a low voice, and she turned her head, but the halls were empty. Then she peered out of the corner of her eye. The dragon's silver eyes blinked.

"Are you talking to me?"

Who else? I'm hungry. Can we get more of that meat with the white in it?

"Yeah, I'm hungry too," Mei replied dazedly. She'd heard

about dragons talking to their partners, but she'd thought it would happen later. "How are you talking?"

The dragon tilted his head. *I've been shut out now and then, but after you hit that girl, the gates flew open.*

"I was blocking you?"

Most can't speak to their dragons until their second year. It takes practice to make that kind of connection.

"How do you know this?"

It is known. I can hear your thoughts.

"Oh." *Oh. You were laughing in my head.*

There. The dragon chirped. *Call me Kuro and wake me for lunch.*

Okay, then. Mei stepped slowly to her next class, staying well behind her classmates in the distance, as Kuro curled around her neck to sleep. Had her standing up to Benio about Kuro made her hear him more clearly? At least she wasn't going mad. Her thoughts raced back to when she'd first heard the dragon, and she vaguely remembered when the priest had been about to beat her. She shook her head and continued down the hall, just out of sight of her classmates.

Mei stepped into her next class and went to the back like she had in the others. The sensei in this class just ignored her. Mei found she preferred that to Sora's and Tomo's attention. After class, Sora stood in the hallway, her arms folded in her sleeves.

"Come with me." Sora's face was pinched. If her face shrank in any more, it would be indistinguishable from a dried plumb.

Mei followed her back to the classroom.

"Did you not understand the rules?" She emphasized each word as she spoke.

"I understood."

"You hit another recruit?"

"Yes."

She puckered her lips. "That's breaking a rule!"

Mei stood in silence. This woman didn't care what she had to say. Mei might be in the wrong to choose violence. Benio had almost grabbed Kuro, and Mei hadn't been about to let her touch him.

"You will apologize to the recruit, and today, you will go without lunch or dinner. You are only allowed food for your dragon. You should be feeding him now."

Mei opened her mouth, then shut it. She could go without for two days. Did they not know that starvation was nothing to an eta?

"Now get out of my sight."

Mei left the classroom and went down to the dining hall to get the meat for Kuro. To avoid the smell of food, Mei tried to breathe through her mouth. Even the air tasted like spices. It might be time to resort to going through the garbage. She gently woke Kuro, and he ate so fast the meat made lumps appear through his skin.

"You'll choke one day," Mei said.

I want more of the white next time. Are you not eating?

She let him nibble her fingers. "I'm not feeling well."

His eyes flashed. *Lies.*

"I am being punished for hitting that girl."

Idiotic punishment. Get me more meat, and I will give it to you.

"I'm fine."

Benio had a bandage on her nose. "Are you really sitting at our table, talking to yourself?"

Mei looked up from Kuro's empty bowl. "I guess I am."

Mei smiled and stroked Kuro. *She can't even hear her dragon,* she thought smugly.

She's lucky. That dragon has nothing interesting to say.

Oh?

It is jabbering on about the girl's ugly nose. Do you think I can get more meat? He padded his claws on her shoulders in an excited dance.

I'll see, but you know they don't like me.

Kuro's silver eyes gleamed and narrowed. *Bakas.*

Mei felt a comforting warmth at Kuro's words as she got another bowl of raw meat. He kept trying to force her to eat it.

You really didn't even want this, did you?

You need to eat, Kuro grumbled as he gnawed at a bit of fat.

She scratched him under the eyes. *I'm tougher than they think.*

Kuro ate the rest of the raw meat, and Mei snorted at his heavy belly. He already seemed longer today, and soon, he wouldn't be able to perch on her shoulder. The day would come when she would be alone in class. Mei shivered at the thought and continued to follow her classmates at a distance to the next torture session.

She sat hunched in the back of each class and avoided the sensei's attention. After the last dragon roar, the recruits needed to clean their main classroom.

They all stood in Sora-sensei's room. Benio pointed at Mei.

"I think the eta should clean the room. The rest of us have rank."

The willowy girl snorted. "We are all the same rank now."

"Watch it, Toshiko, otherwise we'll think that you are on its side."

Toshiko smoothed out her already perfect hair that was held back in a tight bun. "It probably knows how to clean better than you. I doubt you did a day's work in your pampered life." She grabbed a straw broom and thrust it at Benio.

Benio huffed but took the broom.

Mei didn't know whether to be insulted or not. Was this girl sticking up for her or insulting her?

The rest of the recruits grabbed various cleaning tools out of the closet. Mei stood there and stared at the board. Toshiko sighed and smacked the board. "It says desks. You wipe them." She made an exaggerated wiping motion.

"Arigato." Mei took a cloth and bucket from the closet and went out to get water. It wasn't easy only using one hand to carry it back. In the hall Aimi bowled into her, making her drop the water all over the floor.

"Oops."

Benio giggled at the spilled water. "Oh my Kami, it can't even clean."

Mei thought another punch to the face would do Benio some good, but at this rate she wouldn't get to eat again. Kuro woke from his nap and hissed at Benio, and she stepped back into the room.

Mei cleaned the water in the hall then finished the desks. By the time she was done everyone else had already left and her back burned.

She had time before she needed to feed Kuro. One of the teachers had mentioned a place with more books, and maybe something there could help her understand the scribbles. The halls looked the same, but Mei thought they'd said it was on the second floor. A few students were talking in the hall, and when she passed, they would close in and whisper. Kuro slept, still around her shoulders. She found the stairs to the second floor, and there was only one entrance.

Mei pressed the door open and peeked through the crack. A musty smell hit her nose, and she almost sneezed. Beyond the door, in the lantern-lit room, were shelves and shelves of books. She pushed through the door and dust motes floated in the air as the sun lowered outside the windows. An older lady sat to the side and didn't even look up as Mei stepped into the room.

She debated asking the lady for help, but as she walked closer, it appeared the woman was snoring softly. Mei let her rest, not knowing if the woman would have helped her anyway. Toshiko sat in the corner by herself, her sky blue dragon in her lap as she wrote furiously. Mei went to the opposite side of the room. She didn't know anyone's intentions and even though Toshiko didn't seem to care for Benio, it didn't mean that Mei could trust her.

The books before her held knowledge that any eta would be glad to learn. There were no schools for eta, and her father had taught her the basics the best he could, but he'd gone blind while Mei was young and never taught her to read or write. She remembered he'd tried for months, but without his sight, the lessons had gone nowhere.

"I will learn now, Father." Mei wandered through the shelves and tried to pick out a book that looked easy. She found a thin thread-bound volume and went to a low table to stare at it.

Looking at the words, Mei vainly hoped that maybe one would share its mysteries with her.

"I didn't know that the breeding cycle of moths could be so interesting."

Mei jumped at the familiar voice to her left. Emiri was bent over, reading the passage Mei had been staring at.

"Oh? I didn't know."

Emiri tilted her head. "I've been looking for you to check your bandages. It took forever for those nits to tell me where you were."

Mei's stomach clenched. Emiri was the only one who had shown her any kindness, and Mei didn't want to lose it, but it was better that she find out now rather than later. "I'm an eta."

Emiri snorted. "No, you're a shodragon rider. And if I've learned anything from my training in healing, it's that humans are all the same on the inside."

Mei grimaced. "That's a bit gruesome."

"We all bleed. We all die. Will you let me check your wounds? Or are you too proud to let me look? I have to make sure the bones healed correctly. It was hard to tell with all the swelling yesterday."

Mei's eyes widened. She untied her obi and hoisted up her uniform, showing Emiri her back. She touched the bandages in various places, and Mei only winced a few times.

"It's healing nicely. How's the hand?"

"I haven't used it, but there's no pain."

Emiri grinned. "How's the hand that punched Benio in the face?"

Mei held out her right fist, and it was only slightly bruised. "I've had worse."

"Serves her right. I heard you can't eat tonight?"

"And I have to apologize to her."

Emiri dug through her bags. "Don't worry about it. I'm sure you don't have to mean it." She held out a wrapped-up box to Mei. "Go on. Eat something."

With shaking hands, Mei took the box and opened the lid. Inside was a row of rice balls. Her mouth watered, and she took a large bite out of the first one. The taste of pickled plum invaded her mouth, and Mei closed her eyes, savoring the food. She stuffed the rest of the ball into her mouth and reached for another.

Emiri studied Mei as she ate. "I figured it had been longer since you last ate."

Mei looked at her hands. She nodded and finished the food. Maybe the food meant nothing to Emiri but it meant a lot to Mei. When an eta shared food it meant they wanted you to survive. Just maybe Emiri wanted her to make it here. After closing the box, she placed her hands on her stomach and sighed. "Thank you," Mei whispered. "Thank you for this kindness."

"Also"—Emiri glanced at the book—"did you need help?"

The stress that occupied Mei's soul released at that one question. Emiri's lovely round face seemed like a Kami coming down from above. Mei leaned forward. "You would teach me to read?"

Emiri smiled and stared out at the setting sun. "I won't tell you that your life here will be easy." Her black eyes met Mei's. "But you can prove all those nits wrong."

The warmth of Emiri's friendship stayed with Mei as she sat alone at dinner and when she went to bathe and her peers all left the bath. It stayed with her even as she entered the room and the others had shredded all her bedding. She placed the sleeping Kuro on his bed and curled up in her ruined blankets. She stroked Kuro's scales and blocked out their laughter. She would make it. She was strong.

CHAPTER
SEVEN

Chin woke up in his bed, his back wrapped in bandages. Kazu must have come in the middle of the night again to heal him. His homdragon was still learning, so Chin's back contained lines upon lines of old scars. He sucked in air when he tried to get up, but he couldn't stay in bed. It was time to put on the show.

As he dressed, he made sure the obi wasn't too tight around his waist, and taking a deep breath, he slid open the door. His socked feet made no sound as he approached his family.

There was no visual difference from the day before, but the silence spoke volumes. His father didn't meet Chin's eyes, and Kazu was suddenly preoccupied with feeding his dragon. Kazu would leave today to go back with his master, leaving Chin alone. It's not like he could do much for Chin.

He knelt to sit on the warm floor, and his breakfast was placed before him. Chin ate at a steady pace, forcing the food down his throat. Once he finished, he got up to leave, but his mother spoke, making him freeze in mid-crouch.

"You will have new training starting today." She put her chopsticks to the side of her bowl.

Chin sat back down and nodded. His brother quietly glanced back and forth between Chin and Aiko.

"Something must have been defective in your training," she continued.

Chin highly doubted that. He had the best tutors money could buy.

"So you will train with the shodragon riders, since no master would ever take you."

His head jerked. "How? I don't have a dragon."

Aiko waved her hand. "I arranged it through Emperor Xion. You can't take the classes in which you would need the dragon, but you will do all the others. We think that exposing you to more dragons will help you." She sniffed. "In sixth months, this should all just be a nightmare."

Chin lowered his gaze. What did she know of nightmares? His didn't end. It was supposed to have been over last night. Then he would only have needed to come home for holidays. After his training, he would never have had to come here. Now he had to parade around those with dragons. How did this help his mother's pride?

"You will leave at sunrise from now on, but today, we will go learn about your job and training. Be ready to go in an hour. The servant put the uniform in your room."

Chin nodded and got up from the table.

"If this doesn't work out, you'll go live with the eta," his mother called out as he was leaving, her tone dark.

He forced his legs to move; they made it to his room, then he collapsed on the floor. Without a dragon, he might as well be an eta. There was no work for those who didn't have a dragon. His mother wouldn't keep him here to shame her forever. Why hadn't a dragon chosen him? He always tried to be a good and kind person.

He rested his head on his hands, and the door opened, but he didn't jump up. His brother sat next to him.

"I'm sorry."

They never spoke of what Aiko did to Chin. "For what?"

"My training will be over in a year. Then you'll come live with me."

Chin kept his head down and didn't reply. They sat listening to the painfully cheerful morning birdsong coming through Chin's open window. The ever-present spiderwebs gave the morning sparkle where there should be none. Kazu had said it like it was nothing, but Aiko would make sure his brother married after his apprenticeship was over. Chin was certain that the new wife wouldn't want an eta in the house.

"I need to change," Chin said softly. He wanted his brother to leave.

Kazu stood. "Need help?"

Chin's throat tightened, and he shook his head. The bedroom door slid shut, and Chin was alone. He found the uniform on his bed, and he shifted on the hakama and top. The white obi of a novice recruit went around his waist. Once again, he made sure it wasn't too tight. However, if it was noticeably loose, his mother would tighten it for him.

He opened his door, and Kazu stood outside, waiting. Chin sighed and didn't comment as his brother followed him. He slipped his wooden shoes on, and they went outside. Chin sat on the stone steps, and Kazu, his shadow, sat next to him.

After a while, Kazu nudged him, and Chin stood up as the door opened. His mother wore a bright blue kimono today and jerked her head at Chin for him to follow her.

His legs felt like lead, but he got in the rickshaw and tried to put as much space as he could between them. Today, nothing would hold back Aiko's temper, but he always tried to appease her. Ever since he was young, he'd tried to make her happy, but the beatings never stopped.

This time, they went even farther up the mountain, and the rickshaw stopped before the fortress where all the shodragon riders lived. It was a massive honeycomb that came out of the mountain. Shodragons flew through the air, glimmering like jewels in the morning sun. A steady ache entered Chin as he watched the majestic beasts fly.

A man in red met them at the front gate. He bowed to Aiko, and she gave him a deep nod. Chin bowed low, and the man motioned for them to follow.

He had a pleasantly cheerful face, and Chin wished he could read the mood coming from his mother.

"Sora-sensei couldn't meet you this morning since she's with the new recruits, but you will join their class tomorrow."

His mother sniffed, and Chin knew she perceived this as an insult. He supposed Aiko thought the sensei should have dropped everything to meet with her.

At her silence, the sensei kept speaking. "I am Dai-sensei, and Sora-sensei is my wingleader."

The purple obi around his waist clashed with the red. He'd heard that during battle, they wore black, but they wore red until they got assigned their own color as a wingleader.

Aiko remained silent, and Dai strode toward the fortress, his face still holding a smile.

I suppose he deals with worse when the rains come.

"This way to the novice recruit class. New classes start every six months when the dragons—"

"We know," Aiko cut him off. "We know how it works. Just show us what he will be doing." For a moment her eyes flashed green and Chin thought he imagined it.

Dai nodded, and they continued to follow him. Chin bent his head and tried to keep up. The wooden sandals had not been the best choice for rocky terrain.

Dai noticed him struggling. "Most wear cloth shoes. I will have some sent with you."

Chin glanced at his mother's frozen face and responded, "I am fine. Arigato." He would get them later. His mother might see this as another weakness. Her strides were as smooth as ever over the rough stone path. Chin forced himself to walk more deliberately, and his back ached from the strain.

The sensei raised his eyebrow but kept moving forward until they reached the first door. A hint of spice crossed Chin's nose, and Dai opened the door to reveal long tables.

"This is where he can eat his meals. Will he be sleeping in the dorm?"

"No." Aiko briefly scanned the room and walked off, leaving Dai and Chin to run after her.

Dai barely got ahead and gestured for them to go up the stairs. The stone made everything cool and dark. The wooden sandals clacked down the stone halls, and they came to the first floor.

"Classes are in the morning, and the afternoon is reserved for practical dragon training and fighting. Today is more of an orientation."

Aiko glared at Chin. "You missed the orientation."

Chin nodded. "It will be no trouble to catch up." He bit his tongue. How could he have attended a class that he hadn't been aware of until a mere few hours ago? Noticing the steadily increasing stiffness in Aiko's body, he knew there would be no break for his back tonight.

With each step down the hall, Chin's body grew more and more empty from the hopelessness of the path his life had taken. The clatter of their footsteps dulled in his ears, and the faint voice of the sensei muffled in his brain. A bit of sun warmed his face through the paper in the sliding class-room door.

He turned his face, and through the crack, he saw that the class was in session. They all had on white obis like his. Chin didn't want to think about what the reception would be like when he entered the class tomorrow. His back prickled with shame, and before he could lower his eyes, he focused on the slight figure in the back.

It was the girl he had saved from the market. She was much cleaner, but it had to be her. She stood in the back, her shoulders shoved back. Her dark eyes glared forward, and around her neck, a black shodragon rested. It seemed odd that she would stand in the back. Chin leaned toward the crack to see in further. She didn't have a stool to sit on.

He looked away. Now he felt like he'd invaded another private moment of her struggle. The class wouldn't even care that he was there. They might not even notice a drag-onless boy. Everyone's eyes were on the eta girl. If she could stand there daring them to mock her, then he could survive.

He looked up. Dai and his mother were at the end of the hall. Chin straightened and walked as fast as he could before his mother detected that he had fallen behind. Trying to run in wooden sandals without drawing attention wasn't in the stars. Her eyes narrowed at his approach, but they continued to follow Dai.

"After lunch, your son will help in the dragon caves. That way, he can get more exposure to the dragons we have here. Also, he will tend to the different plants for dragon use." They went up more stairs and down a back hall. The air grew damp, and a sheen of sweat developed on all of their brows. "This is where the dragons sleep or stay when they are not sunning outside."

The heat grew stifling as they entered an enormous dome of a hallway. It was big enough for ten dragons to fit through. Chin's head tilted back as they went in farther to see a large hollowed-out portion of the mountain. Inside were hundreds of archways leading to the dragons' dens. The openings went up for spans, and Chin didn't want to look down to see how far they went. It would take hours to walk around. A system of chains clanked on the sides, and he realized that was how those without shodragons got around.

A blue shodragon gracefully landed on the edge of the hall, then wandered into one of the caves. Chin's mouth gaped open. They were huge. Even though his family was part of the daim, he had never gotten this close to a shodragon. His father occasionally mentioned his time as a shodragon rider, but then he would get pensive and down saki. He didn't know how his father's shodragon died but it was before he was born. Chin shivered. These dragons could crush him without a second thought.

"We will head to the recruits' floor. That's where you will help take care of the dragons. A rider is responsible for the majority of the care, but priests in training have to clean out the caves."

Dai clanged a gong next to a chain, and it rose. Chin eyed the chains, and his palms felt damp, and not just from the heat.

"These were forged by homdragons and dendragons." Dai smiled at Chin. "Nothing to worry about."

Aiko frowned, and her eyes narrowed. "He isn't worried."

That cut short any conversation, and they waited in silence until a metal cage large enough to hold eight people approached the docking area. A young man in gray robes nodded to them as he opened the latch. His head was shaved, and the door slammed behind them after they stepped into the metal box. It had a solid metal bottom with open bars around the sides to let air flow around them, and as the chain lowered, the heat rose from the bottom, making his hakama pants flutter. The young man continued to crank the handle, dropping them farther into the pit. Aiko stood still. Not even a hair moved.

They reached a docking station lined with white stone. "New recruit floor," the bald priest said. After they'd gotten out, he continued back up.

Dai pointed to a room with a half door. An older priest was inside talking to someone. "This is where you will report every afternoon and receive your list of tasks. For the first week, someone will be with you, but after that, you will be on your own. Right now, these dens are being cleared out. Soon, the dragons will sleep here and not with their part-ners. Any questions?"

Chin shook his head and chanced a glance at his mother.

Aiko had never been a warm person, but the coldness from home usually never crept out into the world for others to see. Throughout their time with Dai, her eyes would scan the area then move on. Why wasn't she speaking? It wasn't like he expected her to brag about him being here, but she'd forced him into this, and who knew what she'd done to get him to be part of the shodragon recruits. She had influence, but he wasn't aware how much.

Dai tapped his fist against his thigh. "Well, this is it. His day ends around sunset. Will the rickshaw runner be there to pick him up?"

Aiko nodded.

"Okay, then."

Chin could tell that Dai had expected more than this, but they went to ring the gong, and the young priest came down and took them back to the main entrance to the dens. As they came back through, a woman with a sour expression stepped out of an empty classroom.

"Ah, Aiko-chan, I was hoping to catch you before you left."

Chin cringed at the informal honorific. His mother's face didn't flinch, but she showed too many sharp teeth in her smile.

"Sora, it has been many years."

The woman peered around Aiko. "This is your son, then? He's joining my recruits?"

"This is part of his training until he goes to the selection in the spring."

Sora smirked. "Odd training."

Aiko's lips turned up slowly. "It really is none of your concern. All you have to do is teach him."

Sora nodded her head to the side, not quite a formal bow. "I do my best with the quality I get."

"I heard of this quality last night. You have a rodent in your class." Aiko leaned in. "Do you need help to get rid of it? You always attract such types," she whispered loudly in Sora's ear.

Sora's jaw clenched. "You'd know since you are putting one in my class," she said, her words clipped.

Too far. She's gone too far. Chin's gaze darted between the two. Dai stood frozen.

Chin's mother nodded to Sora. "Blessings on your new recruits." Without glancing back, Aiko walked out of the hall, leaving Chin and Dai to trail after her. As they left, faint laughter made his skin crawl, but when he turned, Sora-sensei wasn't there.

The group made quick time back to where the rickshaw waited, and it wasn't even near lunchtime yet. Dai, his face now absent of a smile, bowed low as they boarded the rickshaw and left the walls of the fortress.

Aiko stared straight ahead on their journey back. Chin's eyes followed the ticking rhythm of the rickshaw driver as he ran. The driver had a green dendragon on his shoulder. Chin wondered what type of dragon benefited a rickshaw driver. He closed his eyes and leaned his head on the heavy canvas. He wasn't even suited to run people around town.

He imagined his life with Kazu and his future wife. Maybe they would keep him in a backroom and drag him out so people could look at the eta.

As they got closer to home, they passed by a cliff overhang on the side of the mountain. Chin's eyes widened, and he sat up straight, making his wounds burn. He didn't have to be an eta; he didn't have to be anything. The crisp blue sky behind the cliff as they turned beckoned him. He sat back with a grin on his face. Aiko would have her six months, but in the end, Chin would have his freedom one way or another.

He felt oddly free, and not in the way he'd imagined. When they reached home, Aiko had him get out, and she directed the driver out of the gate. She gave Chin no instructions before she left.

He had nothing to do? This wasn't the norm. He took off his wooden sandals and went to his room. The cloth shoes that he should have worn but had missed were there. He took off the uniform and wrapped an old kimono around his shoulders. There was nothing else for him to do.

Chin went down the hall, and his father and Kazu were both gone. So he went around the house. Even though he could hear padded noises from the maids moving around, the silence and absence of Mother comforted him.

His feet led him to the library. Chin never got to read for enjoyment, and he walked down the shelves of string-bound books, tracing the thin bindings with his finger. Chin paused at a painting at the end of the row. He didn't remember it being there.

The bright silver shodragon gleamed from the picture. A young woman, her eyes on fire, leaned in as the dragon dove downward. Her long black hair ribboned out behind her. Chin stood and felt the movement and rush from their descent. His hand trembled as he raised his fingers to the painting. He traced the woman's determined face. *It was like her, that girl. This is the face of a shodragon rider.*

Chin dropped his hand and shuffled back to his room. He now knew what he was missing, what the eta girl had that he didn't. The sun set as he sat on his bed, his eyes unseeing as darkness approached. Only the clacking of the rickshaw telling of his mother's return jarred him out of his stupor.

He let out a slow breath, and letting the top of his kimono fall down, he knelt on the floor and waited.

EIGHT

A nip at Mei's fingers woke her before the dragon roar.

Hungry.

Mei opened her eyes and wiped away the sleep. "It isn't even breakfast yet. Also, there's food over there." She gestured vaguely toward the bowls left out in the night. The claws clicking on the stone told her that Kuro had headed toward the food. When he came back, he jumped on the bed. His long body stretched against hers.

She sat up. "You're longer!"

Kuro tilted his head. *You're meant to ride me, you know. I will get much bigger than this.* He curled up next to her. Unable to go back to sleep, Mei reached for the oil next to the meat, and she rubbed it into the patchy parts of his scales. With all this growth, he wouldn't fit in the dorm soon.

Mei turned her head slowly, looking at the other dragons and the bodies under their covers. Without Kuro here, she would be alone with them. She went back to oiling Kuro, the mechanical circular movements calming her.

The sun rose as she groomed Kuro, and soon, the dragon roar woke the others. They ignored her as they dressed, and the dragons trailed behind their partners. Mei lightly touched her collarbone, enjoying the fact that Kuro still fit, and she scratched his eyelids. He hummed in response to her treatment. She would miss holding him, but her back would be happier.

In the dining hall, Mei held back her drool as she waited for her breakfast. The rice balls Emiri had given her had helped and was more than Mei usually ate. However, now that good-smelling food was part of her life, she found that going hungry had gotten harder. She bowed as she took the servings of eggs, fish, and rice and went to the table. She sat farther away from the other recruits. Right now, it was more important for her to finish her food than make a point.

Kuro pointedly sat between her and the others, guarding her food. He ate his meat in a few gulps, and then his silver eyes tracked the other recruits. No one looked at him while Mei ate her meal. She smiled at her guardian.

With every bite, a new flavor erupted in her mouth. She'd gone from a life of eating garbage to having warm food. She closed her eyes and savored it. As she swallowed, a vision of her father flashed before her eyes.

Mei's throat tightened, and she pushed the tray away.

You only ate a few bites.

I'm full, Mei replied.

Kuro snorted. *Why aren't you eating?*

My father's probably starving. Had he finished the fish? How would he get food without Mei there? The other eta would help him, but in their harsh world, he needed more.

He wants you to starve too?

Mei shook her head. *I'm sorry. It's hard to eat right now.*

Kuro put his warm head on her shoulder, and Mei ate a few more bites, but it tasted like ash.

She stood, washed her tray, and placed it with the others. Then she steeled herself as she walked to Sora-sensei's classroom. Mei didn't want to be with the others.

In the room, there was still no stool for her, and she stood with Kuro, waiting for the others.

Why don't you take a stool?

I think that would cause problems, Mei thought.

So?

This is not the battle I want to fight. There'll be others.

Kuro tilted his head and curled around Mei's neck as she waited. Loud voices came from down the hall, and Mei squared her shoulders to prepare for the day. *I am the daughter of Rikku and Koji.* She stared straight ahead, ignoring the whispers as the other recruits found their desks.

Everyone in the room quieted when Sora-sensei entered. She pointed to the wall behind her. "This is your schedule for the week. In the afternoon, you are to go down to the dens, and the priests will show you your dragon's lodging during your first year." Her eyes narrowed. "Make sure you oil your dragons every night. If I find any dry patches on their skin, I will skin you."

The class stayed silent as everyone's eyes widened. Mei stroked Kuro's head and smiled slightly at how he gleamed from this morning's oiling. His black scales were the most stunning in the room.

You kind of smell like flowers, Mei thought.

Kuro snorted. *I'd rather smell like that fatty meat I had at breakfast.*

"You will attend classes in the field in the afternoons with your dragons. Those will be centered around fighting and, later, flying." She flicked her long sleeves. "Bring any danger to your dragon or others and you will be grounded."

On that cheery note, the dragon roared, and they went off to their first class. Mei stayed behind, but out of the corner of her eye, she noticed a familiar face. Her brow furrowed, and she turned her head. It was the boy who had bought her the fish. She froze as she watched him walk out with the others. No dragon perched on his shoulders. Why was he here with them? Her face warmed at the thought of seeing him again and the memory of how he had saved her from Fat Choi. She had never dreamed she would meet him here. Maybe his dragon was hurt and not with him at the moment.

While she was still puzzled about his presence, Kuro nudged her to follow the others. Shaking her head out of its stupor, she went into the next class, and her heart sank when it was Tomo-sensei's room. Mei took a shaky breath and went back to her wooden desk and stool. It was covered in slashes and paint splatters. Mei thought some were words, but she didn't know what they said. She did, however, understand that this wasn't a kindness.

She glanced around the room, and everyone was staring at her desk. Benio snickered softly with Aimi and Niko. Kenta nudged Daisuke and pointed. Tomo entered, and he noted the whispers.

"What's going on?" His boney hand waved them to silence. Then his pale eyes took in Mei's desk. "What did you do?"

Mei started. "M-me?"

"Yes, you! Are you not used to having a desk? What did you do?"

Her head wavered from face to face. Kuro growled, and Tomo shushed him. Sulkily, Kuro lay down.

"Your punishment for destroying the desk—"

"Tomo-sensei," Daisuke interrupted. Mei had not interacted with him. He towered over everyone in the room.

Tomo's sharp gaze almost flayed the boy. "What?"

"Didn't you say she can't read or write?"

"Yes."

"Then how would she know how to write those words, and why would she write them on her desk?"

Mei stared down at her desk. From his words, she had a feeling that whatever was written had something to do with her being eta.

Tomo sighed. "Daisuke, we can never know why it acts the way it does."

"Sensei, she didn't do it. She wasn't even here last night."

"Oh, and how would you know?"

Daisuke stood and jutted out his chin. "She was with me until curfew."

The class gasped, and whispers raged like a storm in Mei's ears. She couldn't be sure what Daisuke was talking about. She had been with Emiri in the library, not him. Was he making this up because Tomo wouldn't believe the truth? Mei hunched her shoulders and looked away when Tomo's gaze hit her.

Tomo sucked in his cheeks, making his face look even more skeletal. "I hope you realize there are other women of breeding here and you shouldn't degrade yourself."

Daisuke just nodded and sat back down.

Tomo continued with the lesson, and once more, Mei couldn't focus. The side glances from her classmates worried her. Kenta gave Daisuke playful punches when Tomo's back was turned. Benio's eyes narrowed and jealously radiated from her as she touched her bandaged nose. A tightness formed in her chest. Daisuke had claimed they'd done couple things together.

Living in clay huts close together, and most without doors, left little to the imagination when it came to adults reproducing. Her father had told her that sometimes adults also did it for fun. From what Mei had seen and heard, it never sounded that fun, and her father had laughed when she had said that. He had said that most looked down on women who slept with a lot of men. The impact of that statement hit Mei, and she felt short of breath.

The glances from the other recruits now had new clarity.

What? Kuro's thought speared her mind.

It's nothing, Mei replied.

I don't know what the big deal is. Dragons mate all the time.

Gross.

How do you think I got here? I just appeared?

Mei rolled her eyes.

"Did I say something to amuse you?" Tomo asked.

Mei needed to learn to control her actions when she spoke to Kuro. "No, sensei."

"What's the point of you being here if you won't learn?"

She gritted her teeth and bowed. As much as she disliked Tomo, Jion-sho's face popped up in her head, along with her father's. Her father was starving right now to give her this opportunity. No one could take it away from her if she did so herself.

"Now that I have your attention," Tomo said, "read the next passage on formation."

"I can't read, sensei," Mei muttered.

"Oh, that's right." The other recruits scribbled furiously, while all Mei could do was sit and listen. But she did listen and then repeated the information in her head. She wouldn't give up that easily.

The morning passed without further incident, and after a quick lunch, they all headed to the extensive field. When Mei had first arrived at the fortress, she hadn't seen the flat expanse of land. It was an abnormal sight on the mountain, and they must have used dendragons to flatten the earth.

While they approached, a sensei dressed in yellow robes and a wide black obi waited for them. His arms were crossed, and his face held a sleepy expression. His hair was medium length, and the wavy curls exploded around his face in the slight breeze.

He yawned as they all stood facing him. "Dazai," he said. They all looked at one another, and the sensei sighed. "I'm Dazai. Stand in proper formation."

They all stood still, most of their brows furrowed.

"Do you not understand this class is to learn how to shoot yumi? Form!"

Mei, although still confused, went with it. She held her arms out to her side and put her left foot in front of her. Benio and Aimi laughed at her, but she focused straight ahead at Dazai-sensei.

He nodded and came over to her. He kicked her right foot back and twisted her torso to the side. Then he made her hold her left arm out straight and her right behind her.

"Good." Dazai glared at the rest. "Form! Move it, nits!"

They all stood while Dazai walked around and hit them

with a long branch if they went out of the form. Even in the cool air, sweat pearled on Mei's brow. If someone lowered their arm by an inch, he would smack them and scream, "Form!"

Sometimes, he would stand back and shut his eyes, and a few daring souls would relax, but even though sleepy, he was always aware. The dragons, bored with the activity, romped with each other in the grass. Mei was happy to see Kuro playing with the others.

As Dazai made another round, he briefly nodded to Mei. He hadn't hit her once. He would also look at her. Even though her hand and back ached, Mei pushed herself for the sensei who had noticed her. He was treating her like the others. The coldness in her chest melted for a moment. Her focus renewed, and she smiled.

Then the roar of the dragon rumbled across the field. Some of the recruits gave tremendous sighs as they lowered their arms and placed their feet back. Kenta dramatically collapsed to the ground.

"Did I dismiss you?" Dazai said, voice low.

Mei almost let a laugh escape when they jumped back into their stances. The minutes ticked by, and Dazai nodded. "Go away." Then he turned his back and went toward an equipment building, leaving them all there like absurd kuebiko scarecrows.

When she lowered her arms and moved her legs, the muscles burned. She wobbled over to Kuro. She still wasn't sure what the class had been about, but somehow, she felt she had learned the most from Dazai-sensei.

Everyone's steps were a bit off as they walked back to the fortress. Daim had some sort of training, depending on their money, but it was no match for this class. The fish boy hadn't been with them for the lesson, and as they walked to where the dragons would now sleep, she wondered why he wasn't there now.

Passing the dining hall, they went up to the first-floor classes. Then they kept going into the heart of the mountain. Mei's hair stuck to her neck from the damp air. The heat engulfed them as they entered a large opening. The sound of clanking chains echoed in the abyss, and Mei stayed far from the edge.

A young bald priest bowed and directed them to the dock, where a metal lift waited. Kuro had no problem waddling into the box, and his silver eyes glanced back at Mei.

Coming?

She smiled weakly and got into the lift.

If you are scared, how will you fly?

I'm more worried about falling than flying, Mei replied. Or being pushed. Mei kept that thought to herself. Surely they wouldn't go that far, would they? She pushed the disturbing thought out of her head, and the lift stopped at a dock lined with white stone. Next to a priest in black robes stood the fish boy. She couldn't remember his name. When had he gotten here?

She stepped off and joined the others. The priest nodded to her and directed their attention to the boy.

"Chin will direct you to your dragon's den. It's your responsibility to clean the den and feed your dragon. He'll help you with any task you may need."

Chin didn't meet their eyes. So he wasn't a priest, and he wasn't a shodragon rider. What was he?

Benio and Daisuke nodded to him like they knew him.

Mei could only assume it was daim business. It was better that she stay out of it.

One at a time, the others were shown their dens, and Mei waited until the end. She needed to meet Emiri at the library after dinner, but she couldn't jump the line.

When it was Benio's turn she hissed at Mei. "Stay away from Daisuke, saseko."

Mei didn't even know how to reply to her. But if Benio thought that Mei felt threatened by her, she'd need a lot more noses.

Everyone was gone, and it was finally her turn. Chin directed her to an opening close to the lifts. The torches flickered, and they walked down the wide, dark hall. Then without warning, the corridor expanded into a large dome that could house all the eta on her dirt road. Mei gazed around at the smooth stone and reached out. She jerked her fingers back, feeling the heat from the walls.

"It's heated for the dragons' comfort," Chin said softly, his voice quiet in the den.

Mei watched Kuro curl up in a worn spot on the rock floor, perhaps formed from previous shodragons who had slept here before. "They're comfortable?" She shut her mouth. He probably didn't want to speak to her.

"Apparently, it's comfortable to them." He didn't notice that she'd grown silent and kept talking. "The heat can get pretty intense down here, but farther down in the large dragon bathing area, you could drown in a wave made by a shodragon." He laughed a bit.

He was nice? "You've worked here long?"

Chin's eyes flickered. "No, just started today."

Something had changed in his voice, and Mei didn't

know what to do. She felt like he needed comfort, but he surely wouldn't want an eta to sympathize with him.

Mei scanned the large space, and the heat prickled her skin, but as long as she didn't move much, it didn't bother her. He wasn't leaving, so she thought she could take a chance. "Do you think..." Chin's light brown eyes met hers, making her pause. She took a deep breath. "Do you think I could sleep down here?" She turned her head away, waiting for a sneering reply.

"Actually, it's common for riders to sleep with their dragons. You're a recruit, so I'm not sure. I don't think anyone would stop you..."

Because they'd rather have me out of sight. Kuro lifted his head and snorted.

"You can hear the dragon roar from here, and the bathing area for the dragons is downward. Soon, the dragons will be able to fly there on their own."

Chin bent over, moving stiffly. Was his back injured? Mei peered at his back while he was turned.

"If you bring down some tatami mats," he said, not noticing her gaze, "it should be pretty comfortable." He straightened and bumped into Mei's head.

She stepped back, her face warm. "Sorry. I was just looking at the floor." Mei vaguely gestured to where Chin stood. He probably already thought she had lower intelligence. She didn't want him to know she thought he was hurt.

He raised his eyebrows. "Well, if you need anything, let me know. I'm here until dinner."

Mei bowed. "Arigato."

Chin bowed and left. Mei went over to Kuro, who already snored softly. High windows vented the hot air and let in sunlight, but there were spots for torches and lanterns at night. She ran her fingers across Kuro's smooth scales.

"I'll stay with you tonight." It might be better if she got her clothing before meeting with Emiri. That way, she wouldn't run into any of the others. Mei felt a tug on her heart as she left the den. Soon, Kuro would be too big to go inside the classrooms, but the space felt empty without him by her side. Part of Mei was tempted to go back and wake him so she wouldn't have to go to the room alone. She shook her head and let out a rush of air. She knew how to get by on her own, and she wasn't afraid of the other recruits.

Taking the lift by herself was another matter, though. While the priest lifted them up, she had her hand behind her back, clutching the metal frame. Mei blurred her vision so she wouldn't have to see the wide abyss below. They reached the top, and Mei forced herself to walk slowly to the dock and bowed to the priest.

On her way to the dorm, she grabbed food. The hall was emptier than normal, meaning it had to be already past the evening meal. She ate quickly and made her way up to the sleeping area. Her blankets were still in ruins, but thankfully, her spare clothes were untouched.

She bundled up her clothes in a narrow roll and did the best she could with the mess of blankets. As she turned to leave, a deep voice haulted her.

"They've been rough on you."

Her heart almost stopped. She'd thought she was alone, but blocking the doorway was the tall boy with the long hair from class, Daisuke.

NINE

Daisuke, who had claimed he'd had physical relations with her, now blocked her path. What did he want? His hair was unbraided, and it rested like silken spiderwebs over his shoulders. The light brown strands fell forward as he bent his head down to look at her. With his height and broad shoulders, he dwarfed all the other recruits, and especially Mei, who had never had much nourishment growing up. She supposed with his angular face and narrow nose he could be handsome, but even though his face offered friendship, his eyes twisted Mei's stomach. He was the type that would have made her run down another alley.

"I'm sorry that my excuse for you was so crude." His smile didn't reach his eyes.

Mei nodded and went to walk past him, but he didn't budge from the doorway. She tensed as she drew away. When facing an opponent this large, it was better to run. Her street instincts flared, and her muscles tightened, preparing her to get away from him. There was only one way out.

"Are you afraid of me?" Daisuke tilted his chin, and his hair shifted to the side.

"No." Mei backed away. She felt every point where her feet met the floor. He was large, but she was fast. Kuro's warmth was missing from her shoulders, and his shodragon was also not with him. It was just him against her. She wouldn't let him take her.

His lips turned up, and he pushed his hair behind his back. "I'm making sure they understand what I meant, so you don't need to worry."

Honestly, that was the last thing Mei was worried about. It didn't matter if the recruits thought she'd slept with the whole winglegion. Daim gossip felt pathetic compared to her daily struggle to survive as an eta. "It doesn't worry me. Excuse me, please." She was more concerned with the glint in his eyes.

"You're not like the other girls here." He didn't move. Daisuke studied her like she was a tasty shrimp roll.

Mei's forced smile tightened. "What gave you that clue? The fact that I'm eta?" How would she ever learn to read with this nit standing in her way? "Please, I need to go."

Daisuke leaned against the doorframe. "Oh, do you want to make the lie true?"

A calm flowed through Mei's body. He must not understand words. As an eta, she was used to being ignored. He shifted, leaving the opening Mei had been waiting for. She clutched her bundle and dove toward the gap between his legs. Mei tucked her slight frame and rolled, knocking her knee against his bits as she stopped in the hall. He doubled over, and Mei ran to the library, not waiting for him to recover. *I won't be so lucky if he corners me again. Shells*, she swore to herself. In only a few days, she'd dropped her guard. These stone walls had given her a false sense of security, but they had trapped her, giving her less freedom than before.

Her soft soles made no sound in the hallways as she ran, and after a few glances behind her, she didn't see Daisuke following her. She felt even better about her choice not to sleep in the room with the others.

"Recruit!"

Mei halted, and the sensei with the green kimono stood in the hall. She hesitated. They hadn't had a class with him yet.

His dark face was friendly and he gestured for her to follow him into his room. Mei didn't budge. She wouldn't go anywhere alone with him.

"Ah, I apologize. You don't know me. I'm Washi-sensei. I wanted to find you earlier and I thought it was you... Wait a minute?" He went back into his room. Mei didn't move. He came out with a bundle. "I thought this might help you." He put the bundle in her hands and it was heavy. "These are books that might help you get started with reading. They used to belong to my children..."

Her brows furrowed. "Why?" The other sensei didn't seem interested in helping her read.

"You were chosen and you belong here." Washi bowed and left her in the hall.

It took a moment for Mei to come out of her shock. She didn't know what to think of his acceptance of her as a rider.

Mei reached the library doors, and the same lady slept at the desk. Toshiko was back in her corner and Emiri waited for her at a far table, her homdragon curled up in her lap. At Mei's entrance, she smiled.

"I thought you wouldn't make it."

"They showed us the dragon dens today. I'm sorry for being late." Mei bowed low. She didn't mention Daisuke. Mei still felt unsure about this new friendship. Not trusting kindness had become a lesson early in her life. Father was the only one she'd trusted until Kuro, and Kuro slept most of the time. The eta helped each other, but there were always a few who took advantage. "Also a sensei stopped me to give me these."

Emiri waved off the apology. "Sit." She took the bundle from Mei and gasped at the books inside. "These will help. I'm not a teacher myself, so having these beginner books will help after we learn what the symbols mean."

She put them to the side. "We will start with the kanji, which are the symbols you see that form words. Once you learn those, reading shouldn't be too hard for you, since you already speak well. It will just be a matter of practice." She pulled over a board with light cream sand resting in a frame.

"What's that for?"

"To write. It'll waste less parchment."

Mei nodded, and Emiri wrote something in the sand. Mei looked at the strange lines. "What's that?"

"It's your name." Emiri's eyes glimmered. "I thought you might want to know that first."

Her name? Mei's lips parted, and her fingers hovered over the sand. She followed the curves of the lines, and her eyes softened. A feeling of belonging and pride swelled in her chest. This was hers. No one could take her name. "Arigato, Emiri."

Emiri nodded and started with the first kanji.

Their heads remained bent over books and the sand for hours. Emiri found some text with pictures and words underneath, and once Mei learned one symbol, she would write it and say it ten times. When the sun set behind the mountain, the older lady woke and told them to go to bed.

Mei's brain felt flooded with symbols and lines. She sat up and bent her neck to the side. Soreness burned as she stood to leave the library. Her nearly healed back felt tight. She watched Emiri clear the sand of her last work. To Mei, the end product of her writing looked more like a hen searching for grubs. Emiri seemed more confident in her ability.

"You've made substantial progress!"

"It isn't fast enough." Mei matched her pace as they left the room.

Emiri sighed. "I know, but you'll get there. I can't imagine the surprise on all the sensei's faces when you show them you can read and write."

They probably won't care, Mei thought. But reading would help her study, and if she understood the material, she might have a chance to pass the written tests. Jion-sho believed in her. Her mind drifted to Chin and his unique circumstances of being in their class without a dragon. As she walked with Emiri, Mei thought maybe she would know something.

"Do you know why a recruit was added to our class today? I didn't see a dragon with him. Is it ill?"

Emiri stopped walking. "Ah, you mean Chin? No, he doesn't have a dragon."

"Then why's he in the class?"

Emiri glanced around the empty hall, then leaned in. "A dragon didn't choose him," she whispered, "and his mother made a huge fuss. So he's training with the priests until the next selection. They have never let anyone in here without a dragon." She raised her eyebrows as she started walking again. "And he can leave every night."

"Why would the mother do this?"

Emiri shrugged. "Who knows, but a daim not getting a dragon is practically unheard of. He must feel so much shame in bringing dishonor to his family. Daim are big on honor."

He had probably expected to get chosen that day. Mei had gotten a dragon, and he hadn't. Wouldn't he hate her? Suddenly, his kindness felt strange. It was better to be wary. Once, a gang member had given her clothes and fed her. It had gone on for some time, and then one day, he'd tried to tie her up to sell. Mei shivered at the memory of Chin's wide eyes. There were many instances on the street where kindness meant death or slavery. Yes, she better be careful of Chin. He shouldn't be able to steal her dragon, but he could do something underhanded when she least expected it. She gave Emiri a sidelong look. She was teaching her to read. What if she had ulterior motives too? Now that Mei was healed, there was no reason for Emiri to help her. A tightness grew in her chest as she built imaginary walls to protect her heart. Mei started to go back to the dens.

"Aren't you going up to your room?"

Mei shook her head. "No, I don't think I want to sleep there. It's safer elsewhere."

Emiri nodded sadly, understanding. "I'll see you tomorrow after dinner again."

Mei bowed and let the gradual increase of heat guide her to the entrance leading to the dens. Once again, she clung to the lift as it lowered. She found the den, and a wet Kuro greeted her.

You've been gone forever.

"Really?" Mei quirked her eyebrow. "Did you already eat?"

Not a lot, Kuro grumbled.

Mei laughed and went to the entrance to grab more meat. Kuro chewed and gulped while Mei oiled his hide.

"Did you get bigger?"

He seemed to be about a palm's length wider.

I will fly soon.

"I already miss you being small. You were pretty cute. Maybe you are just getting fat."

Kuro snorted. *I'm not a dendragon.*

Mei rubbed a patchy spot on his scales. The sweet smell of jasmine from the oil hit her nose. "Of course not. It's just that it's easier when you're in class with me."

He stopped eating. *No one will dare hurt you.*

Mei had never heard that tone before. It was protective and threatening. "Don't worry. We'll prove them all wrong."

Kuro nipped at her hair and finished his food. After Mei finished oiling him, white lanterns lit the way to the dragon baths. They were thankfully empty as she dipped in to wash. The water almost burned her skin, so she made it a quick scrub. She removed the bandages on her back, but her hand still throbbed, so she kept those bandages on. She was surprised that Emiri hadn't checked them tonight. With her skin bright red, she made her way back to the den.

A tatami mat was in the corner, along with a folded brown blanket. She inspected the kindness. Chin must have done this. Why was he doing this for her? She looked at the mat warily and curled up next to Kuro. It was better not to get close to Chin. There was no reason for him to do these things. The claws would fall one day, and Mei or Kuro could get hurt. In the heat, Mei's hair dried quickly, and she ran her fingers through her hair, combing it out. Her mind was confused by kindness from others who weren't eta. Did not trusting them mean she showed them that class mattered to her just as much? She would need allies even more here, and they gave no reason for her to not trust them. As long as she tread carefully she could maybe believe in kindness that wasn't from another eta.

She carefully took out the books Washi had given her and her fingers gently traced the words. There were pictures along with them. One picture was of two people smiling above the word... friend? Emiri, Washi, and Chin. Did she dare think of the word?

The overwhelming heat from the den and Kuro's body put Mei to sleep. For the first time since leaving her father, she finally felt safe. Then a stray thought shot through her mind. She couldn't leave the fortress, but Chin could.

THE DRAGON ROAR shook the walls in the morning hours. Mei and Kuro jerked awake. His wingspan seemed larger.

"Still growing, I see."

Are you calling me fat? Kuro tilted his head.

Mei rolled her eyes. "You do eat a lot. More than the other dragons."

Kuro snorted and waddled out the entrance, leaving Mei to chase after him. When they reached the edge, Kuro teetered on the open ledge.

"What are you doing?" Mei's heart sank. He could fall over the edge.

What dragons do. His hind legs bunched, flexing his muscles, and he jumped into the air, expanding his glimmering black wings. The morning sun flickered over his scales, making them look like flecks of obsidian. He beat his wings, and a wave of air flung up Mei's hair.

He was glorious. Mei's eyes followed his ascent to the opening of the large cave, and her heart ached that she couldn't be with him on his first flight.

You will. His voice was soft.

I know. Mei smiled to herself. *I'll see you later. Don't eat too much.*

No promises.

Mei laughed softly. It was weird feeling this happy. The metal box ride almost didn't bother her this morning as she held on to the image of Kuro in flight. Soon, it wouldn't matter what others thought or tried. She would be free in the sky.

After breakfast, she went to Sora-sensei's room. There was still no stool, but Mei leaned against the wall in the back of the room. She gazed out the window, hoping for a glance of black scales flying by. Her stomach clenched when Kuro didn't join her.

Loud voices clamored in the hall, and Mei took a deep breath before the other recruits entered. The usual glances and laughter in her direction from Benio and her face painted followers were nothing new. Without Kuro, Mei fixated on the wall with the writing. A bit of excitement overcame her when she recognized some symbols. She focused on picking out the sounds she remembered and thought she was confident enough to identify a few of the days. Something to the side of the list said something about cleaning? Her brow furrowed as she tried to pick out the next kanji, but Sora-sensei came in and interrupted her reading.

"We're starting our new cleaning schedule after lunch today. Like before you will be responsible for a job, and we will rotate through since we don't need all ten of you to clean everyday." She gestured at the new spot Mei had been studying. "Your name will be under the job listed as usual."

Laughter came from the class as Sora read Mei's name under sweeping.

That isn't my name. Mei's lips tightened, and she could only assume what the sensei had written as her name. As Sora continued, Mei straightened and went to the board. Her concentration was on the word Sora had pointed to, and without stopping, Mei wiped it with her hand, took the talc rock, and pictured the strokes of her name that Emiri had shown her last night.

With a shaking hand, she drew the lines and went back to her standing spot. No one moved or spoke. Mei faced Sora-sensei and tilted up her chin.

"You spelled my name wrong, *sensei*."

Sora's face folded in on itself with how forcefully she pursed her lips. The sour expression turned into a deadly glower. "You assume I care, *eta*."

Mei met her gaze and didn't blink. "My name is Mei." Heat and strength filled her body. This might be a minor battle in the long run, but they couldn't take her name now.

"I'll speak to you after class."

She resumed talking about oiling dragons and proper feeding habits. With the sound of the dragon roar, everyone left the room. Sora called Daisuke to stay behind as well.

Mei had a sinking feeling about the topic of conversation. Sora stood at the front of the class with a condescending smile. Daisuke, hair braided once more, bowed low and stayed in the classroom while the other boys patted him on the back as they left.

"Now, everyone knows that among recruits relationships develop," Sora said, forced sweetness in her voice. "I want to be clear that you are taking the proper precautions to avoid unwanted children." She glanced at Daisuke. "A young man of your breeding, I am disappointed in your taste, but you know you can't breed with it. If you're just using it for release, that's understandable, and I'm glad you found a purpose for it."

A sharp ringing grew in Mei's ears. *Purpose for it.* They could spread rumors all they wanted, but now they assumed that was all she was in this class for? Hatred toward Sora and Daisuke flamed in Mei's soul. She forced her face to remain still, but her eyes gave away her rage.

"Sorry, sensei. I'm taking the proper measures."

"It also may have a disease."

Why had she needed to stay and hear this? Mei's voice was low as she interrupted their sex talk. "We're not sleeping together. I wouldn't choose him."

Sora laughed, and the sound hurt Mei's ears. "Oh, you are lucky that he deems you worthy to release with you. A poor eta such as yourself should consider itself blessed."

Daisuke bowed his head in acceptance of her praise. "Your words honor me, sensei."

Rage boiled inside Mei, and she stormed out of the room. There was no need to stay and hear more. Let them think what they wanted. They were disgusting people. Their smiling, condescending faces teased Mei's mind as she ran to her next lesson.

What happened? Mei's mind flooded with someone else's anger as Kuro's voice pierced her thoughts. Burning fire enveloped her mind, and her insides felt like they were being flayed.

She honored his anger on her behalf. *They think I am nothing more than a daim's plaything.*

Who?

Sora-sensei and Daisuke.

Kuro said nothing more, and the rage subsided in her body. Putting a name to her attackers calmed Mei enough for her to focus on her next lesson. It was almost lunch, then she would have afternoon classes with Kuro. The dragon roar signaled it was lunchtime, but shouts and more roars followed.

Mei heard cries about a fight, and she ran with the others outside the room and down to the front of the fortress. In the middle of a large circle, Kuro's expanded wings shone in the bright sun, and a belly-up dragon was under his talons. The dragon was almost the same size as Kuro, but she was a deep crimson. Kuro's silver eyes blinked at the crowd and focused on Daisuke. He bared his teeth, his burning gaze not letting up as Daisuke backed away.

As the crowd whispered, Mei picked out a few phrases.

"Dominance is already starting."

"When I saw the black dragon this morning, I wondered..." Washi-sensei trailed off and looked at her with something close to pride.

"Isn't that the eta's dragon?"

"Yes, and the red is Daisuke's?"

One by one, everyone turned to Mei, who stood behind

the rest. She forced her face into a neutral expression so she didn't look daft. Was this supposed to happen?

What's going on? Mei asked, hoping Kuro would answer.

Putting him in his place, Kuro replied, and Mei could sense the smugness.

Are you allowed to do this?

Kuro huffed in Daisuke's direction. *Yes. His dragon was considered higher only because of him. Now we're at the top.*

I hate to break it to you, but I'll never be at the top.

According to who?

Mei had no answer for him. These were different rules. They kept telling her she was an eta, but it wasn't supposed to matter. *What now?*

We stay on top.

Mei wanted to roll her eyes, but she approached Kuro and patted his shoulder. He let the red dragon roll away with her head lowered. Now there was something new in Daisuke's eyes as he stroked his dragon. Mei couldn't resist giving him a slight smirk as she walked off with Kuro.

After lunch, they went back out to the field. The terse Dazai-sensei wasn't there, but rather a man with a more cheerful, rounder face, Washi-sensei. As she approached, he gave her a wide smile, showing off his white teeth.

"There they are! The newest class." They all bowed, and he bowed in return. "I'm Washi-sensei, and in my class, we will be focusing on flight and communication."

Mei could sense the excitement from all her peers. The shodragons were still on the small side, but they were dipping and flying in the wind above them.

"Today's lesson is more on communication since they are still too young to have you on their backs." Washi glanced at Kuro. "I have a feeling he will be a big one." He nodded in approval at Kuro's size.

Mei felt like a proud mother, but Kuro snapped at a bug in the grass, ruining his posture.

I think he just called me fat too.

She did her best to keep a straight face.

Washi laughed at Kuro's antics. "The connection for conversation won't be opened up to you just yet. Bonding with your dragon is a process. However, you need to understand how a dragon feels and thinks in order to communicate. They can understand you and each other already, even though you can't understand them."

Mei felt like she held a secret with Kuro. The warmth of their connection had helped her through these first days of training. Even though his presence in her head could be disconcerting, she was happy to have an ally.

"You see the brightly colored flags on the other side of the field? You'll direct your dragon to get a certain color once they are in flight."

It was still warm outside but windy, which would make it problematic for those who had to shout commands.

"We will take it one at a time." Washi went to the end of the line.

It was interesting watching the dragons with the other recruits. It was almost humorous to watch the stoic Toshiko flail her arms after her dragon took flight.

Benio and Aimi screeched in the wind and those next to them backed away to protect their ears.

One after another they shouted the colors in the air, but every dragon brought back the wrong flag. They'd come back and nudge their partner, and the partner would always stroke them.

Even though they were cruel to her, they were good to the dragons.

It was finally her turn and Kuro was in the air. "Mei, go for the green flag," Washi said.

He wants the green flag.

Kuro paused. *I can't see a green one.*

Oh?

There are some shades we can't see. Those all look gray.

Then it's the second flag from the end. It's a bit of an off green.

Kuro flew and grabbed the correct flag and brought it back. When he dropped it in front of her, the entire class and Washi stared at her.

"How did he know?" Washi asked, his tone shocked.

"I told him, then he told me he couldn't see the color."

"That's right. Dragons can't see certain shades of color." Washi clapped his hands and laughed. "Don't tell me you can already speak to him?"

Mei nodded, and Washi slapped his leg. "Well, not only is your dragon at the top, but you are already leaps and bounds ahead of the rest." He glanced at the other recruits, who now glared at Mei. "Don't be a baka and judge her by her upbringing. You'd be fools not to learn from her."

She stood awkwardly as he praised her, unsure of what to make of this sensei. They continued with the lesson, and now that the recruits knew their dragons couldn't see specific colors, they gave their dragons different directions.

Tired and windblown, they returned to feed their dragons and eat. The lesson in the afternoon had stretched late, so everyone ate frantically, then loaded up large buckets of meat for their dragons outside. The other dragons waited to eat after Kuro had started. She shook her head and wondered what this would mean for her. Her classmates' looks were as hostile as ever, so in reality, nothing had changed.

Before her lesson, she wanted to see Kuro settled into his den, so as he flew to the top of the abyss, she took the lift down to his level. He waited for her and nudged her softly.

Good job today, she thought.

You seem worried.

This won't make them stop. I am worried about what they'll do next.

Kuro snorted angrily. *Then I will take them all down.*

Mei smiled and patted his scales as they went into his den. Kuro let out a screeching roar. Mei's heart stopped when Kuro's blood flowed onto the stone ground.

TEN

Chin was in the middle of sweeping when the roar of a nearby dragon in pain startled him. Dropping his broom, he ran toward the noise. A few priests also ran toward Mei's den.

His heart sank as he ran. He stopped at the entrance. The floor was wet with blood. His shoes slipped as he got closer to the writhing dragon. Mei was covered in blood, and he didn't know if some of it was hers. Her frantic face found his. "We need a homdragon! Emiri's in the library!" she shouted.

Chin didn't know who Emiri was, but he turned and ran, leaving the roars of pain and shouting behind him. The lift arrived as he got to the dock.

"Main floor!" From his tone, the priest pulled faster, and Chin ran off before they came to a full stop. He ran to the library doors and burst through, waking an older lady sitting nearby. "Emiri?" he shouted.

A round-faced girl stood, her homdragon wrapped around her neck.

"Mei's dragon is hurt!"

Her eyes widened, and she ran out of the library with Chin. "Where's he injured?" she asked in breathless gasps as they got into the lift.

"I just saw blood."

Her mouth twisted in thought, then she pawed through her pouch and fed the homdragon something green and leafy. They reached the lower level, and she was the first homdragon to arrive. The priests had gathered cloths and were trying to stop the flow of blood from the dragon's clawed feet. Others tried to hold Mei back.

"Let her be with him!" Chin yelled.

They let her go, and she knelt next to the dragon while Emiri approached.

She grabbed cloths from her pouch and knelt next to the dragon's feet. The wild silver eyes of the black dragon swung to her. Mei hugged the dragon's neck and whispered, calming him.

As Emiri wiped the wounds, Chin spotted something gray shining on the ground. He looked closer. A metal ball with thin sharp spikes the length of his fingers was painted the same color as the rocks. Some of them stuck out of the dragon's foot and belly. Emiri applied pressure next to the object, and as she pulled, the dragon roared, but she immediately covered the wound and wrapped it.

The priests and Chin stood by as Emiri pulled out each spiked ball and collected them in a pile. Chin ran to grab a broom and swept the area, uncovering more of them. They were painted well enough that they were hard to see in the torchlight, and the spikes were thin enough to breach a dragon's scales.

They depended on shodragons for protection. Chin's hand shook as he collected more gray spikes. To think they would use the fact that Mei was an eta as an excuse to injure a shodragon. Who would be that foolish?

The sensei and more homdragons arrived, but Emiri had completed most of the healing already. They whispered to each other as he took the spikes to the entrance.

"This is unheard of. She is already causing corruption among the recruits," Tomo-sensei whispered to Dazai.

"Shut your trap, Tomo." Dazai-sensei sounded bored, but his eyes were clear and focused as he examined the scene. "There's already corruption," he said softly. His eyes met Chin's, and he knew Chin had overheard him.

The healers guided the dragon and Mei over to the sleeping area and inspected Emiri's work. Then Emiri fed their homdragons a violet flower, and they went over all the wounds. Chin didn't know the name, but the plant was rare and meant for fast healing. His brother had mentioned that it was kept aside for shodragons and riders for battle.

At least they hadn't denied the dragon healing because of Mei's rank. The sensei questioned the priest who stayed at the main gate of the dens.

"Did you see anyone come into the den?" Washi-sensei asked.

The priest shook his head. "Only Chin has been in and out of the den since I arrived this morning."

Chin froze. There was no way he would ever do this to a dragon. He scanned the room, looking for any kind of hint, and a dark pair of eyes burned into him. She'd heard.

He didn't even have time to think or speak before her compact body tackled him, throwing him off balance. The wounds on his back broke open as he hit the stone floor. Her hands wrapped around his neck, and he gasped for air. A dragon snarled in the distance, and he tried to pry her hands away so he could breathe.

The sudden lack of air made him thoughtless, but he shoved his arms under hers, breaking her hold.

"I-I didn't..." Chin coughed. "Not me."

"Liar!"

Still on top of Chin, her face frozen in fury, Mei pummeled his face in a rage. He blocked most of her hits, but one landed squarely on his nose.

Warm blood ran down his face and into his mouth. Someone pulled Mei off him while she kicked and tried to free herself.

"Recruit, stop." Dazai-sensei stood in front of Mei. "You attack without proof?"

Mei's wide eyes glared at Chin. "He was the only one in here."

"We have barely begun to question! Hold in your rage," Dazai snapped. Shocked at the sensei's outburst, Mei backed down, but her anger still read on her face.

"She most likely did it to the dragon herself. Probably thought it was food," Tomo said from the back.

"Is that so, Tomo?" a cold voice said from the entrance. The room fell silent. A large but slender man stood all in black, his ebony eyes taking in the scene. The Sho.

Chin's heart sank. If they accused him of hurting a dragon, his mother wouldn't wait six months to kick him out. The clear, crisp blue sky would come sooner than he thought.

Jion-sho strode into the room, his aura drawing every gaze. His long tied-back hair swished slightly. His sharp angular jaw didn't move as he took in the room, and his eyes settled on the bloody carnage.

"Who was in this room?"

The priest approached and bowed low. "I was only aware of Chin. If I missed someone, it is on my honor."

Chin took a step back as Jion-sho's eyes met his. He had the sudden urge to confess, even though he had done nothing.

"Did you do this?"

"No," Chin answered, voice shaking. He bowed deeply. "I would never hurt a dragon."

"Even though they didn't choose you?"

Chin's gut clenched at the blunt question. He was glad his gaze was still on the floor as his face reddened. "I would never hurt a dragon."

"Look at me, Chin."

Chin raised his face, and Jion-sho only studied him.

"We will find who did this." He looked at Tomo. "I don't want to hear those words again, Tomo. You know better." He strode out of the room, leaving a roomful of blank faces.

Mei's glare still rested on Chin as other priests directed him out of the den. Chin looked back and had never felt such burning hatred. This was nothing compared to what he felt from his mother.

As he left the den, the priest made a sympathetic clucking sound. "Did she hurt your back too?"

He must have been bleeding through his uniform. Chin avoided the priest's eyes. "I think it's just the dragon's blood. May I go clean up?"

The priest nodded. "A healer will wait to treat your nose. Your mother wouldn't like that, would she?"

"No, she wouldn't," Chin murmured. He went down to the indoor river where they got drinking water for the dragons. He took off the top and washed up the best he could, but the fabric was stained with his own blood.

He would need to sneak in without Mother seeing. She visited him nightly now, and without his brother, the wounds would be harder to keep from bleeding.

"What's that from?"

Chin jumped at the voice from behind him and saw the healer, Emiri, her eyes wide.

He had no excuse to offer. "What are you doing over here?"

"I stayed to heal your nose, but I can also wrap up your back..."

Chin put his top back on, and the damp cloth clung to his skin. "Just the nose."

Emiri nodded, her eyes showing pity, and Chin looked away. He didn't need to see that look on her face. Someone else knew about his injuries, and he didn't even know how to tell her not to mention it.

"I won't tell," she whispered and placed warm liquid on his nose. An odd burning sensation radiated from the salve, but it was comforting.

"She'll understand that you didn't do that to her dragon. Just give her time," Emiri said, breaking the silence.

"It doesn't matter."

She backed away. "It really does. With so many against her, she needs you. Give her time to realize you've been there for her all along."

Why did this girl care? "Don't worry about it." Chin turned, listening to her soft footsteps as she left the hall. Chin shouldn't care that Mei hated him. It upset him that she thought he could do something this extreme. He had been nothing but kind to her, and she was ready to believe that he would hurt her dragon.

Chin sighed in frustration. Mei's fierce gaze haunted his mind from when they'd first met. She was a survivor, a fighter. Her sheer will made him respect her. That was all it was: respect. If she hated him, it didn't matter. She didn't need a dragonless boy as an ally.

He sat on the ground and leaned his side against the wall. Closing his eyes, he hoped the priest wasn't expecting him back soon. He didn't want to go near Mei, and he didn't want to go home. So he sat in the dark and listened to the soft rush of river water over rocks.

Two voices approached, and Chin thought that one sounded like Daisuke.

"You said it was for the girl."

"The dragon didn't bleed that much," Daisuke replied flippantly. "The wounds will heal before tomorrow."

The other voice was female, but Chin couldn't place it. "You were just mad that it's more dominant than your dragon."

"Hush. I wouldn't hurt the dragon. I thought I put the spikes where that thing slept."

"In the entrance! Daisuke, do you think I'm stupid?"

There was a pause, and Chin tried to sink lower into the shadows. How had they placed the spikes in the den without the priest seeing?

Daisuke's voice was patronizing as he said, "You aren't stupid. I just made a minor mistake. Will you forgive me?"

The girl huffed, and Chin imagined her looking away. "It's bad enough that everyone thinks you and that thing are together. Why won't you set them straight? You said you love me!"

"And I do. I was just throwing that thing a bone. Then it had to go after my dragon. You know I love you," he crooned to the young woman.

Chin wanted to gag as smacking sounds came from their direction. He hoped he wouldn't have to hear them kissing all night long. After a few giggles, the two finally walked away.

Now he knew who'd hurt Mei's dragon. Who should he tell? The Sho was impossible to see, so he should tell the priest. Daisuke would deny what Chin had heard. He would also probably use the girl as his alibi. He would just tell the priest and let them handle it. *I can do that much, at least.*

Chin stopped by the main gate, and the head priest for the floor was there in his office with a priest in training. Even though it wasn't a large space, a multicolored glass window made the room not feel so tiny. Bound books and stacks of parchment occupied built-in shelves. A simple wooden desk took up the rest of the space. It had different potted plants that Chin didn't recognize. The priest carefully put plants into a satchel.

"Chin, you may go now."

"Oh." Chin paused. "Is the dragon okay?"

The priest nodded. "He will be. The true tragedy is that whoever did this will not suffer."

"Why do you say that?" Chin asked, giving him pause.

"It's how this world works. Good night, Chin." He turned his back and shuffled around some papers, and a priest in training helped.

What would happen to Daisuke? He had a dragon as well, and he was daim. Chin would have to tell the Sho directly. He took the lift and walked up the stairs past the dorms to where the sensei and the Sho lived. Two guards with dendragons stopped him.

"Where are you going?"

"I need to speak to the Sho about—"

The guard cut him off. "He flew out just now. He won't be back until later this week."

Chin didn't know of any other sensei who cared about Mei, except maybe the one in yellow robes, but he shouldn't risk the information getting lost. For now, he would make sure Daisuke stayed far away from Mei. This would be so simple, especially since Mei hated him.

Chin sighed and went back down the stairs to the front of the fortress. The rickshaw waited for him. He got in slowly and leaned his head against the material as the driver took off running. The sun dipped behind the mountain, painting the sky a deep red, just like dragon blood. Chin let the cool breeze dance across his face. He could pretend in this moment that he was free. It was later than normal, and he was sure his mother was already mad.

It honestly didn't matter. Each lash felt the same.

CHAPTER
ELEVEN

After checking under Kuro's bandages, Mei left him to grab a quick breakfast away from the others. She ate in the classroom. She didn't want to see Chin, but she stood in the back of the room, facing out the window. Instead of the sour Sora-sensei, the chief priest entered the room with the recruits. Mei heaved a sigh of relief when Chin wasn't among them. Had he been taken away because he'd confessed? Her lips formed a thin line, and the memory of Kuro's fresh blood on her hands made her body tremble.

The class felt different with the chief priest among them. No giggles or glances at Mei today; they were all focused on the new guest. He took out a cluster of pouches from the satchel he carried. Something remained folded in a silken cloth away from the rest.

Everyone leaned forward in their seats as he opened the pouches to reveal a group of different flowerlike plants. Toshiko sat straighter in her chair, her paper ready for notes.

Besides studying in the library every night, Mei noticed she was always scribbling furiously on her paper.

The priest bowed, and they all bowed back. "Today, I will talk to you of your duty as shodragon riders."

Everyone glanced at one another, and some fidgeted on their stools. They knew the reason, but most would not utter it, just like one never wrote their name in red or mentioned what came with the rain. It was a bad omen.

The priest gently handled the flowers while he spoke. The bright colors contrasted with his words. "Every spring, when the rains come to flood, the jorogumo awaken, looking for blood."

Silence encased the room as the priest recited a line from a proverb. He took his time to meet all their eyes, as if judging their character as riders. "The shodragon is our greatest defense against those who would attack, kill, and eat us."

The man-eating spiders were bigger than a human and some almost as large as a shodragon. Some believed they could turn into beautiful women to mate, but then they turned into spiders to feed. Mei shivered. The eta lived on the outskirts of the city. They were always at risk during the rains when the creatures broke through the walls. There were stories of those who had just disappeared in the past weeks. No one cared since they were eta.

"Your shodragons are like the homdragons, because once they eat something, they can create. They are also like the dendragons, in that they can manipulate. The shodragon can create and manipulate." The priest gestured toward the plants he'd set down on the table. "These create different types of fire for the shodragons to combat the jorogumo. The most common and easiest to grow"—he pointed to a reddish flower—"to the forbidden." He pointed to the silk-covered plant. He picked it up and held it carefully in his hand, giving them only a brief glimpse before covering it again. The deep red flower with petals shaped like spider legs made Mei shiver. "This forbidden fire cannot be controlled, and a dragon and rider will lose their lives in its use. We hope one day to harness its power."

This time, Mei thought the entire class shivered.

"As soon as your dragons are large enough, you will fly. In the meantime, you'll practice with the different flames that your dragons can use. Like the other dragons, they can only use the most basic forms of fire while they are young. Even though for these next rains you will not be ready to fight directly, this training is important since you will all work together in the future. Learning to trust and communicate with each other is a must."

These people would rather injure my dragon than work with me, Mei thought darkly. *I can in no way trust any of them.*

She glanced over to where Daisuke sat, and he was looking at her. She frowned at him and was thankful Chin wasn't in class.

"In the next days, it will be important not to waste these plants. The priests' primary responsibility is to safeguard and grow them, but there isn't an unlimited supply. So before every training, you will get a certain amount. Use it wisely."

The priest went over more about each flower and the type of fire it created. A blue one was apparently a freezing fire that only the Sho had used to its full extent.

Mei felt a tingle of excitement at the thought of trying out the different fires with Kuro. She wondered how far his abilities would grow.

The priest talked for the rest of the morning, and before they knew it, it was time to head outside to practice with their dragons.

To their surprise, all the wingleaders were waiting on the field. Kuro flapped above Mei as she came out onto the field.

Should you be flying?

Kuro showed off his bandage-less scales. *They didn't give me extra to eat, even though I was seriously injured.*

If you get too fat, you won't be able to fly.

Kuro sniffed and landed next to Mei. As the recruits lined up, a wingleader stood next to them. Mei was glad to see Washi-sensei coming over to her. So far, only two of the sensei had treated her normally.

The priest passed out dried versions of the plants he'd shown them in the classroom. "This is hostas. It's a green leafy plant. We have found that the fire is more powerful when the plant is fresh, but it's harder to keep. For training, we provide dried plants. In battle, it will be different."

Mei looked at the flattened leaf in her hand. This made fire?

"Now feed them to your dragons. Your sensei will help you with the rest. It may be wise to spread out farther."

Mei followed Washi to the far corner of the field where his dark blue dragon waited. Its amber eyes peered at Mei, and Washi fed it some of the green leaves.

"Now," Washi said, "the dragons create the fire, and they can manipulate it to a degree, but you'll notice something happens when you feed your dragon. Go on."

Mei bent down and fed Kuro the leaves. Almost instantly, her body felt warm, like a hot coal had dropped inside her stomach. She gasped and hugged her waist.

Washi chuckled. "The first time a recruit feels that is always fun. Your connection with Kuro is how the fire is directed. If he does it by himself it won't be as precise. You don't have to talk, even though you can. You just have to think of where you want the fire to go." Washi pointed to a target that Mei hadn't noticed. A wave of green fire shot out from his dragon's jaws and hit the target dead in the center, burning the wood.

Mei stepped back in the grass, and Washi chuckled again. Then a slender stream of green fire came out of his dragon and gently tapped the edge of the target.

"You see, you can have much control with practice. Sometimes, you'll want that blast of flame, but in battle, you may run out of fire while the creature's webs are dragging you down. You can spare a small amount of flame to break free from the webs, even if you can't deal a killing blow."

Mei's head bobbed at his words. The warm pit at her center steadily burned. "What happens if we don't release the fire?"

"The shodragon will vomit it up. It does no harm, but it is best to use all of it. Now try to hit the target." Washi directed her forward, and his dragon shifted to the side.

She didn't even know what she was doing, but Washi just smiled at her while she stood there with her burning tummy. *Okay, I guess we're supposed to hit the target.*

Kuro blinked up at her. *How?*

I thought you'd know?

Is it like a burp?

Mei snorted. *I guess?*

Kuro tilted his head, and Mei felt the heat rise in her. She furrowed her brow and swung her arm out at the target, pointing. Nothing happened.

Washi laughed. "You're so serious. Why don't you try to push the fire out of yourself and direct it as if you were the one breathing fire? Feel the connection you share with your dragon. Once your dragon gets the hang of it, he will do it on his own too."

Mei bit the inside of her cheeks, focused on the fire inside her, and then touched the top of Kuro's smooth head. She envisioned the fire coming out of her and hitting the target. To her surprise, she could feel the heat moving in her body. She looked down to see Kuro spit out a bright spark of green fire, which landed about a handspan away from them.

"Wonderful!" Washi clapped and snuffed out the cinders with his foot.

Mei tilted her head, looking at the charred grass. That didn't seem so wonderful to her. The sparks had gotten nowhere near the target.

"You're getting the basics down, and it'll take time to produce a full flame. Now let's keep trying."

Skipping lunch, they worked through the afternoon on getting Kuro to breathe fire. Toward the end, they managed a steady flame that lasted about five seconds. Dripping with sweat and smelling like ash, they stumbled back to the fortress with Washi-sensei.

He paused at the stone entrance. "Great work today, and make sure you get an extra helping at dinner. Now remember, you're only using the green fire while your dragon grows. In the next month, we'll add in the orange and maybe red." He slapped her shoulder, and Mei winced. "Great work today, recruit. And let me know if you need anything else to help you with the other classes."

Mei stood there, a bit startled as she watched him mount his dragon and fly away. Her shoulder smarted where he'd touched her. It was strange that she'd found others to rely on in this prison. She felt a new warmth inside her that wasn't from the fire.

She had only been here a few days, but thanks to Emiri and Washi-sensei, things didn't seem that bleak. Mei had thought that Chin was on her side, but he'd hurt her dragon. She'd almost trusted him to take her father food.

In the dining hall, the food servers were giving everyone double portions for the missed meal. She stared at all the food on her tray, then she discreetly folded up the food inside the rice in a spare cloth. Her father might not have eaten these last few days, and they weren't allowed to leave, but she would not let him starve. When she'd left him, his coughing fits had still contained bits of blood, and there was no way her father would beg on the streets. She shook her head at his pride. The eta would help, but they would also make the call of death. An eta knew when food shouldn't be wasted. They would try, but in the end, they would need the food for someone who had a hope of surviving. They didn't know about her father coughing up blood, but they would find out sooner or later.

She'd waited too long. She needed to get food to her father. Her hands trembled at the risk she was about to take, but after Kuro finished his meal, he glanced at her.

So when are we leaving? His silver eyes were unblinking.

Tonight.

THE FOOD, now cold, remained tucked in Mei's clothing. She snuck into the uniforms room next to the priest's office and found something dark to wear over her white clothes. She thought about having Kuro carry the food to her father, but he was still small, and she didn't want to risk it. This was something she needed to do. Her father needed her, and they'd trapped her behind these walls. She stood alone in the growing darkness, watching the guards patrol the stone wall. In the distance, Kuro gave off the appearance of playing with the other dragons in flight, but he was reporting back to her the guards' movements.

On the far side, there is a dark corner. Can you crawl up the wall?

Mei rubbed her calloused fingers together. *Walls aren't a problem for an eta.*

She crept in the shadows in the direction Kuro had pointed out. He would keep watch from above as she climbed over the wall. If he could, he would join her, but chances were he would have to remain on watch. Mei hadn't wanted him involved, but after a silent argument at dinner, she knew there was no way Kuro would stand by and let her do this on her own.

The wall grew taller the closer Mei crept up to it. Her fingers stiffened in the twilight air, and her entire body shook. The Sho's eyes from her first night haunted her. If she got caught, would it be the end for her? She let out a breath. She would rather see her father taken care of than wonder if he lay dying in a mud hut. Gritting her teeth, Mei placed her fingers in the cracks in the stone and started the slow climb while Kuro watched from above.

It didn't take long to scale the wall—she was used to climbing to get out of situations—but it felt like eyes were watching her the whole time. She hoped it was Kuro. Almost at the bottom, she jumped down and landed softly on her feet. Then she took off at a sprint. There was no time to waste, and if they found her missing, she wouldn't be the only one who suffered, but Kuro too.

Clutching the food, she ran down the mountain without stopping. Her breaths came in gasps, but she stayed in the darkness as the young men lit the lamps with their dendragons. No one paid her any attention as she stole through the closing market. The streets turned to dirt as the hollow faces of the eta shambled to their homes from a day of begging or stealing.

Her feet and heart led the way, and she sprinted all the way to the open door. She choked back a sob at the thin figure in the dark shadows of the hut. Her father sat hunched over on his bed, facing the wall. The green beads clicked through his fingers. His head turned at the sound of her feet coming to a halt at the door.

"Who's there? Yui?"

Yui had been looking out for him. Mei's chest heaved in relief. "No, Father, it is me."

"Mei?" His trembling fingers reached out, then stopped.

Mei stepped into the room, and her father jumped toward her. His arms flailed and caught on her shoulders. "What're you doing back here?" His voice pierced the darkness in a trembling tone that Mei had never heard before.

"I brought you food…"

He shook her shoulders. "Why did you come back? You need to leave now." His white eyes fixed straight ahead. "Get out!" he said, his weak voice breaking.

"Father! I brought you food." Mei pulled out the food and put it near her father's hands.

He shoved it away, and it spilled across the dirt floor. The white rice mixed in with the dirt. Food for the bugs. "No, do not come here. They'll kill you. Don't you know any better? Didn't they tell you what will happen if you leave without permission?"

Mei clutched her father's hands. "I can't let you stay here to starve. Father, why are you doing this? I don't want this." Tears ran down Mei's face. There was no gentleness in her father's face.

His jaw loosened, and he hunched his shoulders. "Mei, it's not your duty to care for me. This was the only thing I could do. The day I found out that an eta had received a shodragon, I knew it was you." He dropped his hands from her shoulders. "Think of me as dead. Do not come back here."

"Father..." Mei choked and bent over to scoop the food back into the cloth. "I can't just leave. Don't you understand?" She couldn't go on in this world, pretending she didn't come from here.

His bent fingers reached out, and Mei put her hands in his. Her father clasped them to his chest. "From the time you could first walk, you've taken care of me. My greatest honor is being your father." He lifted a calloused hand to her cheek and rubbed the tears away. "I'm so sorry that this is another burden you'll need to bear for me. A father wants their young to live a better life. You were not meant for these rags or this shack. You were meant to be your mother's daughter." A whisper of a tear glistened at the corner of his milky eye.

"I don't understand." Mei buried her face in her father's chest. His heartbeat was steady in her ears. "Don't send me away. Don't make me pretend you're dead."

He lifted her face with his bent fingers. Although worn and rough, they were so familiar. "Mei, I know what happens to someone who leaves the fortress. The entire city knows. Did you get permission to come here?" She shook her head. "Then you must run back and pray they never find out you were here tonight. Take me out of your heart and live. Do not come back to this door, or I will take the last walk." His hand gripped her tighter. "You don't know what's at risk. You don't understand what's at stake."

Mei sobbed as her father held her in his arms, then he turned her around and gave her a push out the door. She turned her head. "Father, I don't understand. I'm an eta. There's nothing for me there. We can leave. We can go with Kuro—"

"No, we can't." He left her shoulders cold. "Go now. Find those you can trust. You are everything. Go or all this will be in vain."

Then her father turned his back. Mei could see every one of his ribs through the too thin cloth. She reached out but paused at his stiffness. Her hand dropped to her side, and she bowed her head. Choking down a sob, she ran up the path she'd taken only moments before. Her eyes blinded by tears, she kept stumbling into eta, who drew away from her after they saw her rich clothing and somewhat clean appearance. She gulped in air and sprinted to where she'd climbed over the wall. Her fingers wouldn't grip the stone as she stood there, her hands shaking.

What's going on? What happened?

I can't... I can't climb...

Out of the darkness, a black form approached from the sky. Kuro landed next to her and stuck his head under her hands.

You must climb.

A few more tears leaked out. *I know. I...*

Kuro flew up, grasped her clothing by her shoulders, and

pulled her. He couldn't lift her, but his strength gave her balance as she found the right crevices in the stone wall. They made it over, and Mei fell. She lay on her back on the grass. Kuro curled next to her as she sucked in air. It felt so hard to breathe. Had it always been this hard to breathe?

What happened?

H-he doesn't want me to come back. I'm s-supposed to think of him as dead.

Kuro nuzzled next to Mei and crooned. His warmth comforted her, and she closed her eyes. Her father didn't want harm to come to her, but she couldn't do her best while he was starving. His tone of voice had suggested that something else had happened. She didn't know what he'd meant. How could an eta be important? It wasn't like a wingleader would choose her at the end of all this training.

It felt like a thin line was coming out from under her—a line that traveled over this wall and down into the district that people wished didn't exist. That line had felt tight before her father had cut all ties to him. The eta were her family. Her home.

I can't just leave him.

Yes, but you shouldn't leave again.

Mei sighed. Maybe a sensei would let her leave one day. She thought Washi seemed sympathetic. Could she somehow convince him to give her a pass?

With the invisible chain that kept her here fully in place, Mei stood and walked back to the fortress. Then a dark figure came out of the shadows. In the faint torchlight, she could see Daisuke's cold eyes.

"Going out for a midnight stroll, eta?"

TWELVE

A bitter laugh left her lips. "You're going to tell, aren't you? Go ahead. It's only a matter of time before they get rid of me." Emptiness crept into her heart. She'd tried. She'd pushed forward no matter what they'd said about her. She'd stolen and eaten garbage. She'd made deals. But her father had told her that all she'd done to help him survive was meaningless. Did it even matter if Daisuke told? What did she have left?

"So the eta is giving up after all this? Interesting. No one's on your side?" Daisuke leaned on the wall, playing with a blade of grass, and looked at her like a cat looked at its next meal.

Before Mei could reply, she felt a soft spear of thoughts. Its brightness and warmth beamed up from her. A smooth head nudged her hand.

You have me. The mournful tone made her feel ashamed.

I'm sorry. I'm so sorry. I do have you. In her mind, she could never rise to deserve such loyalty. "What do you want?" The empty ache in her heart lessened as Kuro kept a continued presence inside her mind.

Daisuke flicked away the grass. "You want a deal now?"

Mei blinked and met his gaze.

He leaned in, and his spiderweb hair fell forward. "I'll ask for two things: tell me who you went to visit, and give me a bit of that eta pride since you took some of mine." He paused for effect. "Go out and pick me a gift of flowers. Then come to the room and tell everyone that you are desperate for me."

His face was unreadable. Was he really this shallow? "What do you get out of this?"

"Amusement," he replied in a singsong fashion.

The flower request seemed like something Daisuke would do. But why did he care who she'd seen tonight? A glimmer in his eyes made her think that the request was coming from someone other than him. Who would care about what an eta did?

I can bite him.

He'll tell them I left. You know that anyone who leaves without permission is seen as a deserter.

I don't think he will.

She studied him, and he lounged like he had all night to wait for her response. He knew how to hide his feelings, and Mei thought he would have survived well as an eta. It meant the flower plan was a distraction from his true motives.

"How can I trust you won't tell later?"

He flicked imaginary lint from his robe. "I guess you can't trust me, but this is the only chance you have."

"So you want flowers and a confession?"

His lip twitched. "And who you went to see."

Mei smiled to herself. Yes, that information was what he

wanted. She didn't care about his flower game. "I went to see my guardian."

"Guardian?"

"Does that answer your question?"

His eyes flickered, and she assumed he wanted more details. He could assume that her father had died and left her in the care of someone else. Something told her to keep his existence quiet. Daisuke might just be a messenger.

"Why would you risk death to see a guardian?"

Remain still. "I answered your question. Now do you want your show?"

Daisuke didn't move, and she could see he debated whether to press the issue.

"I'll be waiting." He turned and said as he walked away, "It better be a good show. Doesn't your life depend on it?"

Mei's fingernails bit into her palms. He still wanted to go ahead with it. Without responding, she went out to the field and yanked out some innocent wildflowers. She stood for a moment, gripping them in her fist. She could still feel her father's hands holding her. Something was behind his desperation. What had he meant by risk? She was just an eta. Her life didn't matter. She felt alone, fighting for something, but she didn't know what.

You aren't alone.

She straightened her shoulders and clasped the wilted flowers. *Wait for me in the den. I will take care of this.*

No.

Wait, she snapped.

Kuro eyed her and then snorted as he flew off to the dens. She didn't want him to see her simpering in front of the other recruits. He thought she was more than an eta.

I don't care. I don't care what they think, Mei told herself as her feet dashed up the stone steps. The more she chanted those words, the more she wanted to sink into the stone. Somehow, enduring her classmates' jeers was better than confronting them head-on. She really didn't want to make a spectacle of herself for Daisuke. Her steps slowed as a murmur came from her old room.

This is nothing. I am nothing. As Mei walked forward, she felt like her body had been left behind with her father's hands on her shoulders and the frantic look in his blind eyes. The memory brought unbidden tears, and she blinked them away as she slid open the door.

Every face in the room blurred as they turned toward Mei. Then, at the end of the room, Daisuke sat like an emperor over his tiny kingdom. He leaned against the stone window frame and lightly combed his hand through his long black hair. Benio and Aimi gave him covert looks, but his eyes focused on Mei. She clutched the flowers and forced herself to relax like her life depended on it, because it did. Daisuke hadn't gotten the answer he wanted from her earlier, so this humiliation would have to suffice. Mei put on the blank mask that had kept her alive all these years, the mask that told everyone she didn't matter and shouldn't be noticed. Kenta jeered at her and the other recruits looked up at her approach. Only Toshiko kept her face buried in her book and huffed in annoyance at the noise.

"Why's it back?" Benio asked, crossing her arms.

"I thought it slept out in the garbage," Aimi replied. "It smells terrible in here now, we'll have to leave the windows open all night."

"We should kick it out," Niko joined in. She stopped braiding her hair and stood next to Benio.

All the whispers hit Mei's ears, and she paused in front

of Daisuke. He arched his thin brow and held up his hand, silencing the others.

She almost wished he'd let them keep whispering. The silence burned in her ears and ensured they would hear her words. She forced herself not to choke as the words flew out of her mouth. "Will you accept my feelings?" She thrust out her flowers.

Gasps broke the silence, and she kept her eyes focused on her tormentor. He remained still in the flurry of whispers that broke out. A graceful smile appeared on his face, and he languidly stood and stared down at Mei. She bit her cheek. He loved flaunting his height over her. Another dominance game. She stuck out her chest and met his eyes.

Kento laughed. "It has feeeeelings for you, Daisuke!" He knelt down and threw out his arms. "Will you accept its feelings?" The room burst into laughter at his antics.

"Eta, how kind of you to express your feelings; however, what was between us is now over. I appreciate the effort you have put into your..." He glanced at the sad flowers. "... gift. I'd hate for them to get wasted, so you may enjoy them and then leave."

Enjoy them? Her thoughts rushed to grasp his meaning.

He smirked. "Eat them."

The flower stems bit into Mei's hand. Without moving her eyes, she opened her mouth wide and shoved in all the flowers. She gnashed her teeth into them, and the bitter flavors stung her tongue. Mei gulped down the massive lump as the room broke out into laughter. Mei and Daisuke were the only two not smiling. She gave him a mocking nod and left the room.

With the bitter taste of flowers in her mouth, Mei sprinted down the hall and ran head on into a body.

She gasped and looked up, seeing Washi-sensei's concerned face. "Mei? Why are you running around this late?" He leaned in and saw her watery eyes. His face darkened. "What happened?"

Mei knew it would only make it worse for her if she told on the others. "Nothing. It's cold. It makes my eyes water."

Washi nodded. "I see." He paused for a moment. "I just made some tea. Would you like some?"

"I—"

Washi held up his hand. "You don't need to talk. Just some tea." He slid open his classroom door. The lights were bright in the room. Since he taught them outside, his room was smaller. Clutter of different plants and fire pattern drawings hung on the walls. One formation caught her eye as Washi brought her a clay cup of tea.

"Ah, the Gado formation." He pointed to the dragon below. "If your team runs out of plants, the others fly in above while a runner can deliver more to them. This can happen in longer battles. Usually it's the recruits that run the plants. It can be dangerous, but this formation offers the most protection."

Mei studied the cup and took a careful sip of the tea. It washed away the taste of the flowers and was soothing down her throat from the scratchy stems.

Washi sipped his own tea and continued to stare at the drawing. "I know things are hard for you and I can't be everywhere, but if things go too far, please let me know."

Her throat tightened and it had nothing to do with the scene with Daisuke. "Arigato."

Washi nodded, and they both sat and finished the tea in silence. Mei still held back tears. Seeing her father, the flowers, and Washi's kindness was overwhelming. She stood and bowed to Washi. He tipped his head.

"Sleep well, recruit."

"Arigato."

Mei held back her tears until she got to the lift. In the safety of the den, she fell to her knees. With her head on her arms and sobs shaking her body, tears poured out of her eyes.

"I can't do this, Father. Why did you make me do this?"

A soft head rested on her shoulder while she sobbed into the night. When there were no more tears to cry, she wiped her cheeks and met Kuro's eyes.

"I gave up everything to be here. I won't let them win."

Kuro nudged her with his nose. *I'm with you until the end.*

Wrapped together, they fell asleep in the den's warmth.

CHAPTER

THIRTEEN

Daisuke sighed as he played with the edge of his deep blue kimono. The room where all the recruits stayed was empty. When he'd told everyone to get out, they'd listened to him. He had never shared a room in his life and found it insulting that the fortress didn't provide separate rooms. His light brown hair hung loose and nearly touched the floor. The hair had become so bothersome, but his family always kept their hair long. They expected him to be the next Sho.

The peaceful view outside the window frustrated him. In these passing five months, snow had covered every inch of the fortress land, and the outside lessons were cold. Their dragons were almost flight ready.

No one was doing anything about the eta, and it was the only thing that provided excitement in this stone prison. Maybe he should go thank it personally. He could tell the eta was waiting for him to tell the sensei that it had snuck out those five months back, but what would be the fun in that? He'd enjoyed watching it squirm. The little guttersnipe actually had done a fair job of avoiding him since the flower incident, which had made it harder to find out information.

He smirked at the memory of the eta's rejection and the audacity it had had in kneeing him in his bits. Still, the eta was the most interesting thing around. The daim women fell into his lap and made it almost too easy.

At home, he had other amusements, but at the fortress, there was no privacy. He leaned farther into the stone window frame, clicking his manicured nails against the stone.

A sigh came from the bed, almost startling him. He'd completely forgotten she was there. Daisuke furrowed his brow, trying to remember this one's name. Pulling shut his kimono, he moved to leave the room. He remembered that this one was clingy.

Maybe if he spoke to Father, he could get his own accommodations. The Sho had shut down the first request, but he could always try again. Even though Daisuke didn't wear his uniform, he stepped out in the cool evening air. He supposed he should go check on his dragon. The priests were careful to watch all who came in and out since the eta dragon's injury.

Leisurely moving down the stairs and into the lift, he headed to his den. His dragon lay curled up on the heated stone, and for a moment, a genuine smile passed over his face. With her crimson scales and golden eyes, she was a beauty.

She shifted awake at his approach, and he placed a hand on her head.

"Sorry, I was just checking on you. Get some rest."

She nuzzled his palm and curled up once more, breathing softly. "I hurt the dragon who hurt you," Daisuke whispered softly. He didn't care that she had no marks on her from that fateful dominance fight. In the early days, she'd shown dominance that had rivaled the Sho, and now the eta's rat had somehow grown larger and more skilled, solidifying its ranking.

"Why can't we talk?" Only silence and breathing. What made the eta so special? Why did she get to communicate with her dragon? He would eventually talk to his, but it was hard to believe that an eta had such an advantage. There was nothing special about the wiry eta.

Her flashing eyes entered his thoughts, and he had to admit she was different, to the point he considered her human. He shook his head and stood, giving his dragon one last stroke before he left.

Outside at the entrance, Washi-sensei talked with the priest. In front of them was a pile of tangled leather.

"It is a disgrace that the practice harnesses are in this state." Washi clicked his tongue as he tried to pull one out of the pile, his round face red. "How are we supposed to use these tomorrow?"

"We'll work through the night putting them to rights."

Daisuke came closer, and Washi turned at the sound of his soles scraping the rock. "Oh, Daisuke, checking on your dragon?"

"Yes, sensei." Daisuke bowed. "Did you need any help?" It was so troublesome trying to pretend to care about a servant's chores. If he wanted to get into the best winglegion, however, he would have to play nice for three years. He wanted to fight and battle, but the power that came with being a wingleader was his first goal.

"Oh, maybe a little."

Daisuke let out an inner sigh and went to the harnesses.

He tried to untangle the one closest to him. "Shells, this is a mess. Are we flying tomorrow, sensei?"

"Right you are! The dragons are big enough to support your weight. You'll do drills in pairs of two." Washi frowned. "That may be a problem." Washi dropped the harness he held back into the pile.

Daisuke knew he was thinking about the eta. "My dragon and... *her*..." He tried not to choke on the word. "... dragon are the largest."

"Yes." Washi eyed him, and Daisuke became very interested in the harness in front of him.

"Wouldn't it make sense that we pair up for the drills?"

"It would." Washi tilted his head and studied Daisuke. "You would really partner with her?"

Daisuke shrugged, feigning disinterest. "When the rains come, will it matter if she's an eta? She clearly has the strongest dragon in our group." His throat burned as he said the words. He didn't have a plan—hurting her dragon had been one thing, but if he was close to her, he could do so much more. Swallowing his pride for a moment didn't matter. It was time to think of the long game, and breaking down the eta's fierce eyes would truly be worth it. Broken things sure could be beautiful.

"I don't think your family would approve of *her*." The jovial tone disappeared for a moment and Daisuke thought maybe Washi was trying to communicate something else to him without saying it. But the man's smile reappeared and Washi untangled a harness and hung it on a nearby hook.

"What do they matter when the Sho's in charge at the fortress? He would agree that our dragons should go together." In a normal year, that would have been true. Daisuke was always careful not to do anything malicious in front of the sensei. Kento and Benio could act like the bakas. He wanted to be chosen by the Sho, not Sora or the others. A proper daim knew how to play political games.

Washi nodded and tried to catch a harness that fell. Daisuke handed it to him with a smile.

"Your attitude toward your team will get you far, Daisuke."

"My goal is to be useful, sensei." He finally worked out another harness. Now he just needed an excuse to get out of here and leave this chore to someone else. Where was that dragonless daim? He should have been doing this. Daisuke held back a laugh at the thought of the dragonless daim taking the blame for the dragon's injury. It had worked out too perfectly. It was almost boring when it was so easy.

"Sensei, I left something in my den. I'll be right back."

Washi nodded, and Daisuke left to get away from the labor. Around the bend in the hall, he paused at the entrance to the black dragon's den. He slunk closer and could just see inside with the shadowy lighting. The eta lay on the dragon's forearms, with the dragon's neck stretched out over her. Her bony frame looked so frail next to the dragon's head. She wasn't refined like the daim girls, but to Daisuke, her roughness made her attractive. Too thin, too short, too angular, but one look at her stance and you knew she was a fighter.

Then he met a pair of silver eyes. The dragon watched him, and his head didn't move as his glare pierced Daisuke. It made him shiver and step back from the entrance. To his right, he noticed a large metal hook. That was where the harnesses would be hung. Daisuke smiled, bowed slightly to the dragon, and went back to all the harnesses. Sometimes, a bit of work was necessary.

CHAPTER

FOURTEEN

Over the last five months, Mei had watched Kuro with jealousy as he'd flown out of the dens. Soon, she wouldn't have to take the lift anymore, if Kuro gave her a ride. She almost laughed at the comment he would make over being her transportation to the den.

Dancing with anticipation, she grabbed the harness and took the lift. She ran to the snow-covered field with light steps, and she picked out Kuro's dark scales in the sky. The way he twisted and flew in the air made her heart sing. She would get to be with him soon.

You seem happy today.

I am. We get to ride. She paused. *Are you sure you're ready?*

Kuro snorted. *See for yourself.*

As she ran, he dove at her and pulled up at the last minute, almost making her fall down. When he landed, she thumped his forearm. He dwarfed her now, and she needed to crane her neck to look at his face.

You shelling show-off.

161

Kuro said nothing and stretched out in the sun, preening. She leaned her head on his shoulder and closed her eyes, listening to the thump of his heartbeat. Around him, a calmness settled into her body. After being on alert her entire life, there was something about Kuro that made Mei feel rested. She felt unnerved during most of her days and kept her head down around Daisuke. She didn't know if he would tell the sensei about her leaving, even after his shelling request. Since that night, she'd avoided him at all costs. She also hadn't found a way to get food to her father these past months. She'd thought of asking Emiri for help, but she already did too much for her. And her father might even reject that offering to stand firm in his wish that Mei forget him.

The other students approached the field, drawing her out of her thoughts. They held harnesses, and their dragons landed. All the dragons received scratches and pets while they waited for Washi-sensei. Excitement bubbled out from everyone. Today, they would finally ride their dragons.

"These harnesses are so plain my father said he'd buy me a new one," Benio bragged to her sycophants. "I'm thinking a nice yellow to stand out against his tawny butter earthy scales."

"The word you're looking for is brown, Benio." Toshiko snorted. "And they won't allow it. If you haven't noticed, color has meaning and yellow belongs to Dazai-sensei."

Benio removed imaginary lint from her riding gear. "Like that old grump would care."

"I assure you he would. Toshiko's correct." Washi approached, his green robes fluttering behind him. Benio snapped her mouth shut and got even more interested in the imaginary lint on her clothing. The usual jovial expression graced his face. Behind him, four large shodragons and their riders landed. Mei's hair flew back in the gust of wind from their giant wings.

Over the last few months, seeing full-grown shodragons had become part of their normal lives, but now they were only a few spans away. Their scales glimmered, and their heads were held high in the air. In the middle of them, the Sho's large golden dragon shook out her wings as Jion-sho dismounted.

As Jion-sho went to the head of the recruits, Washi-sensei bowed and stood to the side. In his black riding gear, Jion-sho made a striking image against the pure white snow. The recruits would eventually get better riding gear too, once they began their training runs. The riding gear was tighter than their usual uniforms and insulated with hide and wool against the cold. They also had taller footwear, which went up mid-calf, called boots. Also, all the riders wore a thick pair of gloves. With the unusual clothing, the dampened sound, and the lack of wind, it seemed like they were in their own world.

"From this point on in your training," Jion-sho said, his voice carrying over the stillness, "you will do flying drills to neighboring villages. Some will carry supplies or messages. There are ten of you, and everyone will ride in pairs."

Mei heard a flurry of whispers and caught several glances in her direction. Jion-sho followed their gazes, and his jaw tightened.

"Washi-sensei?" Jion-sho asked.

"Yes, Sho?"

"Are these recruits worried about social class?" The whispers stopped. They all took in Jion-sho's flinty expression as he met their gazes. "If I wanted to be among the first to be selected for a winglegion, I would think it wise to be paired with the best dragon and rider."

Mei's eyes widened. She hadn't even ridden Kuro yet, and he claimed she was the best? The others' gazes chilled. Benio practically looked like she wanted to strangle Mei. Her communication skills had given her an edge over the rest, but that wouldn't last long. The invisible chains felt heavier at the added pressure.

Washi-sensei didn't answer but his face lost his cheerful expression as he looked at the recruits.

"It doesn't matter, but we chose for you." Jion-sho gestured to Washi. "Have the first team step up."

Washi nodded. "Daisuke and Mei."

The gasps didn't surprise Mei. She wanted to gasp too. Throughout the training, she'd tried to ignore the others despite their constant torture. Daisuke had popped up around her the most as she'd tried to avoid him. The other girls in the older recruit years fancied him. Aimi's face flushed red and her livid gaze burned into Mei. Her shoulders tightened at the prospect of what they would do to her since he was her partner in training. *He will have the opportunity to get me alone with him.*

Let him try something, Kuro said, and his undertone made her feel safe.

They both stepped forward with their dragons. Kuro's black scales contrasted nicely with Daisuke's red dragon in the field of white. Hands slightly shaking, Mei strapped on the harness. They'd practiced this many times in class, but this time, it would have to hold her in the air. This harness gleamed and had to be newer. The smooth leather slipped over her fingers as she tightened and checked each strap.

Comfortable? Mei asked.

Yes.

Leg, please.

Kuro bent his leg so Mei could get up around his neck. When seated, she adjusted the straps on her legs and around her waist. She didn't have a place to put her hands, so she rested them awkwardly in front of her. The others would steer their dragons with reins for now, but Mei didn't need to. Washi looked over Mei's work and nodded.

"They're ready," he said to Jion-sho.

"Fly to the other mountain and back. Mei, take the lead."

Mei bowed, and she didn't wait to see Daisuke's reaction to the Sho's proclamation. Some of the sensei's faces spoke enough of their disgust.

"Make us proud," Washi whispered to her as he stepped away.

Her back straightened and she bowed. His belief in her quieted her nerves. *Let's go, Kuro.*

Through the leather harness, Mei felt Kuro's powerful muscles bunching under her. His wingspan stretched out in inky darkness against the snow. He tilted back on his hind legs, and with one mighty push, he vaulted into the sky. His leap couldn't be called smooth, but he didn't have as much power as an adult shodragon yet. Mei could feel his wings strain as they beat to gain more altitude. The lack of wind made it less cold, but there was no push to help lift them. Today, the dragons would have to get in the air on pure strength, and maybe that's what the sensei wanted to see.

Is everything okay? Mei asked. The steady pumping of the wings worried her.

Kuro snorted. *You weigh nothing. Shouldn't you be enjoying this?*

Mei started and twisted her head around. Her class

looked like tiny spatters of ink in the snow. Even the adult dragons seemed small. Daisuke flew on her right flank, a slash of red against the clear sky. But all around her, the world opened, showing a place where she could be an equal. Her heart soared with Kuro as they flew toward the mountain. The city sprawled out behind them, and Mei's vision wandered to its edges. Her father could no longer see, but in some way, she hoped he knew she could see him.

A joyful laugh escaped her lips, and that prompted Kuro to go even higher. Mei craned her neck and let the cold air whip around her hair. She'd forgotten to put on the headgear, but for this ride, Mei enjoyed the briskness surrounding her. The pain of being an eta had stayed on the ground with her classmates.

They reached the mountain too soon, and Mei's heart sank as Kuro turned around to head back. As he turned, she shifted, leaning in with him, but her body kept going.

The sky turned as Mei slipped off Kuro's neck. She scrabbled for the harness, but it fell with her. Kuro's slick scales provided no traction, and with her arms outstretched, Mei fell toward the white world beneath.

No sound left her throat, but Kuro roared in the air as he folded his wings and dove after her. His long claws grasped her arm. He expanded his wings, jerking them up while he latched on to Mei.

Mei screamed as her left shoulder popped, and pain flooded her body.

What's wrong? What happened?

Kuro's questions darted in her mind, but she couldn't focus and gather a thought to send him; only mindless pain consumed her. As he reached for her with his other claws, her arm slipped through his grasp, and she fell again.

The wind roared in her ears, and before Kuro could reach her, a different set of claws came at her side. In trying to grip her body, they left large gashes in her stomach and thighs, but she was firmly in the claws of Daisuke's dragon.

Warm blood ran down the claws, and Mei could hear something in her mind. A black shadow kept popping up in her side vision.

Through her dry lips, she muttered, "I'm fine. It's—" She briefly blacked out as the dragon tried to land on her hind feet, almost throwing Mei to avoid landing on her with her weight.

"Get a homdragon down here now!"

Voices shouted as the cold snow melted into her body. With the blood flowing out, her warmth left too.

Mei! Mei! Mei!

She wanted to answer, but thoughts flicked away like ash in her mind.

A low, warm voice came through her scattered thoughts. "Mei, you need to calm him so we can get close to you."

Calm him? Oh. Mei felt that connection, her Kuro. *It's okay. Let them through.*

Mei!

They need to heal me. It's okay.

Mei.

The mournful tone of Kuro's thoughts broke her heart. *You did nothing wrong. You saved me. Stay back a tad so they can get closer.*

A large body slid against the snow. Then chilly hands touched her, and she flinched.

"Her shoulder is out, but I will stop the bleeding first. These aren't so bad, so no need to waste fast healing on it— her," a voice she didn't recognize said.

"Jion-sho's coming back. I will tell him she'll be fine."

Mei tried to piece together who was talking, but she drifted in and out as they wrapped her up. She felt her body being lifted, and the heat let her know she was finally back inside.

"Okay, hold it down while I pull its arm. Then we can leave."

On the hard stone ground, Mei felt a colossal weight on her body. She gasped as they pushed into her cuts. Tears burned her eyes, and the final pop caused her to cry out. Her brain focused on the pain, but when she glanced around the room, only a large black head with wide eyes was in view.

Mei! You don't seem okay. After they healed me, I could walk. I still smell blood. Didn't they do it correctly?

Mei coughed and tasted blood in her mouth. *They won't waste healing on me.*

Waste! A loud roar resounded in the den, and Kuro stalked around Mei.

I'll be fine. I just need to rest.

I smell fresh blood.

Kuro, it's okay. I'll be fine. I will just sleep for a moment.

You'll be fine?

Mei heard the doubt in his voice. She didn't really know if she would be fine. If Emiri heard about this, maybe she would come to help. Mei squeezed her eyes shut. She couldn't always depend on Emiri. Dragging up resolve, she lied to Kuro. *Yes. Rest will fix this.*

I will watch you rest.

Mei smiled. *Don't forget to eat.*

Kuro snorted. *I will watch.*

In the heat of the den and under Kuro's watchful gaze, Mei tried to sleep. The excessive heat in the den left the bandages drenched in sweat. As Mei tossed and turned, her wounds broke open, sending fresh pain down her side and legs. She clasped onto a hand, but when her bleary eyes opened, only Kuro sat in the den.

Kuro worried like a large mother hen at Mei's moaning, and finally, in the night, she felt a pair of cool hands resting on her head.

"The nits didn't tell me you were hurt." The grumbling voice belonged to Emiri. "They wouldn't give me what I wanted, but this will speed up the healing."

"You're here?"

"Where else would I be? I'm sorry they didn't call me when you were hurt. Whoever did this did a shelling of a shoddy job."

Emiri worked quickly and removed the other bandages, and a cold salve covered her open wounds. The pain immediately lessened to a dull throbbing. The tightness of the new bandages comforted Mei. Emiri rubbed a minty-smelling salve into Mei's sore shoulder.

"I used up my supply of viola those months ago on your dragon, and the nits won't give me any more, saying I wasted it." Anger tinged Emiri's voice. "This will stop any infection, but with how deep the wounds were, they will take a few days to heal fully."

Mei gave Emiri a shaky smile. "Arigato."

Emiri blushed. "I'm just doing what they should have done in the first place. They have no right to be called healers. I should report them to the Sho."

Mei lightly shook her head. "It's my battle."

"Eggs and shards above it is! If they don't heal you, it's my battle too!" Kuro snorted in agreement as Emiri placed her hands on her hips. Now Mei had two mother hens clucking over her.

"I'm not used to people caring about me."

"Well, I care and so does your gigantic dragon. Also Chin."

A flush of anger heated her face. "He hurt Kuro!"

"Kuro? Oh…" Emiri's eyes widened, and she bowed toward Kuro. "I apologize for not asking for your name sooner." Her eyes went back to Mei. "I don't think Chin hurt him. It has been months, and they found nothing."

Mei turned her head away. "I think I should rest now."

"Yes, I'll watch over you with your dragon."

Even though she couldn't see Emiri, Mei felt her presence behind her. A lone tear fell from her eye at the kinship offered to her. Trusting someone outside of her father seemed like a fantasy. A glowing sense of safety surrounded her as she drifted off under the watch of her two guardians.

FIFTEEN

Under protest from Emiri, Mei left the den the next afternoon. She already missed her morning classes. It would take more than this to keep her from her first training run with Daisuke.

"Fine, but if you open all your wounds, I will let you bleed out." Emiri looked at Kuro. "Can you talk sense into her?"

Kuro tilted his head, and his silver eyes glared at Mei.

"I'm fine! You saw for yourself that they were closed, and all I'm doing today is riding. No fight training, just a delivery run. I'll be sitting the whole time."

Emiri clenched her jaw and shook her head. "Fine." She raised her hands and draped her homdragon over her neck. "Don't listen to the healer. Just do what you want."

Mei bowed. "Arigato, Emiri. I don't think I would have made it through the night without you." Mei still felt sore, but she might have gotten an infection if it hadn't been for Emiri.

Emiri sniffed, and they headed out of the den. A new harness hung at the entrance, and Mei took it carefully.

"Did they say anything about why my harness broke?" Mei asked.

"No. When I heard you were injured, I ran down here."

Uneasiness entered Mei's stomach. The training harnesses were used, but priests checked them before each class. Had someone tampered with hers? From now on, she would keep it deeper inside the den. This went beyond minor pranks and slights. They now wanted her dead. Mei put her palm on Kuro's solid body. The feel of his weight comforted her, and he flew out of the den while Mei and Emiri rode the lift.

"I still think I should tell the Sho."

Mei shook her head. "This is only the start. The healers will just claim ignorance."

"That kind of ignorance could get them kicked out, as it should. While you're fighting, you don't want those kinds of healers."

Mei studied the clanking chains as they rose. "I'm sure they're skilled healers for everyone else."

"I suppose I'll just have to stay by you when you go to battle." Emiri crossed her arms.

"I'll feel like a daim with my own personal healer." Mei smiled. Without contact from her father and with the constant bullying, Emiri became one of the few humans she could trust.

Emiri rolled her eyes as they stepped off the lift. She studied Mei before they parted ways. "Just be careful?"

Mei nodded and went toward the field. She didn't run today. Her body hurt more than she'd let on. They were going to do longer flying runs, and she couldn't just sit in the den. From her distance, she could already see everyone's dragons. The snow crunched under her feet, and Mei shivered under her heavy and tight gear. It was harder to breathe under the clothing today, but with the longer run, she needed to wear all of it.

Everyone stared at her as she approached, and Kuro landed majestically beside her. As always, she stood apart from them.

"How are you today?"

Mei jumped at Daisuke's question. "Fine."

He gave what she imagined should be a comforting smile. "I'm your partner, you know. I need to know if you really are okay."

She jutted her chin. "I'm fine."

His eyes lingered on her small body, and to someone else, it might have looked like he was assessing for injuries, but Mei felt naked under his ravishing gaze. Turning away from him, she focused on triple-checking the new harness as she placed it on Kuro's neck. Her hands trembled at the memory of sliding off and trying to grip the glass-smooth scales. Only yesterday, her life had almost ended.

You're shaking.

It's cold. The last thing she wanted to do was worry him. He kept craning his neck around to study her as she adjusted the harness for the fourth time.

It isn't wise to go today. I will not fly. It is best to stay here and eat to gain strength.

Mei placed her forehead on his shoulder. "Kuro, I need to do this today. Please understand."

He snorted, and the cold air fogged up around them, but he remained silent. Mei hoped that meant he would fly. She inhaled through her nose and released the breath in a slow whistle. It helped a bit to remember the feeling from the first part of the flight, but nothing could lessen the tremor in her hands. The trembling crept into her legs, and Mei wanted to slap her cheeks to calm herself down. The eyes on her back stopped her.

Toshiko looked annoyed at being paired with Kento. Kento and Ren were throwing snowballs at each other and finally she snapped.

"Kento, if I get bad marks because of you, you'd better pray to a kami because you will not be safe from me. I will burn all your clothing so you have to fly in the snow naked."

Kento actually stilled and went to stand next to her.

Mei bit her lips so she wouldn't laugh.

Benio and Aimi were taking mail out to the water islands, and when their brown and coral dragons took off, the snow stirred around everyone's feet.

Washi-sensei waded through the rest of the partners, and a wagon held different packages.They attached them to dragons, and as soon as the sensei checked, the pairs would fly off. When he reached Mei and Daisuke, he paused.

"Are you okay to fly today?"

Mei nodded sharply, noting the worry on his face. "I'm healed enough to fly."

Washi said no more and directed the wagon drivers to load packages onto the two dragons and check for balance. Mei appreciated that he never pressed her for longer answers. The packages weren't large since the dragons were still growing, but they were still heavy.

Mei and Daisuke stood at attention as Washi briefed them. "You'll be taking a few supplies of food to a village to the south. You'll travel the farthest today, but your dragons are also the largest. They're giving us unrefined metals in exchange."

"Is there any worry since people have disappeared from that side of the city? Has this village experienced any trouble?" Daisuke asked.

Mei raised her eyebrows. He actually cared about the missing eta? *Doubtful.* His face remained blank, and Mei couldn't read him. He always put on a show for the sensei, and to her that was more dangerous. Somehow, gangsters on the street were easier to handle than the too smooth Daisuke. Her mouth tasted like bitter flowers just looking at him. *The nit.*

Washi shook his head. "This village has dendragons who mine, and they have a better stone wall than we do. Very fortified. Follow your charts and you can't miss it. But be on watch during your flight. You never know if someone will need help. Those are the only stops allowed if in an emergency."

They both bowed and mounted their dragons. Daisuke gestured to her to take the lead. Even though she was injured, Jion-sho's decision was final. Mei was thankful there were no normal classes this morning. She could only imagine the new jealousies she'd face as the lead rider. Kento had finally tired of throwing flowers into her food at mealtimes and dramatically screaming about her accepting his feeling.

She was only the favorite because of Kuro. He'd proved his dominance, and now the little eta was along for the ride. Why had Kuro chosen her? She was half the size of her classmates, illiterate, and not the strongest fighter.

Washi handed her a bow, interrupting her thoughts. She hooked the yumi bow and arrows to the latch on the harness behind her. They shouldn't need them today, but they both had a pouch for their dragons' fire and a quiver full of arrows. Mei could now handle the green fire and had moved up to the red, although for these runs, they'd only given them a small amount of hostas for the green fire.

Even though the rainy season wasn't for a few months, other things could attack them if they had to make an emergency landing.

Mei looked to Daisuke, who was once again watching her, but this time he waited for her signal. She tapped her forearm and put her palm up. *Ready to fly?*

He tapped his forearm. *Ready.*

Kuro, let's go.

No response.

Kuro?

Mei panicked when he remained silent. *Kuro? What's wrong?*

He didn't budge, and he didn't respond. Mei glanced at Daisuke, his head tilted in what seemed like concern.

Kuro, please.

We shouldn't fly today. You're still injured.

Mei calmed her nerves, and relief flowed through her at his response. *I understand your feelings. My falling had nothing to do with you. I need to fly today, and I promise, after we return, I will take it easy and eat so much.*

The long pause made Mei fidget, but he finally said, *You promise?*

Yes, I promise.

It wasn't my fault that you fell?

Her heart ached at the uncertainty coming from her dragon. *It wasn't. The harness wasn't good, but I checked this one over and over, and I'll be safe.*

After another long pause, Mei felt Kuro's muscles bunching as he got ready to launch into the air. Today, a slight breeze flickered across the snow. Then the snow danced in flurries as Kuro beat his wings, gaining momentum. They were in the air once more, and Mei's stomach dropped at the lift.

Today, her hair remained secure under her leather and fur-lined cap, and she clutched the front of the harness with her gloved hands. The view lessened her nerves as she cautiously looked around. She forced her legs to relax against the harness. She had to trust she had inspected it thoroughly.

The sun was high above them and moving to their right. Mei took out the wooden tablet with the landmarks to the mining city. She found the mountain formation and directed Kuro in that direction. Tucking the tablet back into her riding jacket, she took more breaths to calm herself. Up here with Kuro, she was free. Nothing would happen today, and her harness was fine. She attempted to close off any stray thoughts of doubt so Kuro wouldn't hear them.

The beauty of riding with Kuro crept into her body. She belonged in the sky, just her and him flying together. There were no daim, feu, or eta up here, just human and dragon.

As she sat tall, her wounds twinged, and the ache in her shoulder became more pronounced as they flew. After an hour, the walls of the mining village came into view. Washi was right. The stone walls stood taller and thicker than the city's walls. Thanks to the dendragons, the walls were slick and likely hard to scale.

The watchman on the wall waved to them as they flew overhead, and they circled once, waiting for people to clear out of the yard. Then Kuro leaned back, spreading his wings to slow their descent. The landing jarred her wounds, but it was as smooth as Kuro could make it in the tight stone courtyard.

Mei deftly unhooked herself from the harness. She and Daisuke met in the middle and bowed to the man who approached them. He wore a dark gray yukata lined with fur. The colder weather in the mountains required it. His sleek burnt-orange dendragon perched on his shoulder, a lovely splash of color in the gray setting.

"Shodragon riders, you are welcome here." He bowed to them.

"Arigato. We have the supplies," Mei responded. She was surprised that Daisuke let her talk. He stood silently to her right and slightly behind her, showing her authority. Even though his posture was correct, she didn't enjoy having Daisuke at her back.

The man nodded and directed the others to unload the dragons. "We were told to be mindful of the weight since your dragons are still growing."

"We appreciate it. Is there a place for them to drink and eat before we leave?"

He waved another group of people forward. They carried two troughs with long poles attached and placed them before the dragons. They had piles of meat in them, and the dragons crunched happily on the bones while the men unloaded their burdens.

They directed Daisuke and Mei toward a smaller room in the guard tower, where they signed off on the trade and were provided a hot meal. The thick soup contained root vegetables that Mei had never seen before. A strong garlic smell came from the food, and she had no problem gulping it down with the side of rice. The crisp water tasted metallic but was still refreshing.

Daisuke ate silently across from Mei. He held his utensils with delicate precision. Some of the food remained unfinished. Glancing at Mei's empty bowl, he held out his, and she shook her head. She didn't want his scraps. Part of her wished she could take it to her father. The idea of landing to see him before they went home played in her thoughts. However, it went against the rules to go without a sensei's permission, and her father wouldn't be happy to see her if she risked it again. Maybe Washi-sensei would let her visit him. He seemed to be the kindest, and over these last months of training, they had built up a mentor-student relationship.

"You seem lost in thought."

Mei glanced at Daisuke as he pushed away his dishes. "I guess."

He sighed. "You don't have to keep shutting me out. We're partners."

She bit the inside of her cheeks, letting the soft pain calm her anger. "If you want to have a relationship so much, then eat a bunch of flowers."

Daisuke raised his long eyebrow. "I see." He gave her a low bow.

What did he want from her? "You may be my partner, but I will not trust you. But you can trust me."

"Is that how you want it to be?"

Mei stood and took her bowl to the counter. He had a lot of nerve to assume he could be forgiven easily. *He really has the gall to act like I put the separation between us?* "It's just how it is for an eta." Wrapped up in her jacket, she went to stand by Kuro as they finished loading the metals. Her gloved hands went over the harness again as she waited. A crunch in the gravel behind her told her Daisuke was coming behind her. She tilted her body to keep him in her line of sight.

"Your harness okay?"

She nodded.

"Do you want me to double-check it too?"

"No." She couldn't be bought with fake concern.

She heard him walk back to his dragon. Only a few seconds ago, she had told him she didn't trust him. After her fall yesterday, there was no way she would let him near her harness. If he needed to know anything about the eta, it was that they knew how to survive.

The loading done, Mei and Daisuke bowed to the man and mounted their dragons. Mei tried not to flinch as she used her left arm to pull herself up. The steady ache was only getting worse as the day went on. She might have to beg Emiri to put something on her wounds again, even if it meant getting a lecture at the same time. Strapping in her legs, she waited for Daisuke, and he signaled that he was ready.

They took off, and Kuro strained to get over the wall before he could free-fall from the top to get his balance. Mei shouted as her stomach surged and laughed at the thrill. Falling *with* Kuro differed from falling *off* Kuro. The sun now on their left, they headed toward the fortress.

Mei's body felt flushed, even in the cold, and when they got back, sleep wouldn't be far away. Time passed peacefully up in the air, so when a flash of red dove in Mei's view, she gripped the harness as Kuro balked.

Daisuke went to her side, pointed to his eye, then put two fingers down. He'd seen a human? Mei's face burned.

She hadn't even been surveying the area like she was supposed to.

Daisuke ran his hand down his left forearm. *Land?*

If there was a human out here and they weren't in a caravan, they might be in danger. Washi even told them to keep an eye out and she'd let herself get distracted. Many people had gone missing. She raised her right arm and bent it at the elbow. *Yes.*

Kuro, let him take the lead.

Kuro pulled back, letting the red dragon make a slow descent down the side of the mountain. Mei couldn't see the fortress, but the part of the city with the eta was close.

The trees were thick, and it took a bit of searching to find a suitable clearing to land in. There were no roads close by, and under the trees, the day seemed darker. Mei grabbed her bow as she dismounted and strapped the pouch for Kuro's fire across her chest. His fire in the trees wouldn't be the best idea, but if it came to it, Mei would risk it.

"You saw a human?" She studied Daisuke's face, looking for a lie. It was her own fault she'd been daydreaming instead of looking. Now she put herself in a dangerous situation trying to read him.

"Yes. Someone dragged them into the cave up ahead."

Mei's eyes widened. "Someone?"

"Or something. It was hard to see through the trees." Daisuke pulled down his bow. "Our dragons will fit in the cave, so it may be best for them to come in too. Unless you don't think we should save the person?"

They were most likely an eta, and if they found what or who had been taking people, they could put an end to it. Everyone kept talking about the missing eta, but no one had done anything to stop it. Or he could be lying, but Mei believed she and Kuro could take him and his dragon if needed.

"Let's go. If there are too many, we can inform the Sho." *Be on guard.*

I will.

Daisuke nodded, and they headed through the trees. Mei grasped her bow tightly, and she wasn't sure how far she could draw it with her injured shoulder. Her right arm was fine; it was just a matter of managing the pain. The cave entrance appeared before them, and Mei didn't like the look of the loose rock around the opening.

"Wait here." Daisuke stalked through the edge of the trees and approached the side of the cave. He crouched by the entrance and waited. Getting down on the ground, he crawled closer to the opening, and then he came back slowly. "I don't see anyone inside. We may have to go in farther."

Mei nodded. She stepped out of the trees and approached the cave entrance. Kuro followed behind her, scraping against the rocky ground. Sticking her head in the cave, she couldn't hear anything, but the sharp smell of waste burned her eyes. Something was here. She shifted her bow and drew two arrows. "Best to use the green fire. Agreed?"

They gave their dragons a bit of the hostas plant. The green fire would singe whatever it was and wouldn't be too harmful if it rebounded in the cave. She could feel the burning fire inside her. They pulled out torches from their packs, and the dragons let out a spark to light them. Mei and Kuro were ahead of Daisuke and his dragon. She didn't like him at her back but she was appointed as lead. The dragons' claws scraped in the stone cave. She worried that whatever was in here would hear them coming and either hide or jump out and attack them.

The cave split into two paths. Mei paused, and Daisuke came up behind her. "We should split up and scout each tunnel."

"It isn't wise to split up in here."

"Just scouting. Are you afraid?"

Mei clenched her jaw. He'd shown she was in charge all day, but alone in the cave, he wouldn't listen to her. "It's too risky."

"Just for a few feet, then we come back. It won't take long."

"Fine." She didn't want to argue with him in the cave. Mei went left, and he went right. The sound of dragon claws slowly faded the farther she went inside. "I shouldn't have gone in in the first place," Mei muttered to herself. She held up the torch, and it flickered against the wall. The walls narrowed, making it harder for Kuro to pass through. Feeling like she was getting buried alive, Mei struggled to breathe. She didn't have to listen to Daisuke; the Sho had put her in charge.

"We should head back and wait for Daisuke." The last thing they needed was for Kuro to get stuck in a cave. Slowly backing out, Mei kept glancing around and behind them. The feeling of being watched made Mei's skin itch.

They made it back to the fork, and Mei tapped her foot while waiting. She couldn't leave the baka in here, but she didn't want to go down another dark tunnel.

A large crack sounded from the main entrance, and dust flew in the air as she and Kuro ran toward the noise. The rumbling stopped, but in the flickering light, the entrance was completely blocked off.

Mei choked on the dust and put her face in her forearm. They backed away from the entrance.

"Mei?"

She heard a faint shout coming from behind the rock wall.

"Are you outside?" she yelled.

"Yes."

What was he doing out there? Her heart sank. He'd gone outside instead of waiting for her. Had he trapped her inside?

"Mei?" His voice got fainter. "I will get help!"

She slid down the side of the wall. Somehow, she didn't believe him. He'd meant for her to get trapped in here. "Okay." *I was a fool.*

"Don't worry..." She couldn't hear the rest, but Mei knew she would have to find a way out herself.

Kuro, are you okay?

It is hard to breathe, but I'm fine. Should I dig?

Mei examined the fallen rock with her flickering torch. If she could still hear Daisuke, then the rocky barrier must not be that thick. *Maybe. I'm worried our digging will cause more rocks to fall. There is still air coming through, so we may have to find another way out.*

"Let's take the rocks from the top."

Mei scrambled to the top of the entrance, while Kuro stood on his hind legs. She slowly picked her way through the rocks, and after a while, the pain in her side forced her to take a break.

Kuro saw she had stopped. *Are you hurt?*

"Sore."

Kuro leaned down and put his head next to her leg. *Rest. I'll finish.*

She stroked the side of his head, and his eyes closed. "I'm sorry. We shouldn't have come in here."

If we can help people, we help. That is who we are.

Mei closed her eyes. "Yes."

Before Kuro started digging again, Mei's head jerked toward a sound at the back of the cave. It was so faint that she almost thought she'd made it up.

Wait, Kuro.

He cocked his head, and Mei could tell he heard something too.

It sounded far off, but there was a slow, steady clacking against the stone floor, almost like raindrops falling on the stone. The sound rose, and the steady clicking and clacking got louder and louder. The sound rushed toward her and Kuro.

Mei's throat tightened, and she stood and drew her bow. "Kuro, get ready."

SIXTEEN

Chin's back burned as he swept the stone hallway with the straw broom. His mother used to only whip him every so often, but it had become a nightly ritual as the next selection got closer. In the past, he'd survived, but now, without his brother, the wounds never healed.

He shifted his shoulders back for some relief. He'd chosen not to go to class today, and apparently, the Sho wanted to talk to him whenever he returned. He was gone more often than he was here, and in the last months, nothing had been mentioned of the accusation of Chin hurting Mei's dragon. The priests had informed his mother about the incident. From what Chin could tell, he wouldn't take the blame, but it was yet another shame added to the list.

The first recruit ran down to get their harnesses, and Chin walked farther away from Mei's den and slowly dragged the broom across the floor. The throbbing in his back matched the strokes of his sweeping as he continued his chore.

Maybe if I find a dark corner, I can just sleep here and not go home. It would give his back a break. The spring selection grew near, and thoughts of the clear blue sky kept him going.

His pensive mood came to a halt when people gathered outside of Mei's den, causing a commotion.

"What's going on this time?" he muttered. Apparently, she couldn't avoid catastrophe for long. A group of men with homdragons went in and out of her den.

"She's patched up enough," the healer called out to the priest on his way to the lift. "Don't bother us about her again."

Chin clenched his jaw at the healer's tone and approached the priest. "What happened?"

"Fell off the dragon and another dragon caught her. Gashed up pretty bad, it seems."

"Should I go..."

The priest raised his eyebrow. "Best stay away from that den until the Sho clears you from the incident."

Chin nodded and casually ambled over to sweep next to Mei's den. As the afternoon wore on, he ran out of excuses to walk by the den. The sun set, and the priest said nothing as Chin sat next to the entrance.

He peered inside. The black dragon towered over Mei's slight frame. Every time Chin peeked in, the dragon would catch his eye and stare him down until he glanced away.

In the middle of the night, Chin woke from his doze and heard moaning coming from inside. The dragon paced around her, and Chin stepped inside. The dragon's wide eyes surprised him, but he made no move to stop Chin's approach. Mei lay on the ground, flush with fever.

Chin put the back of his hand on her head, and as he took it away, Mei grabbed his hand. He tried to remove her grip gently, but she held fast.

"She needs a healer." Chin made eye contact with the dragon. Just how much did he understand? "I will go get Emiri." He pried her hand from his and ran to the lift to find a healer who would actually help.

As he ran down the hall where the healers slept, someone pointed him to Emiri's room. He knocked on the door and heard a slow shuffling. The door opened, and a round face poked out. Emiri's hair stuck up from her loose braids, and her homdragon padded around her feet.

"Mei's hurt, and she needs a healer."

The sleep cleared from Emiri's eyes, and she grabbed her bag of plants and herbs. "How bad?"

"I'm not sure. There were healers with her today, and they said she would be fine."

Emiri's eyes narrowed. "I need to get more supplies." She wrapped a thick plain kimono around herself, and Chin followed her down to the main floor. An older woman dozed behind a short counter.

Emiri smacked her hands down on the wooden surface, and the woman jumped. "I am out of viola, and I need to restock."

The woman frowned and stood, taking her time to stretch. "I was told not to give you any more, and you know it."

"Why?"

The woman's lips tightened. "We have this conversation every time. You used too much, and you know it's scarce.

What do you need it for? I've heard of no new injuries of any severity."

"Mei, she's injured!"

"Mei?"

Emiri bit her lip, and she tensed. "The eta girl, her name is Mei." Each word left Emiri's mouth like chips of ice.

"Oh, the eta. She was treated."

"Not well enough."

The woman raised her eyebrow. "According to whom?"

"She's hot and her wounds are still open," Chin said.

The woman smirked. "So the dragonless boy knows all about healing."

As a daim, Chin had never felt the rejection of someone outside his house. Low bows had followed him on the streets before his rejection, and this woman's gaze now caused him to shrink away.

Emiri leaned in and met the woman's eyes. "She needs healing. She's a shodragon rider."

"No more until they give me the all-clear. Waste your other supplies."

Emiri clenched her fists, and he thought she might punch the woman in her face. He also felt the urge to smack the woman's smirk off.

"Let's go." Emiri stalked out of the room, and Chin followed close behind.

In Mei's den, Emiri got to work.

"Get these clothes off her." Chin froze. Emiri glanced up at him. "Blood is crusting through her clothes, and they need to be removed. You're the only one here, and I need help."

Chin nodded, took a knife from Emiri, and began cutting off Mei's clothes as Emiri fed her homdragon. After he was finished, Mei seemed so small. Three large gashes bled from her midsection, and a large one ran down her thigh. Emiri handed him a wooden bowl.

"Is there any clean water?"

Chin fetched water from the underground river and placed it next to Emiri.

She took a cloth and handed it to Chin. "Help me clean the wounds. I doubt they even did that much." Her eyes were flinty as she took another cloth and wiped away the blood and dirt.

"Did they really not heal her?"

Emiri focused on her job, and her words were clipped as she said, "They didn't."

After they cleaned the wounds, the homdragon spit a blue paste onto the clean bandages. Chin helped Emiri wrap them around Mei. He could see every rib.

"Is she not eating?" he asked.

"Not enough."

Emiri went to Mei's belongings and found a sleeping robe, and Chin helped dress her. They sat down, and Emiri leaned against the wall while Chin remained sitting straight. Mei's dragon, after a nod from Emiri, wrapped himself around her body and huffed.

"Will she be okay?" Chin asked.

"It will heal slower, but yes, she should be fine. Knowing her, she'll go out training tomorrow."

Mei's hand stretched out, and Chin felt himself reaching toward it, but he stopped himself and stood. "Thank you. I better go." He went to the entrance.

"I'll let her know you were here."

Chin paused, his back to them. "Don't." He left the den. He didn't want to go home, and the priest let him rest in the back. Chin couldn't sleep, and the image of Mei's hand kept fluttering across his closed eyelids. When the priest came to get him, he was already up and putting on his uniform.

Going by Mei's den, he glanced in. She slept with Emiri by her side. Chin went up the lift to go to class. He tried to focus as the sensei spoke, but his mind had a mission of its own. Leaving to go back to work was a relief, and he focused on cleaning out some of the older shodragons' dens for the rest of the afternoon.

When he returned to the novice level, it was already late, and he needed to go home tonight. The last thing he wanted was for Mother to come and get him. He shuddered at the thought.

He rode the lift up, and as he walked toward the rickshaw, a red dragon landed in the courtyard. Guards ran toward the tower and the dragon. Daisuke dismounted, and a rush of people surrounded him.

Brow furrowed, Chin went toward the commotion. Other sensei ran toward Daisuke.

Washi spoke first. "Daisuke, where's your partner?"

Daisuke's eyes widened, his face full of fake fear. "She ran off! I chased after her, but her dragon is just too fast. I don't know where she went, but it was toward the west."

The sensei exchanged looks and burst into action. They were going after Mei. As everyone ran around asking questions about Mei's location, Chin focused on Daisuke's face. He thought he saw a slight grin.

"I need to go feed my dragon. Is that permissible?" Daisuke asked.

"Yes, yes, go. We will head after the dragon."

Rickshaw forgotten, Chin watched Daisuke mount his dragon, and Chin went back down to the dragon dens. He waited close to the food supply, and when Daisuke strode past, Chin yanked him into an empty den and blocked the entrance.

Daisuke molded into a fighting stance, but when he recognized Chin, he dropped his arms to his sides. "What do you want?" His fine brows arched.

"I want to know what really happened to Mei."

"She ran off."

Chin's lips thinned. "So I heard. I find that hard to believe."

"Oh?" Daisuke smiled. He leaned casually against the stone wall. The torchlight flickered against his angular face. "It's just an eta."

"Where is she?"

"She probably missed her hovel and went back."

Chin stepped forward. "Where is she?"

"Are you, the shame of a daim household, going to fight me?"

"Where is she, Daisuke?"

Daisuke darted away from the wall and tried to shove past, but Chin blocked his way, his eyes even with his. "It's probably dead by now, so you can go find another eta trash to mess around with, Chin-*san*."

Chin clenched his fist and swung at Daisuke's jaw. In one fluid movement, Daisuke leaned back, and his knuckles only grazed him. Daisuke retaliated by jabbing Chin in the stomach. Chin bent to avoid most of the blow, but he still let out a gasp of air.

Chin kicked out his foot, trying to trip Daisuke, but he danced away from him. Daisuke dashed forward and tried to kick Chin in the side. Chin turned away and grabbed at Daisuke's foot, but only found air. In his rush to catch his foot, he'd missed the fist coming at him from behind, and Daisuke landed a blow to Chin's back.

His back wounds broke open, and he fell to the floor from the shock.

Daisuke chuckled. "Failure at this too?"

Chin stayed down because someone like Daisuke always wanted to get in one more kick. Slow footsteps approached, and he didn't move, waiting for the right time.

"Vermin like you don't belong here, and if I had your shame, I'd have killed myself long ago."

Chin waited, and then he heard the scrape of Daisuke lifting his leg. In one movement, he turned and grabbed Daisuke's foot before it connected. Chin yanked on the limb, and Daisuke fell with a thud. He quickly pinned Daisuke down and pressed his forearm against his neck. Daisuke gasped for air, and Chin glared down at him.

"I wonder how long it takes for someone to suffocate." Daisuke's eyes widened, and Chin increased the pressure as he struggled under him.

Chin put his face close to Daisuke's and whispered in his ear, "Where is Mei?" He leaned up, watching Daisuke struggle to talk. "You want to tell me now? Or should I just rid the world of a scab like you? You seem very concerned about vermin, so I might want to help you out."

Daisuke struggled, but Chin held him tight. When he was close to passing out, Chin lifted some of the pressure.

Daisuke inhaled. "I know. I know where she is!"

"She's alive?"

"I-I don't know. Maybe."

Chin clenched his jaw. "Where?"

"From the tunnels inside the fortress, you can get there. She is caved in."

"Did you set this up?"

When Daisuke didn't answer, Chin put more pressure on his neck, making him gasp. "Yes. I know the location, and I can give you a map."

"A map?" Chin replied dryly. "So I can disappear too?"

"I never went there..."

Chin let out a breath. "How did you know about the tunnels?"

"One of the older healers told me about it," he whispered, his voice small. "The servants found it easily from her instructions."

"An old healer?" Chin leaned to cut off his air again. He felt him swallow, then let up so he could talk.

"She gave it to me in case I got trapped too."

"Who?"

Daisuke turned his head away, and Chin didn't want to waste any more time. Someone wanted Mei gone and had used Daisuke as bait. Chin didn't trust that Daisuke would lead him to the correct location, but he didn't want Daisuke at his back the entire way there. "How far?"

"In my sleeve."

Chin carefully shifted to grab a book out of Daisuke's sleeve. "I'm going to tie you up and leave you in a dark corner. If I don't return, no one will find you."

Anger shot from Daisuke's eyes, but he remained silent. Chin took his time gagging and tying him up with strips torn from Daisuke's clothes. Chin hoisted him like a sack of potatoes and darted through the halls, avoiding people. Once he'd dumped Daisuke, he went to grab a bag and stuffed it with supplies and a short weapon. He stole them all from the armory while the priests were occupied elsewhere.

Now that he was armed, he placed the bag on his back. His constantly burning wounds reminded him yet again that he wouldn't be going home. No one else would help Mei. He glanced at the map, and it looked like he would have to follow the instructions backward. The exit was past the lower levels of the caves. Grabbing a torch and the map with the instructions, he headed into the dark and abandoned emptiness of the fortress.

SEVENTEEN

In the flickering torchlight, Mei focused on the narrow entrance to the right. The light clicking sound and her own breathing became her center as she drew her bow. Monstrous shadows slunk across the rocky walls, and in the shadowy lighting, a single black leg arched out of the right tunnel. Then another leg and another. Mei took a deep breath, and with trembling hands, she took aim. Kuro arched his neck.

"Let me shoot first. There may be more." They would need his fire against multiple foes. The jorogumo always lived in packs. Following the black legs, the elongated torso of a woman stretched out from the bulbous spider bottom. Her black eyes reflected in the light, making them greenish. Her mouth gaped open, showing obsidian pincers moving in slow revolutions. The body seemed shiny and more armored than the top. Mei aimed for the dilating mouth, and her side burned with the effort of keeping the string taut. With a slow exhale, Mei let the arrow loose. The jorogumo bolted toward her and Kuro with a screech. The arrow whisked past her face and barely grazed the side, leaving a dark ichor on the jorogumo's cheek. Before Mei could draw another arrow, Kuro released bright green fire. The flames caught the jorogumo in the torso, and it let out another screech but fell over, its legs flailing in the air. The acrid smell of its burning body made Mei's eyes water, and she nocked another arrow. This time, her aim was true, and she shot the creature through its eye. The crackling of the burning body echoed in the space, and Mei ran to grab her two arrows.

The arrow was lodged in the head, and Mei grimaced as she put her foot on the body to yank it out.

Only one? Kuro asked.

"I doubt it." Mei stiffened. Kuro's fire had proved effective, but they only had a tiny amount of hostas plant. He'd fired without her, and she found it hard to aim the fire and shoot. In this space, it was okay, but she would need to help direct the fire. The other arrow lay broken on the ground, leaving her with nine arrows. She tucked the arrowhead into her obi. Mei avoided looking at the burning body on her way back to Kuro. The smoke made it harder to breathe, but the light helped her see.

"Do we keep digging?"

We could try going into the cave to find a way out.

Mei shivered as she glanced into the dark tunnels. The jorogumo had come out of the right side, and earlier, they'd gone down the left tunnel. The left tunnel had gotten too tight for Kuro, so they would have to go down the path the creature had come from. The narrow path would be easier to fight in, but she had only nine arrows. Her hands trembled as she realized she was facing every child's nightmare. The green fire slowly ate away at the body, and with shaking hands, Mei tore off a bit of her uniform to tie around her nose and mouth.

"Does the smoke bother you?" she asked, her voice muffled under the cloth.

No. There is fresh air coming from somewhere. We need to leave here.

I know. Mei sighed. Kuro would follow whatever she suggested. During the fight, more rocks had fallen in the entrance, and she didn't know if they could dig a hole big enough to get out in time.

"Let's go down the tunnel. Can your nose follow the fresh air?"

It's hard to find, but I believe so. Also, I can find raw meat too.

Mei let out a shaky laugh. *I don't think there's any raw meat.*

There is.

Mei's breath froze. *Maybe we should avoid that smell, then. It-it may be human.*

Could be.

Mei gripped her bow and grabbed the torch from where she wedged it in the rocks. They left behind the still burning body of the jorogumo and headed into the black. Kuro trailed behind her. She would have to drop the torch if another one attacked so she could shoot. "Do you need to eat another plant?" The burning felt small inside her, and she didn't know how much flame he had left.

Not yet.

Mei nodded, and they kept going into the dark. The air smelled stale to her, but she trusted that Kuro's nose was better than hers. Once in a while, she would pause in the black, and Kuro would gently press his nose against her shoulder, comforting her. With every breath, her side ached sharply, and she could feel her skin breaking open with each step. Blood had soaked through her uniform.

Mei?

"Yes?" she gasped with effort.

Should you get on my back?

She shook her head slightly, blurring her gaze. "I need to be ready."

Kuro remained silent, and the dark tunnels stretched on. The one they'd killed must have been a scout. She didn't know how smart the jorogumo were. From her classes, she'd learned they could fully transform into a human, but the thing they'd killed had seemed more like an animal.

The tunnel slanted downward as they walked, and the air chilled. Mei wasn't sure if she shivered from the cold or from the shock of having fought her first monster. The torch turned into a slight flicker, and they only had one more in Kuro's pack. Up ahead, there was a large space, and five tunnels branched out from the main entrance.

Kuro paused in the dark, and Mei let him smell each entrance. He came back to Mei.

"Well?" Mei crouched to rest.

They all smell like those things. One smells slightly of dragons, and one of them smells of fresh air.

"Dragons?"

Yes.

Do you think one might lead to the fortress? When they'd landed, they'd been close to the city. *The missing people are probably here.*

It could be.

"Should we go down the path that smells like dragons or air?" The thought of these creatures having a path to the fortress sent chills down her spine. How did the wingleaders or priests not know this? No one went into the depth of the mountain. There could be anything down there. It seemed stupid that the shodragon riders would leave themselves so vulnerable.

The air could be from a crack in the ceiling or wall. There's no promise that it is a way out.

You're right. Let's go toward the dragons.

Mei reached into the pack on Kuro's back and lit the last torch.

Kuro? I'm sorry I followed Daisuke.

You already said this.

Mei didn't think they would make it out alive. Her heart ached at the thought of never seeing her father again and that Kuro would be trapped down in the dark, dying with her. She didn't know how to lead. She even knew Daisuke acted differently in front of the sensei, but when he challenged her she backed down like an eta in the market. She should have told him they would report back. If the Sho believed her to be a leader, then she needed to lead.

"Kuro?" Her voice was soft in the darkness as they headed toward the fourth entrance.

Yes?

"Thank you for choosing me."

A nudge brushed against the back of her head. *Don't speak like this is goodbye. There is still more food to be eaten.*

Mei smiled. "Is that all you think of?"

Yes. And you.

Her heart warmed, but her fear also grew at the thought of losing him. If he had chosen someone more capable, then... Taking a deep breath, she shook away the thoughts, and they headed farther into the dark. The entrance was wider, which both relieved Mei and scared her about its defensibility. Her ears pricked at any sound that differed from the scrape of Kuro's claws or her soft footfalls. No clicking sounded in the silence. Her whole side was damp, and it took more effort to keep the dizziness at bay.

She paused to tighten her obi, hoping that would slow the flow of blood. Her wound openings kept getting wider, and she didn't want to leave Kuro alone.

Wait.

Mei glanced up at Kuro, his silver eyes gleaming in the dark. *What?*

I smell them. A lot of them.

Her throat tightened. How far?

Before Kuro could answer, a clacking sound came from the tunnel. Her heart thudded against her chest. Bending down, she leaned the torch against the wall and prepared two arrows. *It's better if we hit them with fire first.*

Yes.

Kuro's neck stretched past Mei, and his eyes focused as the clacking increased. The clacking became a tidal wave of hail against the rock. She tried to focus on connecting with his mind so she could aim the fire. Her stomach clenched, and she drew back her first arrow, holding the other in her spare fingers. Missing wasn't an option.

The clacking grew, and Mei could hear it all around her. *Kuro?*

They are coming. Get on my back, Mei.

Ignoring the pain, she grabbed the torch and flung herself up onto Kuro's back as he charged forward. The jorogumo came into view, and as Kuro let loose a blaze of bright green fire, he dodged forward, running through the flaming bodies. Mei focused the fire on as many heads as she could see. The surviving jorogumo clawed at his body.

Mei felt him flinch as they struck him, but he kept running past the first wave.

More.

Mei plunged her hand into the bag, and as Kuro ran, he craned his neck back and snatched the plant out of her hands. The fire burned inside her, and with effort, she clenched her legs against his side, drew her bow, and leaned around his neck. Another burst of flame, which she directed to the left. Mei steadied her hand and shot the remaining jorogumo on the right before it could claw at Kuro as he ran. The clacking behind them grew louder.

No more ahead. But they will catch up to me.

We have to stop and fight.

Kuro ran until the cave narrowed, and Mei jumped off his back, her focus on the fight. Her wounds no longer hurt as the thought of battle flared through her mind.

With their backs against the wall, Mei and Kuro fought the nightmarish creatures. Kuro's flames lit up the cave, and Mei could see the carapaces. The creatures screamed, showing their pointed teeth, and their glowing greenish eyes became Mei's targets. She found it harder to branch off the fire and could only do direct hits before aiming at the glowing eyes with her arrows. That the tunnel was so narrow had saved them so far.

Mei had five arrows left, and only a few plants remained of Kuro's dwindling supply.

Mei, you should run.

In the midst of battle, the lone thought cracked through Mei's resolve. Kuro leaned around, grabbing the last of his plants all at once.

I can hold them off while you run.

No.

Mei, you can save yourself.

No. She drew her arrow but missed the charging jorogumo. It ran at Kuro, and Mei jumped forward. The claws slashed at Mei, striking her in the shoulder. Ignoring the pain, she tackled the large body and flung it to the side.

Frantically feeling for the broken arrow in her obi, she clasped it and tried to stab the creature. More of the creature came between her and Kuro, and he loosed his fire, trying to get to her. He lashed out with his claws as they surrounded him.

The smoke from the burning jorogumo thickened in the air. The creature knocked the arrow out of her hand, and raising one of its sharp legs, it dove toward Mei. She rolled, but the other legs blocked her under it.

The leg gashed into her arm, and she screamed. Then before it could hit again, a bright sliver of light flew out of the dark and blocked the leg. Then it swung under, gutting the jorogumo.

A hand reached for her, and Mei stared blankly at it.

"Come on!" The voice shocked her into grabbing the hand, and he hoisted her up.

Chin's face loomed out of the dark, and they dashed toward Kuro. He slashed his sword, knocking the last jorogumo out of the way.

The smell of the burning bodies filled the cave, and in the eerie silence, Mei stared at Chin like he was a spirit come to haunt her.

"How? How?"

"I got the information out of Daisuke. He said you'd run off, but I didn't believe him."

Chin pulled bandages out of his pack and quickly

wrapped up Mei's arm. "We need to get moving. There are probably more."

Mei nodded, and she and Kuro followed Chin. He ran at a fast clip. Mei's vision blurred, and she collapsed to her knees.

"Mei?" Chin looked up at Kuro. "Can you carry her? I should leave my arms free."

Kuro leaned down, and Chin helped her onto his back. She wrapped her arms around Kuro's neck as he ran after Chin. After a while, Chin paused at a fork in the path and took out a book.

"What's wrong?"

"I dropped it in the fight, and the map got smudged."

"Map?"

"Apparently, Daisuke got it from someone to help him out of the caves, but I didn't know there were jorogumo. Your group was the first I saw."

"Kuro, which path is better?"

They both smell like dragons and creatures, he responded.

Mei glanced at Chin, "He said they both smell the same."

Chin swore under his breath. "I'm sorry I can't remember."

"Pick one and we'll follow." Mei's head felt light, and she couldn't think. Somehow having Chin here reassured her.

Chin chose the path on the left, and they followed him through the darkness. He held up his torch as they jogged. They kept up a fast pace, and Kuro's gate seemed off.

Are you hurt?

Only a little. Rest.

Mei frowned, and her hold tightened around Kuro's neck. Then they all came to a halt. Chin flung himself against the wall and stopped moving.

"What—"

He put his finger to his lips, silencing Mei. Her eyes focused ahead, and below them, long strands of sticky web covered everything. Hundreds of jorogumo crept through the webs in the wide pit. Above them, the webs stretched on, but Mei couldn't see the end. Chin snuffed out the light, and they fell into sudden darkness, but not before hundreds of eyes gleamed in their direction from the pit below.

In the dark, the clacking of the legs grew louder and louder.

Tell the boy to get on my back.

Without hesitation, Mei yelled at Chin, "Jump on." She gripped Chin's fumbling hands and pulled him up.

His embrace around her waist made her want to scream, but as the clacking sound grew louder, Kuro vaulted into the air. The sticky webs clung to Mei's face. He struggled to fly in the enormous pit and tumbled onto a ledge.

Kuro let out a flame, and the fire burned through the web. The cavern lit up, and the jorogumo approached them from the webs. Kuro's wings were covered in sticky strands. Chin jumped off Kuro's back and lit his torch from the remaining flames. Then he took his sword and cut through the web, trying to free Kuro's wings.

Mei slid off the dragon's back and pulled at the thick web with her hands. They had barely freed Kuro when the first jorogumo arrived, slashing at Chin.

Fresh air ahead!

Kuro's voice broke through the battle.

"Chin!" He glanced at Mei. "Fresh air ahead!"

He gave her a slight nod as he dodged a slash from a creature. Kuro took the lead while Chin and Mei brought up the rear.

Mei forced her feet to move, and up ahead, sunlight came from the ceiling of the cave. The opening was wide enough to get through. She pushed herself forward. The clacking grew louder behind them, the sound of their gasping drowned out by the approaching wave.

When they reached the hole in the ceiling, Kuro arched up, carefully grabbed her and Chin in his claws, and pushed them up. Scrambling against the crumbling dirt, they cleared the opening. Mei turned toward the entrance just as a flood of webs encased Kuro. A jorogumo vaulted onto his back and bit into his neck. Kuro roared in pain, and with a heave, he knocked the creature off.

"No!" Mei screamed and tried to jump down after Kuro.

Arms wrapped around her as she struggled. "Mei, we can't fight them all."

Kuro's soft voice came into her thoughts. *Run, Mei.*

She froze, and Chin loosened his hold. Her dark eyes flashed. "Never tell me to leave you again." She broke out of Chin's grasp and jumped back into the dark, landing on top of Kuro's back. Taking an arrow, she jammed it into the nearest creature. "Fight, you damn dragon! Or we'll die here!"

With a roar, Kuro strained against the webs coating him. Mei jumped down, grabbed the flickering torch, and ran it against the webs. Kuro broke through, flinging back and smashing the jorogumo against the wall. They scraped at his back, and he roared in pain. With his wings almost free of the webs, he clawed up the side of the cavern. Mei clung to his tail, waving the torch at the jorogumo like a madwoman.

Half of Kuro's body broke through the surface, and more webs shot out, clinging to Mei. They pulled at her, while Kuro pulled her in the opposite direction.

He flopped over the edge, and Chin ran around, cutting at the webs and trying to knock down the jorogumo.

"Can you fly?"

Yes.

She crawled up Kuro's back, and Chin followed behind. Kuro staggered as he pushed off his back legs, but he made it off the ground as more webs shot toward him. Chin cut them away the best he could, but Kuro veered to the side, and Mei slid off his neck. As she fell, a hand clutched her wrist. Her shoulder screamed with pain as Chin held on.

They cleared the trees, and in the distance waited the edge of the city. Kuro's wing strokes trembled in the air. The large wounds in his black scales were visible in the twilight.

We are almost there. Keep going. We are almost there. Mei chanted in her mind to Kuro as he fought to keep flying. Chin's hand slid down her forearm, and he pulled her back onto Kuro. She lay over his neck like a sack of laundry, too tired to right herself.

The minutes felt like hours, but they eventually landed in the courtyard. Kuro collapsed onto his side in the snow, and Mei and Chin slid off his back. In moments, healers surrounded them and were patching up Kuro.

A large dark blue dragon bloomed into view as Emiri rushed over to bandage her wounds.

Washi stood over her, his eyes solemn. "You're to come with me." Tomo and Sora stood next to him. They almost looked gleeful, which worried Mei more.

"Okay," Mei replied as she remained on the snowy ground.

She heard Emiri's angry voice in the fog of her mind. "She can't go anywhere right now! Can't you see she's barely alive?"

"Emperor's orders," Tomo snapped.

"I'm sorry, Mei. Can you make it?" Washi asked.

Sora sniffed. "It's fine. She can handle a bit of pain."

"I can go," Mei answered before Washi could respond.

She didn't want to cause trouble for Washi and she could tell he was unsure about taking her. He was an equal to the other sensei in rank.

Emiri sucked in her cheeks, and she helped Mei to her feet and handed her over to Washi-sensei. His brow furrowed. "I can tell the Emperor to wait. You're too injured."

"The Emperor shouldn't be kept, Washi. If you care about what happens to the eta you know it will only be worse if you wait." Sora brushed snow from her purple kimono like that was the thing that mattered now.

Mei reached for Kuro, and Tomo shoved her. "He will be fine. They are using viola."

She recognized the purple flowers they'd fed the homdragons. Her eyes overflowed with tears at the sight of Kuro's wounds bleeding onto the snow.

"He isn't moving," she cried and tried to head toward him, but Tomo cut her off.

"We have to go now. I'm sorry. The healers will fix him." Washi bent to her ear so the others couldn't hear him. "I hate to say it, but Sora-sensei is correct. It's better to not keep the Emperor waiting." Washi carefully hoisted her up onto his dragon, and they flew to the top of the fortress. Mei's eyes never left the black figure in the courtyard. Tears fell from her eyes.

EIGHTEEN

They landed at the summit of the mountain. Mei's memory flashed back to her first night here. It remained the same, but this time, she had Washi-sensei by her side instead of Jion-sho.

She wanted to lie down in the snowy courtyard and sleep, but whatever waited for her would require her remaining strength. Washi offered her his arm, but she shook her head and limped slowly next to him. She would meet the Emperor on her own two feet.

"Let's get this done quickly so you can return to your dragon and get healing." Washi's voice was laced with anger at her expense.

Kuro? She sent out the quiet thought, but the silence made her stomach clench.

The guards opened the doors as she approached, and in the great hall, no other sensei was present like last time. Only the Emperor was, and he sat in an opulent red kimono tied with a black obi. He had a long dark beard, and he leaned back in the Sho's chair. As she staggered closer, his black eyes followed her, and there was no hint of kindness or mercy on his stark face.

Washi stopped, bowed low, and knelt, facing the Emperor. Mei followed his example, and her knees ached from the cold stone.

Time passed as the Emperor remained silent. She wished she could lie down while he finished his inspection.

When he finally spoke, his voice came out calm and composed. "Where were you, shodragon rider?"

"I was trapped in caves just south of here, Your Highness." Mei's voice cracked as she spoke, her throat feeling raw.

He paused, and his fingers tapped lightly on the wooden armrest. "Your partner claims you ran off."

Her eyes flicked up, and heat filled her body. "He said he went to get help."

No emotion showed on his face. "Your stories differ, and he's now missing."

Missing? "I don't know where he is, Your Excellency."

"Convenient."

Mei didn't respond. What did he want her to say?

"You have sustained multiple injuries. This is the second time your shodragon has been injured badly."

"We were fighting the jorogumo."

Washi gasped next to her, and the Emperor stood.

"The rains haven't arrived yet," the Emperor stated.

"They're in the caves just south of here. We barely escaped with our lives." She gestured to her bloody clothes. "As you can see."

The Emperor sat back down. He studied her once more and placed a hand to his chin. "Or you got in a fight with Daisuke. His dragon's also missing."

Mei's gaze darted around. "I haven't seen him since he left me, saying he was seeking help."

"Emperor, Mei has no reason to lie," Washi responded.

The Emperor's lips tightened. "You will remain silent."

Washi bowed as the muscle in his cheek twitched.

The door opened behind them. Mei glanced back to see a tall form enter. Daisuke.

Her jaw clenched as he approached, and he bowed and knelt next to her. His clothing was wrinkled and torn, a far cry from his usual put-together appearance.

"Oh, you're back now?" the Emperor said, his voice devoid of emotion.

"I apologize, Your Imminence. I was looking for Mei and got delayed."

"Your parents are anxious."

Daisuke bowed once more. "I'm sorry. I felt responsible for my partner's disappearance."

Mei clenched her jaw. "Because you were," she said softly.

"Do not speak, rider," the Emperor said. "What happened?"

"I think I misunderstood the signal from my partner," Daisuke said, his voice ever confident. "She must have seen something and flown off, and I didn't want to disobey orders, so I returned, thinking she ran off."

Surely the Emperor wouldn't believe this nonsense?

He nodded with concern on his face. "I understand it must be hard to communicate with this partner of yours. The Sho claims she's the best we have in your class." The Emperor glanced down at Mei. "She just learned to speak, I heard."

Daisuke bowed his head. "I will continue to do my best."

Mei shot to her feet and squared her shoulders. "Do you not care that there's a herd of jorogumo not far from here? Do you not care that he left me to die in a cave? What about my dragon, who's struggling to survive? When did this become about me being an eta?" The words flew from her mouth, and Washi tried to tug her back to her knees, but Mei planted her feet.

The Emperor folded his hands into his sleeves. "Washi-sensei, please take your charges away. Make sure you teach the eta how to address others above her station. It needs to become more like other humans. Rider or not, I'm still Emperor."

Mei clenched her jaw, and before she could speak, a hand covered her mouth. It was Washi's. He bowed and forced her head down as well. "Forgive our lack of training her, Emperor." His voice was stilted as he replied. Only Mei could see the anger on his bowed face.

As he pulled her toward the door, the Emperor's voice reached out. "Be warned, eta. This time you have my mercy."

Mei's heart grew bitter as they went out the gates. Her eyes met Daisuke's, and he smirked as he mounted his dragon and flew down the fortress. She paused before getting onto Washi-sensei's dragon. The attacks on her character and the physical abuse—she'd handled it all by believing she could live through it. But if Daisuke had caused the cave-in on purpose... She stiffened. They were trying to kill her, which she'd already known, but they would blatantly get away with it.

"If the Sho were here, it would be different. I don't have the power to face the Emperor. I'm sorry, Mei. I will report this all to the Sho. There are too many politcal games that you're getting dragged into."

"I understand."

They landed and Washi helped her down. "Do you? It's dangerous around the Emperor. We all have to watch our words. You need to live to continue to fight another day."

Mei's chest tightened. She not only came close to death from jorogumo tonight but also desertion. The Sho wasn't here to stop it. Seeing the fear in Washi's eyes now made it very clear.

"I understand."

He let out a sigh. "He didn't try anything tonight. We got lucky. Now heal up. There will be more battles tomorrow."

Tiredness leaked into her bones and Mei walked to Kuro. Mei sat next to him in the snow. She mutely let Emiri treat her wounds. Kuro finally opened a silver eye and raised his head.

Food?

Mei rested her head on his large forearm. *Okay.*

They ambled away from the rush of people. Kuro wobbled as he launched into the air, and Mei went around to the lift. Down in the den, a few more healers rushed around Kuro as he gulped down whole shanks of meat. A lone priest shoved a bowl of porridge at Mei, and she sat, leaning on Kuro while she drank the meal.

The last healer left, and Mei's eyes closed. She'd almost drifted off to sleep when feet scraped at the entrance.

Washi-sensei nodded to her. "Did you eat?"

"Yes." She studied his now somber face. He was the only sensei who treated her somewhat equally. "Sensei?"

"Yes?"

Mei took a deep breath. "Are there more eta going missing?" When she'd left months ago, some older eta leaders had gone already.

Washi tilted his head. "I'm not sure on the exact report. No one will report an eta..." He trailed off.

"I know I'm in trouble, but may I go check on my father? I can leave with your permission." In these last months, she hadn't even tried to escape to see her father. His warning that she needed to stay away still rang in her ears.

His brown eyes grew curious. "I think that should be allowed. I will try to get permission. I think it's best if the Sho is here to back me up, so you may need to wait a few weeks or more."

"But—"

"Rest."

It didn't take any effort to follow Washi's order as he left the den. Her eyes closed, and Kuro's warmth comforted her.

How do you feel? she asked before sleep claimed her.

Very fuzzy and full.

Mei curled up next to Kuro and welcomed the blackness of sleep.

AFTER WATCHING Mei take off to the top of the fortress, Chin ran down to the bottom. He needed to untie Daisuke. Chin didn't want to free him, but it might look worse for Mei if he went missing.

Chin's footfalls thudded against the stone floors as he ran into the abandoned room where he had left him. It was empty. He scanned the room and turned around. It really was empty. Chin ran his hands through his hair, backed out of the room, and bumped into something.

"Are you looking for me?"

Chin spun around to face a rumpled Daisuke, his large dragon looming behind him. "I told you I would come back."

Daisuke stroked his dragon's neck. "You know, dragons have an excellent sense of smell." His eyes focused on Chin. "And you don't have a dragon to find you should you go missing."

Chin gripped the hilt of his katana, and Daisuke let out a short laugh. "I'm not going to kill you. Now..." Daisuke straightened and folded his arms. "Did you save it?"

"Yes."

"Oh?" The corner of Daisuke's mouth tilted up. "She's full of surprises." He invaded Chin's space, not caring that he was weaponless. However, anyone with a large dragon behind them would feel confident. "How does it feel, dragonless boy, that it has surpassed you?"

"You should know." Chin didn't back away, meeting Daisuke's dark gaze. Daisuke's hand lashed out and clutched his neck. The icy fingers only let a bit of air through. He backed up, but the stone wall stopped him, and the red dragon loomed from behind. Chin clutched Daisuke's wrists, but they felt like iron shackles. When he reached again for his sword, Daisuke kneed him in the groin. Chin doubled over, wheezing through the tight grip.

Daisuke leaned in, his breath tickling Chin's ear. "She'll never surpass me, you failure of a daim." Daisuke squeezed Chin's neck one last time and released him. Chin fell to the ground as Daisuke stood over him. "Where's the eta?"

A foot landed on his chest. In his training, these situations had happened many times. In a rush, he grabbed Daisuke's ankle and twisted it sharply. He rolled to the opposite side as Daisuke fell. Chin jumped to his feet and drew his sword as the dragon pounced. He shuffled back from the dragon as Daisuke pushed himself up.

"Bringing a sword to the fight?"

"You brought a dragon."

Daisuke held his hand up to the dragon, and it stopped moving toward Chin. "Let's have a fair fight, eta lover."

Chin narrowed his eyes. "Send your dragon away, then."

"Aw, you don't trust me?" Chin didn't reply. "Fine." Daisuke faced his dragon. "Go to the den."

After she'd shuffled off, Chin placed his katana down and lowered his stance, facing Daisuke.

Daisuke smirked and mirrored Chin's stance. "We may have had the same trainer."

"Most likely."

They circled each other, judging the other's stance. The injuries on his back and the bruising from his recent fight with the jorogumo put him at a disadvantage. If Daisuke saw him favoring any body part, he would exploit it. That would be what Chin would do. Chin studied his movements, but Daisuke flowed over the stone floor like he was familiar with their fighting ground.

Daisuke lunged at Chin, and he stepped back, letting the kick slide past him. Instead of going for the leg, Chin countered with a jab, but Daisuke dodged the punch. Daisuke used the momentum to spin forward, and he elbowed Chin in the small of his back.

Chin bit his lip and twirled away from the hit, but his vision blurred. Daisuke followed up with a swift kick to his side. Chin flowed with the attack, but the kick still stung. A whoosh of air left his lips, but he swerved his leg into the back of Daisuke's knee. Too slow. Daisuke pivoted out of the way, and Chin's back was left exposed again. Daisuke took advantage and landed a kick there.

Chin fell with the blow, and his face hit the cold ground. Hands trembling, he pushed himself up, but Daisuke stomped on his back. His wounds cracked open. Gritting his teeth, he tried to get away.

"Stay down. Your back is quite the weak spot."

Shards, he could tell from the start. Clenching his jaw, Chin pushed up with all his strength and rolled under the foot. Daisuke's foot dragged across his wounds, but Chin broke free. He stood and faced Daisuke, warm blood dripping down his back.

Daisuke tilted his head and charged at Chin, his movements fluid. Daisuke raised his arm and slashed down at Chin's shoulder, but he blocked it with his forearm. Chin's back burned, and he felt every movement.

Focus on the fight. The pain is nothing, Chin chanted to himself. His mind back in the fight, he focused on Daisuke's relentless attacks and went on the defensive.

Chin could tell that Daisuke was playing with him. His blows came down lighter as he wore down Chin's stamina. It worked. Chin had already fought all day, and his movements to block Daisuke's attacks slowed down. From the side, a jab caught him in the jaw. His eyes lost focus, and before he could see again, another punch slammed into his face, knocking him down. A final kick to his side made Chin go completely still.

In the quiet, Chin could hear Daisuke's soft breathing and footfalls.

After a moment, Daisuke spoke, but from far away. "You can't protect her. She will die. There's more to this than even I know."

"I wasn't... trying... to..."

The footsteps faded away, and Chin was left alone in the darkness of the stone hallway. He blinked and moved his arms and legs. The soreness from Daisuke's swift kicks and punches ached, but Chin felt a faint burning in his chest at losing. He pushed up his battered body, already worn, and placed his hand on the wall for support. Taking short steps, he reached the lift. The priest stood and gestured for Chin to come to him. Next to the priest, his mother stood still and collected, her blue kimono a bright spot in the darkness ahead.

Chin stopped, and his heels slid backward on their own. What was she doing here? "Your mother was worried about you," the priest said from down the hall, even though Chin was far away. "She came to take you home today."

Chin scanned his mother. She stood with her hands tucked in her sleeves. The picture of daim elegance sent a stab of fear down his spine. He wanted to run. A flame of rebellion grew in his chest. Chin took a deep breath and angled his foot back toward where he had come from. Then he looked into his mother's eyes.

Her eyes flashed greenish as they took in everything, down to his rebellious feet. She didn't need to move to stop him. Chin's quiet rebellion ended in seconds, and he carried himself over to Mother.

The priest glanced at them, and Chin lowered his gaze to his shoes. "I'm sorry, Aiko-san, that you were worried. I let him stay a couple times. He's a very hard worker."

"He will overwork himself if I let him." His mother's kimono rustled as she bowed. "Thank you for your help." Her voice had a kind lilt. Chin shuddered. "Let's go, my son." Her hand rested on his shoulder. It was cold.

Chin followed her to the lift and out into the snowy courtyard. Smears of blood stained the snow, but Mei's dragon was gone. Snowflakes fell from the sky to cover up the carnage.

Aiko took delicate steps, and by the time they got into the rickshaw, Chin couldn't stop his trembling. He huddled to the side and closed his eyes while the runner took them down the mountain to his house.

The driver stopped, and Aiko got out of the rickshaw, but Chin remained curled inside. Her wooden sandals clicked on the stone walkway and then paused. Her voice brooked no argument with one short word: "Come."

Chin unfolded his body and staggered after the bright blue kimono. They paused in the doorway, the warm heat hitting Chin's face as he slipped off his shoes. He stood in the hall, not looking at his mother.

"Clean yourself up, then come see me. Do not keep me waiting."

He nodded and walked toward the bath. Warm water greeted him, and his sore and bloody body relaxed in the tub. Chin methodically ran a cloth over his arms and legs. His back smarted in the water, but the sensation helped clear his mind. He continued to shiver, even though he was warm.

He slowly slipped out of the tub, dried himself, and put on the fresh yukata that waited for him. His bare feet hugged the warm wooden floor as he went down the hall to his room, where she would be waiting.

He slid the door open and knelt in the usual spot.

"Where were you?"

"I slept overnight since there was an emergency."

"What emergency?" she asked, her sharp teeth nearly snapping at him.

Chin paused. "A shodragon rider was hurt, and I helped take care of them."

"Them?"

"Her."

"Her? Don't you mean *it*?"

She knew. "She needed help."

Aiko stood and ran her cold hand through his hair. "Why are you helping an eta? The eta who stole your dragon?"

"You can't steal—"

A sharp tug on his hair stopped his words and yanked his neck back. "Why are you helping an eta?" Aiko's voice pierced through the room.

Chin swallowed, his neck throbbing. "I-I don't know. She needs me."

Aiko shoved his head as she let go. "Do not see that thing again, my son." An animal hiss escaped her lips.

The small rebellious fire rekindled in Chin's chest. "You don't get to decide for me."

Aiko sniffed and strolled to the bench in the room. She tapped it with a slender metal rod. "Come."

Chin's eyes met hers, and he gritted his teeth and stood. "No."

She stepped forward. "Think wisely, my son."

A shuffling noise came from outside his door, and he knew from experience that house guards waited outside. He stiffened and lay down on the bench, his stomach flat against the wood. Cold hands came to tie down his wrists and legs. His robe still clung to wet patches on his back.

The metal whip whistled through the air and struck him, cutting through the robe and skin. Pain bloomed through his back and down his legs while Aiko showed no mercy. She always paused between strikes, getting the most out of his pain.

The last blow fell, and her soft breathing mixed with Chin's ragged breaths.

"Don't help that thing again." She left the room, and the door slid softly shut.

Chin remained tied to the bench. The small fire inside him became no more than a puff of smoke.

NINETEEN

Darkness permeated the den when Mei opened her eyes. The slow rise and fall of Kuro's chest told her he slept. She stroked the ridges of his jaw, and a smile curved her lips.

"You know I won't ever leave you to die, you nit," she whispered.

Kuro snorted and continued to sleep. She left him to rest and ran out to dunk her body clean, then put on her last fresh uniform. Mei needed to get more clothing but didn't want to ask. Her riding robes lay in ruins in the den's corner. She sighed and took one last look at her sleeping dragon before going to the dining hall. She was the first to arrive. Mei got her food and sat down, relieved she didn't have to deal with her class just yet.

Mei moved stiffly, and she longed to go lie back down next to Kuro. The food melted on her tongue, and she tried to gain strength from its warmth. From what the Emperor had suggested, no one would believe her about the jorogumo. They would rather believe she had run away than the fact that the monsters were awake. *Bakas.* Maybe it would be better to take her father and leave.

The thought grew in her mind. They could leave and go north. There were large patches of land where they could hide. Kuro could now fly. Nothing was keeping her here with the rest of them. She could wait until Washi-sensei let her go and then tell her father to be ready. The hope of freedom glowed through Mei's body. Then the memory of her father's face and his tight grip flashed in her mind. He wouldn't leave. There had been something behind his words, and she needed to find out what.

Mei took her dishes to the servers and bowed to them. She went to her first class and her place at the back of the room, still with no chair. Mei thought about leaning against the wall, but she remained stubborn. Small defiances kept her going, and she needed to keep her spirit up. She put on her mask. *I'm just an eta. Ignore me.*

The other recruits entered with Sora-sensei on their heels. Sora took one look at Mei, and the sour expression that Mei knew all too well appeared on her face. Mei searched the room for Chin, but he was nowhere to be seen. Was he more injured than she'd realized?

The whispers and glances in Mei's direction were nothing new as Sora talked.

"Rules have been broken recently." They all made angry faces at Mei. "I never thought I would have to broach the subject of desertion."

Mei stiffened. Had Sora read her mind? She realized they all believed Daisuke. It didn't matter. There was no way she could win against all of them.

"It's sad that you cannot bond as a group should. These are the people who will fight side by side with you against the jorogumo, the creatures that wake with the rains."

They are already awake, bakas.

"I want to make it clear that there is one among you who you cannot trust. It's just in the nature of what it is."

Sora's words jarred Mei's thoughts.

"It will leave us. It has no loyalty to the city or you." Sora's eyes met Mei's. "It's what eta do."

Mei pulled the sides of her uniform. "Sora-sensei."

"I am talking. Please be quiet."

"No." The word of defiance rebounded in the room. "I am always quiet." Her voice trembled. "This time I will only speak once." All eyes focused on her. "You will not believe me. That's *your* nature. The nature of those who think they are better. However, I've just fought the creatures and survived. I survived to tell the Emperor that they are already awake and near the city, taking those you consider worthless." Mei's gaze flicked across the room. "I will not leave." Mei forced out the words. "I have more honor and loyalty than every monster in this room."

She trembled and tried to breathe to control her shaking limbs, but the best she could do was clench her teeth to keep them from chattering.

"Lies," Sora-sensei spat.

Mei didn't respond. She only shook her head and directed her gaze out the window. She might as well have spoken to a wall.

"They are not awake!" Sora's screech hurt Mei's ears, but she still didn't look at her sensei. Benio snickered and whispered something to Aimi. Kenta laughed and did a standing impression of what Mei assumed was herself, and Daisuke's lips curled at the corners knowing that he'd won this battle.

Toshiko remained silent and her measured look was unreadable. The rest of them joined in with the antics until Sora shushed them and continued on her rant.

It didn't matter. The ones who would die weren't important to them. She was the only one who cared for the eta. No one else in this fortress would lift a finger.

Her father's words echoed in her mind: *You don't understand what's at stake.*

It's not my responsibility, Mei argued.

Isn't it? Kuro asked. It was faint but still filled her with the same warmth.

The eta are not my responsibility, she repeated. *We can get my father and leave.*

After a brief pause, Kuro answered, *I could see you before I left my shell. I saw you stumbling in the dark. Your brave spirit called to me.*

Kuro... I...

You are meant to break the world. We can fly away, my partner, but I don't think that is what you want.

You chose me because I would break the world? A flood of fear entered her shaking limbs.

Kuro huffed. *Don't you think it needs to be?*

Mei didn't respond. The clear blue sky out the window appeared too calm for the anguish in her mind. Sora-sensei was still ranting, but she wasn't listening. *I don't know.*

Why don't we find out together?

She'd never understood why Kuro would choose an eta. Being here had made her realize that she really was no different from those in her class.

Okay. She smiled to herself. *We can stay for a little while.*

Kuro sent warmth through her mind. *Also, how would you feed me out in the wild? Am I expected to hunt too?*

You're a dragon, after all. Although a lazy one.

He didn't respond, and Mei was alone again. She looked toward the front of the room, and Sora-sensei's red face glared at her.

"Oh, was I supposed to be listening?" Mei asked.

A communal gasp sounded, and Sora-sensei's mouth gaped open. Mei shook her head, and as she went to look out the window, she met Daisuke's eyes. He smirked, and his eyes glittered. Mei jutted her chin and stared him down. Daisuke raised his eyebrows and gave her a deep nod.

A challenge. He wouldn't hold back anymore. She would need to be careful around him. Easier said than done since they were flying partners.

Sora-sensei concluded another rant about something or other and dismissed them outside.

Dazai-sensei's class over the last months had focused on shooting the longbow. They would always have to hold their stance for what seemed liked hours, then shoot targets while standing.

Even though they killed Mei's shoulders and arms, Dazai's lessons had saved her in the caves. The hours of holding her form had helped her in the heat of battle. This time, their dragons waited for them, already harnessed next to upturned targets in the snow.

Before Mei could even ask Kuro what was going on, Dazai shouted, "Form!"

They all lined up with their legs and arms outstretched. Dazai strode past them, whacking a few with a long stick. "Form!" Mei held back her laugh when he struck Kenta.

Mei stiffly adjusted to the second form and waited for Dazai to inspect her.

"Injured?" His sharp eyes missed nothing.

"Yes, sensei."

"Can you fly?"

"Yes, sensei."

He frowned and walked on to the next recruit. They went through all the forms before grabbing their longbows. Then they stood and waited at attention.

"You will shoot from your shodragon. This is how you will help your dragon in battle. Follow my forms on the logs."

Over to the side, there were thick logs with another log sticking out of them. Mei supposed this was to simulate the dragon's neck. It felt comical sitting on the wooden logs, but they all got on as Dazai stood in front of them.

"Form!"

They leaned into form one. Following Dazai, they shifted forward, and keeping their backs straight, they leaned to the right of the fake dragon's neck. The recruits balanced through the forms on the back of the logs. Satisfied, Dazai permitted them to mount their dragons.

Kuro lay in the snow as Mei approached.

Are you okay? she asked.

Yes.

He said no more and slowly got to his feet to let her mount. Mei patted his side and pushed her worries away. He was probably still tired from the battle, but he was healed, so there shouldn't be any problem.

After this, I will make sure you get extra fat on your meat tonight.

Kuro snorted, and after Mei latched herself in the harness, they took to the air. The transition to the air seemed harder for Kuro.

Should we just land? Mei asked him.

No.

Mei bit her cheeks and focused on the upturned target. When she shot from solid ground, the beat of the wings didn't mess with her aim. She matched her breathing with Kuro's wingbeats. Mei leaned over the right side of Kuro's neck and took aim. She couldn't pull back the string far enough, and the arrow fell limply to the ground. They flew on to the next target. Kuro varied his tilts so Mei could work on each side. She finally pulled the bow to a full draw, but her arrows hit the ground and not the target. Upon landing, Kuro stumbled, almost crashing forward.

Mei jumped down and went to his face, putting his head in her hands. "What's going on?"

Tired.

Emiri had been there during the healing, so nothing should have been amiss. "Let's go back to the den and rest. I'll get Emiri."

Mei put her bow away and bowed to Dazai before walking back up to the fortress. Kuro trailed after her instead of flying.

"It'll be okay," Mei said while facing forward.

A loud roar sounded behind her, and two objects collided. Mei turned around. The red dragon pounced on Kuro, and they flailed in the snow. Mei ran forward, only for a muscular arm to hold her back.

"It's their battle."

Mei shrugged out of the grip and looked up to see Daisuke. She knew that, but she also knew he'd seen Kuro was weak today. "A low trick."

Daisuke faced forward. "That's how life is, eta."

She stepped away from him, and her eyes locked on the two dragons. Kuro struggled to get off the ground, and the red dragon kept bowling him over while they rolled in the snow. Kuro was larger than the red dragon and tried to use his weight to steady himself, but his slow movements gave the red dragon the advantage.

The red dragon lashed out with her tail and hit Kuro in the side. Kuro tried to lock his neck with hers, but she squeezed out and used her forearms to roll Kuro onto his back. She lightly clamped her jaws around Kuro's neck, and he quieted.

The dominance fight was over as quickly as it had begun, and the other recruits applauded as Daisuke waved to the crowd. He smiled, gave a slight bow, and walked over to his dragon.

Kuro lay still in the snow. In the middle of running over to him, Mei paused, and the smirk on Daisuke's face burned into her mind. She slipped in the snow as she changed directions and plowed into Daisuke, wrapping her arms around his waist. They fell onto the snowy earth.

He broke free from her grip, shoved himself up, and glared at her. "Don't do something you'll regret."

Mei stood slowly and brushed the snow from her uniform. "This fight proved nothing, other than your dragon can beat a sick one."

Daisuke snorted. "They healed him."

"Not entirely."

In a rush, Mei crouched and flung snow at his face. He turned away to avoid getting it in his eyes. She took his moment of blindness to throw a quick jab near his groin.

Daisuke doubled over and lashed out blindly with his arm. Mei quickly ducked and jabbed him in his lower back.

He turned and backhanded her in the arm, knocking her over. Mei rolled with the tumble and bounced to her feet.

She faced him and smiled, then put her hand up and pulled her fingers down to her palm, gesturing to him like one would a dog.

His eyes flashed, and he rushed in to chop her in the neck, but her neck was no longer there. Instead of trying to block his attack, Mei flattened to the ground, grabbed his ankle with both hands, and jerked it to the left. His body fell with his forward momentum, and he landed next to her in the snow.

Before he could get up, Mei jumped to her feet and kicked snow mixed with dirt in his face, then jumped on his groin. Her body wasn't very heavy, but it still caused Daisuke to cough and gag. He curled up in the snow, with his knees to his chest.

Mei danced away from him. He rolled on the ground and staggered to his feet.

"Do you want to die, eta?" His voice shook, and snow and dirt dripped from his face.

"Not today."

He spat on the ground and faced her once more. Mei smiled as she observed he kept his arm low to protect his groin.

Daisuke circled Mei, his steps uneven. She had fought larger and more skilled opponents before. Her lips curved as Daisuke molded into a formal fighting stance. Mei sank low and forgot all about her teachings. If she fought him like they'd trained her, she would lose.

Daisuke came forward with a long kick aimed at her head, and Mei ducked. Bold of him, but stupid. Mei effortlessly fit under the kick and rolled. She took advantage of her momentum and slapped his left ear. He wobbled, and Mei slammed her fist against his nose. Blood spurted out, and Daisuke fell down heavily. She stood over him and kicked him in the throat. He gasped, and blood poured down his face.

"She cheated!" Benio shouted from the sidelines. "Dazai-sensei, she hurt a recruit!"

Dazai folded his arms and focused on Benio. He said nothing until Benio looked away, her face red.

Mei glared at her. Then met the eyes of the rest of the recruits, daring them to attack her. They all looked away. Mei walked over to Kuro.

"Let's go," Mei said to her dragon, resting her hand on his shoulder as they walked up to the fortress. No one followed them.

Sorry.

"Stop it. We're getting you help."

Kuro quieted, and when they reached the mountain, he struggled to fly over the top so he could get down to the dens.

After watching Kuro, Mei ran to the healer hall and ducked through the doors, looking for Emiri. Other healers shot dirty glances at her, but she ran, and no one stopped her.

Emiri was in a room with a guard, placing a bandage on a dendragon's wing.

"You can take this off tomorrow morning, and he'll be just fine."

The guard nodded and stepped aside as Mei ran into the room.

"Something's wrong with Kuro."

Emiri's eyes widened, and she grabbed her bag and bowed to the guard before following Mei out of the room.

They ran down the hall and to the lift. Kuro was

stretched out near the entrance. He hadn't made it to where he normally slept.

Mei rushed to his face, and he didn't open his eyes. "Emiri." Her voice cracked as Emiri rolled up her sleeves.

"Help me check his body. We must have missed something in the chaos of last night."

Mei nodded, and she removed the harness as she ran her fingers across Kuro's smooth, cold scales. They were normally warmer. Mei's heart clenched as she helped Emiri.

They found nothing, and then it took Mei a long time to get Kuro to roll over so they could check his other side. Mei stopped herself from panicking over her dragon's languidness. She ran her fingers under his belly and next to the back of his wing. She felt something soft. With a gasp, she drew her hand back and peered under his wing. A white mound no bigger than a chestnut appeared.

"Here!" Mei shouted to Emiri, and she ran to Mei.

Emiri's eyes focused, and she took a thin silver tool out of her bag. "I will need to lance it, then drain it. Kuro may wake up."

Mei nodded and braced herself against Kuro's wing. Chances were he would toss them off in his daze, but Mei hoped Emiri wouldn't get hurt.

She watched Emiri pull under the tender scale and break the outer barrier. A putrid smell filled Mei's nose. It reminded her of rotting flesh from the garbage piles. Emiri wiped away the pus as it oozed out of the wound. She took a pair of clamps and pulled against the whitish sac. It popped out of Kuro's body and remained intact. It was the size of Mei's fist.

Emiri placed it on the ground, then cleaned out Kuro's wound. He didn't wake, but snored softly.

"Mei." Emiri's tone darkened.

"What?"

"There are more."

All along the underside of Kuro's wing, white bubbles popped up under the scales. Mei bit her lips, and tears burned her eyes. She hadn't even noticed these. One by one, Emiri traced along under his wings and scales, pulling out the white sacs. By the time they finished, the putrid smell had saturated the den, making it hard to breathe. They checked Kuro's entire body and didn't find any more. Emiri placed salve under the scales.

Mei brushed her hand against his head. He felt warm again, and her chest relaxed.

Emiri folded up the white sacs in a cloth.

"What are those?"

Emiri shrugged. "I haven't seen an infection like this before, except with certain bugs planting their young in a host. I will take this to the healer—"

Before she could finish, Mei stomped over to the sacs and smashed them under her feet.

"What are you doing?"

"These are jorogumo eggs."

Emiri gasped and smashed them with Mei. Then a few of them hatched.

"We need fire!" Mei diverted one of the hatched creatures as it tried to scuttle out of the den.

Emiri ran out the door and returned with a loose torch. They scorched the runners, and they died simply enough. They took the torch to the remaining egg sacs. Thick smoke filled the room, and they coughed from the fumes. Kuro opened one eye and surveyed their frantic squishing.

Mei?

"Eat some plants and help us out!" Mei yelled at the dragon.

He leaned over to the flight pack and ate something. Then Mei jerked Emiri toward the wall. She and Kuro connected, and with a burst of green flame, the rest of the eggs were destroyed.

Mei and Emiri fell against the wall, gasping, and Kuro studied them with a confused look on his face.

Is this a ritual of some sort?

Mei let out a tired laugh. "No, just killing your passengers."

Kuro sniffed the charred eggs and sneezed. *They smell like bad meat. I'm hungry.*

Emiri glanced at Mei, and she let her in on the conversation. "Kuro says he's hungry."

Emiri's face looked slightly green. "He's not going to eat them, is he?"

Mei laughed and grabbed her stomach, while Kuro and Emiri looked at her like she had lost her wits.

I don't think I could ever eat that, Kuro grumbled.

"Did I say something strange?" Emiri asked.

Mei continued to laugh as her friends exchanged glances. It felt good.

Once she'd settled down, she thought Emiri might know about Chin. "Um, so today in class..."

Emiri made a face. "I heard about what happened. Are you okay?"

"Oh yeah, I was just wondering if you saw that guy.."

"That guy?"

Mei focused on the wall while Emiri studied her face. "That guy who's always around."

"Chin?"

"Is that his name?"

Emiri rolled her eyes at Mei's obvious lie. "No, I haven't seen him. After he flew back with you, he disappeared. I know he goes home at night, but he's always here early in the morning."

"I didn't know if he was injured or something."

"I thought you hated him?"

Mei kept avoiding eye contact. "Well, I don't think he hurt Kuro. Why would he save us if he had?" She shrugged. Emiri raised her eyebrow knowingly. "I just wanted to thank him! Stop looking at me like that." Mei tried to battle with her own pride. She had to admit that Chin had only every helped her. It might be better to not push away those who seemed to be on her side.

They sat in silence before Emiri spoke. "So what happened?"

The darkness, the screeches, and the smell of smoke entered Mei's mind. "I was trapped in a cave with them." She tensed. "I thought it was the end, but out of nowhere, Chin appeared."

"So they're awake." Emiri shuddered next to Mei.

"Yes, and no one will believe me."

TWENTY

Daisuke glared in the blurry-looking glass. The idiotic healers wouldn't use their precious viola on his nose. He stalked away from the cheap glass and kicked his tiny bed. This place was horrid. Even though he'd won the dominance fight, the little snipe had beaten him in front of the entire class. The only thing the sensei would do was take away a few of her meals. When her dragon regained its strength, it would reclaim its top spot.

He slammed his fist into the stone wall. Pain flared in his arm, and a bloody smear remained on the stone.

"I'm going to go."

The girl hastily adjusted her yukata and left the room.

Daisuke's confused gaze followed her out. Where had she come from? He plopped down on his peasant bed and rested his face in his hands. When they'd arranged the caves, they'd told him he would not be in danger. The people he had used had sworn that the caves were empty, but Mei had come back raving about jorogumo. What if he had stayed inside and used the map? Would he be dead?

It had to be a stupid eta trick. Eta were all insane liars. Then he'd given that daim bastard his map. He clenched his fingers, stabbing them into his skin. He was better than the both of them, but somehow, they still needed to be stamped out. The daim betrayer was no better than an eta.

A soft throat clearing interrupted Daisuke's thoughts, and he raised his eyes to see two city guards standing at the entrance.

"The Emperor requests your presence, Daisuke-san." They both bowed.

Daisuke sighed and tucked his injured hand in his sleeve. "Fine."

He was a bit surprised when they took him up a lift to the top of the fortress. Why was the Emperor still here? Didn't he have his own palace?

When he reached the hall, the Emperor still sat in the Sho's chair, wearing a deep green kimono. Daisuke knelt, the cold stone bruising his knees.

"Stand."

Daisuke followed his orders but kept his eyes low. He heard the Emperor stand and walk toward him.

"Walk with me, Daisuke."

Without saying anything, he followed him, pacing in a circle around the large hall.

"There's no denying that the Sho rules over the shodragons while I rule over the city and the army. The balance is necessary for our country." The Emperor halted, and they looked out the window, the vast city sprawled before them.

"Now there's a threat to the balance, and the Sho is

doing nothing about it. Some sensei are worried this will look bad on the riders and upset their authority with the daim class."

Did the Emperor think he could take on shodragons? The Emperor had the city guard but shodragons could wipe them out in a blink. "I'm sorry, Your Excellency, but what does this have to do with me?"

"I've enlisted your help to find information about the eta, and you've given me nothing. I have been informed of your clumsy attempts to solve the eta problem and, through other sources, how you botched the cave incident. I will take a direct approach with you so I can resolve the problem. Permanently."

Daisuke shifted his eyes, peering at the Emperor. "She's really that big of a problem?"

The Emperor leaned back on his heels and kept studying the city below. "The shodragon recruits are cut off from the rest of the city. There's a purpose to that, besides training you." The Emperor turned his head and met Daisuke's eyes. "Shodragon riders are to stay out of politics. However, with an eta upsetting the balance, there are murmurs throughout the city that the eta think they are human. That they deserve dragons."

"Anyone who can pay can get a dragon. The eta can never afford it."

"Yet one did. Despite the higher cost in silver." The Emperor turned away and walked to the center of the room, and Daisuke followed. "I am not here to discuss these matters. I am here to make sure the eta meets its end."

Daisuke raised his eyebrow at the Emperor's back. There was something he wasn't saying, but Daisuke could try to glean that information later. When the Emperor had approached him to find out about the eta's family, he'd just wanted better sleeping quarters. Then she'd pissed him off, and he'd wanted her to fail. His attempts hadn't really been meant to kill her, just injure her or make sure she didn't take his place on the dominance issue. When he'd been approached about the cave, he'd just followed orders. "You are telling me to kill h—it?"

"I would never tell you to kill one of the precious shodragon riders. They are, after all, very important to our survival from the jorogumo. The rains will be here after the winter thaws." The Emperor moved to sit back in the Sho's chair. "I think you will need to watch the problem and wait for a moment to arrive."

"A moment?"

"You're not the only one working to have this problem meet its end. Some are more discreet than your blatant attempts."

"Who?" Daisuke should have realized that he wouldn't be alone. The Emperor wouldn't be foolish enough to depend only on one person to get rid of the eta. His mind swam with who it could be, but the Emperor did give something away. It would be someone who didn't make their hatred known to the eta. They would be working on earning the eta's trust. It was too late for Daisuke to have Mei trust him unless something drastic happened.

The Emperor smiled and waved his hand in dismissal. Daisuke bowed low and left the audience chamber. He took the lift back down to his floor. If he told them she'd run out all those months ago, it would be the end. There was something more to this, though, and Daisuke didn't like being used without knowing the purpose. Would the Emperor kill him too to hide evidence? Maybe it was time to think of his other options. Distracted, he ran into a girl who might be in his class.

He bowed and walked on toward the room.

"S-sorry," the recruit stammered.

Daisuke looked back at the girl, and she blushed. He sighed. He had time to kill. A charming smile graced his face, and he aimed it at his next target.

TWENTY-ONE

Mei leaned against the stone wall and rolled her eyes. She had made the mistake of trying to tell Sora-sensei about the jorogumo again.

She had only gotten a shrill response: "Don't start here with your lies and fantasies."

Sora's words still invaded Mei's head.

Even bringing the charred bodies of the infant jorogumo hadn't helped her case. "Why are you bringing filthy dirt in my room?" They really didn't look like anything anymore, but Mei had thought she should try. Eta were being taken, and no one cared, but if they thought others were in danger, they might check out the caves.

After all that, Sora-sensei spent the better part of an hour demeaning her and telling her she didn't get to eat for the rest of the day. Missing a meal after breaking Daisuke's nose seemed worth it in Mei's eyes. She bit her lip to keep from smiling at the image of his perfect face smeared in blood and his wide eyes at her attack.

She snuck down the hall so Sora wouldn't catch her

smiling after a lecture. It was time to meet Emiri in the library. Reading was getting easier, but Mei's writing looked more like an animal scratching the ground to get away from a dragon.

The library and the den were the only two places Mei found comfortable. The dust motes in the beams of light eased her as she entered. The lady at the entrance snored softly, and Mei went to their usual table. Toshiko sat in the corner. Mei had worried at first about the other recruit studying in the library, but Toshiko kept to herself and bent over her books with almost a fevered approach and ignored Mei and Emiri.

Emiri was already there, and when Mei sat down, she placed some rice balls near her.

"Arigato, Emiri." Mei stuffed the food in her mouth and chewed loudly. "You already knew I wasn't getting dinner?"

"That seems to be their favorite punishment. You're already too thin."

Mei shrugged. "I should be used to not eating, but the longer I'm here, the harder it is to go without food." Mei placed the sand tray on the table and began working first on her name. She smiled softly as she rendered the smooth lines.

"That's looking great." Emiri leaned in. "You're really getting the hang of those kanji."

"Now, if only all the answers to the questions were my name, I would be good to go." On the last test Mei had completed, Tomo had claimed he couldn't read her savage writing. "It isn't like they'll give me a score."

Emiri bit her lip and wrote a symbol for Mei to copy. "This means *bastard*. Maybe they'll understand that."

Mei snorted, and with the diligence of the best student, she copied the kanji carefully.

"It's good to hear you laugh."

"Kuro's recovering, and Washi-sensei is working with the Sho to give me permission to check on my father." Mei glanced up. "I honestly feel a bit relieved. Everything else is just normal, but if I can see that my father is okay, I will be able to go on here."

Emiri nodded. "I can't believe they are letting you go. They never let anyone leave, even Daisuke."

"Washi-sensei seems more understanding than the others. I think I can trust him but I'm not sure he would want to cause dissent by letting me go. Maybe if I promise not to mention it to the others." Mei pictured the jovial man in her mind. He never cringed away from her and always taught her fairly along with the rest. She placed her hand on the books he gave her. Only two sensei seemed to want her to do well. "I think he sees me as human."

"You are human, Mei." Emiri placed a hand on Mei's wrist. It felt so calming and warm.

"Arigato, Emiri. I didn't know why you helped me, but I wouldn't have made it this far without you." The two shared a quiet moment. Despite the treatment of the others, Mei knew Emiri wouldn't betray her.

"It's what anyone should do." Emiri took her hand away and nodded. "Your writing is better with swear words. Do you want to try another one?"

The after-dinner hours passed peacefully in the library. Mei giggled with each new word, and she had to agree that her writing was better when it came to swear words. They stopped at "Your family came from dragon dung," since their laughter woke the lady at the front, and she told them that the library had closed ages ago. They both bowed and left.

Mei's heart felt light, and after bowing goodbye to Emiri, she ran all the way to the lift. In the den, she found Kuro eating.

"Are you feeling better?"

There isn't enough white in this meat. His voice came through clearly.

"I guess you are feeling better if you can complain about the food. Kuro?"

Hmm?

"Have you seen that boy who was with us in the caves? Did he come by tonight, by chance?"

Someone smelly brought the food tonight, not him. Kuro paused in his eating, and a large silver eye homed in on her. *Do you like him now?*

"I might be stubborn but I should admit when I was wrong about someone. So many people are wrong about me."

Mhmm.

Mei threw up her hands. "I just want to make sure he's okay. Shells."

Kuro snorted and went back to eating. Mei took the moment to run her hand along his full body again. After she made him lift his wings to check for a second time, he nudged her out the door with his head.

Go bathe. You're smelly too.

"Fine, fine." She grabbed her yukata on the way out and went down to the dragon baths. A couple of dragons splashed on the other side of the pool. Mei stripped and watched their movements. Flashes of color in the torchlight made them seem like giant koi. Their play made waves ripple up Mei's ankles as she entered the scalding water. Her body was now used to the heat of the pool, but it still bit at her skin when she submerged herself. Gasping, she lifted her head out of the pool and jumped when a dark figure stood at the edge.

"I should just drown you and save us all the trouble," Daisuke said, his smooth voice echoing over the water.

Mei placed her feet firmly on the ground. The water got deeper, and she couldn't swim. She glanced at the playing dragons.

"They won't help you."

"What do you want, *daim*?" Mei sneered the last word like everyone did when they said *eta*.

He laughed. "You really are getting out of place."

"What do you think my place is?" When she stood up to anyone, it felt like she was fighting her own nature.

Daisuke stepped closer so that his toes touched the water's edge. "What do eta do? Steal, mate, and die? Kind of like animals, don't you think?"

"So what do daim do? Eat, sleep, and walk around with a bamboo pole up their bum? Kind of useless, don't you think? I mean, even animals have more purpose."

"You seem to have found your voice, little eta."

"I had to since I was tired of hearing yours."

He stepped into the water. Mei took a shaky step back. "Sometimes, it's better not to squawk so much." Daisuke removed his yukata and strode into the water toward Mei.

She treaded away from him, but the water slowed her retreat. Out on the streets, being fast was something she could count on, but if she tried to skirt past him, he would cut her off. His dark brown eyes flickered in the torchlight. She couldn't read them, but he had tried to kill her once.

"Scared, little eta?"

"It's wise to fear things that want to hurt you."

He swung his arms along the surface of the pool, sending out ripples. They lapped at Mei's neck. The hot water made her feel light-headed, and her stomach clenched at the situation she'd found herself in. He could drown her and leave her body to float in the pool, and no one but Kuro would care. *Kuro!*

What?

Come to the pool! Daisuke has trapped me here.

He didn't respond, but she felt a flash of anger through their bond. Mei let out a sigh.

Then she felt a firm grip on her bare arm. Daisuke loomed over her.

"You know I could make your life easier here if you would just be my little toy."

Mei tried to jerk her arm out of his hand, but her feet slipped. "You have everything you want, Daisuke. Why do you have to take everything from me?"

His brow furrowed, and his hold lessened. "What's so important about you, eta?"

She was about to speak when a large black object flew over the surface of the water. Kuro's head rammed into Daisuke's body and sent him sprawling over the water.

In the midst of his flailing, Mei pushed through the water to shore. She wrapped herself in her discarded yukata without drying off. The thin material clung to her skin. "Let's get out of here."

Without looking back, she ran to the den, with Kuro flying at her heels. The sound of Daisuke sputtering chased her.

TWENTY-TWO

With the panic over Daisuke having again trapped her, Mei could hardly sleep. From now on, she would take Kuro with her to the baths. It was foolish of her to go down by herself and not watch her back. Daisuke's poor attempt to get her to trust him on the supply run hadn't worked, and he'd revealed his claws with the cave. Her life was at risk, and it would be foolish to think otherwise.

Mei got dressed and took a breath to steady herself. The fallout of her confronting Sora and fighting Daisuke would rile the recruits. She didn't know how they would retaliate but they would. The bullying would only get worse. It was better when they ignored her.

She took the lift and made her way to the dining hall. The food always smelled amazing to her as she got her portions of fish, miso soup, egg, and steamed rice. So far she could eat like the others. The kitchen staff didn't get involved in recruit politics. They only made Mei clean up the mess that others made when they threw things at her.

The tables were empty and Mei ate as her classmates appeared. Benio sneered at her and sat at the other end of the low table. Mei always shoved the food in her mouth before they could do something to it, and that drew even more disgust from Benio.

Daisuke entered and all the girls whispered and giggled. Some offered him their side dishes and meat, and he smiled at them.

Mei rolled her eyes. Who would give up food for that nit? She picked up her tray and cleaned it. While she washed her tray, a body knocked into her and hot liquid burned her back. Mei yelped and the other recruits laughed.

She turned and Kenta stood there and let out a fake cry. "The eta spilled my food." His eyes glimmered and Mei bit her lips.

The staff huffed and handed Mei a cloth to clean up the spilled food. Mei threw the cloth at Kenta.

"Why should I clean up his mess?"

Silence. Not even the clink of chopsticks from the other recruits could be heard as Mei stared down the kitchen staff.

"You spilled it, you clean it."

"No. I was cleaning my dishes, and he spilled it on purpose." A voice in Mei's head was screaming at her it wasn't worth it to fight about. But after standing up to Sora yesterday, it unleashed her mouth, apparently.

"Recruit, clean up this mess before you leave or I will tell your sensei."

Kenta took a new tray from the worker. "Eta, we have to clean up our own messes." Kenta's tone dripped with condensation. "You may be used to living in trash, but we aren't."

With shaking hands, Mei placed her clean tray on the rack. "If anyone here is trash, it's you, *daim*." Mei wished the others would continue to eat again, but they all watched the show as she and Kenta faced off. "What are you but a joke? Following Daisuke like a dog? Not good enough to find your own way? You feel bigger spilling food on me? I may be an eta, but at least I don't need to work hard at beating you *in every way*."

The words fell out of her mouth and Kenta's face burned red against his tan cheeks as the veins popped in his neck. Before Mei could dodge, his arm flexed, and he smashed his tray into the side of her head.

She gasped as more hot liquid splashed over her face. Her ears rung with the impact and her body fell over with her hands landing on the floor. The rice squished in between her fingers. She gripped the food in her hands and in a smooth movement stood and flung the food at him. It splattered across Kenta's face, and some of the food entered his open mouth, making him cough.

With that, he hurled his body at her, using his weight and height to his advantage. There was no skill, just rage, and they pummeled each other. Mei, already against the wall, didn't have time to back away and let herself fall with him. Using the momentum of his weight to keep rolling him as they fell, she flipped him to the ground. He landed on his back with a thud and let out an oomph of air in surprise at being floored.

Taking advantage of the movement, she rolled to her feet and landed a kick to his side. She then tipped one of the large containers of dirty, soapy water and dumped it on the prone Kenta.

His clothing stuck to him as bits of food clung to his

skin. To Mei's surprise, the recruits in the room let out a laughing cheer at the soggy Kenta.

Hatred flooded his face. Mei changed her stance as he shoved himself up to charge at her.

"Enough!"

Mei stopped a groan from leaving her mouth. It was Sora.

Quiet once again fell on the others, but this time the older recruits found their food very interesting.

"I cannot believe the havoc you bring to the recruits!" Her pinched face took in the mess. "I've never been so ashamed of my recruits."

"Sora-sensei, the eta makes us look bad." It only took a moment for Kenta to change his anger into the demeanor of a victim.

Mei scoffed.

"Hush, eta. Clean this before the morning class. You will be on time, so you better hurry."

Mei swallowed all the words she wanted to say as Sora turned her back. Kenta made a face at her. Her fingernails dug into her palms and she grabbed the discarded cloth and got on her knees to clean up the mess. Why did it have to be Sora? The others stepped around her as she cleaned. Benio washed her tray and splashed water over Mei's head.

"Oops." She giggled with Aimi and Niko as they left.

Mei ignored them and finally finished cleaning the floor, but she looked down at her uniform in dismay. She didn't have another one, and this one was full of stains now. With another cloth, she did her best to clean it off, but she knew the back of it was dirty too. She would spend the day covered in food stains, but she would go to class on time.

Sora said nothing about her not getting lunch, so as long as she wasn't late she could still eat.

Mei?

It's okay.

With a growl in his voice, Kuro replied, *Who?*

Mei grinned despite her damp clothing as she went to class. *Are you going to fight them all?*

The humans might not be fair, but with dragons it's simple. They know I'll win all the dominance fights when I'm well again. The red dragon's time won't last long.

Hold off on Daisuke's dragon. One front at a time.

Kuro hummed low in her head and Mei went into the classroom calmly and stood at the back of the room.

"Oh my kami, it rolled around in trash," Aimi whispered loudly to Benio.

"I think it sleeps in trash. Sensei, it smells so bad, can't someone teach it to bathe?" Benio asked. She acted like Mei's smell was comparable to death. If they fought in battle, they would get dirty. Taking in Benio's, Aimi's, and Niko's painted faces and fixed hair, Mei would give them two minutes in the first fight before they cried and quit.

Sora sympathetically shook her head. "I know this is a burden we must all bear. I will speak to the Sho and see what we can do about its hygiene habits."

It's not worth it to respond. She smelled like breakfast, not trash, but Mei would not point that out.

I'll show them smelly.

Kuro, what exactly are you doing?

He didn't answer her.

"I know you all have to go through so many trials in your first cycle as recruits—"

Mei inwardly sighed. How many times did Sora need to act like the other recruits had it harder than her?

"—but every sixth months, before the next selection, are exams."

The class groaned. Kento, wearing a fresh uniform, pretended to faint. Toshiko sat straighter and poised her ink over the paper. Toshiko studied the hardest out of all of them. It was like breathing to her.

Sora ignored the theatrics from Kento. "These will be not only practical exams but also written exams." Her lips pursed at Mei. "Your dragon rank's important, but if you wish to join a winglegion, your scores must reflect your knowledge. Dragon care, fire, the yumi bow, formations, history, and signaling will all be on exams."

Benio raised her hand, and Sora called on her. "Sensei, if our dragons can speak to each other and us, eventually, why do we need to worry about signaling?"

"You never know what will happen in battle. We fight more than the monsters that come with the rain. Sometimes our telepathic signals can get blocked. Nothing you learn here is wasted effort."

It was maddening to worry about tests when jorogumo were awake before the rains, but Mei knew if she didn't do well things would only get worse for her with the sensei. That is, if they would even score her fairly. Dazai and Washi might, but Tomo and Sora always claimed they never understood what she wrote.

Sora wrote on the board. "Now we'll review all the aspects of dragon care today. Take careful notes."

As Sora taught, Mei slowly wrote the notes on spare paper she snagged from the back. She didn't have much from the earlier classes, but she could try to write what she could now. Trying to make the kanji legible was difficult and by the time the dragon roared, her hand cramped but she had some notes finally.

A hand reached out and took the papers in front of Mei.

"I thought we weren't to give paper to the eta. Since it's a waste." Benio held up the paper with her perfectly manicured fingers. "Look at its writing! It's like an animal language." She passed the papers to Aimi before Mei could grab them.

"Give it back."

Aimi held them between two fingers and reached out the window. The wind ripped them out of her hands. "Oh no, I think I dropped them. It's not like you can use them, anyway. You can't read or write. At least we know you'll always be at the bottom of the ranking."

The other recruits laughed.

"That's one good thing about having an eta," Kenta chimed in.

"If you're not worried about me beating you in rank, then why throw away my notes? I guess I'll have to score better without them." Not waiting for more jibes, Mei turned and left for the next class, which was Tomo's unfortunately.

He warned them too about exams and Mei got ahold of more paper and tried to take careful notes. His class was more difficult than dragon care. She performed those tasks with Kuro daily. The formations Tomo taught were harder to remember since she'd only been on one flight. Also, the history was in a dry, boring book that had complicated words that were difficult for Mei to decipher. Maybe she could ask Emiri to help question her on the history if she could get hold of a book.

For the rest of the day, the sensei poured information down their throats. The rest of the recruits didn't have energy to pester Mei. While they cleaned the classrooms after classes, Benio and Aimi skipped out and left. She was surprise Niko stayed to help. Usually she followed Benio.

Mei's brain felt like it weighed her down, but she didn't dare skip cleaning and tidied with the rest of them. They all avoided her until they heard a shriek coming down the hall.

Benio burst into the room and pointed her finger at Mei. "What did you do, eta?"

Mei paused, holding her wet cloth, and it dripped onto the floor. "I don't know what you mean."

"Everything in our room is ruined! It smells like roasted dragon dun. It's burned!" Aimi cried next to Benio.

Niko stepped up to Benio. "What do you mean?"

Benio actually looked frazzled. "Our room's destroyed!" she said, spit flying from her mouth.

The other recruits dropped their cleaning tools. Mei knew she shouldn't follow them, but she didn't know what Benio was rambling about. When she got blamed for it, she might as well see what it was. She hadn't been to the old rooms since she moved out months ago. The smell greeted them first as they reached the hall. Smoke and feces. They all coughed and held their sleeves over their noses as they reached the room.

Mei kept farther back and glanced into the room. It was filled with smoke and the pungent smell of what could only be kasu. Something that probably was dragon dun was tossed in the room, but then all the beds were burnt and the feces cooked into the frames and cloth. The trunks were black and ash floated in the air.

She shouldn't take pleasure in the destroyed room, but

she swallowed her laughter at their faces as they took in all their items. They loved wrecking her things. Now they knew how it felt.

Kuro... How?

Dragons can open windows.

Open? More like smash.

Benio finally noticed Mei in the doorway. She shook a blackened cloth at her that might be clothes. "You owe us new things!"

Mei shrugged. "I was with you the whole day. How could I manage to do this?"

"Your dragon did it!" Her voice rose in pitch, making everyone wince.

"I have no clue what you mean."

Benio raised her hand to slap Mei, but Mei leaned her face forward. "Just try it," she hissed.

Benio paused, and her eyes widened. She lowered her hand. "You'll regret this."

Toshiko kicked over a ruined book and it melted into ashes. "This wouldn't have happened if you'd just leave the eta alone."

"Don't tell me you're on its side, Toshiko." Benio spat out the words and her followers fell in behind her and nodded.

"I'm on no one's side, but if you keep this up we will all do badly on exams." Toshiko nudged more items as they dissolved.

"Who cares about exams? My silk is ruined." Aimi wailed.

Toshiko's face remained bland. "Oh yes, the silk that all shodragon riders need. Maybe if you spent more time studying than combing your curls, your marks would be better."

Aimi's mouth formed an O and Toshiko stepped out of the room, leaving small puffs of ash behind her. "I'm going to the library."

"No one will marry a try hard, Toshiko!" Aimi stomped and shrieked when ash got on her uniform.

"Good." Toshiko strode down the hallway.

With the looks the rest of the recruits were giving her, Mei took off after Toshiko. Benio may not have hit her but Mei knew they outnumbered her.

"Are you sure it's wise to retaliate?" Toshiko asked as Mei passed her.

"My dragon has a mind of his own."

Mei thought she saw Toshiko's face soften for a moment. "Ah yes, they are quite protective." She nodded to Mei and entered the library.

Mei got something to eat before meeting Emiri in the library. Thinking back on the faces of the recruits made her laugh while she enjoyed the warm meal.

CHAPTER
TWENTY-THREE

Mei flopped her head on the table. "It's pointless. I'm never going to remember all the past Sho. I know Jion-sho, isn't that enough?"

"History's important. We learn from it to avoid our past mistakes." Emiri pointed at another drawing of some man with a beard and long hair. "Now who's this and what years did he rule from?"

"History may be important to daim and feu, but it never mattered to an eta." Mei glanced at the man, who looked like all the rest. "I don't know. Longhair beard-sho, and he probably ruled two hundred years ago."

Emiri shook her head. "Tomo always likes to have the former sho on his test. And you're a dragon rider now, so you have a chance to change history. Who knows, they may study about you someday."

Mei doubted it. If she somehow survived, what wing-leader would pick her? "Eta won't be mentioned, and according to these histories, we don't even exist."

Toshiko snorted from the corner of the library. "Whining

about the lack of eta in our history won't help you on the test."

In all their study sessions, Toshiko never spoke to them. Emiri and Mei exchanged a look.

"I'm pointing out the inaccuracies of the text."

Toshiko huffed. "But my point still stands, you're wasting time. Eta won't be on the test, so get over it."

"Noted." Mei held back further words and went continued to study.

A shuffling noise from the corner drew Mei's attention as Toshiko plopped next to Emiri. "You'll also want to take note of the shodragon names. They'll be just as important."

Emire froze. "Ah thanks, anything else?" She didn't know what to make of the tall girl either.

"You've been ignoring the priests that made important plant discoveries. Aoi was the first to cultivate the lycoris, or as we like to call it, the spider lily. Testing, however, went badly." Toshiko shoved a notebook into Mei's hands. "You can read now, correct? My notes are better than yours."

"Ah... Arigato?" Mei opened the notes, and they were clear and well written and she could understand them. "Why are you giving me these?"

"I don't like you."

"Okay."

Toshiko huffed again and smoothed back her perfectly kept hair. "But I recognize you will be the best competition, including Daisuke. And I like to win in a fair fight. Although destroying a lot of my notes in the kuso fire in the room was pretty clever of you."

"I didn't—"

"Yes, so you said. Get to studying. The exams are approaching."

Mei didn't dare look up from the notes in her hands now that Toshiko sat there. Not only were they good notes, they explained different theories. Mei didn't know Toshiko's game yet, but she needed the help. The normally warm atmosphere was dampened, but Mei got a lot of history done. When the sleeping librarian woke and shooed them out, Toshiko took her notes and placed them in a drawer under the other books.

She pointedly looked at Mei. "It's a good thing I made two copies. But I store these here. Hopefully there won't be a fire in the library?" Her brow raised while she waited for an answer.

"Ah, no."

With no more words, Toshiko left the room.

"She's interesting." Emiri gathered the paper and books from the low table and handed them to Mei.

"Do you think she'd give me wrong information?"

Emiri arranged her homdragon around her neck. "I don't think so. I can look over it too, but it has also been a few years since I took history."

As they left, Mei remembered she had no spare uniforms. "Do you know where I can get more uniforms and riding gear?"

"You'd have to go through the priests. I think they might be more understanding. In the past, students would need to pay for replacements."

Mei had a bit of money left over from the selection. She'd practically forgotten about it, which was strange. She'd cursed herself when she found it after seeing her father. She should have brought him the money, not food. The plan she made was to give it to him if Washi and the Sho let her go see him.

"I guess I can see if they have mercy on me. I have a feeling I'll be going through a lot of uniforms."

"Did you want to keep any spares with me? The dens are watched but not really guarded. No one dare hurt a dragon before..."

"Before me." They made it to the end of the stone hall, the lanterns giving them light but not much warmth. "That might be a wise idea. I don't have much, but they like to destroy it."

Emiri placed a hand on Mei's arm—a soft touch that she wasn't used to here since leaving her father behind. "I will do what I can. Don't let them win, Mei."

Mei put her hand over Emiri's. "You've been a true friend to me. I struggled to believe I could trust you."

"I think when the Sho told me to tend to you the first night, he knew who in the fortress didn't agree with the treatment of eta."

Before going to the lift, Mei paused. "Have they treated you badly because of me?"

"Let's just say I never fit in any way because of other reasons... We can get into that after your exams are over."

Mei realized Emiri had been a good friend to her, but Mei hadn't returned the favor to her friend. "Sorry, that it's always about me. You always do things for me, but what have I done for you?"

Emiri took her hand away. "Friendship isn't transactional. And Mei, you defend those you love with your whole body and soul. I know when I need you, you'll be there for me."

"I will, Emiri, my friend, my shinyuu."

They grasped hands. "Shinyuu," Emiri repeated.

They parted, and Mei went to the lifts. Mei didn't feel as

worried about the exams with Emiri by her side, a true friend since the beginning. Sora and Tomo probably wouldn't pass her no matter what she wrote, but she knew the information and it pushed her further. What eta would have the same opportunity? Eta may never be in history, but maybe Mei could write her own.

As she entered the lift, the hot air gusted around her hair that came loose while she studied. During the winter, the warmth was welcome. Mei had a feeling that the summer might be miserable down in the dens.

A rank smell reached her as she stopped on her floor, and before she even got to her den, she knew what to expect.

Kuro?

Yes?

Where exactly are you?

I've been eating, then swimming with the others.

I have a feeling they retaliated.

Mei walked to the den to find it had been covered with rotten food scraps. Mixed in with the heat of the den, it was pungent. They'd covered everything in old food waste. She closed her eyes and sighed. There wouldn't be much rest tonight while she tried to clean it out.

Kuro landed behind her on the ledge and snorted.

Bad meat.

This happens when we fight back.

Kuro tilted his large head, and his silver eyes swirled. *We only need to land the last punch.*

Mei wasn't sure what trouble her dragon would land her in but dominance seemed more ingrained in him. *Well, you can help me clean up this mess. I'm actually impressed that they worked this hard getting this down here. I didn't know Benio had it in her.*

She knew she needed to get started, but her body stayed frozen outside her door. The tatami mat Chin had given her was covered in rotten meat. She would lose the mat too. Good news for her, she hadn't gotten any spare uniforms yet. But her throat tightened when she saw the scraps of the white yukata her father had given her for the selection. They really took everything from her.

"I thought I smelled something." Washi's usual happy face was fixed in a frown as he looked in her destroyed den. "This is unacceptable. The others will clean this up."

Mei stepped out in front of him and bowed. "No need, sensei. It'll only make it worse. It was my dragon who wrecked their den."

After the incident, no one could actually find proof Kuro did it. Normally, that wouldn't bother Sora to pin it on Mei, but since all the other sensei knew about it, she couldn't make Mei clean it. In that matter, luck was actually on her side.

"I see."

"I didn't help them clean their room, so I guess this is my mess."

Washi shook his head. "No. As a sensei, I need to make sure the appropriate people get punished."

Mei's gut clenched as he walked away. He was on her side, but she wished he wouldn't do this.

He waited for the lift. "It isn't just about you now. They disrespected a shodragon."

Mei bowed again as he took the lift. It only felt like minutes as the other recruits came down in their sleep wear holding shovels and buckets. They all glared at Mei as they walked by. Washi stood behind them, as if daring them to make a comment.

Toshiko clutched a brush and took to what was scrawled on the walls. Ironically, Mei could now read the insults.

"I don't see why we all have to clean this when we all didn't do this. Some of us have better things to do than attack the eta," Toshiko muttered.

Washi tucked his hands into his green kimono. "I will meet any more attacks with this as long as I know about it. This has gone on long enough. There are only shodragon riders here, not eta, daim, or feu."

Mei took an extra brush and scrubbed next to Toshiko. Daisuke barely gave any effort at cleaning but Washi missed nothing.

"We'll stay here until it's spotless, Daisuke, so I suggest you use those muscles."

A muscle in his jaw ticked, but he didn't respond. Benio and her two loyal followers, Aimi and Niko, whined the whole time about the smell.

Daisuke was finally tired of it and snapped. "Just clean. We all know you three arranged this."

The smooth daim never snapped. The mask slipped when cleaning was involved. They did the rest of the cleanup in silence.

Mei wasn't sure how many hours passed but as the others took away the last of the smelly buckets, the air cleared out.

Washi bowed to her.

"Washi-sensei?"

"Yes?"

"Have you heard back from the Sho about getting leave?"

He sighed. "Do you want a cup of tea? It might be awhile

until the smell goes away. I also think I have a spare tatami mat in my room."

Mei was taken aback by his comment. "I guess?"

They went to his empty classroom and Washi slid open the door but left it open. With careful movements, he lit a fire under the clay kettle. "Now, tea can be sent for, but I still find making it myself gives it a different quality."

Mei nodded her agreement, but she didn't have a clue about what he meant. Tea wasn't really something she got to enjoy growing up. There wasn't a high demand for leaf water.

He poured them cups and the steam rose and curled in the air. Mei held the warm cup in her cold hands.

"I didn't mean to give you false hope about you getting to see your father." Washi took a careful sip of his tea and stared out the window. "I have the authority to give you permission myself, but as I said, I wanted backup from Jion-sho since it's already rare that recruits leave, especially in their first year. I thought that way it wouldn't create even more dissent with you and the other recruits."

"I don't think that's possible." Mei didn't drink from her cup but steeled herself for bad news. Was Washi trying to get out of asking the Sho?

"The Sho isn't around much these days. That's all I can really say. I didn't mean for it to take this long. But in the end you could still get a disappointing answer. Is there a way I could check on your father?" He said the words carefully, almost like he didn't want to offend her.

Mei held the warm clay cup. "I wouldn't even know how to direct you and it's asking too much from you, sensei." She wanted to take back those words as soon as she said them. He was offering to take a note to her father or maybe she could give him the money. Why did she turn him down? Something tugged at her to wait for the Sho.

Washi gestured for her to drink. "I'm hoping for good news. But it's more important right now that you do well on your exams. Your father would want you to."

An ached filled her heart. "How would you know what he wants?" The bitterness at being in the fortress leaked out. Even though she knew he was right, anger at being stuck here boiled in her body, and she couldn't hold it inside. "The eta just want to live like everyone else. Who decided that we don't get dragons? Who decided that we were less?" Tears leaked from her eyes and she gasped for air. Why did it become so hard to breathe? She didn't have time to melt down but she couldn't stop. "It'll never matter that I have a shodragon. I'm still an eta, and my father's dying. And they will still torture me until I break. I can't care about exams."

"I understand."

"Do you?" Mei couldn't believe she was practically shouting at the sensei who'd tried to help her.

Washi placed his cup down and reached into his obi and pulled out a small piece of cloth. There was nothing special about it. It was worn and looked like cheap material.

"You're a rider now, but at heart, you're an eta. As an eta, I'm going to trust you." He gently held the cloth in his fingers. "I'm here today because my mother gave me up. She left my father, who would have burned the world down for her. Even when loving her meant he would have to give up his status." Washi closed his eyes. "But eta are stubborn about those they love. And my mother knew there wasn't place for her son if she stayed in his life. It was better to pretend that my father adopted me from a dead family member from up north. She disappeared, and I have a feeling your father would do the same."

Mei placed her full cup of tea down to avoid dropping it. "Your mother was an eta?"

"Yes. But I got to grow up as a daim. I didn't have to fight in the same way as you, only live in fear of someone discovering who my mother really was. Keep fighting, Mei. Not all the sensei and recruits are against you. Some may need to see you prove more than others. But don't worry about Sora or Tomo. Prove to the Sho and me you are worthy of being in a winglegion. And yes, that means passing your exams. The Sho will be back and I will go to him then. But don't throw away what your father gave you."

"I don't mean to, but I can't just let him go."

Washi put the cloth back in his obi and smiled. "No one wants you to forget him. Trust the eta to help him until you can see him again."

"What if he dies before I see him again?" she asked, her voice shaking as she whispered the words she didn't dare to think.

"Then he will live on in you. It will hurt, but the ones who die never truly leave us."

Mei left her tea untouched and sat for a quiet moment in Washi's classroom. The world felt different in here.

"Arigato, sensei."

He stood and bowed as she left. "It will all come out right in the end."

"I would like to believe that, sensei."

TWENTY-FOUR

Daisuke wasn't worried about the exams. His only competition would most likely be the girl whose parents cremated the dead. Tosh-something. He may not make the appearance of studying, but he learned all this information long before he got a dragon. The real joke would be the eta and the practical exams. Somehow the eta mastered the yumi bow in these last months and he still couldn't even communicate with his dragon.

The annoying girls brought him his food, and he ate it in the room, away from the others. He wrinkled his nose. Did the kitchen only know how to make miso soup? And he swore the room still smelled of dragon kasu. He ate the rice and pushed the rest away as Benio twittered next to him. Did she ever shut up? In his worst nightmare, his parents were talking about an arranged marriage with her. Being a shodragon rider saved him for a while, but her father ran the largest pleasure street, and his parents only saw money.

"Maybe we could put something in the dragon's food to

make it sick," Benio stated, and the curly haired girl laughed in agreement.

Daisuke snarled and gripped Benio by her uniform, almost knocking over his food as he stood over her. Her feet barely touched the ground. Her loudly painted lips trembled. "Don't go after the dragon."

"But you..."

"I will not lose rank because you killed a dragon. Washi's now watching all of us, and we all will be punished if something happens to that lizard."

Benio's face paled, and she quieted. Daisuke shoved her away. "Leave."

The girls ran out of the room. Playing politics was a dangerous game. If he'd gotten caught when he'd injured the dragon the first time, he would be over. He was an idiot. The Emperor clarified that someone else was doing a better job than him getting rid of the eta. For a bit he thought it might be the dragonless daim, but he'd rescued her, and now he'd disappeared somewhere. Then there was the healer that the eta hung around, but she was lacking in motivation. He'd sent out feelers, and nothing in the healer's history would let him believe she cared about the Emperor's approval.

He would lose any boon if he wasn't the one to take care of M—the eta. But it would have to be done without harming the shodragon. They would shun those that killed a dragon almost as bad as an eta. He'd let his anger get the better of him before, but this time he wouldn't. When he became Sho, he wanted the Emperor on his side.

The dragon roared, and Daisuke made his way to Sora's room. Half of the exam would be in her room and the other half in Tomo's. Sora made comments about cheating and basically directed them all at the eta. Well, it couldn't be Sora who the Emperor was talking about. He studied the eta, who stared straight ahead like always, standing in the back of the room as if it was making a point. The eta got mouthier and mouthier as the days passed. There was danger in letting it think it was human. He would need to stop admiring it. He didn't need a conquest with it. Not if he had to get rid of it. When the eta was gone, it would be terribly boring though.

Sora placed the exam in front of him. He pushed out thoughts of the eta and got to work. The time went by quickly and the dragon roar shocked most of them. The idiot Kenta dramatically sighed and flopped over on his desk.

"I think there's nothing left in my brain."

True, but was there anything to begin with? "This is only the first test."

Kenta groaned and followed him out of the room.

As much as he didn't care for any of the other recruits, he would need them. They were fodder in his political games. He would be good, as long as Benio didn't open her mouth about him hurting the dragon and he didn't make any other mistakes that others knew about. They all took a short break and the tall girl was muttering to herself about something on the test. Didn't the other families prepare them for this? Poor feu shouldn't be allowed here either.

Daisuke sat in Tomo's room. The sensei didn't even give Mei—the eta—a test.

"I need a test, sensei."

"You can't write. I won't grade it, anyway."

The eta stood there until Tomo thrust a test at it. She didn't give up, that's for sure.

This test was harder. The past Sho didn't stand out as

much. The Sho and the Emperor ruled in harmony according to what history they learned.

After the dragon roared, they all went out into the fields to show their control with fire and shooting the yumi. Dazai and Washi would grade Mei fairly. Annoying. Her control of fire beat out all of them.

"Form!"

Daisuke held in his sigh and held his body still as the sensei moved around.

"Shoot."

At least Dazai didn't prattle on. They all took their turns shooting. Kenta missed the target entirely. What did that baka do these last months? Next to him, the eta laughed. Daisuke held his lips still. It was funny. Kenta really was an idiot. How on earth did a dragon choose him? But considering that one picked an eta, the standards must be falling.

Now their shodragons joined them, and he ran his hand along his dragon's scales. She was stunning. The only chore he enjoyed was seeing to her scales and hide. She nudged him with her head, and he let himself show emotion behind her neck.

"Hey, beautiful. Let's show them what we got." Her eyes whirled, and he scratched under her eyelid.

He fed her hostas, and the burning flames filled him in his chest. They focused on the target and she hit it dead on.

"Perfect," Daisuke murmured to his dragon. They were each given three tries, and Daisuke hit the center every time.

Now it was the eta's turn. Washi stood and watched her while holding a book bound in twine marking down the score. He smiled at the eta as it approached.

The sensei pretty much adopted it like a pet. Daisuke fought to keep his face from showing his disdain.

Some are more discreet than your blatant attempts.

Daisuke's eyes widened. He drew his gaze away from the eta. That's right, there were only two sensei who treated the eta with respect. Two sensei who were the head of their own winglegion and would have the most immediate promotion to being Sho. And one sensei who treated the eta with special treatment.

As the eta's flames hit the target center each time and Washi nodded his approval, Daisuke held back his laugh. Could it be Washi this whole time?

Daisuke didn't know anything about him, but something told him that if he didn't act quickly, he might just lose the game, and he hated losing.

TWENTY-FIVE

Mei didn't know it was possible but the food tasted sweeter after the exams finished. The others ate quietly, too exhausted to bother her for once. It was nice hearing the sound of chopsticks and spoons against bowls as all the recruits ate. Toshiko barely touched her food while Kenta shoved rice in his mouth like an eta eating for the first time in days.

After Mei finished, she saw Washi standing in the doorway. He made eye contact with her and tilted his head to the side.

She cleaned her dishes quickly and went up to his classroom.

His face broke out in a grin. "The Sho came back an hour ago."

Mei could feel every beat of her heart.

"Not only is he making some other sensei grade you fairly, but he also spoke with me about a pass."

"Washi-sensei, please..."

"As long as it's only for an hour, he gave you a pass. Only

the guards that morning will know of it. He doesn't want the other recruits to know. However, I have a feeling they will find out eventually. Nothing stays a secret long here."

Mei stopped herself from throwing her arms around the sensei. "He said I could go?"

Washi held out a red pass with a black dragon marking. Under the dragon it had the number one. "It isn't much time. But you did very well on your exams and usually there's some sort of reward for good marks. This might not happen again, recruit."

Mei took the pass with shaking hands. "It will be enough." She could take her father the money.

"Go early."

"I don't think I will sleep tonight at all."

Washi smiled. "It was well earned."

Mei swallowed and bowed before she left. Even if it was only for an hour, she could have some time with her father. The pass was more than silver to her. She could keep going as long as she knew her father would be okay.

IN THE EXCITEMENT of soon seeing her father, Mei hardly slept. When light peeked through the window, Mei jumped out of bed and left her sleeping dragon to go grab breakfast, her pass and money carefully tucked away in her obi.

The scents of fresh fish and eggs occupied the air as Mei approached the silently working staff. They grabbed a tray, and Mei asked, "Could I... package this up to eat outside?"

The lady quirked an eyebrow at Mei and glanced out at the snowy grounds. She shook her head and muttered to herself as she filled up three bowls. After stacking them and covering the top one, she wrapped them in cloth. "Bring the dishes back clean."

Mei nodded and dashed out the door. She could at least give her father something to eat. Yui had said she would look out for him, but extra food was scarce and the communal food only offered tiny portions.

She approached the guards at the gate and bowed. "Washi-sensei told me I could go out this morning." She showed them the pass.

They took the pass and eyed it carefully and didn't hand it back. "You only have an hour." She bowed again and passed through.

Mei took off down the hill at a fast clip, her feet crunching through the hardened snow. She clutched the food and shivered without an over robe. Her riding jacket remained bloodstained and torn in the den. Half a year ago, the cold had been part of her eta life. Now, with clothing that covered her and the hot den she slept in, the cold came as a shock to her. She had cleaned these clothes every night and still needed to see about getting a spare set.

The temple entrance appeared on her right, and the red torii gates with fluttering lanterns winked at her as she walked. Her life as an eta had changed at that moment, and she'd left behind her father. Mei's heart burned as she picked up her pace. She'd had zero contact with him or other eta in months. She'd followed his instructions, but this time, she could see him without worrying him.

Her breath fogged in the air. Mei longed to wrap her father in her arms and watch him eat the food she'd brought.

Merchants with their dendragons set up for the day, the bright colors of the dragons flashing against the snow. The fish smells greeted her, and Fat Choi put out his daily catch in his stall. When she caught his eye, she froze, but he bowed low to her and continued filling his bins.

Mei's lips parted in confusion, and then she realized he only saw the uniform of a shodragon rider. He didn't recognize the girl who'd stolen a fish. She bit her bottom lip and kept moving down the hill. The snow and dirt mixed in the road, making the path muddy as the sun came up over the mountains. The buildings turned into a maze of shacks, but Mei's heart knew the way to the worn-down hut in the middle of the chaos.

Her heart skipped a few beats as she ran toward home. She ran to the door of the familiar shack and burst inside. A startled family's round eyes peeked at her from the floor.

"Who are you?" Mei asked.

The family glanced at her clothes, and they all bowed low to the dirt floor. "No one."

Mei waved her hand in frustration. "Where's the man who lives here?"

They all glanced at one another, and the woman in the back held her children close. "This was empty."

Empty. Mei blinked in the dark room and staggered a step back out of her old home. Still at the door, she whispered, "Do you know where he is?" Her hands trembled. "Do you?"

They all bowed low. "We go missing," the woman said, head to the ground. "There's no difference."

"It makes a difference to me," Mei muttered as she left. She stumbled away from the hut, her body numb from the cold. She shuffled her feet through the mud. Where could he be? He had to still be alive somewhere. When a place emptied in the eta district, it was open to whoever wanted it. Mei ran in a panic toward Yui's house.

Yui stood outside the door, and when Mei approached, she backed up into the house.

Mei burst through the door, and again the family inside backed against the wall. "Yui?" Mei asked.

Yui's eyes widened. "Who are you?"

"It's me, Mei."

Her mouth gaped, and she scanned Mei's clothing. "Why are you here? Where did you go? What?"

"Please, come talk to me." Mei grabbed her hand and dragged her outside. She pulled Yui between two shacks, and Yui glanced around, fiddling with her fingers.

"You just vanished. We thought they got you."

"No, I got a dragon, but that isn't important." Yui's eyes shot open. "Where's my father?" Mei asked.

Yui shook her head. "More of the eta vanished in the night. You know how it looks."

Mei's throat tightened. In the morning hours, after the rains, there were sometimes marks in the ground—large marks left by a body being dragged through the dirt. Odd round footprints would follow. Mei had seen for herself what left those footprints. The jorogumo never took too many, but the shodragon riders couldn't stop them all. Somehow, it was always the eta who were taken. Disposable.

"There were... drag marks?"

Yui didn't look at Mei as she softly said, "When I went in the morning to take him some spare food, there were those markings in the snow."

The world around Mei turned into a nightmare. Her father had been taken, dragged away by those creatures. He wouldn't even have seen what had grabbed him in the night. Mei's legs gave out, and her knees hit the cold, muddy ground. She dropped the food, and her hands clenched in the rocky mud. Everything around her blurred, and the sounds of eta waking and moving flitted through the silent screams in her head.

"Mei?" Yui squatted next to her and shook her shoulder. "You know there's nothing we can do."

Mei mutely nodded. "But I can do something," she said, her voice cracking. She needed to get Kuro and go back to the caves to find her father. She bolted up and shoved the discarded food into Yui's hands. Her body burned, but she ran all the way back through the streets. The market now full of people, Mei shoved her way through the crowds, leaving muddy handprints on their clothing. They all shouted at her back as she tore her way through. *I need to get Kuro.*

Slipping and sliding up the mountain, she reached the gate. There was no time to collapse, and she screamed in her mind, *Kuro!*

No response.

Kuro!

Nothing.

Kuro, I need you! Kuro!

Her mind was empty. She continued through the gate, and a large crowd of recruits and sensei blocked her way.

"Excuse me." She pushed her way through.

"Stop," a voice called out. The Emperor stood to the right, surrounded by guards.

Mei froze and hastily bowed. "I'm sorry. I need to get my dragon. My father—"

"Your dragon was taken away."

Mei charged at the Emperor, but the guards threw her down. "Where is he?" Her voice was tense in the quiet courtyard.

"You again deserted your station, recruit. Your shodragon was taken, and you are to be punished."

Mei jumped up and ran at him again, and again she was thrown into the slick snow. Her back skidded along the stones. She got to her feet. "He's mine. He believes in me! You can't take him away."

"There's no use for a recruit who cannot follow the rules. I warned you about desertion."

"Desertion? What do you mean?"

"Where were you?"

Mei's mouth gaped, and she searched for Washi-sensei. His green robes were missing from all those who had gathered. The fortress guards and their dendragons circled her like she was a wild animal trying to escape. "Washi-sensei gave me permission to leave. The Sho as well. The guards have my pass."

The Emperor tucked his hands in his sleeves. "He said nothing to the other sensei, and the Sho isn't here."

She looked over the crowd, and finally, she spotted green. Not caring who was in the way, she shoved her way toward Washi-sensei. There he was, but his face had no smile. She bowed. "Washi-sensei, tell them you allowed me to go see my father."

Washi blinked in fake concern. "I'm sorry, I don't think you understood me. It isn't allowed for recruits to leave while they're in training. No exceptions."

"But—" The man before her changed in an instant. The books, making the other recruits stop bullying her, his mother being an eta. Lies. All lies, and she'd believed him.

Mei stepped back, her throat closing. *Kuro, Kuro, Kuro!* she screamed in her mind. What had they done to him? She turned back. "Is my dragon dead?"

"No," the Emperor responded. "It is a bad omen to kill a dragon. He will be kept until he fades away."

Her father. Her dragon. Mei stood still, and her fingers traced the hem of her uniform. The dry mud cracked off her skin and flaked to the ground. She grasped her elbows, hugging herself to keep her insides in her skin. The betrayal of Washi spread in her bone.

"I'll kill you, sensei."

His face stayed cold but a tiny smile stretched on his lips. He bent over and whispered harshly so only she could hear, "Good luck with that, eta."

With an animalistic cry she threw herself at him but the guards blocked her way and held her down.

"Due to the choices of this one recruit, we are forced to punish the entire class," the Emperor said to the crowd. "However, after three days, the eta will be executed. This is the policy with those who betray the shodragons."

Words hit Mei's ears, but only emptiness remained. She'd lost everything already. Her mind filled with images of the jorogumo ripping her father apart. With a choking sob, she fell, and footsteps surrounded her, but she didn't care anymore.

Mei let them lift her and take her to a group of wooden poles in the dirt. She let them strip her naked in the cold air and tie her to the pole. Her classmates stood naked around her. They were to stay out until the next day as punishment for letting one of their own fall. Benio, Aimi, and Niko tried to cover themselves as they shivered. Toshiko held herself tall, and with disappointed eyes she watched Mei.

Their hate-filled gazes didn't bother Mei. She wanted to die. *Kuro, please.* Nothing. Her mind was as empty as it had been before Kuro had chosen her. Her worthlessness poured into her mind. *You shouldn't have chosen me. I'm just an eta. I am nothing.*

A warm hand jarred her out of her thoughts, and her bleary eyes saw a kind round face. "Emiri?"

Emiri nodded and made a show of checking Mei's body. "I'm supposed to keep you alive until the execution." Her voice faded at the irony of her words.

"I don't mean to be a burden. I'm sorry I wasted your lessons." Her tone was dull and indifferent.

"What can I do?"

"The creatures took my father, and the monsters took Kuro." Mei peered at Emiri. "Is there anything you can do?"

"Mei…"

Mei closed her eyes. "Arigato, Emiri. Seeing my name for the first time was a genuine gift."

Tears ran down Emiri's face as she finished checking Mei. A guard escorted her away.

During the day, the sun warmed their naked skin. When the sun set, the wind blew against their flesh in an unforgiving manner.

Mei's numb body would revive a bit with periodic treatment, but she wished for the numbness. It was time for her to die. This was what happened to eta who rose above their station.

In the morning, the crisp snow gleamed as the sun glistened overhead. From the fortress, a group of sensei strode toward the shamed recruits.

Sora-sensei studied all her students gravely. "You all bring shame to shodragon riders."

They all bowed their heads, but Mei raised hers. "Sensei, I think it is you who brings shame."

Everyone looked at Sora, their eyes wide. "What do you have to say, eta?"

Mei smiled. "Not much. I'm dead, after all." She met Sora's eyes. "What does it matter what I think?"

Sora pursed her lips. "Exactly. Come, recruits. You are now to clean the fortress for the rest of the day."

"Don't worry, the eta will be gone soon," Mei called out to their backs. "You can live in your ignorance."

They kept moving, and Mei was alone with the expanse of white before her. The guards didn't bother standing close to her, as if they knew Mei wouldn't even try to escape.

When Emiri would come to do a slight healing on her fingers and toes, Mei wouldn't speak. Her mind was occupied with her father's death and Kuro being trapped and alone. Throughout the second day, Mei called to him in her mind. It felt like he had never been there to begin with. She moistened her cracked lips and leaned against the ropes. Her body was so exhausted and drained that it fell into a fitful sleep.

A WOMAN STOOD *at the edge of a cliff, her dark hair blowing in the wind. She wore the fighting robes of a shodragon rider, with a black and silver obi around her middle. Mei frowned and stood at the edge with her.*

"Why are you here?" Mei asked.

The woman continued to look forward, and she didn't answer. Mei followed her eyes and saw nothing but water. She gazed at the woman.

"Who are you?" Mei asked.

There was no answer. The woman turned, and her dark brown eyes stared at Mei. The wind blew against them in powerful gusts. She didn't speak, but she raised a hand and cupped Mei's cheek. Her eyes held the words she wanted to say.

"Tell me. Tell me what you want."

MEI'S EYES OPENED. A face hovered mere inches from her.

TWENTY-SIX

Chin had lost track of time. After a servant would come to feed him, he would sleep again. He had refused to eat at first, but then his mother had come back. So now Chin ate every meal. Trapped on his stomach with his ankles and wrists chained down, he didn't know if his mother would let him out. The short bathroom breaks were his only mercy. This locked room with the chains bolted to the floor haunted his dreams, and as a child, even the mention of it had caused him to shake with fear.

His wrists chafed under the bonds, and he gave up trying to loosen them by reaching his fingers down. They just weren't long enough. He painstakingly let slight movement into his shoulders, the muscles tight from being in one position for so long.

He closed his eyes and wished he were trapped in the cave with the jorogumo. The door slid open, and socked feet approached him. A servant knelt to spoon-feed him his meal.

"I guess it is better to sleep through all this," he muttered.

The servant didn't answer but held the spoon to his mouth.

Most of the food dribbled out the side of his mouth as he tried to eat while lying on his stomach. He only had a few moments of consciousness to eat. When the servant finished, she lifted his head to wipe the food from the side of his face. Then she wiped the floor and placed his head back down.

His eyes felt heavy, but then he heard a commotion outside his door.

"Mother, you can't keep him in there!" Kazu shouted.

A loud slap sounded outside, and Chin recoiled. "Stay out of it."

"Why are you doing this to him?"

"I already explained it. You know what's inside him. It has to be this way. Your meddling will doom us all."

His brother paused, then said, "You can't really believe it. I'm going in there—"

Another slap sounded. "Get out of this house and don't come back until I'm finished. I'm the only one who will take care of this. Your father's too weak-willed."

"Because he's sane!"

"Take him out, now."

Shuffling, then silence. When Chin's torture had started as a child, he would always ask, "Why are you doing this?" As he drifted off, he wondered what his mother had meant and what good it would do him to know any more.

He woke to yet another sting on his bare back and accidentally yelped from shock, which made the next lash fall down harder against his skin. He bit his cheeks, tasting blood, but he stayed silent.

When Mother finished and he heard her cleaning the strap, he took a risk and asked, his voice cracking, "What's inside me?"

His mother stopped cleaning. "What do you mean?"

Don't talk. Stop now. Chin ignored his voice of reason. "You told Kazu that something is inside me. Is this why you do this? What evil is making you do this to your son?"

Aiko's soft footfalls approached until her toes were next to his nose. "You aren't supposed to know that. Forget what you heard."

Chin squeezed his eyes shut, and his voice shook as he said, "Just tell me what it is, then I can live with this. Tell me there's a reason for all this. Tell me I'm not going through this for nothing. Tell me, please."

"No." She nudged his face with her toe. "Because of this, we will need more sessions."

"Mother, please."

She stepped away and hung up the strap. "Accept your plight with thankfulness. Be grateful I'm strong enough to do this for you." With those last words, she slid the door shut and left Chin alone.

Tears fell from his eyes, and he wanted to curl up in his bed. One time, when he was young, he'd had a terrible fever. He remembered the comfort of his mother's cool hands on his head. She'd stayed up at night, watching over him as he'd almost died. His mother even protected spiders, but not her own son? What had happened? What was inside him that could make his mother do this to him? If she let him out, he wouldn't wait. He would brave the blue sky and leave this world.

His food came in, and after the humiliating wipe down of his face, Chin looked forward to being lost in sleep. However, the grogginess never came, and Chin was left to study the wood floors. He turned his head back and forth to stretch his neck. Had they forgotten to drug his food? Chin laughed sadly. For once, he would have welcomed the nothingness. It was like his mother always knew how to increase the pain.

Time passed, and Chin's mind didn't let him rest. His body shivered from the cold. Then the door slid open, and quiet footsteps padded into the room. Chin craned his head, but then his brother's face appeared right before him.

"You need to go," Kazu whispered.

"What are you doing? If Mother finds you here—"

Kazu's hand clasped over Chin's mouth. "I am getting you out of here. A friend of mine needs your help."

My help? Chin thought. His brother moved his hand away and unlocked the manacles. He would finish one and set it down as carefully as possible so as not to make a noise.

Chin wanted to moan as he stretched his body. His brother helped him stand, and Chin needed to lean most of his weight on him.

"I will heal you when we get out of here," he whispered.

Chin nodded but could barely move. It would be better if he healed him before, but who knew when Mother would come back for another session. Kazu wrapped Chin's arm around his shoulders, and they headed out the door. Kazu shut the door behind them. They headed to the backyard and not the front. Did Kazu expect him to get over the wall in his condition? Chin thought it might be better to go back rather than risk getting caught. He could only imagine the punishment.

They reached the yard, and a rope hung over the side with loops attached. Kazu lowered one loop over Chin and tucked it under his rear. Then he did the same with the other one. His brother then pulled them both up with his arms. His brother's arms bulged from the strain of lifting two bodies, but they reached the top of the wall.

"This is where we jump down," Kazu said.

"Great."

"What are you doing?" The shout came from the direction of the house. In the doorway, the lamplight from inside outlined their mother's figure. For a moment her eyes almost glowed green in the dark night.

"Leaving," Kazu shouted back.

"My son, if you leave, you have no idea what will happen."

"I think I do."

"Chin, I'm doing all this for you."

Chin stared at his mother. She seemed smaller from up on the wall. "I'm going, Mother. Just let me go."

"Guards!" she shrieked into the night.

Kazu leaped into the darkness and rolled when they hit the snow. His brother stood, but Chin lay on the ground, unable to stand. He could hear the clacking of his brother's homdragon as she came up to Chin.

"We can't heal him now. We need to run."

Run? Chin laughed. Then his brother yanked him up and tossed him over his shoulder. The jarring movements of Kazu running on the slick snow sent constant jolts of pain through Chin's body. Shouts came from behind them as the house guards started after them. Following them in the snow would be easy, as they were leaving an obvious trail.

Chin's voice warbled as he said, "Leave me. You'll get away faster. You have an apprenticeship, and you'll be—"

"Shut it." His brother ran faster.

The homdragon chittered next to them and bounded ahead, leading them through the thickening trees. The incline steepened, and his brother slipped in the wet snow. Chin looked back and guards closed in on them. They swung their kusarigama.

"Kazu, leave me."

Kazu gasped for air as he reached out for a tree to steady himself. "I came to get you. I won't leave you."

All at once, the guards released the chains, and the hooks latched on to Kazu's legs. They yanked back, and Kazu fell on his face, dropping Chin in a heap on the ground. Chin rolled down the mountain, and a tree stopped his descent toward the guards. The four men approached and stared down at their victims.

"You boys know better than this," the head guard chastised.

"Let us go. You know what she does to him," Kazu said. He turned, but they still had his legs locked with the kusarigama. Chin felt a slight warmth growing in his body. Kazu's homdragon had spat a green salve on Chin's back. Some of the pain released, but his legs and arms didn't want to push up his body.

"You know why she does it." The head guard directed his words to Kazu. They weren't worried about Chin.

Kazu met Chin's eyes, and he kept shifting his eyes in the direction they'd been running before the guards had caught them. Chin shook his head and rested it on the ground. He couldn't move anymore. His body had taken on too much, and even with the bit of healing, he couldn't outrun the guards. He should just go back to Mother.

Then he felt a sharp bite on his ear, and he flinched. The angry eyes of a homdragon glared down at him, reminding him of Mei in some way. She'd stood up to the fish vendor despite her bleeding back. Chin gritted his teeth and pushed his arms under him. He bit back a gasp of pain as he stood unsteadily on the snowy ground.

Kazu bolted up and flung himself at the guards, bowling them over, and they all rolled down the hill. Chin wanted to make sure his brother was okay, but the homdragon tugged at his leg, and he started the painful jog up the mountain.

The red torii gates of the temple appeared out of the darkness, and without pausing, the homdragon kept going toward the temple.

Chin held his side as he ran after the dragon. He assumed she knew where Kazu had been taking him. So far, he didn't hear any guards behind him, and the stone path was clear of snow, so he wouldn't leave a trail for the guards to follow. The guards' dendragons might smell him, though. They veered off the path and came to a building beside the temple.

The homdragon bounded through the door, and Chin gasped as a cloud of incense greeted him.

A round face with wide eyes met him, and Emiri bowed quickly. "Scatter these in different directions," she said to her homdragon and his brother's. They looked like pieces of Chin's clothes. The two dragons scampered off, and Emiri approached him.

"Let me wrap your back now."

Chin shivered as she wrapped his wounds. She made no

comment about how he'd received them. She handed him a thick top.

"Anything else?" she asked, her tone leaving no room for lies.

"Just stiffness in my arms and legs."

She lifted his pant legs and rubbed a different salve over his legs and shoulders before he put on his jacket. He still hurt, but a blooming sense of relief flowed through his body.

"What's going on?" Chin asked.

"Mei needs you."

"Mei?"

Emiri bit her lip. "The Sho is gone and the Emperor ordered this. They're accusing her of desertion for going to see her father. They took away Kuro and are going to kill her. She's tied out in the snow, and the creatures took her father." Emiri's dark eyes met his. "You know how to get to the creatures' nests. You can help her find him, can't you?"

Shells, how many days was he gone? Go back to the jorogumo? Chin let out a bark of laughter. He'd just mentioned that he would rather die with them than stay with his mother. Why not? Might as well die helping Mei.

"How am I supposed to free her?"

"Only two guards are watching her, and I can drug their food so they'll sleep. Do you know a way to the caves?"

"Through the fortress."

"We need to leave now. The guards your mother sent won't be tricked for long, and your brother's homdragon probably wants to be with him again. What happened to him?"

"He threw himself at the four guards."

Emiri's eyes widened. "That sounds like him."

"You know him?"

She nodded. "We don't have time right now. Let's go."

Chin obediently followed Emiri out of the building, and they headed up the mountain. Emiri must have gone to Kazu. How did she know they were brothers? How did she know Kazu? They both had healing homdragons, so they must have met that way.

Chin wanted to lie down in the snow and sleep, but he forced his legs to follow Emiri up the mountain. They reached the fortress gates and knocked on a wooden door.

A voice came from the grate. "Is that you, Emiri?"

"Yes."

The door opened, and Chin and Emiri went through. A tall, lanky guard appeared on the other side. "You're out late."

Emiri gave him a flirty smile. "You know, only the rarest plants bloom in the moonlight and snow."

The guard smiled back and leaned toward her. "Who's he?"

She waved off his question. "He works down with the priests. I met him on the way up here."

The guard gave Chin a hostile glance but accepted Emiri's story. "You better get inside. It's cold out."

"Don't worry, I will."

They headed off toward the fortress, then Emiri veered left, into the kitchen. A tired-looking servant was putting together some bento meals.

"You up late, Nona?"

The lady sighed. "I'm on the night shift for the two watching the eta."

Emiri stepped close to the food and slipped something in the rice when the lady's back was turned. "Let me know if you need more of that salve for your back."

Nona turned and smiled. "You're a gem for checking on me so often. Get some rest." She glanced at Chin. "Both of you."

Emiri bowed and left the kitchen, with Chin trailing behind her. They entered an empty classroom that overlooked the field, and she handed him a satchel.

"These are some pre-made bandages. They will not be as strong as freshly made ones, but they will help. I labeled them." She stood closer. "I stole this. It has plants in it for the dragons, but you may not have Kuro with you. I don't know where they put him. Also clothing for Mei."

Chin thought he recognized the satchel, but he wasn't sure where he had seen it before. He slung the satchel over his back, wincing as it brushed against his slightly healed wounds.

"Still hurts? I'm sorry I have nothing stronger to use."

"I'm used to it."

It was obvious she wanted to say something more, but she clenched her jaw and faced the open window. A lone pole waited in the distance. From inside the room, Chin couldn't tell who was tied to the pole, but the small body belonged to Mei. His chest tightened. She was already too thin to be out in this cold weather.

Chin gripped the strap of the satchel until his knuckles turned white. "Why did she leave? Didn't she know they would do this?"

"She got permission from Washi-sensei to check on her father since the eta are disappearing. He told her she was cleared to go."

"Washi?" Chin pictured the teacher's jovial face. "I thought he supported Mei."

"Apparently not."

They stayed silent, and finally, the serving woman headed toward the two guards.

"Get ready."

They left the room, and in the hall, they ran straight into Daisuke. He glanced between them and then at the empty classroom behind them.

"Good on you. I didn't think you had it in you, Chin-*san*." Daisuke smirked.

Chin went to step around Daisuke, but he got in the way. "Step aside."

"Where are you off to in such a hurry? You know women like to cuddle after."

Chin lunged at Daisuke, but Emiri put a hand on his elbow. She bowed to Daisuke. "He's escorting me to treat the eta. Excuse us."

Daisuke bowed, but Chin didn't like the way Daisuke's eyes followed them as they left.

TWENTY-SEVEN

"Mei. Mei, wake up. We need to go."

Her eyes opened from a dream, and Chin's face was mere inches from her own. "What?"

"The guards are out. We need to go."

She raised her arms, and they were free. "What are you doing?"

"Saving you. Come on. I can't lift you." He threw a yukata over her naked body. Chin was saving her.

She leaned her head back against the pole. "I don't want to be saved."

"What?"

Mei shoved him away. "Let me die."

He grabbed her shoulders. "After everything, you're giving up here?"

"There's nothing left. The jorogumo took my father, and the Emperor took Kuro. I'm an eta, Chin. This is what we do. We die."

Chin grabbed her jaw and glared at her. "We'll find your

father and get Kuro back. But right now, I need you to walk. You didn't want to die the day I met you, and I'll be damned if I let you give up now!"

His words and anger cut through Mei, and she grabbed his arms. "You'll help me?"

Chin clenched his fists. "If I have to go back to that hellish cave to save your father, I will do it. Just move."

Mei's sore and frozen body didn't function very well, but the thick yukata Chin had brought felt so comforting against her skin. Chin pulled her along toward a back entrance of the fortress.

Mei jerked against him. "Why are we going there?"

"Supplies. Also, the entrance to the jorogumo caves is down there."

"What?"

"No one uses this door, and if you keep behind me when anyone approaches, you should be fine. It's late, and no one will be around."

Mei followed him through the twisting tunnels. After a while, he was still holding her hand. She let herself tighten the hold, taking a bit of strength from him. She wasn't familiar with these tunnels, but she trusted Chin.

He paused, then turned back to her and whispered, "Up ahead is a room full of spare gear. I know the priest who's in charge of it, so let me go get something stronger for us to wear in a fight." Mei nodded. "Besides a bow, is there another weapon you would like?"

"A short sword, and also some knives." Just in case there was close combat.

Chin raised his hand to make sure she stayed there, and he disappeared around the corner. His voice traveled through the tunnel as he said, "They requested me to get some gear and deliver it up to the second-year rooms."

The priest clicked his tongue. "They are more than capable of getting it themselves. It's late for them to be making demands. I also haven't seen you in awhile."

"Family emergency. It's fine. I like to stay busy."

Mei could picture the priest shaking his head. "Very well, get what you need."

A few moments later, Chin thanked the priest and came back to Mei. He led her to an empty room where they could change.

As she dressed, she quietly called out to Kuro in her mind. Chin must have sensed her worry.

"We will find him, but we may need to go without him to get your father. They won't kill him. I'm guessing they are keeping him sedated until you were to be put to death."

After tying her obi, Mei swiped away a stray tear. "You're right. I can't wait any longer to go after Father."

They finished latching on their weapons, and Chin took them to gather some food and torches. He was apparently well-liked by all the priests and had no trouble with them believing him.

He had a familiar satchel on his back, and with a grimace, he adjusted it to fit more of the food. Before Mei could ask about the satchel, Chin directed her to go deeper into the mountain's catacombs.

Tired and sore, she kept going. They went deeper and deeper until the darkness became an inky blackness beyond the beam of the torchlight. After a few hours, Chin stopped.

"We should rest for a bit."

"Probably wise," said a voice from the dark.

Daisuke stepped into the light.

Chin stood in front of Mei, blocking her from Daisuke. He placed his hand on the hilt of his katana.

Daisuke smiled. "I'm not here to fight you."

"Then leave." Chin backed up and directed Mei to do the same.

Daisuke crossed his arms and leaned against the wall. He had his own pack and weapons. "I'm here to help you."

"We'd rather not have to watch our backs and our fronts. Leave," Mei said from behind Chin. Her arm burned from where he had grabbed her in the pool. She would bet that once their guard was down, he would attack. If Washi betrayed her, she could never trust Daisuke. He was wasting their time.

"The longer you argue with me, the less time you have to save her father."

Chin gritted his teeth. "Then leave."

"No."

"I will make you leave."

Mei placed her hand on his arm. "My father, he's already been..." The rest of Mei's sentence drifted off. She couldn't choke out the words. She didn't even know if they would find a body.

"He will kill us," Chin replied.

She rose onto her toes and whispered in Chin's ear, "Let them handle him. He doesn't believe they're awake."

Chin's brows furrowed, and his eyes flicked back and forth between Daisuke and Mei. She set her jaw. If it was between Daisuke dying and her father, she would leave Daisuke behind. Wasn't it what he deserved?

Chin leaned down, his lips near her ear. "We can't just let him die."

Mei stared blankly back at him. She'd suffered at

Daisuke's hand more than he had, and he must have seen her answer in her face, because a look of resignation crossed his features. She sighed. "We won't let him die," she whispered in his ear. *Maybe.* Didn't Chin understand that Daisuke would kill her if given the chance? She couldn't talk to him about it now. The minutes wasted were already eating at her.

Chin cocked an eyebrow at her but motioned at Daisuke. "Fine, you can come, but walk in front of me."

Daisuke shrugged and went to the front. He gave Mei a sly smile as he passed, then continued in the direction they'd been heading before he'd interrupted.

Mei held up a torch. Chin kept adjusting the pack on his back like it hurt him.

"Do you want me to carry the pack?" She walked next to him. Neither of them seemed ready to fight the monsters.

He shook his head. "You need to rest as much as you can. We should stop soon and get a bit of sleep. Then I can put on the bandages that Emiri prepared for us."

"We can't sleep with him around." Mei jerked her head in Daisuke's direction.

"I'm more than happy to take watch while you both sleep," Daisuke responded without turning around.

"We'll let you know if we want our throats slit, arigato," Mei replied. She took Chin's hand in hers. His face turned toward her, but he let her hold on to his hand. She looked away from his gaze and stared forward. She was ready to meet death, but she would live long enough to save her father and Kuro. Kuro believed in her; he saw her as more than an eta.

Daisuke looked like he was going on a short stroll. Mei narrowed her eyes. He was here for a reason, but he was going to a lot of effort to kill her, just like Washi. Their footfalls sounded loud in the dark tunnel, and every time a new noise hit her ears, Mei would tense and reach for her bow.

"How far until you ran into them?"

Chin frowned. "It's hard to tell how much time passes down here. Also, I was running. Honestly, the fact I found you was sort of a miracle."

"Why did you come for me?"

"Why wouldn't I?"

"Because I attacked you and I'm just an eta."

Chin's hand tightened around hers. "You're human. I may have been raised with more privileges, but it doesn't make me better than you. I see something in your eyes that makes you more human than most daim I know."

Something fluttered inside her. Then something felt like it would break. "Then why do they treat us this way?" She bit her tongue and drew in a shaky breath. Now really wasn't the time to have a breakdown over the way the world worked. She thought of Washi, and his coldness at the end. How he'd helped her only to end her.

"I don't know. There isn't a good reason. It's just how it has always been."

She didn't reply since she was dangerously close to sitting down and bawling. She focused on her father. The warmth of Chin's hand allowed her eyes to close. She forced her feet forward, her body tired from its days out in the snow. When she tripped a few times, Chin stopped walking.

"Let's just take an hour to rest."

Mei shook her head. "I'm fine. We can keep going."

He studied her eyes. "Are you planning on saving your father or dying with him?"

"Fine. A short break."

They found a turn in the path, and Mei sat next to Chin, across from Daisuke. Chin passed her some bandages from Emiri, and Mei pushed them back. Her body was just worn. There was no need to waste them.

"I'll watch so you can rest," Chin said.

"I'll watch you too," Daisuke commented.

Mei scooted closer to Chin and rested her head against the stone wall. The rock felt cold, and she shivered slightly. Even though sleep evaded her, her body relaxed. Her eyelids shut, and she took deep breaths. They must have thought she'd fallen asleep since they started talking.

"What do you want with the eta?"

Chin shifted beside her. "I don't want anything. I just want to help her."

"It doesn't make sense. You're a daim, correct?"

"So I'm supposed to not care if she dies?"

Daisuke laughed. "Do you feel sad when a bug dies?"

"I don't need to talk about this. Just go to sleep so we can leave you behind."

Daisuke remained silent for a while. "How long are we going to go through these tunnels?"

"Until we get her father back. Why are you here?"

"I'm bored."

"So you want to have a near-death experience?" Chin asked, disbelief tainting his voice.

"You believe it?"

"I was there, and even if I hadn't been, I would believe her."

Chin's words wormed their way into Mei's thoughts. It was odd trusting someone besides her father. Emiri and Chin had come into her life and had every reason to leave her. Unease grew through her. She wasn't worthy of their trust or belief in her. She shifted, and Chin put his arm around her. Her heart pounded, and she wondered if he could hear it.

"It won't work."

"What?" Chin asked.

"You and the eta."

They remained silent, and Mei tried to puzzle out Daisuke's meaning. The rest of the time passed in silence, and when Chin gently shook her awake, Mei stretched. They ate a quick rice ball, gathered their equipment, and started back down the tunnel.

At each intersection, Chin would take out a paper and make a mark, and then they would head down a tunnel. They needed to find the main tunnel they'd stumbled upon after Chin had rescued her. That was where the jorogumo nested.

Chin slowed down. "We're getting close."

Mei drew her bow and readied an arrow. She left the knives and sword tucked under and in her obi. "Do you remember which direction we ran?"

Chin shrugged. "I'm hoping once we get there something in our memories will jog."

"Oh good, lost in a cave is so much better," Daisuke said.

"Then leave." Mei followed Chin and hoped Daisuke would turn around, but he stayed next to them. "Will you fight when they attack?"

"Sure."

If he didn't believe her, he should believe Chin. Nothing looked familiar as they walked. Before they'd turn a corner, they would listen for the telltale clicking of the jorogumo's legs. Mei wondered if the creatures could already smell them.

Even their breathing seemed too loud as they walked, and Mei thought they would meet the monsters around every corner. Eventually, they turned a corner and walked into sticky flyaway webs; they were getting closer.

"We should turn back now," Daisuke stated, his eyes tracing the webs with a flicker of uncertainty.

"We told you to leave. We aren't going with you," Mei replied.

Daisuke hesitated. "I'm going back." As he turned to leave, a long web shot out of the darkness and clung to his face. If he screamed, the sound stayed trapped in the webs.

Mei darted forward and grabbed his arm. They ran away from the firing web. Map forgotten, they made their way through the thickening web. The torch burned it, but it took too long to get off their bodies. Sticky threads slowed their movements, but the jorogumo stayed in the darkness —for now.

"Should we be worried that they aren't attacking?" Mei asked.

Chin glanced around and nodded grimly. "A trap?"

They couldn't see farther ahead because of the darkness and the webs closing in around them. Mei had forgotten she still held on to Daisuke's arm as he tugged it out of her hand.

Daisuke ripped the webs off his face. "I say we keep going. We know they're back there."

Mei had to admire the way he remained calm even though he hadn't believed they were awake. Or he was that stupid not to believe evidence when it was right in his face. "It's getting too thick to move. We should go back and fight our way out."

"You don't know that there's a way out."

"You don't know that it's better that way."

Chin stepped between them. "I'm going with Mei. Do what you want, Daisuke."

Daisuke pounded his fist on his thigh and drew his katana to cut through the web. It fell away effortlessly under his sharp blade. He turned back to them. "See, not that bad."

Out of the dark, two long legs grabbed his middle and pulled him away. Before Mei could think, she locked in her arrow and shot it at the jorogumo's eyes. The arrow hit its mouth, and it made a sick gurgling sound. It dropped Daisuke and fled back into the dark.

"Still want to go that way?" Mei asked.

Daisuke brushed himself off and followed Mei and Chin. Before they could make any progress, glowing jorogumo eyes surrounded them. The green disks didn't blink as they closed in on them. Chin and Daisuke put their backs to Mei, and she stood with her back to the wall behind them. Without speaking, they understood their roles.

The creatures lunged forward. Chin and Daisuke parried the blows from the jorogumo. Mei stayed in the back, shooting at the creatures. Their reflective eyes made easy targets, but the height of the cave limited her bow draw. Chin's sword flashed as he went for the jorogumo's vulnerable torsos. Their long legs reached farther than his sword, and he twirled between the attacks to get in close.

The narrow cave gave them some advantage, in that only a few could attack at a time, but there seemed to be a never-ending stream of the creatures.

A loud clang sounded from Daisuke's side as his sword hit one of their hardened legs. His katana cracked, and the top part of the blade was flung into the darkness of the cave. Daisuke dodged to the side and attacked with what was left of his weapon. He slid under the outstretched legs of the jorogumo and thrust his weapon upward. Blood streamed down and covered him, and the screeching jorogumo fell on him. He rolled under, drew another short blade from his obi, and headed to the next one. Another came up behind him, and Mei took aim, fired the arrow, and hit the jorogumo in the neck. It sputtered blood. Daisuke turned and saw that she had saved him.

He nodded, then got back to the battle. Mei reached back for another arrow, but her hand felt nothing left in her quiver. She drew her short blade and joined Chin in his fight as two jorogumo closed in on him.

Mei twisted through the legs to get at their vulnerable middle, but their attacks were relentless. The blade was too short, and the flickering torchlight dimmed. They would be in darkness soon.

"Daisuke, to us," Mei yelled. She heard an answering call but not what he said. With his back to them, Daisuke defended the rear, while Mei and Chin pushed forward through the mob of monsters. Daisuke would fight because Mei knew he also needed her if they were going to get out of this alive. But if Daisuke found an opening it wouldn't go well for her and Chin.

The hardened legs hit Mei in the side, and she fell but rolled to her feet before another blow could land on her neck. From the side, webs shot at them and slowed them enough for the jorogumo to jab at them. Blood leaked from all their wounds, and then the torch they had set against the wall flickered out. Left in complete darkness, Mei stopped swinging her blade for fear of hitting Chin.

"Chin?"

"Here!"

He was close. She stumbled toward him, but thick web caught her, anchoring her down. Her limbs were stuck to her side, and even her mouth was blocked, so she couldn't scream. *Father, Kuro, I'm sorry.*

Then out of the black, a voice shouted, *Mei!*

TWENTY-EIGHT

Kuro. Kuro? You can hear me? Where are you? Are you okay? What happened?

I'm in the mountain far below. I don't know how I got here. Where are you? Did you eat?

Mei wanted to laugh from relief. *I'm back with the jorogumo. They took my father. I'm stuck in their web, and they are dragging me somewhere. Can you move?*

She tried to take a breath through the web but only managed gasps as they dragged her along.

I'm chained down. Anger flew through their connection. *I can free myself. I will come to you. I can smell you now.*

Frustration burned inside Mei. When they had been walking around under the fortress, Kuro must have been close. *Kuro, this may be the end for me.*

You said you wouldn't leave me to die. I won't leave you to die. Stay alive.

Kuro...

She was left in silence again, and the strength she had lost while tied to the pole back at the fortress returned to her limbs. Gritting her teeth, she wiggled her fingers toward her obi. The hard form of the knife brushed against her fingers as she worked it into her hand. She edged the point up and felt the pings of the webs snapping as the knife cut through them.

While being dragged, she sliced the knife up to free her other hand and grabbed another blade from her obi. Armed with two knives, she made quick work of the webs and freed her legs. In the hazy light, she glanced up. The underbelly of a jorogumo was above her. Gripping the knife in her right hand, she thrust it toward the creature's underbelly. Her hand plunged through the soft flesh, and thick ichor splashed over her face and body. The dying moans of the jorogumo reverberated in the tunnel, and Mei rolled away as it collapsed. Another one carried a body right behind her, and she slid under it and slashed the cord that connected the body to the monster.

The body fell, and she heard a muffled shout of surprise. She swiftly ran the blade along the web, hoping she didn't cut the person since it was hard to see in the shadowy light. She wrapped her arms around him and rolled away from the remaining jorogumo. They both hit the wall, and she came face-to-face with Chin.

Before they could run, the jorogumo was on them. Chin threw her under him and gasped as he got hit in the back.

Mei pushed a knife into his hand, and he stabbed at the center of the beast. The knife got stuck in the underbelly, and they crawled out before it trampled them while it writhed in pain.

Chin made it to his feet first and hoisted Mei up. They ran, and they didn't see any other jorogumo.

After turning the corner, Mei gasped. "Where's Daisuke?"

Around the corner, they skidded to a halt, facing a row of open entrances. A quick look told them the horrible truth. Each one was filled with oblong objects wrapped tightly in web. A rotting stench permeated the air near each pathway, and she covered her mouth to keep down the rice ball she'd eaten. After hearing skittering sounds down the pathway, they ducked into a room. The scent of decay overwhelmed them, and Chin gagged, trying not to make a noise.

Using her gut-encrusted knife, Mei sliced off two pieces of her yukata and gave one to Chin. They tied it around their noses. The light came from round web-covered holes in the cave's ceiling. Mei was thankful for the light. They'd lost their packs in the attack. The only thing that remained was Chin's satchel, which was tight around his chest.

Mei wiped her knife on her obi and searched for the last knife she'd tucked in before they'd left. It wasn't there. She clasped her last weapon, and Chin now held a longer dagger.

He noticed her weapon. "Do you want to trade?" His voice was quiet in the room of rotting corpses.

She shook her head. "I'm better with a bow. You'll do more damage than me with that."

Chin looked around the room. "Do we start... looking?"

Mei bit her lip. Her father might be in here. If he was dead, he would be here. "Let's search for the living. Daisuke will be there too... maybe. He did help us fight," Mei added grudgingly.

"True. I suppose we can help him."

Mei squeezed Chin's forearm. "I heard Kuro. He's coming."

Chin's eyes widened, and he hugged her. Mei tensed and then relaxed in his embrace. "That's wonderful. We could use his help, honestly, and I still have this." Chin held up the satchel. At Mei's questioning eyes, he said, "It has the different plants for fire. I forgot where I saw the satchel, but it is the same one the priest had." He handed it to Mei.

Various plants were inside. Her shaking fingers found the wrapped one at the bottom of the bag. She would need to be careful not to grab that one by mistake. Some of the others she had never used. Shifting through the plants, she put the ones she'd used on top and the others that were too strong for Kuro to the side. Having this would make her feel more confident when Kuro came. *Are you near?*

No response. If he'd run into the jorogumo, he might be in trouble. "Let's hurry and look. We don't have time, and I want to make sure Kuro is okay."

Chin nodded, and they ducked out of the room. Mei followed him down the hall. They only briefly glanced inside each room to scan the oblong objects for any movement or sound. The smell permeated the thin cloth, wrapped around her nose and mouth. Mei breathed out of her mouth. The scent seemed to cling to her tongue. In the next room, she signaled to Chin and quietly whispered in his ear, "We aren't making progress. Do you think we should divide?" They hadn't run into any more jorogumo, but Mei's chest pinched at their slow progress.

Chin studied her face and looked off down the hall they still needed to cover. "We really shouldn't split up, but you are right, we aren't moving fast enough."

Mei knew what Chin had left unsaid: they were already too late. "I'll go down the right and you take the left? Head back here when we are done?"

Chin nodded and tiptoed away from her. He disappeared from her view in seconds, and now that he was gone, she wished he was still beside her. If she found Daisuke he might slit her throat. They should have left him. Could she kill someone like that even knowing they would kill her? She shivered at the surrounding emptiness. The dead bodies were her only companions now, a graveyard of eta.

In the faint light of the caves, Mei jumped at every sound. She padded along as quietly as possible, but even the scuff of her footfalls was loud in the darkness. Her nose had adapted to the smell and the slight musk coming from the damp cloth on her nose. She realized it was soaked through with her sweat. Some rooms now contained more circular webbing with larger egg sacs. She ducked out of those rooms, not wanting to be in them if a bunch of hungry jorogumo hatched.

The holes in the ceiling widened, and more light filtered through the thick webs. A child could fall through those holes. Maybe that was the purpose. When she was growing up, parts of the woods had been forbidden and now she understood why. There was also the theory that when an eta gave up, they went for a long walk in the woods, never to return. Mei grimaced and kept moving.

She turned into the next room and scanned the interior. This one didn't smell as bad as the others, and movement caught the corner of her eye. Mei gripped her knife. A body stirred again. She rushed forward, knelt next to it, and cut along the thick webbing. She tore the web away from the face with her hands, and Daisuke's body fell on top of her, knocking her to the floor.

Mei shoved him off, and he rolled onto his back, gulping in air. His eyes focused on her, and he grabbed her arm.

"You came for me?"

Mei shook herself out of his hold. "You were on my way."

"Why didn't you leave?"

Why didn't I leave? Good question. Mei stood up and brushed herself off. "Can you walk? I can't carry you. I have a few more rooms to check, then we need to meet up with Chin."

"He's okay?"

"They captured us together. I don't know why they brought you here."

Daisuke grimaced, his face a sickly pallor. "This room is different. It isn't for eating." He didn't meet her eyes.

Mei's upper lip curled in disgust. "Let's move out while we can and find Chin."

"You shouldn't have separated."

Mei ignored him because she agreed with him. "Do you think the others are alive in here, then? Also, how do you know this is their breeding room?"

"They were transformed, so they were talking. They said the rest were already used. Once they use them, then..." Daisuke stumbled. She'd never seen him so scared. His whole body shook.

On the ground next to the bodies, Mei saw round objects. "Are those—"

"Heads."

"Let's go."

"Right behind you."

Mei led the way out of the room and went into the next one. Daisuke stayed close to her. He didn't have any weapons. She kept an eye on him and hands on the hilt of her weapon. *He needs me to get out of here. I think.* He wouldn't be stupid enough to stay alone and try to get out by himself would he? If anything, Daisuke was a survivor. They made it to the last room in the hall, and Mei scanned it. It seemed so pointless. Then a glimmer of green caught her eye.

Mei froze in the room as Daisuke turned to leave. Realizing she'd stayed behind, he followed her eyes. "What's that?"

"Jade."

Her feet shuffled on their own as though through a dream. Mei brushed the web away from the green jade beads. Her throat closed up as they clattered to the stone floor. The jade beads clinked with the finality of death.

The hands that had held hers through all the nights of her childhood were now in front of her. The familiar bent fingers and the rough callouses. Even the light blue veins. Months had passed, but Mei would always recognize those hands. Hands shaking, she lightly touched the fingers and waited for them to clench around hers like they used to. Cold.

They couldn't be the same warm hands that would brush through her hair or feel her face. The hands that would gently wipe away her tears. Cold. They were too cold, so they couldn't belong to him. Warm hands didn't belong here, so they couldn't be his.

Mei pressed her thumbnail into the skin of her hand. Her insides cascaded and her soul twirled into a maelstrom. Pain emanated from her hand, but she couldn't stop moving her fingers toward the answer she already knew was waiting. Her damp hands clenched the sticky web near the face, and she ripped it away.

A silent scream opened in Mei, and she collapsed. No sound. No warmth. Cold hands.

Her father's unseeing eyes looked past her in death. She couldn't move. A hand touched her, and she twitched, having forgotten that Daisuke was in the room with her.

"Mei?" Daisuke's voice reached her in the turmoil of her racing thoughts. "Do you know this person?"

She choked, curled up on the ground, her forehead against the freezing stone. The chill shot through her body, and she squeezed her knees into her stomach.

Daisuke shook her gently. "Is this your... father?"

A strangled gasp left Mei's throat, answering his question. Mei heard him stand, and she remained unmoving. There was shuffling in her father's direction, and she glanced up to see that Daisuke had laid out her father. The web no longer covered his body, and his eyes were closed. Daisuke removed the outer layer of his rich kimono and placed it over Kaji's body.

Mei sat up on her knees and looked forward blankly. Daisuke's kindness seemed bizarre, but he honored her father. Tears poured down her cheeks. Daisuke knelt next to her, and he bowed his head toward her father. They sat in silence, Mei not daring to utter a sound.

"Mei, we need to leave, Daisuke finally said."

That was the second time he had said her name, an odd thing to notice when half her soul lay dead in front of her. "I c-can't leave h-him h-here," Mei said, voice trembling.

"You know we can't carry him." Daisuke's voice was gentle yet firm. "You also know we need to leave."

He was right. Her father wouldn't want her to stay here and die. And she was right, Daisuke needed her to get out of here alive. But her body wouldn't move. The more she stared at her father, the more he looked like a stranger. "It's not him. It's not him."

Daisuke nudged her arm. "Do you need me to carry you?"

Mei again ignored him, and she crawled forward and curled up next to her father's body. She studied the lines of his face, searching for proof that he wasn't Kaji.

Daisuke got up and tried to lift her away from her father, but Mei clawed at his hands, forcing him to drop her.

"We need to leave."

"Then leave!"

A billowing breeze entered the cavern, and Mei felt a mixture of mourning and urgency flow through her.

We need to leave.

Kuro's voice resounded through her still body. His large frame pushed into the room, and he dwarfed them, barely getting through the door. He somehow curled up and placed his head in Mei's lap. She wrapped her arms around his neck and buried her face in his smooth scales. His physical warmth soaked into her slight frame. Her tears fell onto his scales. He must have fought his way to her.

"I can't leave him here to be eaten." Mei's words were muffled as she spoke into his neck.

Do you have anything I can use?

Mei lifted her head and gripped at the satchel Chin had given her. *You mean burn him?*

It is all the honor we can give him, the father of a shodragon rider.

"He would have liked you." Mei opened the satchel. She clutched the yellow plant that produced the hottest fire she and Kuro could use.

I would have liked him too. Kuro gulped down the plant,

and she stood next to him, her head lowered. She connected with Kuro, and as he released the fire, they aimed it at her father's body.

Large tears rolled down her face as what was left of her father burned to ash. The acrid smell of burning flesh replaced the scent of rot. Daisuke placed the cold jade beads in her hand. She held back more tears as she tucked them under her robe. Their coolness made her skin shiver.

The fire ran out of fuel, and Kuro nudged Mei. *We need to go. I'm sorry.*

Mei stepped forward and knelt, placing her fingers on the pile of ash. Her tears fell and created small craters in the burnt remains. "Father, I did it. I have a dragon. His name is Kuro, and he loves to eat the fat off meat. I'm still fighting, Father. It hasn't been easy. I don't know what's at stake, but I'll try to understand what you meant. I'll try..." Mei choked. "But I'm going to be the greatest rider, and you will see me riding with the Sho."

She bowed, and carefully, she swept up the ash and folded it in the cloth that used to be around her face. Mei placed her father in the satchel and turned to face Kuro and Daisuke.

"We need to find Chin and get out of here."

They nodded and followed her out of the room. With her ash-stained hands, Mei clasped the strap of the satchel and walked forward, leaving her heart behind.

TWENTY-NINE

Chin grew uneasy as he left Mei behind in the room of dead bodies. With his long dagger, he would need to be awfully close to a jorogumo to kill or injure it. Their long, hard legs would stab through him if he made a mistake. Mei, however, only had a knife.

Chin turned back, then paused. Would she think he didn't think her capable? He gritted his teeth. It would be better to find survivors as quickly as possible, then head back. *She'll be fine.*

He continued to search, going in and out of rooms. He felt thankful for the holes in the cave ceiling. With all the webbing, he assumed they caught little forest animals. He made sure not to touch the webs. If they were anything like actual spiders, they might sense the vibrations.

In another dark room, he found a couple of bodies. Some appeared to be half eaten, and he choked back bile. In the darkness, he could pretend he didn't know what the dark stains on the floor and walls meant. The farther he went, the more body pieces he found. Chin stepped on what looked like a hand and jumped aside. He decided not to study it and go on. If Mei's father was here, there would be nothing left of him to find.

The trouble with splitting up was that he didn't even know what her father looked like. If anybody moved, he supposed he would save them. It would be pure luck if it was her father. The tunnel widened, and there were no more side rooms to check out. Chin stayed close to the walls. The stone lightly scuffed his arm as he walked. Damp air, mixed with the coppery scent of blood, hit his nose. It might be better to go back. Chin had turned to leave when a female voice came from up ahead.

He frowned at the calm-sounding voice. Something was off if someone sounded that relaxed down here. He crept forward, and two women talked to each other, their backs to Chin. He could barely make out that they wore kimonos. One of them had hair down past her waist, and the other's was tied back. He turned his ear toward them but only heard faint murmurs. Then the long-haired lady left and the other turned to Chin.

Chin choked. From the curve of her nose down to the way she held her hand—

"Mother?" His voice echoed in the dark cavern, and Aiko turned her neck. Her eyes widened when she spotted Chin. It was no mistake of the light—they glowed a brilliant green.

Chin stood taller and came away from the wall. "Mother? What are you doing here?"

Aiko's hand remained folded, and she studied Chin from across the cavern. Drips of water rang in his ears. She took one step forward and paused. "You should never have come here."

A dark wave of questions entered Chin's mind. He put his hand to his dagger, and his shoulders tensed. If his mother was here, did that mean she was helping the jorogumo? Chin stepped aside and drew his weapon. "What are you doing here, *Mother?*"

Aiko took another step forward and bowed her head. Chin had never seen her lower her head to him before. When she raised her face, her eyes were closed. Her lips moved, but no words came out. She opened her eyes, and they looked like cold bits of metal. "It's over." Her arms stretched open. Something flickered under her kimono.

Chin felt the urge to run, but his feet remained rooted to the stone floor. He watched as hard black legs expanded out of the side of his mother. The kimono ripped with the extra body mass. The legs planted themselves on the ground, scraping against the surface. Then her top half elongated, squeezing up, and her hair remained tied back, but the kimono lay in tatters against her body. Long claws grew from her fingers, and he stared as the last part of her, her face, grew wild and animalistic. Pincers dilated out of her mouth. The mother he'd known his entire life was truly a monster.

His palms sweat as he grasped his weapon. He could run, but it was time he faced his mother.

Aiko's long legs paced around the cavern. In the dim light, she probably knew the terrain better than Chin. With each footstep, his ears twitched. He waited for her to strike first. Her eyes reflected the animal green glow, and Chin's stomach clenched. Nothing was recognizable about her. But at the same time, this felt more like the mother he knew.

She skittered left, and Chin curled under her outstretched leg. The hard surface of her outer shell scratched along his side, but he continued to roll under. He gripped the dagger and dashed for her unprotected underbelly. Aiko read his intention and pushed her legs up, springing onto the large webs that decorated the room.

Chin grimaced as he watched her circle him from above, his neck craned back. He backed up, hoping he could dodge any attack. Instead of dropping onto him, Aiko tilted her underbody and shot out a stream of sticky web. He twirled out of the way, but thinner strands clung to his clothing. He tried to brush them away, but they clung to his hand, making it difficult to separate his fingers.

She continued to shoot web at him, and he continued to run and dodge. The whole cavern became layered in webbing, and it blocked his view of Aiko, who still hung above him.

Chin's gaze darted around the room, and he felt trapped, not unlike his complete life with his mother. A large leg struck out from the webbing, and Chin balked, moving too slowly. It hit his shoulder, and the force knocked him to the ground. As he fell, the web tangled around him. He slashed at the bindings and rolled away as another leg came out of the darkness toward him. It brushed against his back, and he stifled a shout. She knew where to hit. More legs appeared from the shadows, and his dagger clanged against the hard surface. His weapon would do no damage against them unless she held still—an unlikely prospect.

He fell onto his belly, exposing his back, and crawled out of the webs on his elbows and knees. Sweat dripped into his eyes in his frantic escape. He needed to get somewhere he could see her. A break showed in the webs ahead. Reaching it, he jumped to his feet and cocked his ear, listening for sounds of Aiko approaching him. The only sound he heard came from his heart thudding against his ribs.

He reached through the web, pushing it aside as he carefully listened for any sign of attack. A colossal figure loomed over him and knocked him to the side. Aiko, now in front of him, raised her legs and stabbed them at his body. Chin forced his arms up to deflect the blows. His dagger, useless against her hard shell, was in the way. The constant barrage of attacks from her legs shredded his sleeves. Scraping off more of his skin, he grabbed one of her legs, and as Aiko retracted it, Chin went along for the ride. He held her leg with his left arm and stabbed at her side with the dagger. A gash appeared in Aiko's side, and she gave a painful screech as she shook her leg, flinging Chin off. His body flew through the webs until a thick mass caught him. He skidded to a stop, and his feet didn't touch the ground.

From out of the shadows, Aiko darted in toward him. The more Chin struggled against the web, the more entangled he became. The web clung across his body, and the back of his hand, in which he held the dagger, was stuck firmly.

Aiko paused and looked at her prey trapped in the web. Chin gritted his teeth, feeling his skin pull away as he tried to break free. Her eyes glinted, then she pushed forward on her back two legs, the sharp bottoms of her four front legs reaching forward. They were headed straight for his heart.

With one last push of strength, Chin yanked his hand out of the web and pointed his dagger at his mother. Her leg reach was longer than his arm. It was over.

At an abnormal moment, he thought he saw her smile. Then right as her legs reached him, she spread them out, letting his dagger plunge into her middle. Aiko gurgled, and her body sagged onto the dagger, plunging it in deeper. Her weight pulled against Chin and freed him from the web, ripping off skin and the top of his robe. When he landed, Aiko melted under his body, and the face of his human mother stared up at him.

Blood bubbled out of her mouth, leaving a red trail down the side of her pale cheek. Her mouth moved and rasping sounds came out as she struggled to speak. "My... son..."

Chin knelt over his mother's body. His hand pulled back from the dagger. It glistened red with her blood. "Mother." She was dying, and something broke inside him. He felt free, but his mother's actions at the end tore at him. "Why?"

A trembling smile answered him. Her eyes held secrets he tried to understand. She drew a shuddering breath, lifted her arm, and pointed to her left. "The spiders... never harm you. Follow... get... out..." More blood gurgled down her face, and with a sad smile, the light left her eyes.

"Mother?" Chin's hand shook as he placed his fingers to her neck. No thudding heartbeat. Dampness hit his knees as Aiko's blood pooled around her, her beauty now broken and bloody before him. He pulled the dagger out of her, and it squelched as he removed it. He stood on trembling legs and gazed down at the person who had abused him his whole life. Why had she let him kill her? He looked at her pointing fingers. Did she want him to survive?

His hatred toward the broken woman and his desire for her approval clashed in his soul. He reached down and brushed his mother's hair away from her forehead. She wouldn't like the stray strands. Methodically, he covered her in what was left of her elegant kimono. He laid her right arm next to her body, but he kept the left arm pointing toward the tunnel at the end of the cavern. The last act of love toward her son.

Emptiness overcame him as he wiped the dagger on his clothing. He found himself unable to leave, but then the sound of running claws hit his ears. Chin swung around. A dark form loomed ahead. He stepped over his mother's body and prepared for battle.

THIRTY

As Mei fled past the point where she'd left Chin, a burst of worry entered her thoughts. If Chin hadn't made it back yet, he must have run into trouble. Daisuke jogged beside her, and Kuro rambled on behind them, his claws scraping against the stone floor. Mei clutched her knife as she ran. It seemed like the tunnel would go on forever.

The webs grew thicker, and Kuro struggled to get through. The webs didn't stick too much to his scales, but some would hit his eyes and obscure his vision. Mei had to stop and wipe the clinging threads away.

"Be careful."

It's not like I can help it, Kuro grumbled.

Mei patted him, and they resumed their pace.

"Do you know where he is?" Daisuke asked.

"Down this tunnel." Mei thought she sounded confident. The truth was, she didn't know where he'd ended up. If they continued any farther, Daisuke would tell her it was time to turn back. Mei didn't want to hear it. She would escape with Kuro, Chin, and her father. Her hand pressed against the satchel.

The tunnel widened, and they slowed their pace. The cavern ahead grew darker, and a wall of web extended across the space. She could hardly see in front of them.

Daisuke paused at the thick strands. "I don't think we should go in there."

This was probably another trap. "Kuro, can you burn away the webbing?"

"Are you sure you want to do that?" Daisuke gestured in front of him. "They are probably behind it," he said, voice lowered.

"I'm going in farther." Kuro burned the web away before Mei continued.

Daisuke sighed and followed them, now behind Kuro.

"Scared?" Mei asked.

"Yes."

Mei smiled wryly. She wasn't about to tell him that the sweat forming on her forehead was also from fear. Mei pushed her hand through the web, and it clung to her. She was about to turn back, but a thick liquid stopped her feet. Blood? She reached forward, and a figure lunged out at her, brandishing a dagger. He swiveled at the last moment.

"Mei?" Chin's shocked eyes met hers. "You're alive?"

Mei frowned. "Am I supposed to be dead?"

He stepped back. "No. I, uh... I just..." He took a deep breath. "I'm glad you're here." He glanced up at Kuro. "I thought his shadow was one of them."

Kuro snorted.

"I'm sure he doesn't mean that you look like one," Mei commented.

"Can we go?" Daisuke asked.

"You found him? What about your father?"

Mei nodded to Chin. "My father is no longer alive." She looked behind Chin to find the source of the blood. A beautiful woman lay in a pool of blood. Her face seemed familiar, and Mei stood over her. One of her arms seemed to be reaching for something. "What happened?"

"My mother." Daisuke's and Mei's eyes focused on Chin. "She transformed back after her death."

"Transformed?" Mei glanced at all the webbing. "Your mother was a jorogumo?"

Chin didn't reply and shifted his dagger in his hand. "That is the way out."

"She told you this?" Daisuke asked.

"I'm going to believe her."

Mei glanced from Daisuke to Chin. She could see that Daisuke wanted to go in the opposite direction from where Chin's mother pointed. Chin's steady gaze persuaded her. He believed his mother. She would trust his judgment.

"Let's go."

"You're going to trust a jorogumo?"

"I trust Chin. You can always go your own way, but I won't return for you this time."

Daisuke frowned but followed them down to the tunnel. Mei placed her hand on Kuro's shoulder. "Is it too narrow for you?"

No, but it will be hard to turn around. It is a good thing I didn't get any fat today.

"Yeah." Mei smiled, and Chin took the lead down the dark tunnel.

They continued on, and the round holes in the ceiling diminished. They grabbed each other's hands and stumbled through the inky darkness. It was odd holding onto both of them even thought it was for safety. In this moment she felt strangly close to her former tormentor.

If there was a turnoff anywhere, they would likely miss it. Chin kept one hand on the edge of the wall, and they all followed. The whistling wind gave Mei some hope that they were nearing an entrance.

"Can you see anything, Kuro?"

A little. I can smell the city.

"What did he say?" Chin asked.

"He can see a bit, and now he can smell the city." Daisuke's hand clenched in her grip. "We must be close to an exit."

Then the sound they'd all been dreading echoed through the caves—jorogumo legs skittering against stone. They all had the look of a panicked animal before death. They stumbled in the dark as they ran.

Their gasping breaths mixed with the sound of an avalanche of jorogumo. They frequently tripped and dragged each other up, then fell again.

"Stop!" Mei yelled. "Kuro, can you turn now?"

They heard scraping as Kuro turned in the cave. She felt her connection to him and the orange fire left in his body. *Ready?*

Ready.

Together, through Kuro's body, they swirled out the fire. Mei directed it forward and to the edge of the cave. This was different from Kuro just trying to blow out fire. The reach expanded, and their eyes were flooded with light and the glowing retinas of the jorogumo.

The jorogumo screeched in pain as the hot orange fire burned through them. Their glowing bodies lit the tunnel.

"Move backward. Chin, direct us. Daisuke, help guide Kuro."

Moving at a fast backward clip, Kuro kept flaming, and Mei remained attached to his shoulder. With the light, they didn't stumble, but there was a flood of jorogumo.

"There's a wider opening ahead!" Chin shouted.

The narrow tunnel benefited Kuro's fire. If the jorogumo could have spread out, they would have had the advantage.

Mei lost focus on her fire attacks and shouted back, "Then we try to run?"

Kuro flamed, and one that got too close to the fire bounced off the stone and almost rebounded onto Mei. She ducked and tried to bring her focus back to aiming the fire. They hadn't had enough time to practice with distractions. Kuro snaked his claw forward and slammed it against a jorogumo. It tried to bite him. Mei threw her knife at the beast's eyes, only for the handle to bounce against the side of its head. That was enough for her to connect with Kuro, and then a burst of flame hit the jorogumo's midsection. The acrid smell of burning flesh filled the tunnel, and breathing became difficult with all the smoke. The breeze from outside was too weak to shift it away.

"We have to run!" Daisuke shouted.

Mei agreed but didn't respond.

Getting low.

Mei reached into the satchel for more plants, and only one was left that they could use. It was the green fire.

Not as strong. Kuro tilted his head down and ate it while the jorogumo flooded forward.

"Opening ahead!" It sounded like Chin, but Mei wasn't sure. If they survived long enough to reach it, Kuro could fly above the creatures.

Get ready to turn and run, Mei thought.

The chilly breeze at her back told her they'd reached the larger opening. Mei and Kuro sent one last burst of flame down their path before turning around. To her left and right were other entrances, but she ran on, taking off after Chin and Daisuke, who were farther ahead. Chin turned back. "Keep going!" Mei shouted.

Chin nodded and turned around. Kuro loped easily in the tunnel, keeping pace with her. Then the clacking behind them slowed, and an eerie keening hurt their ears. It traveled through the tunnel, and Mei's skin crawled.

It took all her nerves not to turn around and see what was behind them. It sounded different from the jorogumo. Then Daisuke faced her, and his eyes bulged and his mouth gaped open. He turned back, and his pace increased. Mei pushed her burning legs forward. According to Daisuke's face, whatever was behind them was far worse than what she could imagine. The keening continued, and it only got louder.

"The sky," Chin yelled.

They would make it, but what about the things that chased them? Would they follow them to the surface? The jorogumo came out at night, but she knew they sometimes fought during the day.

We can't let these things follow us, Mei thought.

I agree. Any fire left?

Yes. The spider lily. Kuro... If they used it, they could die. No shodragon rider had survived using the forbidden fire.

Let's see where the tunnel ends.

The sky appeared ahead, but Kuro jerked back. Something had his tail. She spun around to face the creatures. They had the bulbous bodies of a spider and only a humanoid face appeared at the front. Eight large unblinking eyes stared her down. Hundreds of bodies pushed forward, with their mouths gaped open in their keening. Their sharp pincers dug into Kuro's tail, scraping off his scales. Kuro thrashed against them but couldn't reach to claw them off.

Mei threw herself against one and stabbed her fingers into its eyes. They popped, and the creature let go. Slime stretched from her fingers. Another grabbed her and dug its pincers into her shoulder. She screamed in pain. It dragged her away, and from above, Chin leaped over and dug his dagger into its back. It threw him off, and the dagger stayed lodged in the creature. Chin hit the stone wall and fell. Daisuke stood frozen at the entrance.

"Get him out!" Mei screamed. Blood poured from her shoulder, and her eyes blurred. *Kuro?*

We must. Kuro roared and tried to shake them off him, but he couldn't. Mei dug through the satchel for the spider lily. Its red petals, even though wilted, gleamed in the sun.

Daisuke finally moved, and he dragged Chin toward the entrance. He came back as the creatures overran Mei. She clenched the flower in her hand, but she couldn't reach Kuro.

"Are you insane?" Daisuke yelled, seeing what was in her hand.

A creature lunged at Daisuke, and he ducked out of the way, but another clung to him from behind and dragged him toward Mei. He lashed out at the things holding him, and Mei snatched his hand as he passed her. Mei and Daisuke kicked and clawed. She kept the lily protected in one of her hands, until Kuro loomed over her. Kuro planted his claws and ripped the creatures off them while his own back remained covered. Mei held up her hand, and he ate the flower.

Power like she'd never felt before coursed through her and Kuro. Her insides boiled with fire. She gasped and doubled over from the pain. Kuro's feelings flooded through her, and she felt the burning lava coursing through them both.

"Focus, Mei!" Daisuke's voice rang through the cave.

Mei only saw red. She wiped her face, and blood coated her hands from where it leaked from her nose and mouth. She connected with Kuro.

"Release."

It scorched up Kuro's throat, and no bright fire left him, but rather thick lava that melted all the surrounding creatures. Mei dropped to the ground, and Daisuke had to lift her while she kept a hand on Kuro. The lava kept pouring out of Kuro and down the tunnel. The creatures ran, but it flowed over them, melting their bones to ash. The fire didn't end. It consumed her and Kuro.

"Get it all out, Mei!"

She couldn't reply. Her throat ached, and she wanted to dunk herself in ice. Her skin was slick with blood; it was coming out of her pores.

Kuro.

He couldn't respond. She could feel his insides boiling just like hers.

With one last push of her will, she forced the rest of the lava out of him, but she lost control, and a portion splashed on her face and right side. She screamed, and Daisuke threw her in the snow. In her blurry thoughts, she realized the snow meant they'd made it outside the cave.

Kuro collapsed next to her. Mei reached out a shaking hand, and his eyes closed.

No, Kuro. Stay. Don't leave.

Shouting came from the distance, and the earth felt hot under her skin. Daisuke kept bringing snow over and covering her face and side. It melted the instant it touched her.

Kuro?

He didn't respond. Mei's insides felt like burnt mush, and the last thing she saw was Daisuke's dark eyes.

THIRTY-ONE

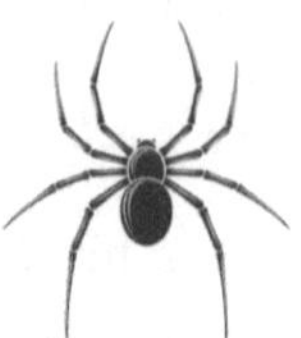

Chin's body ached as he tried to move. The sun burned behind his eyelids, and the smell of burning flesh made him peel his eyes open. Kuro's dark body lay next to him. Steam rose from the dragon, and Daisuke ran back and forth, holding snow. Chin shook his head and pushed himself up. The ground under his fingers was warm and wet from melted snow. He stood. They were above the city and near his home. Throughout the forest, fires burned brightly and the melting snow evaporated into mist.

He turned to Daisuke, who was piling snow onto Mei. Chin balked at her raw skin. It looked like undercooked meat. The right side of her face was melted, and her shoulder wasn't any better. Kuro's tail had been ripped clean of black scales, and he wasn't breathing.

Chin couldn't move and watched as Daisuke ran back and forth. His brain finally caught up to what was happening, and he joined Daisuke in putting snow on Mei.

"What happened?" Chin gasped as he ran.

"They used the spider lily."

Chin dropped the snow he carried and glanced over at the burning forest. It must have come out through the holes in the ceiling. "Is that from them?"

Daisuke shrugged and dumped more snow on Mei's face. It melted instantly. "Yes."

"We need to get her to the fortress."

Daisuke glanced back at Chin. "They will kill her."

In all their running and fighting, Chin had forgotten that Mei was facing death for desertion. "You could just tell them the truth?"

Daisuke leaned over Mei and touched her skin. He jerked his fingers back. "That's up to Washi-sensei. We shouldn't move her. They need healers."

"I'll run ahead and send them here so they can help carry Mei. We will have to leave the dragon." Chin glanced again at Kuro's too still form. If Mei lost Kuro too, she might not make it. He pushed his tired body up the mountain. Overhead, shodragons flew, carrying large vats of water to dump onto the burning forest. They didn't want the fire to reach the city. The snow slid under his feet. It melted from the heat of the boiling fire in the mountain. Chin didn't know how long the forbidden fire would burn, but a fog rose as the snow evaporated. Though he yearned to lie down in the snow and sleep, he pushed forward until the fortress walls rose before him.

Chin burst through the doors, and in the courtyard, healers rushed around, getting ready to help the public or dragons as needed. He scanned the crowd for Emiri. With the wave of healers, he didn't spot her right away, but out of the corner of his eye, he saw a round face. He darted in her direction.

"Emiri!"

Her face jerked toward his voice. "What are you doing here?"

"Mei's badly burned, and Kuro isn't moving or breathing. Can you help? Is there anyone who will help Kuro?"

Emiri surged into action and grabbed a parcel that the healers were preparing. "You and you, come with me now. A shodragon is hurt. Get the stretcher." The two healers nodded, and the homdragons curled around their necks as they all grabbed more supplies and followed Chin.

Chin wiped the cold sweat off his brow and ran through the steam. Emiri and the other healers kept pace behind him. *One more step. One more*, Chin chanted to his legs. They felt like overdone soba noodles. Kuro's body came into view, and Chin collapsed onto his knees in the mud.

Emiri ran to Mei, and the other two began working on Kuro. Chin stared at the moving figures, blinking slowly.

"Need help standing?"

Chin glanced up to see Daisuke blocking the sun. "I don't know if I can stand." Emiri calmly fed her homdragon. "Will she be okay?"

"I don't know if the eta can even be killed."

A hint of amazement tinged Daisuke's tone, and when he said *eta*, it didn't sound like an insult. He remembered the fire in Mei's eyes. "You're right. I don't think this will be her last day on earth."

A loud huff interrupted Chin's focus, and Kuro rumbled as the other two worked on him. They laid white cloths on his tail and back. After they removed them, they came away black, and the fluid dripped into the snow. The healers handled the cloths carefully.

"Poison. They were able to bite him after they ripped off his scales," Daisuke said.

Chin shuddered, but seeing Kuro move gave him hope that Mei would come back to them. Emiri worked steadily over Mei's still body. Chin tugged at Daisuke and pulled himself up, using him as a brace.

Daisuke stumbled slightly, and Chin fell against him. "If you're going to make a move, at least warn a guy."

Chin glared at him and tried to walk closer to Mei. "Can we help?"

"We will need people to help carry her to the fortress." Emiri didn't look up as she spoke. "The Sho has returned, so I don't think they will try to kill her now."

"I'll go," Daisuke replied. "This one is useless." He dropped Chin in the mud. Without glancing back, he ran toward the top of the mountain.

"Will she..."

"She will live. Her face will not heal fully." Emiri placed more cloth onto Mei's face and shoulder.

The skin changed from an angry crimson to an inky black with reddish veins. It looked like spider lily petals.

"That is the last of the viola for Mei. The rest is for Kuro. Thankfully, they didn't notice me taking it in all the chaos."

Chin watched the faint rise and fall of Mei's chest while they waited. More people arrived, and they placed Mei's body on a cloth stretcher with two long bamboo poles.

Emiri glanced back at Chin. "Are you coming?"

He waved her forward. "I will soon. I need to stop by my home." He had a few questions for his father.

The healers disappeared up the mountain, and the ones who helped him finally coaxed Kuro into a staggering walk.

Normally, other dragons would have helped, but they were still trying to put out the fires below.

Moments passed before Chin pushed his way up from the mud. He was closer to home than the fortress. He wanted to stay by Mei, but his mother's transformation was burned into his mind, and his father owed him answers. The smoke mixed with the steam from the snow. Ash clung to his throat, and he coughed as he limped down the mountain. The gateway guarding his house seemed more like a protection from the truth. It had kept him in his hell for eighteen years and held more secrets than he had ever known.

The house guards made no move toward him as he entered. They glanced away from Chin's gaze. Did they already know that Aiko was gone? It had only happened an hour ago. Chin clenched his hand, and his skin felt tight with dried blood—his mother's blood.

He pushed open the door to his home and took off his mud-encrusted footwear at the door. His socks were just as dirty, and he smiled sadly. The walls of his home had never offered him safety, but his body took him down the wooden floors to the room where his father spent his days. He slid open the doors, and Masuo sat on the tatami mats as always, looking at the painting of his lost shodragon. Incense burned in front of the memorial. The cloying scent had always made it hard to breathe.

Chin bowed to the painting and sat on his knees next to his father. He stared at the burning incense and watched the smoke dance in curls, only to disappear as it rose in the air. This silence was normal from his father. He'd become a living dead man the day his shodragon had died.

"I killed Mother." The words burst out of Chin. They

hung in the room like an evil omen. Imaginary cracks broke through the walls of their home.

Masuo looked away from the image of his dragon, and his empty eyes found Chin. "Oh."

Chin gritted his teeth. "Did you know what she was?"

A long pause filled the room. The walls in his mind broke down around him as he sat in seeming calmness with his father. "Yes."

"Yet you..."

A sad sigh interrupted Chin. His father turned to face his son. Chin did the same. This was the most attention he had ever received from him. "It was my last order as a shodragon rider, for my betrayal."

"What do you mean?" Questions flooded into Chin's mind. It was the job of shodragon riders to kill the jorogumo, not sleep with them.

Masuo's eyes glazed over in memory. "This was before Jion-sho took power, although he holds to the promise."

"Promise?"

"I can't tell you the details. It's forbidden."

Chin laughed as his rust-colored hands clenched his clothing. "Does it matter?"

Masuo blinked. "Maybe not. But I was ordered to marry the creature and give her a female child." He gave a broken smile. "It didn't work."

"Kazu..."

His father shook his head. "He's your half-brother. My first wife was a shodragon rider like me." His gaze traveled back to his dragon, and a tear appeared in the corner of his eye. "I couldn't put her likeness here to hold up the lie to you both."

Kazu was only his half-brother. It was Chin who was the monster. "So I am a jorogumo?"

"Only women turn into the jorogumo. The men's fate is different."

The monsters they'd faced at the end of their journey with the gaping mouths and animalistic nature flashed into Chin's thoughts. *Is that my fate?*

"Your *mother* believed she could save you from turning," Masuo said. He smiled sarcastically. "Did that work well for you?"

"The punishments?" Chin winced at his father's sneering face. "That was the purpose behind all those beatings?"

He shrugged and turned back to his memorial. "It didn't matter. I had two monsters in my home. Now I have one less. *Arigato.*"

Coldness entered the room as the last imaginary walls fell around Chin's childhood home. In his mind's eye, all he saw was the rubble of a fake family. In Aiko's last moments, she had let Chin kill her. How could it be that this entire time she had been trying to save him from turning into something monstrous?

His throat closed, and he forced his legs to lift him. He stared down at the father who had never protected him or cared. The father who had just called him a monster. He padded to the sliding door. He didn't turn back to face his father, but spoke to the cold walls of his home. "Now you will lose another one, *Father.*"

Chin slid the door shut and walked out of the crumbling home for the last time.

THIRTY-TWO

The clean, crisp smell of linen reached Mei's nose as she blinked her eyes open. The room was long and separated by white curtains. She recognized the healing room, and then her eyes met the Sho's. He stood before her, intimidating in his usual black. A beautiful woman with flinty black eyes stared down at her. Her long hair rivaled Jion-sho's. Her hands stayed tucked in her kimono, but it looked like she wanted to strangle Mei. They were the only two in the room. Jion-sho stepped forward to block the woman from view.

"You burned down a good portion of the forest."

Mei's throat felt raw as she said, "I-I just wanted to make sure..." Flashes of the creatures flooding after them rushed through her mind. "... that they wouldn't come to the city."

Jion-sho nodded, his eyes distant. "Did you plan to die?"

"I didn't know it would burn so much. I didn't think."

He backed away so the woman could see Mei. He turned to her. "I will make reparations."

The woman hissed at him, then bolted out of the room.

Mei's insides churned. "Is she okay?"

"Do you know what she is?"

Mei tried to sit up, but her body fell back down. "Why do you have a jorogumo with you?"

Jion-sho studied her face. "There are some things you don't need to know, recruit."

"Does anyone else know that you deal with them?"

"Deal? I guess." He sighed. "I had to make many deals to get this far, and you will see why in time."

"You knew they took the eta before the rains. You knew this whole time." Her hoarse voice cracked. Her body tensed as she stared at the man she used to admire.

"I do not have to explain myself to you." His words came out formal and cold.

Mei forced her shaking arms to support her as she sat up. "The eta are not something to be used and discarded! You will answer for this! I thought you were on my side." The betrayal shot through her. First Washi and now this.

"You have no idea what I have done to keep you alive, Mei, daughter of Rikku and Koji."

"Then tell me!"

He pulled up a bundle that lay at his feet and placed it next to Mei. She glared up at him and opened it. The black uniform of a shodragon rider fell out. A jade pendant rested on top. "What is this?"

"This is what your father sold that day. It was a signal that his daughter was of age. We hoped you would take after your mother."

The fine material slipped through her fingers. "My mother?"

"She used to ride a shodragon, before she was killed."

In her father's stories, her mother had sounded like more than an eta. But a shodragon rider? How could this be? "Then why am I an eta?"

"Your father was an eta."

"How was my mother killed? Was it in battle? Why didn't my father tell me?"

Jion-sho held up his hand. "I think you will get your answers from that. Your father had me write it for him." He pointed to a letter folded in the cloth. "I will leave you here to rest, but you will have a trial in a few days."

"You still haven't answered why you did this to the eta. I can't be loyal to someone who is sacrificing them. Also, when did you see my father? You brought the jorogumo here, so you wanted me to know. What do you want?"

"The deaths of the eta are regrettable. I am sure your mother would also never forgive me for them." A deep sadness flashed in his eyes. Then he met her gaze. "I am not asking for your loyalty, but I will ask for your obedience."

He left the room. Mei stared blankly after him. So many questions flooded her mind. How did he expect her to just accept his words? He dealt with the jorogumo. Her hands shook as she reached for the letter. The script was plain and somewhat easy to read. It still took Mei a while to work out the kanji. How did the Sho already know she could read?

My daughter,

It is my regret that my part in your journey will end. I kept my promise to your mother and raised you as an eta. You needed to become an eta. You needed to see what your mother fought for in the end. She fought for more than just our love. She fought for change. We had a quiet hope that with our defeat you could rise. I'm sorry, my daughter, that you will have to fight. You don't have to take up any of this and can let things stay the way they are. However, I think you will find your purpose in all this. Make your own path to what you believe is right. You know who to trust and you will make the right choices.

Remember, my daughter, you are more than what you claim to be. I am sorry I had to turn you away. In my selfish heart, I wanted nothing more than to fly away and leave this city to rot. This was my path. I'm sorry to have put you on it.

I will always be with you. My greatest hope is that you will live and be happy. I love you.

Kaji

~

M*ei's eye* blurred with tears, and she carefully held the letter away so as not to smear her father's last words. *This doesn't answer anything, Jion-sho.* She curled up, holding her mother's uniform and the letter. *Kuro?*

Yes?

Relief filled her at the sound of his voice. *Can we leave?*

I will go with you, to the end.

She closed her eyes and let her tears flow down her face as she fell asleep.

~

DAYS LATER, Mei stared at her reflection in the looking glass Emiri held for her. Her skin on the right side of her face and shoulder remained black, with red cracks laced throughout the damaged skin. She had never cared about her appearance, but she swallowed tightly at the ugliness that marred her face.

"I suppose I wasn't that much to look at to begin with." Mei had never had time to really see herself. Her features seemed childish, but now everyone would only see the dark splotch on her face. Her hair had turned to ash on the right side, leaving bare burnt skin with a little hair growth. Emiri was about to trim the rest.

"Hold still. Otherwise, I will just shave it all."

Mei put the looking glass down and sat up straight as Emiri worked on her hair. "Isn't that what you are doing?"

"I'm trying my best to salvage it."

Most women kept their hair long in daim society, although female shodragon riders were the exception to the rule and often kept their hair either in a tight knot or short. Mei had never seen a female head shaved, though. She sighed inwardly. It didn't really matter; she wouldn't fit in whether her hair was long or short.

"Do you think they will put me to death?" In a few hours, they would summon Mei to the top of the tower with Kuro. She had woken up a couple days ago and spent the time sorting out her feelings about the Sho, Washi, her father, and her mother. The forest still burned, and all the riders would be on rotating shifts until they put out the last of the fires. She didn't know what kind of devastation her use of the fire had caused, but she had a feeling she was about to find out.

"I think the charges for desertion will be put to rest, but

as for the fire... I don't know. I've heard rumors about the destruction."

"How many people..."

"No human deaths."

"That's a relief."

Emiri rubbed something in Mei's hair that smelled of jasmine. Then she grabbed the looking glass and held it up.

Mei cautiously glanced at her image, and her eyes widened at Emiri's handiwork. The right portion of her hair remained short as peach fuzz, but the rest of her hair was brushed over to her left and feathered down. The longest layer reached her jawline. It looked different, but not bad.

"I blended the short styles I see with the shaved head. I think you look ready for battle."

Mei smiled softly. "Arigato, my shinyuu."

Emiri put the looking glass down. "Why did that sound like goodbye?"

Mei let Emiri help her into her new uniform. The tightness of the obi around her waist made her feel steady as the guards came to get her. She turned and gave Emiri a half wave as she left with the two men. The lift to the summit seemed long, yet so short. She disembarked, and Kuro stood at the entrance to the grand hall. His black head nudged her shoulder.

They looked into each other's eyes, and no thoughts needed to be exchanged. They entered the hall together. This entrance mirrored Mei's first time in the grand hall, except all the dragon riders' shodragons were behind them. The grandest was the large golden shodragon of the Sho. Her violet eyes swept over everything, and her forearms rested on either side of Jion-sho's chair. A new chair had been added beside the Sho's, where the Emperor sat with his homdragon draped around his neck. His lips were in a thin line, and his eyes narrowed at her approach.

Mei kneeled and placed her hands in front of her. She touched her forehead to the stone. After a moment, she raised her head and sat back on her heels with her head lowered.

Jion-sho studied her before speaking. "Your use of the fire has sealed off many entrances that the jorogumo were using to abduct their victims. You have shone a light on how they were taking people."

Did I also solve how you were helping them? Her lips pressed tightly together. Her gaze flickered, and her insides dried up like ash. How could she serve a man who thought it was okay to sacrifice people? Was there anyone with honor among the shodragon riders?

"We heard from Daisuke," Jion-sho said, "and he confessed to his lies and how he set up the trap to scare you. Also"—he waved to a guard—"bring him out."

Daisuke confessed? Why would he do that? A new game she wasn't prepared for yet.

Washi-sensei appeared between two guards. His jaw was clenched, and he glared at the Sho.

Jion-sho stood and strode down to stand in front of Washi. In one swift movement, he drew his katana and swung. No one moved, but Washi's obi fluttered to the floor. "For your lies against Mei, who is a shodragon rider, you are henceforth stripped of your position as wingleader. At this time, any wingleader may speak for you to join their winglegion. And those in your legion will need to be spoken for by others."

Sora-sensei stood. "I will speak for him."

Jion-sho didn't look surprised, only resigned. He then

turned to the Emperor. "Although your services were appreciated, you will no longer be needed at the fortress. It's the duty of the Sho to handle the recruits."

The Emperor gracefully rose from his chair and barely bowed to the Sho. "For now."

With all wingleaders watching, the Emperor departed. "I guess the eta wins this time," he said softly as he walked by Mei.

Mei didn't bother to look up at him but spoke her words to the floor. "The eta don't die easy."

"We will see."

After Emperor Xion left, Jion-sho bowed to the wingleaders, they got on their dragons, and flew away. Without the shodragons, the space felt empty.

Jion-sho glanced down at Mei. "Stay."

She hadn't planned on going anywhere; her legs ached from kneeling.

The Sho motioned for her to come closer, andMei took careful steps toward him, her legs numb.

"Even though there's a high cost as an eta, you didn't take long to overcome their ways of not being noticed. You are the only one who has lived using spider lily, and you wiped out thousands of jorogumo."

Her eyes shifted to him. "Isn't that good?"

Jion-sho's face became unreadable. He glanced out the open doors to the city below. Near the eta district, Mei could see dark patches of burnt land. "Yes, according to most it's good." He smiled, but it didn't reach his eyes. "That'll help the riders accept you. But I hope the trade-off will be worth it."

"Trade-off?" Her fists clenched.

"You better prove to me you are worth it." He tilted his head. "Have you made your choice?"

"I wasn't aware I had one."

"Will you obey?"

Obey? Could she even chose not to? Mei didn't understand why he bothered to ask again. She was stuck here. But his eyes searched, looking for something, and Mei didn't know the correct answer.

"I will never do anything that will bring harm to the eta. If you plan on dealing with the jorogumo, I won't be a part of it."

Jion-sho bowed and placed his hand on the golden dragon. "Maybe you can help me find another way to stop what's coming." With no other words, he swung onto his dragon's back. The sun glittered off the golden scales as he launched away from the top of the fortress and flew away.

"What does he mean?" Mei asked.

Maybe he wants to trade for some fatty meat.

Mei sighed. "I doubt it. Are you actually hungry after all this?"

Nothing really happened.

Soft footfalls came from behind her, and she turned to see Chin. A wave of relief filled her. "Emiri told me you were okay, but I didn't see you after..."

"Whenever I stopped by, you were always asleep."

"I'm sorry."

Chin waved his hand. "There's nothing to be sorry for, except maybe to your dragon, since you do snore."

"I do not!"

They met each other's gazes and laughed. It felt good to laugh.

She glanced out the wide-open doors again. "What do you think will happen?"

"I'm not sure. It seems strange the Sho isn't happier that you killed off a lot of jorogumo."

She glanced out over the dark district, where people stole and ate garbage to survive. Her home. Mei's eyes softened. Her father had raised her as an eta, and she had an odd sense of pride. It wasn't easy to kill an eta. What would she choose? She didn't have to—she already told the Sho.

She turned back to Chin. "I'm choosing the eta."

Chin nodded, and Kuro snorted in agreement.

Can we go eat now?

Yes, let's go.

"Do you feel like fish for dinner?" Mei asked as she mounted her ebony dragon and pulled Chin up behind her.

"I have been craving it from Fat Choi." He grinned.

She gave him a wry grin and softly whispered, "You know I can't leave."

The invisible chains were firmly in place around her, tying her to the fortress. She signaled Kuro to fly. Together, they flew down from the fortress, the red glow from the sun casting a dark shadow.

THANK YOU

Thank you for reading! Please leave a review! It really helps new authors and means the world.

If you want updates on future releases, sign up for my newsletter:

https://subscribepage.io/63Pam5

Chin's mental battle is very personal to me. I want you to know that you are not alone.

If you're thinking about suicide, are worried about a friend or loved one, or would like emotional support, National Suicide Prevention Lifeline is available 24/7 across the United States. Please call 988.

ACKNOWLEDGMENTS

The best surprises are the ones you haven't planned on. This book is something that came out when I needed a break from a series. Then it turned into something more, and I can't wait to take you along for the journey with Mei, Kuro, Chin, and even Daisuke.

I wrote this book back in 2020 and life had many ups and downs for my writing and my health. I'm happy to finally let this book out into the world.

I want to thank all my awesome alpha readers. I never got such a reaction before, and it makes me think I'm doing something right. So to Sarah, Jamie, Tanner, Katie, Angela, Bobbi, Nicollee, Bryan, Jayden, and my mom: thank you so much for giving me your time and comments. You all helped me make this story better!

As always, I need to give a special shout-out to my work wife Katie and the Wednesday Women Warriors. Thank you for keeping me going and not letting me give up.

To my wonderful editor, Elizabeth, at Arrowhead Editing: you are the main reason I can publish with success and without fear. Thank you for helping me clean up my mess and making my sentences coherent.

Also to Jennifer, thank you for your edits so I can finally publish.

Thanks to my fantastic cover artist, Logan Keys. My

characters came to life thanks to you, and I can't wait until everyone sees your art!

Last of all, thanks to my wonderful readers. As a new author, your support means so much. I wouldn't have made it this far without you, and I hope you keep enjoying my stories for as long as I can write them.

This is only the beginning!

ABOUT THE AUTHOR

Mari Dietz wrote her first poem about crickets when she didn't even know how to write. Her mom typed it up for her on an old typewriter. From then on, she was a goner to the written word. Over the years, she fell in love with the world of fantasy and thought maybe one day she could write something too.

She took a few side roads and got a major in Theater and English. Then she somehow ended up teaching in South Korea for three years. Now back in the middle of nowhere, she teaches Creative Writing and writes her own books in her "spare time," when not distracted by lesson plans, anime, or K-dramas.

Four rescue dogs give her the privilege of living with them, and they keep her sane-ish.

https://maridietzauthor.wordpress.com/

https://www.facebook.com/groups/1408237512699059